SCARLET SPIRITS

SCARLET SPIRITS

A DAISY GUMM MAJESTY MYSTERY, BOOK 15

ALICE DUNCAN

ePublishingWorks!
love what you read.

Book and cover design by eBook Prep
www.ebookprep.com

January 2020
(Paperback) ISBN: 978-1-64457-026-5
(Hardcover) ISBN: 978-1-64457-027-2

ePublishing Works!
644 Shrewsbury Commons Ave
Ste 249
Shrewsbury PA 17361
United States of America

www.epublishingworks.com
Phone: 866-846-5123

DON'T MISS AUNT VI'S STEW RECIPE

You can enjoy Aunt Vi's Stew and Dumplings just like Sam Rotondo. Go to the end of the book, right after the excerpt for *Exercised Spirits*, where you'll find the directions for Sam's favorite stew.

Email a photo along with your Stew Making Story, and Aunt Vi just might share her recipe for Scotch Shortbread Cookies in return.

ACKNOWLEDGMENTS

Many, many thanks to Elizabeth Delisi, Maven of the Mystical Arts, whom I always consult when Daisy needs to read tarot cards for someone. Liz understands tarot. So does Daisy. I…don't.

I'll never be able to thank Peter Brandvold sufficiently for giving me Lou Prophet, even if he did wait until Lou was old, weathered and on his last leg. Literally, since his other leg was replaced by a peg.

And for my beta readers: David Bedini, Lynne Welch, Sue Krekeler, Roberta Langman and Gina Gilmore. I don't think they believe how much they help me, but they do. Truly. A lot.

ONE

March 1925, didn't barge into Pasadena, California, like a lion. Which was a darned good thing, as I'd had an unpleasant experience with a lion not a month earlier. No, siree. This particular March tiptoed into our beautiful city more like a fluffy little kitten, warm and soft and pretty. With exceptionally short, dull claws.

Earlier in the year—on New Year's Day, in fact—someone had tried to kill me via a motorcar. Several other attempts on my shortish life—I'd only just turned twenty-five—had followed, but I'd recovered by March. In fact, by the second week in March, the world felt like a safe and comfy place in which to live. It's true I jumped approximately twelve inches into the air and squeaked every time a motorcar backfired in my vicinity, and I continued to have the occasional nightmare about a lion ripping off and devouring one or more of my body parts, but my nerves had settled down a whole lot and my physical self seemed to have healed completely.

What's more, my wonderful fiancé, Detective Sam Rotondo of

the Pasadena Police Department, had bought the house directly across the street from the one in which my family lived on South Marengo Avenue. I loved that house, and I loved Sam. And I don't think he bought the place merely because he could thereby continue dining on my aunt, Viola Gumm's, magnificent meals. Vi is a genius in the kitchen. I'm...well...not.

One of these days, when people stopped trying to injure Sam and/or me, we even planned to get married! Our engagement seemed to be dragging on for quite a long time, but that's mainly because an evil woman had shot Sam in the thigh several months earlier and, as mentioned above, I received my own packet of injuries on and shortly after New Year's Day. While I was all better—barring the afore-mentioned backfiring motorcars and nightmares—Sam still had some healing to do. He'd almost died on the day he was shot, and he'd had a couple of frightening relapses after being released from the hospital. Still, he was getting stronger with each passing day, and he didn't need to use the lovely Malacca cane with the horse-head handle I'd given him for Christmas nearly as often as he'd first had to do.

I had resumed working once more, as well. This made Mrs. Pinkerton, my best client, extremely happy. You see, I'm a spiritualist-medium to many wealthy ladies in Pasadena. Unfortunately for her, Mrs. Pinkerton had been cursed with a ghastly daughter, Anastasia "Stacy" Kincaid. Stacy was the reason Mrs. Pinkerton telephoned me almost every day claiming to be in dire need of advice from my spirit control, a Scottish gentleman named Rolly.

That was all right. I didn't mind too much. Having a daughter like Stacy—who, at the time, was behind bars for a series of nefarious criminal deeds—was a sore trial for Mrs. P. Truth to tell, Stacy was a sore trial, period. In fact, it wouldn't surprise me much to learn Stacy was a changeling. This is especially true because Stacy's brother, Harold Kincaid, is a superb human being, a prince among men, and one of my very best friends.

We also had an interesting new addition to our South Marengo Avenue neighborhood. Actually, we had two of them; at least, I sure hoped we did. The first one, Mr. Lou Prophet, originated in Georgia before the Civil War (he preferred to call it the War Between the States). By the time he hit Pasadena, he was old, but he still boasted a slow, deep southern accent and was a fascinating relic. I don't think he'd like me calling him a relic, so pretend I didn't write that. After he'd been hired by a motion-picture studio to give advice on the sets of several western flickers the studios were churning out, he'd been in an accident and lost one of his legs. As a result, he'd relinquished not merely one of his more important limbs, but had also lost his job. He now boasted a leg and a peg, and he wasn't happy about it. He'd ended up at the Odd Fellows Home of Christian Charity, where he didn't belong. Trust me about this.

But Sam and I had sprung him from that awful place, and Mr. Prophet now resided in the little one-bedroom cottage behind Sam's (and my, if we ever managed to tie the knot) new home. There he acted as a caretaker of sorts, since Sam's job as a homicide detective entailed odd hours. Mr. Prophet had already proved himself to be resourceful and handy several times.

Honestly? I think Sam felt sorry for the poor old guy—as did I —and let him live in the cottage because Sam possessed a kind and tender heart (please don't tell Sam I said he had a kind and tender heart. He'd kill me). It had to be galling for Mr. Prophet to be an old, one-legged artifact of days gone by. He'd once been a wild and woolly bounty hunter straight out of the Old West.

In March 1925, I had reason to believe another relic from the Old West had just purchased the gigantic house down the street from us. This new relic was female, and her name was Mrs. Evangeline Mainwaring. The house she'd just bought had been the first-ever built in our neighborhood. Other houses, including ours, had sprung up around it when its original owner had sold off parcels of land.

Therefore, and because I *really* wanted to meet the lady, I persuaded my mother, father, aunt, and fiancé into giving Mrs. Mainwaring a welcome-to-the-neighborhood party. It hadn't taken much persuading, since giving folks welcome-to-the neighborhood parties was a fairly well-established tradition. Harold Kincaid had told me Mrs. Mainwaring used to be something of a scarlet woman in old western towns like Tombstone, etc. I didn't know if Harold's understanding was based on anything other than gossip, but I kind of hoped it was. To the best of my knowledge, I'd never met a scarlet woman, and I wanted to see what one looked like.

That sounds awful, doesn't it? Well, too bad. It's true.

Be that as it may, except for Harold—who was almost always a credible source—everyone else in the neighborhood knew her only as a wealthy woman who had earned her vast fortune in the burgeoning Southern California orange industry. Pasadena brimmed full of orange groves and poppy fields, although by 1925 there weren't nearly as many of either of those things as there used to be.

Therefore, after church on the third Sunday in March my mother, aunt and I decided to toddle down the street to Mrs. Mainwaring's house. We brought with us a batch of Vi's outstanding Scotch shortbread cookies, and we aimed to ask Mrs. Mainwaring if she'd like to meet more of her neighbors. Her house sat on a much larger parcel of land than others in the area, and the house and grounds were surrounded by a six-foot wrought-iron fence. When we walked up to the gate, we found it locked. There was, however, a newfangled buzzer-thing on a wooden post next to it; therefore, being braver and more daring than my aunt and mother, I buzzed the buzzer.

After a few crackling noises, a voice came through the speaking tube! I was impressed. Except in huge mansions owned by some of my clients, I'd never seen one of those speaker boxes. They certainly didn't proliferate in our staid and middle-class neighborhood. The voice issuing therefrom said, "Mainwaring residence," and sounded neither friendly nor unfriendly.

"Yes. Good afternoon. My name is Daisy Majesty. My mother, Peggy Gumm; aunt, Viola Gumm and I have come to introduce ourselves to Mrs. Mainwaring and welcome her to the neighborhood."

"One moment, please."

Ma, Aunt Vi and I exchanged a glance or two. I whispered, "Snooty?"

"Daisy," said Ma. She does that when she thinks I'm being rude or unkind.

"I didn't say she *was* snooty," I said in my own defense. "That was supposed to be a question, Ma."

"Well, it wasn't a very nice—"

The speaking tube crackled again, and the same voice said, "Mrs. Mainwaring will be pleased to meet you ladies. Just press the big black button on the gate, and it will open for you."

I said, "Thank you," glad both for the invitation and because my mother didn't have a chance to finish her sentence.

So I pushed the black button and, sure enough, one side of the gate opened.

"Fancy," said Vi, watching the moving wrought iron with interest.

"Not as fancy as some. Mrs. Pinkerton has an entire gatekeeper just to open and close her gate, don't forget." My aunt cooked for Mr. and Mrs. Pinkerton as well as for our family, bless her. What's more, I knew and liked Mrs. Pinkerton's gatekeeper, Mr. Joseph Jackson.

"True, true," said Vi with a smile.

The grounds of Mrs. Mainwaring's estate were lovely. In March, daffodils and irises were beginning to bloom, and a whole row of rosebushes lined the brick-paved walkway to the house, a three-story number complete with a porch that wrapped itself around the whole structure. I noticed a fellow clad in white working with some flowering bird of paradise plants in the far north end of the property—in other words, the end closest to our house. He looked Chinese. Maybe Japanese. I'm no expert on Asians, although I did know a few of each. Chinese and Japanese people, I mean. White clothing seemed to me an odd choice for a person doing gardening work.

"Hmm. Look at that guy. The one working on the bird of paradise plants."

"Yes?" said Ma.

Vi glanced at him and said, "What about him?"

"He's wearing a white uniform. In the garden. I mean, won't white clothing get really dirty? I always wear old clothes and gloves when I do gardening work because I don't want to get my good clothes all mucked up."

Both Ma and Vi shrugged. I guess they didn't consider the fellow's choice to wear white whilst gardening anything out of the ordinary. Of course, I did more gardening work than either of them, so maybe they'd just never thought about it before.

Anyhow, who cared? Evidently, only I.

When we reached the wide front door of the house—I think people called those wide doors "coffin" doors back in the days when folks laid out their dead loved ones on the dining-room table before their bodies were placed in a coffin; so the doors had to be wide enough to accommodate a coffin—a pleasant-looking Negro woman greeted us. Ma, Vi and I all smiled at her, and I stuck out my hand. The woman seemed a little surprised, but she shook my hand anyway.

By the way, not that it matters, but I'm glad we no longer laid dead folks out on our dining-room tables, but have them taken to mortuaries instead. The notion of dining where a dead body had rested, no matter how beloved the corpse had been in life, gives me a funny feeling in my stomach.

Back to the front door of Mrs. Mainwaring's house.

"I'm Daisy Gumm Majesty," said I to the woman after we'd shaken hands.

"Pleased to meet you, Miss Majesty."

Fiddlesticks. I was actually *Missus* Majesty, but I didn't want to correct the woman. I should have been more specific to begin with.

"And this is my mother, Peggy Gumm. And my aunt, Viola Gumm."

"How do you do? Just call me Hattie, and please come along with me."

Very well then, I deduced Just Hattie to be more or less the equivalent of Mrs. Pinkerton's butler, Featherstone. Only Hattie allowed herself to smile at people. Featherstone might have been stuffed and mounted for all the animation he showed. But he was a crackerjack butler. He even had an English accent! I adored the man and wouldn't have minded having a butler like Featherstone. I'm almost positive Lou Prophet didn't count.

We followed Hattie down a hallway lined on both walls with gorgeous paintings. Hattie then ushered us into a pleasant, airy sitting room, its windows open to admit a gentle breeze, and lacy curtains dancing gracefully on the same breeze. A woman rose from a chair and came forward, holding out her hand and smiling.

Now I hadn't had a clue what to expect of Mrs. Evangeline Mainwaring, but her appearance surprised me. A tall woman, she wore an elegant day wrapper that looked to me as if it were genuine Chinese silk. The pattern on the fabric was certainly Chinese, and the fabric itself clung to Mrs. Mainwaring's body in all the rounded places women weren't supposed to have back then. As a really good seamstress myself—that's not a boast; it's the truth

—I *really* wanted to ask her where she'd purchased so comely a garment. She wore her shiny dark hair in a classic Castle bob, with loose curls and a side part. She might have been any age from thirty-five to sixty, but I guessed she was probably somewhere in her fifties.

Both my mother and my aunt were also in their fifties, but they sure didn't look like this woman. Mrs. Mainwaring had skin like creamy magnolia petals, eyes as dark as her hair, and hands as graceful as a dancer's. I noticed her delicate hands as she held one of them out for us to shake.

"It's so kind of you to call," she said in a voice that also reminded me of magnolias: smooth and mellow. "My name is Evangeline Mainwaring."

In short, the woman was beautiful. Even in her fifties! I was impressed. And, truth to tell, a little jealous. I took care of my appearance due to the nature of my business, but I doubt I'd look as good as Mrs. Mainwaring when I reached whatever age she was.

Being me, I held out my hand and spoke first. "I'm sorry we didn't visit you sooner, Mrs. Mainwaring. We…well, I was recovering from an accident. I'm Daisy Majesty—Mrs. William Majesty—and this is my mother, Margaret Gumm; and my aunt, Viola Gumm."

"How kind of you to call," she murmured, shaking each of our hands in turn. "Won't you take a seat? I'll have Hattie bring in some tea."

"Thank you." I remembered the Scotch shortbread. "Oh, and please accept these from us. My aunt, Vi, made them, and they're delicious."

"Thank you. Such a thoughtful gesture," purred the lady of the house, accepting the box, which I'd tied with pink ribbon.

Mrs. Mainwaring didn't have to signal Hattie; the maid—I assumed she was a maid—appeared in the sitting-room doorway as if her mistress's wishes had been received by her through some kind of spiritual signal.

Nertz. I hoped like heck Mrs. Mainwaring didn't aim to set herself up as a spiritualist-medium!

But no. What a silly thought. The woman was obviously rich as Croesus, whoever he was, and didn't have to work for a living.

"Will you please bring tea for our guests, Hattie? And please take this box to the kitchen, too. Mrs. Gumm has kindly baked us some shortbread."

I liked that she said "please" to her servant. Lots of rich folks weren't so polite to mere underlings.

Hattie said, "Yes, Miss Angie," took the box, and vanished.

Ma, Vi and I sat on a magnificent sofa, and Mrs. Mainwaring took a chair opposite us. I noticed a grand piano in the corner of the sitting room. Boy, you didn't see too darned many grand pianos in people's sitting rooms. We had an upright piano, which I played, in our living room at home. I'd love to get my fingers on that grandie, though.

"So you live north of us here on Marengo?" Mrs. Mainwaring said in her magnolia-petal voice.

"Yes. Four houses up, on the same side of the street. The bungalow with the hydrangea bushes next to the front porch."

"Oh, yes, I've noticed your house. It's a lovely bungalow. In fact, the entire street is charming with its canopy of pepper trees. I'm pleased to have joined you here."

"Um…have you lived in Pasadena long?" That wasn't pushy, was it? According to Harold, she'd moved here in 1896 after having lived a scandalous life in some of the rougher western towns in what we civilized folk think of as the "old days." Again, Harold's understanding might be based on gossip and speculation. I hoped it wasn't, though, for reasons already stated.

"I moved to Pasadena in 1896, Mrs. Majesty, and I used to live in a house on my property at Orange Acres."

"Oh, I've heard of Orange Acres," I said, pleased at recognizing this bit of history as the truth.

"As have I," said Vi. "My employers, Mr. and Mrs. Algernon Pinkerton, always order their oranges from Orange Acres. According to Mr. Pinkerton, your oranges are the best."

Not sure if Vi was telling a slight stretcher there. I mean, oranges were oranges. I personally loved them. What's more, we had both a Valencia and a navel orange tree in our own yard, so we had fresh oranges almost all year round. But if it was a stretcher, it was kindly meant and I doubted God would care much.

"Ah, yes. I've met the Pinkertons," said Mrs. Mainwaring. To my astonishment, her eyes crinkled a little, and I *swear* I saw a twinkle in them. "And I know Mrs. Pinkerton's son, Harold Kincaid. He's a nice fellow."

"He certainly is," I said. "He's one of my very best friends."

"So he told me." More twinkles from Mrs. Mainwaring.

Golly, maybe Harold *did* know what he was talking about!

Hattie appeared in the doorway bearing a tray holding a perfectly glorious tea pot and four cups in an elaborate design that had an Asian look about it. I'd seen the pattern before and knew it had been manufactured by Coalport—in other words, wildly expensive—but I couldn't recall the pattern's name. It sure was pretty, whatever it was.

"Let me help you with that, Hattie," a deep masculine voice said from outside the sitting room, surprising me into a smallish start.

"It's all right, Mr. Judah. I can manage."

"Nonsense," said the voice, and darned if a tall man with a rakish air about him—unless that was my vivid imagination playing games—didn't take the tray from Hattie and carry it to the tea table in front of Mrs. Mainwaring.

When I glanced at the mistress of the house, I thought I saw a flash of irritation in her expression. It vanished so suddenly, I might have been mistaken. My imagination occasionally—only occasionally, mind you—gets out of control. A little bit.

"I beg your pardon, ladies," said the man, setting the tray gently on the table. He stood, bowed, and smiled at us. Goodness gracious, but the man was handsome! Probably as old as Mrs. Mainwaring, he too was remarkably well-preserved. Dark hair and green eyes graced a slightly weathered-looking face. The weathering didn't decrease his handsomeness, but rather added to it.

Which is just unfair, darn it! Why do women get old and worn-out looking, but men get old and remain good-looking? I didn't approve, curse it. Not that my approval has ever mattered to anyone, much less God, who'd probably stopped listening to me whine years ago.

If Mrs. Mainwaring had been irked by this fellow's sudden appearance, she recovered her poise at once. Smiling graciously, she said, "Mrs. Majesty, Mrs. Gumm and Mrs. Gumm, please allow me to introduce you to Mr. Judah Bowman. Mr. Bowman is…an associate of mine."

An associate, was he? Oh, boy, I could hardly wait to telephone Harold!

"How do you do, ladies? Happy to meet you." He started with me, so I stuck out my hand. He had a firm, but not punishing, grip and his smile didn't waver when he asked, "And which one are you?"

"Daisy Majesty," I said and gulped. I swear to heaven, that man's smile ought to be outlawed!

"*Missus* Majesty," said Mrs. Mainwaring. I got the impression she was warning Mr. Bowman to keep his distance from me.

"Very pleased to meet you," said he, and moved on to my mother.

Once introductions were complete, Mr. Bowman sat himself on a chair near Mrs. Mainwaring, giving her a sidelong glance that also should be outlawed. These two weren't married or they'd share the same last name—unless Mrs. Mainwaring was an extremely modern woman—but I'd have bet my last dollar they were lovers.

Lovers. I don't know why, but the word sounds ever so much more romantic than man and wife.

Perhaps it was I who needed to be outlawed. Grim thought.

TWO

Anyhow, by the time Ma, Vi and I had remained a polite thirty minutes, all of us present had managed to glean some —not much—information about each other. For instance, I now knew Mr. Bowman worked as a private investigator and had an office in downtown Pasadena. I'd bet Sam would love that.

I'm joking. Sam loathed private detectives and claimed they interfered with police business. He might well be correct. Everything I knew about private detectives had been harvested from the rows upon rows of detective novels in the fiction section at the Pasadena Public Library. If those detective novels were as accurate as some of the dime novels about characters in the Old West I'd read recently, fiction and fact didn't spend a whole lot of time together.

As already stated, Mrs. Mainwaring owned and operated—in association, I'd learned, with Mr. Bowman—Orange Acres. So I guess she'd been telling the truth about the two of them being associates but, as also already mentioned, I'd bet anything they were more than mere associates.

Mrs. Mainwaring and Mr. Bowman now knew I had a dachshund named Spike, played the piano, sang alto in our church's choir and worked as a spiritualist-medium. Both parties appeared interested in my profession; I don't think they were fibbing.

They also knew Ma was the chief bookkeeper at the Hotel Marengo, and that Vi worked for the Pinkertons. They both claimed to know and like Harold Kincaid, and neither one had ever heard of Harold's evil sister.

Best of all, Mrs. Mainwaring said she'd love it if we threw a welcome-to-the-neighborhood party for her. This made Ma, Vi and me happy, and we chatted merrily as we walked back up the street to our bungalow.

As we approached the house, Mr. Lou Prophet limped across the street to greet us. We'd seen him not long since, as he and Sam had come to take dinner with us after church. Neither man had attended church with us, mind you, but they'd both managed to be free of whatever they'd been doing in time for Vi's magnificent pork roast with mashed potatoes and gravy, early asparagus and Harvard beets.

As he neared us, Mr. Prophet said, "Sam asked me to let you ladies know he's about finished with the bookcase, and did you want to see it." He hesitated for a second and then asked, "Did you meet the new lady down the street?"

"Yes. To both of those questions. Thanks, Mr. Prophet."

"Welcome. What's the lady's name, by the way?"

I wondered why he wanted to know, but figured he might have met her in the "old days," although Mrs. Mainwaring's old days weren't as old as Mr. Prophet's. Did that make any sense? I was pretty sure—although I'd never yet been rude enough to ask—that Mr. Prophet was in his mid-to-late-seventies. Mrs. Mainwaring wasn't nearly so old.

"Her last name is Mainwaring," I told him. "Her first name is Evangeline, which I think is a pretty name."

"Yeah, it's nice," said Mr. Prophet, who seemed to have lost interest in Mrs. Mainwaring. Guess he didn't recognize her name from his rowdy days in the Old West.

"Do you want to come over and see the bookcase?" I asked my mother and my aunt.

"Not right now, sweetheart," said Ma. "I'm going to take a little nap."

"As am I," said Vi. "We'll be able to see it later."

"Absolutely."

Mr. Prophet tipped his hat—a truly disreputable derby—at my mother and my aunt, and he and I turned to walk across the street to *my* new house. Well, it was Sam's, but my name would go on the deed as soon as we were married. Sam had also told me he aimed to set up a trust, whatever that was, to enable me to live well should anything happen to him. I didn't want anything to happen to him, curse it, but at least I understood why he wanted to establish the trust.

I'd learned about a month or so earlier that my Sam had a whole lot of money and didn't need to live on the pay he earned working as a detective in the Pasadena Police Department. He and his father owned a chain of jewelry stores in New York City and elsewhere in the eastern states. In fact, Sam's father had designed my engagement ring, which boasted a glorious gold flower pattern with a spectacular emerald in its center.

It was nice to know Sam had money. I still didn't want anything bad to happen to him. I loved him. I'd lost the only other man I'd ever loved, thanks to Kaiser Wilhelm and his ever-accursed mustard gas, and Billy's death had nearly killed me, too. The mere thought of losing Sam gave me the staggering fantods.

"Fantods" is a word I'd learned from Mr. Prophet, by the way. I'd begun writing down the quaint expressions he used, although I hadn't told him I was doing so. I doubt he'd have appreciated me calling them quaint, either. But really. He had more strange, old-western expressions in his vocabulary than I'd ever heard, even in the dime novels a friend of mine, Robert Browning (not the poet), had lent me. He had a whole collection of the things. That is to say Robert had a collection of dime novels. Shoot. The English language is sometimes difficult to manipulate.

Anyhow, on this particular lovely Sunday afternoon, Mr. Prophet opened the gate leading to the porch for me in a gentle-man-like fashion, and I smiled at him. Then we walked to the front door, which he also opened for me. Therefore, I said, "Thank you."

"You're most welcome, Miss Daisy." He gave me a sly wink. Shoot, even Mr. Prophet could be appealing when he did stuff like that.

The sound of hammering led us to a back room, which Sam had designated as the library, on the first floor of our new home. Sure enough, when I walked in, I saw Sam standing on a tarpaulin sprinkled with sawdust, in his undershirt and trousers, hammering a nail into a board. Sam had an impressive set of muscles. He wasn't lean and lanky as my late Billy had been, nor was his skin the ivory white of Billy's British ancestors. No, indeed. Sam's family was pure Italian, and he looked... Well, he looked really good with his muscles bulging and so forth. He also sported quite a bit of chest hair. Billy hadn't. And yes, I know decent women aren't supposed to notice things like chest hair, but Sam and I had been engaged for a long time by now, and we occasionally did things together my parents might have found shocking had they known about them.

Or maybe they wouldn't. Heck, people have been doing what Sam and I had been doing ever since the dawn of humanity. How else could the human race have survived, you know? But you weren't supposed to do that particular thing until you were married, at least in these enlightened times.

Sam and I, however, had both been married before, Sam to his Margaret and I to my Billy, and both of our late spouses had suffered years of torment thanks to the ailments sickening them.

Margaret had succumbed to tuberculosis, and Billy had finally tired of his life as a pain-wracked, shell-shocked invalid and taken his own life. Dr. Benjamin, our wonderful family physician, had written "accidental death" on Billy's death certificate so he could be buried in Mountain View Cemetery and prayed over by the minister of our Methodist-Episcopal Church, Mr. Merle Negley Smith.

Anyhow, the point to all of the verbiage is to explain that, while Sam and I had both been married to people we'd loved, we hadn't been able to enjoy all aspects of married life for long. We were, darn it, two healthy adults, and we enjoyed the heck out of one of those aspects.

And I also say to heck with what the moralists of the world preached. Sam and I would be married as soon as we could be, we'd been engaged for what seemed like forever, and we knew what we were doing, confound it.

Not that I'm the least little bit defensive about my behavior, you understand.

"Afternoon, sweetheart," said Sam, laying his hammer down and coming over to give me a kiss. "Look at this."

I looked. And I felt my eyes open wide. "Oh, Sam! Did you do that scrollwork at the top of the bookcase yourself?"

"Guilty as charged," said he, pleased with himself.

"I didn't know you were a wood-carver. That takes real talent, Sam. I'm impressed."

"Learned when I was a kid. My father taught me, just like his father taught him. Dad uses his artistic ability to create jewelry these days, but he's still one hell of a woodworker."

"As are you," said I, running my fingers along the delicate scrollwork at the top of the bookcase. The bookcase, by the way, was about as tall as I, if you count the scrollwork, and I'm about five feet, four inches tall.

"I sanded the thing and varnished it," Lou Prophet said at my back.

I turned around and gave him a hug, which startled him and almost made him lose his balance. I hadn't intended the last part. After making sure he could stand on his own, I said, "Thank you, Mr. Prophet!" Turning and hugging Sam, I said, "Thank you both! This is just…" Tears began dripping, and I felt stupid.

"Shee-oot," said Prophet. "Don't cloud up and drip on us, honey. It's bad for the varnish."

Laughing, I plucked my hankie from my pocket. "It's just that it's so pretty, and I love it so much. Oh, Sam, I can never thank you enough for buying this house for us."

"Oh, I bet you can. I'm sure I can think of a way or two." He gave me a suggestive leer.

"Why, Sam Rotondo, what *do* you mean?"

To explain his meaning, he pulled me into a rather intimate hug, which I returned with gusto.

"Want me to leave the room?" asked Lou Prophet drily, thereby succeeding in separating us.

"Spoilsport," Sam said to Prophet.

"Yeah. Sorry about that. But you guys are making me jealous."

"I'm sorry, Mr. Prophet," I said, recalling from several yellow-back novels about his exploits in the Old West that he'd once been a flagrant womanizer. I have a feeling those parts of the books, if none of the others, were true. He just had that…I don't know…air about him, if you know what I mean.

"I'm sure we can find a lady for you somewhere, Lou. You just wait," said Sam, brushing sawdust from my shoulders.

"Guess I'll have to, won't I?" said Mr. Prophet with a sigh that sounded the least little bit discouraged.

"We will," I told him, sounding more determined than I felt. Where the heck were we supposed to find a woman for old, one-legged Lou Prophet? I sure as heck wasn't about to introduce him to any of *my* friends. Despite his relatively old age, I wouldn't be surprised if he could lead a young lady astray, even a devout Methodist-Episcopal one like me.

Please stop laughing.

"Thanks," said he. "Think I'll retire to the cottage. We old folks need our rest, you know."

"Nonsense. You're not old!"

I'd just told a massive lie, and Mr. Prophet knew it. Giving me another wink he said, "You fib pretty good, Miss Daisy, and I know your heart's in the right place."

He limped from the room, and Sam and I toddled upstairs where we finished what we'd begun in our library. Pretend you didn't read that last sentence, okay?

"I think we should hold Mrs. Mainwaring's party in our new bungalow," I said one afternoon as I contemplated life.

"It's not furnished," said Ma.

"Actually, that's kind of the point," I told her. "This house is full of furniture. Sam's house—well, and mine, too, eventually—has two stories, not much furniture, and lots of space."

After contemplating my reasoning for a second or two, Ma said, "Hmm. I think you're right."

"I do, too," said Vi.

"Sounds like a good idea," said Pa.

"Okay by me," said Sam.

"Huh," said Mr. Prophet.

And thus the party venue was selected.

My darling aunt, Vi, expected to have to prepare and supply all the foodstuffs for the party. When Sam and I walked across the street one afternoon after having enjoyed some perhaps-illicit jollifications in our own home, we found her at the dining-room table, making a list.

"Whatcha doing, Vi?" I asked.

"Thinking about what I should fix for the party."

Snatching the list from under her pencil, thereby creating a big leaded streak across the page, Sam startled both Vi and me. She looked up at him, her eyes as round as pie plates. "Whatever did you do that for, Sam Rotondo?"

"You're not going to work at this party. You're going to come as a guest and enjoy yourself. I'm getting the shindig catered by the Hotel Castleton."

"Oh, Sam! That will cost a fortune," said Vi, sounding horrified.

"Sam's got a fortune," I told my wonderful aunt.

"You do?" Vi blinked up at Sam.

"I don't advertise it," said Sam. "But I don't want you to have to do the work this once. Just mingle with the neighbors, meet Missus... Well, I don't remember what her name is—"

"Missus Mainwaring," I prompted.

"Yeah," said Sam. "Her. And whoever lives in that mansion with her." He glanced at me. "Is there a Mister Mainwaring?"

"Not that I know of. There's a Mister Bowman, but I don't know if he lives with her."

"Daisy!" said my aunt, shocked.

"I didn't mean it in a bad way. I only meant that you and Ma and I met Mister Bowman, and it was clear he's on friendly terms with Missus Mainwaring. I have no idea what his living arrangements entail, but we should invite him."

Squinting at me, Sam said, "Bowman?"

"Yes. Mister Judah Bowman."

"Ah, shee-oot," he said, sounding remarkably like Lou Prophet, only less rusty. "Is he Judah Bowman, the private detective?"

"One and the same."

"Aw, shee-oot."

Told you Sam didn't like PIs.

"Well, if he's her… That is, whatever he is to her, I suppose we'll have to invite him, too. And all the neighbors for…how far? I mean, should we invite the entire block, or just the people who live around here?"

"Vi, Ma and I can come up with a list of people to invite. Are you sure you want to spend all that money to have the Castleton cater the party?"

Sam gave me one of *those* looks, and I threw up my hands. That is to say, I lifted my arms in an I-give-up gesture. Every time I read in a book that someone threw up his or her hands, my imagination provides ugly images including both vomiting and hurling body parts around. As my mother had no imagination at all, I think I inherited mine from my father.

"What about folks from your church?" asked Sam.

"What a lovely thought!" said Vi, giving Sam an almost worshipful smile.

"It is, Sam. Thank you. Inviting folks from the church would be kind. And, of course, Missus Pinkerton, Missus Bissel, Missus Chandler, Marianne and George Grenville, Missus Hastings and Flossie and Johnny, too.

Flossie and Johnny Buckingham were two of my most special friends. Johnny ran the local Salvation Army Church, and Flossie worked at his side, helping folks who were down on their luck. I'd introduced them, and I sometimes congratulated myself for doing so. At other times, I remember I'd been trying to get rid of Flossie at the time—she'd wanted to make herself over in my image, for sweet glory's sake—and had sort of thrown her at Johnny. However they'd got together, they were now happily married and had an adorable little boy named after my own darling Billy.

They also credited me with being the person who'd brought them together and thanked me for doing so all the time. I aimed never to tell them the precise truth. Yes, I'd introduced them, but my intentions hadn't been entirely altruistic when I'd done it.

"Oh, yes! We need to invite Doctor and Missus Benjamin and Harold and Del, too." I smiled as I thought about the kindhearted Dr. Benjamin and my best friend, Harold. He was *such* a great fellow. "And Dr. Fred Greenlaw and his sister Hazel."

Sam grunted. Although I don't think he disliked Harold as much as he had when they'd first met, Sam still didn't approve of him. Or of Dr. Greenlaw. That's because both men are fellows who prefer other men to women as objects of their affection. Personally, I don't care whom anybody loves, and believe no one should be ostracized because of his or her preferences. Besides, Harold had told me more than once his condition had nothing to do with personal preference.

"Why in the world would anybody *want* to be like me?" he'd demanded one day when we were together. "For God's sake, it's still *illegal* to be me in most states and countries."

"Good Lord," I said, my voice small.

"I could be jailed if anybody turned me in. So could Del! So could Fred! Cripes, I think they put people like us to death in the Soviet Union!"

Merciful heavens. I'd had no idea. "I'm sorry, Harold."

"Well, you should be! I had absolutely no choice in the matter. I was born this way. If I could go back and dictate how I should be, I wouldn't be the way I am." He squinted at me. "Did that make any sense?"

"Yes," I said, feeling kind of sad, "it did."

And thus I saw then, and I see now, no reason to doubt him. Put to death? Good Lord. I'd bet anything, if I did such stupid stuff as bet on things, Jesus Christ wouldn't punish a person for the way he—or, I guess, she—was born.

Even though Vi didn't have to prepare all the food for the massive party, she, Ma and I worked our respective tails off getting Sam's house ready for the shindig. Sam hired a couple of cleaning ladies to come in and help make sure everything was ship-shape. Mr. Lou Prophet sanded the banister to the second story and varnished it a beautiful cedar-wood color that matched the floors in the house, all of which were made of cedar. Sam had hired someone to sand and varnish the floors since Mr. Prophet couldn't bend or kneel well, thanks to the absence of one of his legs. His peg didn't bend at all, of course.

I absolutely *loved* that house and could hardly wait to get married and move in to it.

After discussing the matter amongst ourselves, we decided to hold our party on a Saturday. Most folks went to church on Sunday, except for the few Jews we knew, and they worshiped on Friday night and Saturday. I don't think they're supposed to work on Saturday, either, but nobody would be working that Saturday except the catering staff of the Hotel Castleton. And, of course, Ma, Vi, Sam, Pa and me.

"And you won't have to do a thing, Mister Prophet," I told him, smiling up a storm. "But it will give you a chance to meet all the people in the neighborhood and for them to meet you!"

Several of our neighbors had already mentioned Mr. Prophet to members of my family, most of them not in a cheery manner, probably because he looked out of place in so civilized a city as Pasadena. Still and all, nobody had anything against him. Well, except for the one time he'd shot a man in our back yard—but that was only because the man he shot had first shot at me. Mrs. Long-necker, who lived down the street, had been peeved then. But she was an old grouch anyway, so she doesn't count.

My life isn't usually as exciting as the above paragraph sounds. Things just happen every once in a while.

"Oh, I don't think I'll stick through the whole party, Miss Daisy," said Prophet. "But I'll make an appearance and say howdy to folks. Don't want 'em to think I'm a total hairy dick."

I felt my eyes go wide, and I tilted my head back a bit. "I beg your pardon? You don't want them to think you're a *what*?"

"Um... I mean... I mean a heretic. I do apologize, Miss Daisy."

"You don't want people thinking you're a *heretic*?" I'm pretty sure I goggled at him.

"Well, yeah. You know. Heretic. Not a religious-like heretic, but...well, a loner-like fellow, if you know what I mean."

"I guess I know what you mean now," I said a trifle frostily, unsure whether I should include "hairy dick" in my dictionary of old-west sayings. It sounded rather vulgar.

As Mr. Prophet and I carried on this conversation, Sam stood at the back of what was going to be our front parlor, his arms crossed over his chest, grinning up a storm. In fact, he chuckled once or twice.

"But I'll do my best not to embarrass you or Sam, Miss Daisy. Cross my heart," said Prophet.

"If you can find it," muttered Sam, still grinning.

After shooting a "behave yourself" glare at Sam and a "You'd better" one at Mr. Prophet, I said, "Thank you."

Sam laughed out loud. I'm pretty sure I heard Mr. Prophet giggle like a girl as he left the house to go back to his cottage.

I swear. Men.

THREE

We set the date for our party on Saturday, April fourth.

Lots of things happened between the time we planned the party and the party itself. For one thing, Sam's sister, Renata Pagano, visited Pasadena. Not for fun. Her son, Frank Pagano, had tried to murder me in January. Threw a big knife at me and, if I hadn't turned my head at a crucial moment, I'd have been a dead duck. Or a dead Daisy.

When asked why he wanted to kill me, he'd claimed it was because he and his family didn't approve of me. *Me*! Daisy Gumm Majesty, who'd never done any harm to anyone, at least not on purpose. The reasons he cited were two-fold: I was neither Italian, nor was I a Roman Catholic. When questioned fully, however, Frank admitted someone had hired him to do the evil deed. He still occupied a cell in the city jail, but his trial was coming right up. Renata aimed to visit Pasadena for the trial and to try to figure out why her son had turned out so badly. According to Sam, Frank was the only bad apple in the family. I had no reason to doubt him.

It came as a blow, however, to learn Renata Pagano disapproved of me, too.

"Told you she would," said Sam as we sat on the porch of my parents' home one evening after dining on one of Vi's magnificent meals.

"Yes, you did, but I didn't think... Well, I can't imagine not approving of someone because of his—or her, of course—nationality or religion."

With a shrug, Sam said, "You don't know many Italians."

"No, I don't. In fact, I believe you're the only thus far. Except for your rotten nephew." Frank Pagano had not only tried to kill me, but when he'd visited Pasadena several months earlier, he'd stolen a darling painted statue of Buddha I'd bought in Chinatown in Los Angeles. Worse, he'd pilfered one of my church's silver candlesticks! The young man was a total failure at being a productive member of society. I didn't tell his mother that, because it was clear she wanted no input from me.

"It makes me sad that your family doesn't like me, Sam, just because I'm neither Italian nor Catholic."

Another shrug, "It's just one of those things. People seem to stick with their own kind. It's not just Italians and Catholics. For instance, lots of people hate Jews just because they're Jews. Look at Shylock in *The Merchant of Venice*. Even Shakespeare hated Jews, I suppose."

"I don't."

Sam gave my shoulders a squeeze. "You're an open-minded human being, love."

"Piffle."

"And a lot of folks don't like men like Harold, either."

"But that's *totally* unwarranted prejudice! Harold and I have discussed this countless times."

"Yeah?"

"Yeah. He said the Soviet Union actually *executes* homosexuals. I guess somebody would have to turn him in or something, but that's horrible."

"True, but the Soviets aren't alone in their distaste. Remember Oscar Wilde?"

Sighing, I said, "Yes. I remember his story. *So* unfair."

"Then there was Henry the Eighth's dissolution of the monasteries."

"But...but that was because he wanted to marry Ann Boleyn, wasn't it?"

With a shrug, Sam said, "Caused a huge upheaval in the church, whatever his reasons were."

"Yes, I know, but..."

"And don't forget the Crusades in the Middle Ages. Those gallant lads wanted to wipe out all the Muslims they could find. In turn, of course, the Muslims wanted to kill all the Christians."

"But..."

"And remember when Mary was Queen of England?"

"Of course, I don't!"

"Well, she burned Protestants right and left. Just because they protested the greediness of the Roman Catholic Church."

I stared at Sam, something having hit me right between the eyes, in a manner of speaking. "Is the word protest where we get the word Protestant?"

After glancing at me for a moment or two, Sam said, "Yes."

Shoot. I was usually the one who knew etymology. I hadn't pegged Sam for possessing such knowledge. Another huge sigh escaped my lips.

"And don't forget the Turks killed a million or so Armenians during the Great War because Armenians are culturally Christian and the Turks feared they'd join forces with Britain and the USA against Germany and Turkey."

"Culturally Christian? What does that mean?"

"It means that if you're an Armenian, your family and friends are Christians. Unlike, say, the Turks, who are Muslims."

"Oh. That's...awful."

"I think so, too, but I'm not Turkish. In New York City, most rich folks hate Italians and the Irish."

"Why?"

"Italians and Irish are considered poor and dirty, not to mention...ta-da!...Roman Catholic."

"That's terrible!"

"Or something like that. As far as I'm concerned, religion has caused and continues to cause more trouble in the world than pretty much anything else."

"Well, I wouldn't go *that* far."

"You would and did about a month ago, if you'll recall," said Sam, thereby making me remember an unhappy episode in my life. Not that the episode in question was far from my thoughts in the first place.

"Yes, but there were extenuating circumstances."

"Huh."

"There were! Several people were trying to kill me at the time, if you'll recall."

"How could I ever forget? And now even Christianity has its various sects and cults."

"Well, I don't know that I'd call them *cults*. Precisely."

"What about those fellows in the Appalachians who handle snakes? Are they like the run-of-the mill Methodist-Episcopals who attend your church?"

"Ew. I read about them. No, they aren't like us. And we aren't like them. I don't know what to call them, actually."

"You don't have to call them anything," said Sam, "but you can't deny the truth, unless you want to fib to yourself."

"How depressing."

"Just the way things are."

"Which doesn't make it any less depressing."

Sam shrugged and said, "Huh." "Huh" was his favorite word, by the way.

"But getting back to you and your own family, you'd started attending services at the Unitarian Church with your wife even before you and I met. She was an Italian Catholic, too, wasn't she? To begin with? Margaret, I mean?"

With a sideways squint at me, Sam said, "I've only had one wife so far, Daisy. And yes, she was both Italian and Catholic. Neither of us cared much for the Catholic Church, although I don't have anything more against it than I do any other church, so Margaret found West Side Church for us." With another squint and a slight frown, he added, "The truth is, I prefer the Congregational/Unitarian Church to the Methodist-Episcopal Church, but I'll join the Methodists if it'll make you happy."

"Thank you, Sam." I squeezed his arm and asked primly, "Will you also join the choir?" Sam possessed a wonderful bass voice. So, in fact, did Lou Prophet, although his vocal chords were not as pristine as they'd once been and his voice sounded a little scratchy. I believe this had to do with his love of "quirlies." "Quirley" would definitely have its place in my dictionary. A quirley was a cigarette. It was also a coffin nail.

Told you Mister Prophet was quaint.

"We'll have see about Lou and your choir," said Sam. I heard the grin in his voice. "Don't press your luck."

"Um…" I began, not sure how Sam would react to the question I aimed to ask him next. "Would you like me to get in touch with Harold to work with the Castleton in catering our party?"

"Sure," he said to my astonishment. "In fact, I was going to ask you to ask him. He knows a hell of a lot more about parties than I do."

"Yes, he does." I decided to leave the matter there.

"Pretty night," said Sam, looking skyward.

"How can you tell?"

I felt his shoulders shake as he snickered. "I know there are stars up there. Just because Marengo's planted on both sides with pepper trees and we can't see the sky doesn't mean it isn't there. The weather's pleasant."

"It is," I agreed upon a satisfied sigh. Life was good. For the most part. "I've finally started making Regina Petrie's wedding gown. She's going to be a beautiful bride."

Regina Petrie was not merely going to be a beautiful bride, but she also worked at the Pasadena Public Library and was my favorite librarian on the face of the earth, which was saying something, since I equate librarians with goddesses. An unfortunate act had been committed in the biography section of the Pasadena Public Library, which I loved almost as much as I loved Sam, during which another librarian had been foully done to death. Also unfortunately, my friend Robert Browning had—foolishly, I admit—picked up the murder weapon and had thereby become one of Sam's primary suspects. Which was silly on Sam's part, but he didn't know Robert as well as I did. Anyway, things turned out quite well as a result of the incident—barring the murder of Miss Carleton, the murdered librarian—because by the time the real culprit had been caught, Robert and Regina were engaged to be married.

Whew! That seems like a long explanation, but it wasn't meant to be. Just thought you might want to know why I told Regina I'd make her wedding gown and the dresses for her bridesmaids. I did mention I'm a crackerjack seamstress, didn't I? Well, I am. I have so few true talents and/or virtues, I don't mind touting my ability as a seamstress.

Anyhow, thanks to various people wanting to do me in during the first part of the year, I'd feared I wouldn't be able to finish Regina's wedding togs in time for the ceremony. I'd been proved wrong and remained happy about it.

"You'll be a beautiful bride, too," said Sam, who wasn't generally mushy.

"Thank you, Sam. And you'll look like an Italian duke."

Sam chuffed out an annoyed breath. "I wish to God Harold hadn't coined that phrase. You've been telling me I look like an Italian duke ever since, and I'll wager neither you nor Harold has ever seen an Italian duke in your lives."

"You're right. The only Italian duke we've ever seen is you."

"Cripes."

We sat in silence for a few minutes and then I remembered something interesting. "Oh, Sam, guess what?"

"What?"

"Missus Mainwaring telephoned me today and asked if I'd be free to bring my Ouija board over to her house tomorrow. She wants to consult with Rolly."

"Have I ever mentioned I think Rolly is a stupid name for a spirit control, even one that doesn't exist."

Ah, yes, there we were. Sam was back to his old self. I didn't mind. This was the self I'd fallen in love with, after all.

"Not my fault. I was ten years old when my agile brain created Rolly. Anyhow, most people think his name is spelled like Sir Walter Raleigh's, and not R-o-l-l-y."

"Yes. I know the story. Desdemona."

I sighed deeply. "Desdemona's not my fault, either! How the heck was I supposed to know when I was ten that Desdemona was a world-famous murder victim? After all, we weren't forced to read *Othello* until eighth grade or whenever it was."

Sam hugged my shoulders. "Don't get miffed, sweetheart. I just like to tease you, is all."

"I know. And I don't mind. Too much."

"So what does Missus Mainwaring want Rolly to do for her?"

"I won't know until I visit her."

"Valid point."

Lou Prophet, who had been playing gin rummy with my father while Sam and I enjoyed our privacy, opened the front door. "Is it

31

safe for me to go home? Don't want to interrupt anything interesting."

"Mister Prophet!" I cried, trying to sound scandalized and not succeeding.

With a sigh, Sam rose to his feet and helped me to mine. "Yeah. I guess it's time for bed. I've got to get up early."

"Are you working on a homicide?" I asked him, not expecting an answer. Sam didn't like me to get mixed up in his cases.

"Not at the moment, but now that you're up and around, I suspect there will be one soon."

Mr. Prophet laughed.

I didn't. "Sam!"

My darling fiancé had called me the Typhoid Mary of Murder in Pasadena a couple of times. But it's wasn't my fault I keep stumbling over dead bodies, confound it!

Drawing me into his arms and planting a kiss on my cheek, Sam murmured, "Don't forget to call Harold."

"After your last comment, maybe I'll just let *you* plan the party."

"Oh, don't do that, Miss Daisy. You want all your guests to survive, don't you?" Mr. Prophet asked jokingly.

"Most of them," I said scowling at the two men.

Sam and Lou chortled as they walked across the street to Sam's and my new house. I'd be *so* glad when Sam and I could walk into that house, bold as brass, as a married couple. Oh, well. *Won't be long now*, I promised myself.

I probably shouldn't have made that promise.

FOUR

Because the weather on Tuesday, March 31, remained fine, I tucked my tarot cards and Ouija board into the gorgeous embroidered bag I'd sewn for the purpose and walked down the street to Mrs. Mainwaring's mansion.

The elegant wrought-iron gate had not been locked against me, so I carried my bag of tricks up the wide porch steps and approached the coffin door—and I really wish I'd stop thinking of the thing as a coffin door.

In spite of my thoughts, before I could either knock or ring, Hattie opened the door, a big, beautiful smile on her chocolaty face. A little hefty, Hattie probably shared the same age as her mistress but, like Mrs. Mainwaring, she remained lovely even in her fifties.

Mind you, my aunt and my mother were also lovely ladies, and both were well into their fifties, but for some reason—I believed I've mentioned it before, in fact—Mrs. Mainwaring and Hattie wore their years particularly well. I suspect having a lot of money helped them in this regard and that they both, even Hattie, slathered creams, lotions and other helpful gunk on their faces nightly. Even daily. I'd learned quite a lot from Harold about how makeup artists dealt with stars in the flickers, so I knew there were many tricks and products useful for keeping the skin upon which the tricks and products were used healthy-looking and…well, not wrinkled or saggy anyway. If you know what I mean.

"Good morning, Miss Daisy. Missus Mainwaring is waiting for you in the front parlor."

"Thank you, Hattie."

Rather than leading the way, as Mrs. Pinkerton's Featherstone invariably did, Hattie walked by my side as we moseyed to the front parlor. Sure enough, Mrs. Mainwaring occupied the room, only today she sat on the bench before her magnificent grand piano, occupied in playing chords. She saw us enter the room, rose from her bench, and approached us, smiling and holding out her hands for me.

"Thank you so much for attending on me today, Missus Majesty—"

"Oh," said I, interrupting, which wasn't very nice of me but my heart was in the right place, "please call me Daisy. Everyone does."

"Daisy," said she, her glorious smile in place. "Madeline Pinkerton told me Daisy is short for Desdemona."

The words were a statement rather than a question but, after taking a glance at the woman who'd spoken, I took a larger chance and answered her unspoken query anyway. "I selected the name Desdemona when I began practicing my craft. I was only ten at the time. If I'd been older or had known better, I'd have selected a more appropriate—or less deadly—appellation."

Our voices joined in merry chuckles.

"I'll call you Daisy only if you call me Angie," said she.

"Very well, Angie. I think your name, Evangeline, is lovely. I'd much rather be an Evangeline than a Desdemona."

"Yes, well, I was rather older than ten when I selected it."

Huh? Hadn't she been named Evangeline by her parents? I

34

didn't ask, because I thought it might be rude to do so, but only continued to smile. However, her comment made me wildly curious.

Hattie said, "I'll go make some tea," Miss Angie.

"Thank you, Hattie. Bring in some of the lovely pound cake to go along with the tea, please."

"Yes, ma'am."

"Thank you."

Golly, I just *loved* the way Mrs. Mainwaring said please and thank you to her servant. Servants. Perhaps Hattie was the only servant in the place, although I kind of doubted it, the house being huge. Also, it was abundantly clear Mrs. Mainwaring—Angie— suffered no paucity of funds. Nor did her hands look red and raw from scrubbing floors and washing dishes, etc.

"I hope you'll enjoy the pound cake, Daisy," said Angie, leading me to a couple of chairs not far from the piano. "Missus Jackson dehydrated some apricots during last year's growing season, and this pound cake is one of the marvels she makes with the dried fruit."

"It sounds delicious. Um… Did you say your cook's name is Jackson?"

Giving me a beautiful and somewhat knowing smile, Angie said, "Indeed, you're probably familiar with Missus Jackson's sister-in-law. I believe you also know Missus Jackson's—sister-in-law to my Missus Jackson—son, Joseph. He guards the gates to the Pinkertons' property." She gestured to one of the chairs and took another one opposite. She'd either set or she'd had someone else set a piecrust table between the two chairs.

"Indeed, I know both of those Jacksons," I said, pleased to have yet another connection in common with this…unusual woman. And don't ask me why I considered her unusual, but I did. Perhaps her rare beauty colored my attitude, although I suspect Harold's hints about a possibly-wild past on her part played an even bigger role in my conclusion. "Missus Jackson and her son, along with a large number of their other relations, came to Pasadena from New Orleans, Louisiana. Well, and some of them came from Tulsa, Oklahoma."

My nose wrinkled in spite of myself. The Petrie clan also hailed from Tulsa. The Jacksons were much nicer than the Petries. Except for Regina, of course. "Joseph Jackson has taught me a lot about Caribbean voodoo. Missus Jackson, Joseph's mother, is an honest-to-goodness voodoo mambo, and she made this juju for me. It's supposed to keep me safe from harm." I fished around at my neck, found the chain upon which I'd hung my juju, and lifted it out to show her.

"Interesting." Angie reached out and fingered my juju. "And has it worked?"

Thinking back over the last two or three months, I said honestly, "Well… I supposed it could have done better, but I do believe it has helped once or twice." After a tiny pause, I added, "I'm not dead, anyway."

"*Very* interesting. And lucky."

I hadn't thought so at the time. However, when Sam, Harold, Mr. Prophet and I had set foot onto the grounds of Gay's Lion Farm in Westlake Park, the blasted voodoo juju had darned near burned a hole in my chest. It's doing so, I admit, had sent a pretty clear message, but the rest of the scene had played out downright terrorizingly, if you were me.

For the record, I'd clad myself in a perfectly splendid sky-blue linen day dress I'd fashioned on my (well, my mother's, but we shared) White side-pedal sewing machine when I was recovered enough from my injuries to sew once more. The fabric had been clumped in with a year-end sale at Nash's Dry Goods and Department Store in December, and I'd snapped it up. The color of the dress matched the blue of my eyes, and my tasteful, flesh-colored stockings and bone-colored shoes, cloche hat and handbag went perfectly with the ensemble.

I then wished I hadn't thought about anything as being bone-colored.

What the heck was wrong with me that day? There's no need to search for an answer to the question. Left-over anxiety still plagued me quite often back then.

As for Angie, she wore another spectacular Chinese-type outfit that clung to the curves women weren't supposed to have in 1925, and which didn't match her eyes, but brought out their dark-coffee coloring anyway. The woman was exquisite, darn it.

Not that I was jealous or anything. I mean, perhaps I wasn't a certified beauty, as was Mrs. Evangeline Mainwaring, but my business demanded I keep up my appearance. So, while not precisely gorgeous or glamorous, I was pretty. Very pretty, according to Sam on those rare occasions he didn't want to murder me for "interfering" in his police cases. Nertz. I never interfered.

But enough of that. I set my embroidered bag at my feet and drew out the Ouija board. "You did say you wished to consult Rolly via the Ouija board, right?".

"Yes, thank you. Um…do you also work with tarot cards?"

"Indeed I do," said I, withdrawing my tattered tarot deck. I'd been meaning to get a new one for months, but events had intervened, and so far I still had to use the old one. Anyhow, it didn't matter. Whatever board or cards I used, I could interpret them any old way I wanted to, spiritualism being the utter nonsense it is.

Please don't tell my clients I said that.

"Would you rather begin with the Ouija board or the tarot cards?" I asked politely.

Pressing an elegant and beautifully manicured finger to her lower lip, Angie tilted her head as she thought. "How about the tarot cards?"

"Happy to oblige," I said, and put the board back into its bag.

Before we could begin, Hattie re-entered the room bearing a tray upon which sat the same elegant china tea service I'd seen on my last visit, along with a plate holding substantial slices of apricot pound cake.

"But let's have a cup of tea and a slice of cake before we begin," said Angie, smiling at her servant.

I removed the deck of cards from the table, put it back in to its bag and allowed Hattie to serve us each a cup of tea and a plate holding a slice of apricot pound cake.

Boy that cake was good! I'd have to tell Vi about it.

As we sipped tea and ate pound cake, which we both did with the delicacy of royal princesses, Angie asked me a few questions. I didn't mind.

"Harold Kincaid told me you play the piano beautifully."

"Let's just say I play the piano," I said with a smile after swallowing a heavenly bite of pound cake.

"And you sing, too, according to Harold. He said, in fact, you played a role in a Gilbert and Sullivan operetta a couple of years ago."

"Now *that*," I said with more candor than was usual for me during my first visit with a new client as spiritualist-medium, "was fun. I didn't want to do it at first, because I don't generally sing except in a choir and was nervous about having a solo part. But Harold talked me into it, and I was fortunate enough to play Katisha in *The Mikado*. I'm not allowed to be mean and nasty in my every-day life, but I had to act like a vicious harpy in order to play Katisha. I loved it."

Angie laughed. What's more, her laugh sounded genuine. "What a charming tale," she said.

Very well. If she said so. "It turned out to be more fun than I'd bargained for." If, of course, one didn't count the nest of murdering scoundrels we'd uncovered during the same eventful span of time.

"After we finish with the cards and the board, would you like to play my piano? I play, but not well, and the instrument deserves better than I can give it."

"Oh, I'd love to!" I cried, again being more candid than usual. Did Evangeline Mainwaring cast spells over people who walked into her house or something? I told myself to act normal. In my case, normal wasn't candid. Normal for me was as unreadable as a blank page.

"I have some sheet music in the bench. Perhaps you can play, and we can both sing something together."

"Sounds lovely," I murmured, trying to curb my emotions, which leapt and skylarked in my bound bosom like fairies playing a silly game.

The conversation, tea and pound cake over with, I got out my tarot deck once more as Hattie cleared the piecrust table of clutter. If you can call a million-dollar silver service and a billion-dollar Coalpoart china service clutter.

I'm probably exaggerating.

At any rate, I shuffled the deck, had Angie cut the cards, and I said, "Is there any particular question you'd like to ask of the cards? They can only give answers to the person for whom I'm reading, so don't ask about anyone else." I had to keep reminding Mrs. Pinkerton of this salient fact, because she kept forgetting. I sensed Angie Mainwaring didn't possess Mrs. P's memory problems.

"Let me see." Angie tilted her head again, giving her the appearance of an elfin sprite or some other vaguely ethereal being. Wish I could do that. "I'd like to know what's in store for us in our lovely new home."

So I guess she wasn't as unlike Mrs. Pinkerton as I'd thought. Clearing my throat, I said, "The cards and the Ouija board can only answer questions posed by the person for whom I'm doing the reading. In other words, while you can *ask* either tool to offer information about others, you'll only get answers pertaining to yourself."

"Hmm. In that case, what do the cards see in store for me?"

"Excellent question."

I aimed to deal out a five-card horseshoe pattern. Not that it mattered, since I was the reader and could get the cards to say anything I wanted them to say, but I do believe I subconsciously decided on the horseshoe pattern because of Harold's suspicions about Mrs. M's background. You know: horses, the Old West, cowboys, gunslingers, bounty hunters, scarlet women; things like that.

But darned if the cards didn't prove interesting all on their own.

The first card I dealt, which resided on the lower left of the horseshoe—Angie's left, not mine, since I could read both the cards and the board upside-down as well as upside-up at that point in my career—turned out to be the Magician.

"Interesting," I said, trying to sound mysterious.

"What does it mean?"

"The first card dealt shows your present circumstances. When the Magician turns up at the outset, as it did here, it signifies a new beginning of some sort. However, you might not want to follow the Magician's guidance. We'll know more when I've dealt the rest of the cards."

The second card showed the six of cups, reversed. This was most unusual, and I felt my eyes widen.

"What does it mean?" asked Angie, as if both the card and my reaction to it worried her.

"At this point," I told her honestly, "I can't say, but it usually means, especially in the reversed position as it is here, that something from long ago might be approaching you."

She sucked in a breath, as if she didn't care for my interpretation.

"Anyway, let's move on. We won't know what everything means until we read the entire layout."

At the top of the horseshoe as it faced Angie, the Tower showed its lightning-struck features. Oh, dear. "Um… the position of this card indicates something unexpected will come your way. This card might signify the possibility you'll have to tear down or demolish old ways or thoughts in order for new ones to prevail."

"Lovely," muttered Angie. She didn't sound surprised, though. Or happy.

The fifth card turned out to be the Knight of Swords. Hmmm.

"Yes?" said Angie as if she weren't sure she wanted to know.

"This card signifies your immediate future, and it indicates movement. The Knight of Swords is brilliant but sometimes unkind. I think, in this layout, it means either you or someone near you—or who might be or become near you—will create some kind of change. Um…perhaps it will be positive change, but it's liable to be somewhat painful before it succeeds in its mission."

"Delightful," said Angie, now starting to sound a little grumpy.

Therefore, I laid down the last card gently, because I didn't care for this layout so far. The stupid tarot cards seldom sent such clear messages. I darned near huffed out a breath of relief when the battered old sun showed up. Battered only because my deck was elderly and well-used. "This is a good card," I said with quite a bit more enthusiasm than I'd meant to show. But golly, until that stupid sun came out, the future had appeared more than a trifle grim for Angie.

"It's about time," said she.

With a short laugh, I said, "Yes, it is. Anyway, the sun indicates a source of energy and strength. And, if the cards are correct, you'll probably be needing both of those things." I hadn't meant to say the last part of that sentence. Honest.

"Yes, so I gathered. I had no idea you were so proficient at your chosen art, Daisy."

"I'm glad you look upon it as an art. I've worked quite hard to achieve whatever proficiency I possess."

"I can tell."

We both sat back and stared at each other, then glanced at the horseshoe pattern made of tarot cards lying on the piecrust table. Then we looked at each other again and Angie cleared her throat.

"Is there any point in consulting your spirit control with the board after all the tarot reading?" she asked, waving a graceful hand over the tarot layout. "Raleigh, or whatever his name is?"

"Oh, most definitely," I said, attempting good cheer. "According to the cards, you might be in for some rough going... um, fairly soon. But Rolly may well be able to steer you in the right direction."

"He may be, eh?"

"Most certainly."

I think we both knew I was lying, but I could tell Angie half-way—or maybe more than half-way—wanted to believe me.

Bless his heart, Rolly didn't fail me, although he did spell out a few things I hadn't intended him to spell out. Once I got home again, I intended to have a stern chat with him. I'd threatened him before, letting him know in no uncertain terms that *I'd* invented him, and I could jolly well *dis*-invent him if he kept doing things of which I disapproved.

Good Lord, I'm talking as though I really believe in him. I beg your pardon.

FIVE

W hat happened then occurred as follows:

After I positioned the Ouija board on the piecrust table facing Angie, she and I placed our fingertips lightly on the triangular wooden planchette. This object, infused with the spirit of Rolly, would zip—or dawdle, depending on his (my) mood—around the board and spell things out, visit the words YES or NO painted on the right and left of the board's upper corners, or use the numbers printed on the board to answer whatever we asked him. It.

Bother.

"Would you like to ask Rolly a question?" I queried Angie politely.

Visibly skeptical—no dunce, she—she said, "Why don't you ask him something? Based on the message delivered by the cards. Well, you know what I mean."

I sensed this was some kind of test.

"Yes, I believe I do." Therefore, carrying on not quite fearlessly, I said to my fictitious spirit control, "Rolly, the tarot cards told

Missus Mainwaring she might be in for a bit of…well, bother, fuss and…perhaps upset. Soon. Were the cards correct?"

The planchette raced to the YES on the board and stopped dead. I don't mean dead. Crumb.

"Hmm," said Angie. "Can you tell me what kind of bother it will be, Rolly?"

The planchette zipped to the NO. Then, as if on its own—it honestly felt as though I weren't manipulating it, although I hate to admit it—the blasted thing spelled out, "D-a-n-g-e-r."

"Danger?" I repeated weakly.

Again the planchette zipped to the YES. This time it didn't move from the spot.

Lifting her gaze from the board and peering hard at me, Angie said with a trace of tartness in her voice, "That's not a lot of comfort. Or help."

"No," I agreed, "it isn't. Um… Let me try a different question."

"Please. Feel free."

So I did. "Rolly? From whence will the upset and danger heading into Missus Mainwaring's life come?" That sounded downright literary, by golly!

Although it took Rolly a little longer to spell things out than to answer yes-or-no questions—say I, who invented the lousy spirit control in the first place—the planchette eventually spelled out, "Long ago and far away." How poetic.

Feeling edgy and as if, so far, I'd not done a very good job with this spiritualist-medium session, I glanced at Angie. "Um…Does that make any sense to you? I'm sorry. I'd expected—"

"No," she said, interrupting me. I didn't mind. "I mean, yes. It makes sense to me. I don't like it, but I think I know where at least some of these various dangers and upsets will come from."

"Oh."

"Mind if I ask Rolly one more question?"

"Not at all. This time is yours to do with as you please."

"Rolly." she said, her voice grim and determined, "will this… threat come from somewhere I've lived before?"

Zooming to the YES, the planchette hesitated on the word for a moment, then zoomed to the NO.

"Oh, dear," I said, noticing frown lines furrow Angie's perfect ivory brow.

"Hmm," said she. "Rolly, will some of this difficulty hail from Arizona?"

This time the planchette stopped, quivering, on the YES and stayed there.

"I see."

"Arizona?" I asked feebly.

Angie ignored my not-quite question. "But other…people… who wish me ill will also arrive to bother me?"

The planchette sat firmly on the YES.

"Hmm. Rolly's given me a clue," said Angie, astounding me, since I was about to stomp on the cursed planchette and smash it to splinters.

"He has?"

"Yes," she said. With great fortitude, by gosh. "I do believe I know where some of these upcoming so-called problems will hail from."

"Really?"

"Yes." Lifting her fingers from the planchette, Angie said, "Thank you very much, Daisy. I do believe Rolly's given me some sound information."

"He has?"

With a tightish smile, she said, "Oh, yes. At least I now know to expect some of my past life to catch up with me, and from whence it will come. At least I hope I do, so I can prepare myself."

As much as I wanted to ask her what her past life entailed, I curbed my curiosity. Doing so wasn't easy.

"But enough of this," said Angie, standing and smiling at me. The smile didn't appear to be forced, but by then I'd already determined this lady to be an extremely talented performer. "I promised you a turn on the piano."

"Are you sure? I'm sorry if you didn't get the answers you wanted. We can ask Rolly——"

"Oh, no, my dear," she said. "I got precisely the answers I'd hoped for—or expected, at least—and I won't need to bother Rolly any more today."

If she said so. I was monumentally grateful for her forbearance, because I'd pretty much lost all of mine. I couldn't take much more of Rolly's rebellion, blast him to a thousand hecks.

I don't think I meant that. Or maybe I did. Actually, I believe I meant something far worse than hecks. I'm not very nice sometimes.

Whatever my muddled state of mind, I thrust all my muddle-puddles—I'm sorry; couldn't help myself—aside. I'd been itching to get my fingers on that grand piano since I'd first seen it. As I packed away the tools of my trade, Angie lifted the lid to the piano bench and selected some sheet music. "Do you like show tunes?" she asked.

"You mean music from musical stage plays, like those that originate on Broadway? Like *The Student Prince* and so forth?"

"That's exactly what I mean."

"Oh, my, yes," I said, my enthusiasm unfeigned. "I have the sheet music to *No, No Nanette*, several Gilbert and Sullivan operettas, *The Merry Widow, The Chocolate Soldier,* and I adore 'The Charleston,' which was introduced in *Runnin' Wild* last year."

"I love that tune, too," said Angie, still smiling.

As she smiled, I sensed all remaining tension in the room dissipate. How odd.

"I have just the thing!" she said after a moment of shuffling through papers. "Here's 'The Merry Widow Waltz,' from *The Merry Widow*."

"One of my favorites," I said. What's even better was I'd just spoken the truth. It really *was* one of my favorites. "The waltz, along with 'I'm Off to Chez Maxim's.' In fact, *The Merry Widow* contains a lot of great music."

"It certainly does. Let's do 'Maxime's' instead of the waltz," said Angie sounding honestly pleased, which pleased me. "That way we can sing together."

I'd feared we'd part mortal enemies after the dismal reading I'd given her, and to which Rolly had added all on his own.

"Oh, but wait a minute!" Angie cried, lifting another piece of sheet music from the piano bench and waving it at me. Then she gazed at me with what I could only call a whimsical twinkle in her beautiful dark eyes. "Have you ever heard the 'Whiffenpoof Song?'"

Blinking, fearing she aimed to play some kind of hideous joke on me in retaliation for the rotten things I'd told her would stalk her near future, I said, "Um...No, I've never heard of it."

"Oh, we must sing this one." She gently placed the sheet music on the piano's music rest. "Perhaps you might want to play it through a time or two so as to familiarize yourself with it, if you don't know it already."

"Sounds like a good idea to me," I said doubtfully. Nevertheless, I sat on the piano bench and scanned the score to—Angie had been absolutely correct—something titled "The Whiffenpoof Song." And, by golly, after playing it through once, I decided it was a great song. Glancing up at Angie, who held her hands folded at her waist rather like an operatic diva, I asked, "What range do you sing? I mean, are you a soprano or an alto?"

Dropping her arms and laughing, she said, "I have no idea. I usually just learn the melodies to songs. I've never taken lessons. I expect I'm somewhere in the soprano range."

"Excellent. Why don't you take the melody, and I'll see what I can do about harmonizing."

"You can do that?"

"Oh, yes. It's one of my few skills."

"My dear, you have many, many skills."

If she said so. Anyhow, I played an introductory few bars, then nodded at Angie, and she started singing the melody in a delightful soprano voice. She might not have taken music lessons, but she had a great voice. The music being easy to follow, I did a pretty darned good job harmonizing with her. I was busy playing and singing, so I don't know this for a fact, but I think we sounded good together— at least as good as Lucy Zollinger and I. Lucy and I were often asked to sing duets by our choir director, Mr. Floy Hostetter.

"This is such a fun song!" I said, nearly giddy with glee. Not only had Angie forgiven me for my pathetic spiritualist output for the day, but I absolutely *loved* this song.

"Believe it or not, it originated in one of those ritzy universities back east. What is it? Princeton? Harvard? No, that's not— Oh, yes! Yale."

"Really? I had no idea it had such a prestigious beginning. It has a better education than I, for sure."

With a laugh, Angie said, "Me, too. It's supposed to be an acapella number, but who cares? Let's sing it again." She sounded almost as eager as I.

So we did. We'd just finished the last verse: "'Gentleman song-sters off on a spree, doomed from here to eternity. Lord have mercy as such as we. Baa, baa, baa,'" when I was nearly startled off the piano bench by applause coming at us from the door to the front parlor. When I looked up, darned if Pa wasn't there! And Spike! And, not as surprisingly as the other two, Mr. Judah Bowman.

"Well done, ladies," Mr. Bowman said, still clapping.

"Well done, for a fact," said Pa, grinning like mad.

48

Spike only wagged, but I knew he appreciated our rendition of the song, too. However...Well, what the dickens were Pa and Spike doing there?

"My goodness, Pa, you nearly scared me to death! And—" I turned to Angie. "Um...Do you mind having a dog in your house?"

"Not at all," said Angie, hurrying to the door. "And this one is perfectly charming."

I hurried after her, hoping to forestall any leaping on Spike's part. I definitely didn't want his little doggie claws shredding Angie's gorgeous Chinese silk...whatever it was.

The first thing I said when I reached the three men—I count Spike as one of the men, because he was a male—was, "Spike. Sit."

Spike sat.

"What an obedient dog!" said Angie, either genuinely impressed or giving a darned good imitation of impressedness. I'm pretty sure that's not a word.

"Yes, he is," I said, proud of my hound. "He placed first in his group at the Pasanita Dog Obedience Club's training class a couple of years ago. And that was in spite of a Great Dane named Hamlet who wanted to play with him."

"Mercy sakes," said Angie.

"Tell the truth now, Angie," said Mr. Bowman. "Have you ever seen a dog like this one before?"

"No, I haven't."

"I hope you don't mind me saying so," added Mr. Bowman, "but he's...an unusual shape for a dog. I guess I'm just used to being around...larger animals."

"Judah," said Angie in a scolding tone.

"It's all right. Spike doesn't mind being unique. In fact, he's proud of it."

"He looks as though he admires himself," said Mr. Bowman,

gazing at my darling dog, his forehead creased in what looked like puzzlement.

"Spike, you see, is a dachshund," I told my audience, also peering at my wonderful hound, only I did so with adoration rather than Mr. Bowman's bewilderment.

"A what?" asked Mr. Bowman, as if he thought I was telling a tall tale. Which is supposed to be funny, because Spike is so short.

Never mind.

"A dachshund," I explained. "Dachshunds are probably the only good thing ever produced in Germany. Well, Spike wasn't. He's from Altadena, but they were first…what do you call it when you create a new dog breed, anyway? Well, they were either discovered or invented in Germany, according to Mrs. Bissel, who possesses show dachshunds."

"Show dachshunds?" said Mr. Bowman, obviously still befuddled.

"Yes. You know. Some people with lots of money and time on their hands actually enter their dogs in dog shows. The Pasadena Kennel Club holds a dog show every year, and Missus Bissel's main goal in life is to have one of her dogs earn enough points—or whatever they are—to attend the big Westminster Kennel Club Dog Show in New York City."

"I've heard about show dogs," said Angie. "I think."

"Anyhow, Spike was bred by Missus Bissel—well, I mean she bred two of her dogs—and she gave Spike to me as a reward for…"

Blast. The explanation of Spike's entrance into my family's life sounded extremely odd. But what the heck. Mrs. Mainwaring—I mean Angie—had hired me in my role as spiritualist-medium, and the almost-true story might well garner more work for me in that capacity.

Therefore, I continued, "She gave me Spike for ridding her basement of a ghost. Or a spirit. Not sure what it was, really, but I got rid of it for her, and she gave me Spike. I wanted him mainly for my late husband, because—" I had to stop speaking because a lump suddenly lodged itself in my throat.

Patting me on the back, Pa said, "It's all right, Daisy." He spoke to Mr. Bowman and Angie next. "Daisy's late husband was in pretty bad shape after the war. Daisy thought a dog might comfort him and bring him some peace." Bending and stroking Spike lovingly, he added, "And she was right. Spike helped Billy a lot."

"For a while," I said, still trying not to cry.

"For a while," Pa agreed.

"Oh!" said Angie, as if she'd just remembered she was the hostess in this grand home. "Won't you come in and take a seat, Mister Gumm? Judah, will you please ask Hattie—"

"I'm sorry, but we can't stay," said Pa. "I only came here to fetch Daisy, if you're through with your session. One of your clients has called five or six times since you left the house this morning, sweetheart."

"Oh. Thanks, Pa." I didn't need to ask the client's name. The only person who'd telephone our home five or six times in the space of an hour or two was Mrs. Pinkerton.

"I'm sorry, sweetie," said Pa. I knew he meant the words sincerely.

"Daisy," said Angie, "I can't thank you enough for coming here today. You performed a valuable service, and I believe I'm prepared for whatever will come."

"I hope so," I said, telling the truth. I really liked the woman.

"You have. Believe me."

A glance passed between Angie and Mr. Bowman. Taking what I presumed to be her silent cue to him, Mr. Bowman continued into the parlor, and Angie saw Pa, Spike and me to the door.

"Thank you *so* much for letting me play your piano. It's a grand instrument," I said as we shook hands.

51

"I hope you'll come again," she said. "I loved singing with you."

"The two of you sounded very good together," said Pa.

"Thank you, Mister Gumm." Angie bestowed upon my father a glorious smile. I hoped to heck Pa, as an old married man—well, not old; middle-aged. But you know what I mean—was incorruptible. A smile like that might be devastating to a man who was vulnerable to feminine wiles.

But no. My father would *never* cheat on my mother. Anyhow, why would Angie want him when she could have Mr. Bowman?

Well, horse feathers. *That* wasn't very nice, was it? I apologize.

"I do hope everything will work out smoothly," I told Angie, taking Spike's leash from Pa. I'd bought the bright red leash as well as Spike's bright red collar, because red was his color. Really. It's the truth. I'm an expert at costuming, and I know these things.

"Thank you. I do, too. I'm glad to know you live right up the street, in case I have a spiritualist emergency."

We both laughed, but I don't think she was kidding.

SIX

S ure enough, the telephone began ringing the minute Spike, Pa and I entered the house. With a sigh, I bent to unhook Spike's leash from his collar, walked into the kitchen and plucked the earpiece from the cradle. "Gumm-Majesty home. Missus Majesty—"

"*Daisy!*" wailed Mrs. Pinkerton. I believe I've mentioned before she was a first-class wailer. In fact, if the Pasanita Dog Obedience folks ever decided to give wailing lessons, I'd wager everything I own on the probability she'd win the gold star and come in first.

"Please, Missus Pinkerton. Tell me what's wrong. I sense you're upset about something." I could sense her trouble because I'm an expert spiritualist-medium. No one else in the entire *world* would assume from her pitiful wailing she was upset about something. Yes, that was supposed to be a witticism.

Another not-funny one. I apologize again.

"Oh, *Daisy!*" Mrs. P continued, still wailing. "They've locked Stacy up in solitary con*fine*ment!"

About darned time. "Oh, dear. I'm so sorry. What…That is to say, why did they do that?" I'd been about to ask what her

53

disgusting daughter had done to warrant such punishment, but this was the disgusting daughter's mother, so I didn't.

"They claimed she *hit* another inmate! Oh, *Daisy*! I can't even *visit* her!"

As Stacy had conked me over the head with a kitchen chair once, I could easily believe the Stacy-striking-someone part of this scenario. Another part of it puzzled me, however. "Have you been visiting her?"

"Well…" Mrs. P hesitated. "Not really, but I've been sending emissaries."

Aha. Thought as much. Harold had told me his mother wouldn't be caught dead visiting anyone in jail. "And they aren't allowed to see her while she's in solitary confinement?"

"*No!*"

For the record, I always prepared myself for Mrs. P's answers to any of my questions by holding the earpiece a foot or so away from my ear. While I'll always appreciate Mrs. Pinkerton for wasting so much of her money on me, I didn't want to lose my hearing because of her. "Would you like me to bring Rolly over for a visit?" I asked gently and soothingly. I always spoke to her thus in the unceasing hope she'd one day take the hint and stop screeching into the telephone. That day my hint didn't work any better than it ever had, which was never.

"Oh, *would* you, dear? That would be *so* kind of you!"

So I did. I already wore a suitable costume for performing my duties as a spiritualist-medium, so I merely picked up my handbag, bade my father and my dog a fond farewell and exited the side door. Our side porch led to the driveway, where our almost-new Chevrolet sat.

As part of my *adieus*, I said to my male kin, "I'm so sorry I have to leave you again, Pa and Spike. I'd much rather be home with you than visiting Missus Pinkerton, especially when she's in a tizzy like this one."

"It's your job, sweetie," said Pa, who understood the working classes. "Although it sounded as though you were enjoying yourself at Missus Mainwaring's house today."

His words brought a smile to my lips. "Oh, I did enjoy myself. She's a lovely woman. I hope— Never mind." It wasn't my place to tell other people's stories to my father. My dog, maybe, but not my father. Not that Pa would blab, but Spike *couldn't* blab, so he was a safer bet.

In any case, spiritualism was total nonsense.

This fact didn't negate the itchy feeling I got when I recalled what the tarot cards and the Ouija board had told Mrs. Mainwaring. I hoped she wasn't really in for a hard time ahead.

I spent the remainder of the morning and most of my afternoon condoling with Mrs. Pinkerton. First she wanted to ask Rolly questions. Then she wanted to ask the tarot cards questions. Then she asked if I'd brought my crystal ball, and when I said I hadn't, she burst into tears. Oh, boy, what a jolly time.

"I'm so sorry, Missus Pinkerton. I didn't realize you'd want a reading from the crystal ball. If I'd known, I'd have brought it with me. Although," I said because it was true and because I wanted her to know, confound it, "it's very difficult for me to lift that heavy ball, even now."

"Oh, dear, really? Because of that ghastly accident you had?"

It hadn't been an accident. What's more, I had good reason to believe her daughter had been mixed up in it, even though none of the main players had turned out to be in Stacy's direct employ. "Yes. Only it wasn't an accident. Someone ran into me with that motorcar on purpose and squashed me up against a pepper tree, thereby dislocating my left shoulder, which is still awfully tender. My fiancé remains quite worried about my overall health and has asked me not to lift heavy things." Mind you, Sam had never said any such thing, but the sentiment sounded good. Sam was much more likely to tell me not to be an idiot and quit trying to lift the damned ball. I didn't say things like that, being a well-brought-up Methodist girl.

"What a sweet man!" cried Mrs. Pinkerton who, until recently, hadn't been able to recall Sam's last name. If she even made a stab at it, she'd call him Mr. Rotund or something equally appalling.

"He's very sweet to me," I said, smiling gently and wondering why some women had such good luck in finding good men and others didn't.

On the other hand, Sam and I had loathed each other upon first meeting, and I'd continued to dislike him after he'd overcome his dislike of me. Anyhow, the person of whom I'd thought when I thought that thought—the thought about some women being bad selectors-of-mates—was Miss Betsy Powell. Miss Betsy Powell had been in love with at least three honest-to-goodness rats, two of whom had murdered people. Was that just lousy luck on her part? Or was there something inside a person's innermost workings that accounted for his or her attraction to good or awful people? Not that it matters. I attempted to focus my wandering wits on the matter at hand.

"I'm so happy for you, Daisy!" Mrs. Pinkerton gasped through her sobs. "My Algie is good to me, too."

Truer words had seldom been spoken. Mrs. Pinkerton's second husband, Mr. Algernon Pinkerton, was a kind and loyal man. Round and roly-poly, he had a cherubic pink face, a vast fortune, and two relatively nice sons who played polo. Mrs. P's first husband —whom she'd divorced for excellent reasons—Mr. Eustace Kincaid, had been a total rotter. I think Stacy came by her beastly qualities from her father, while Harold came by his sterling ones via his mother. Only Harold also possessed more than a few brain cells to rub together, unlike Mrs. P. Not sure about Stacy's overall intelligence, although her behavior always had been and continued to be abominable.

"I know he is, Missus Pinkerton, and everyone who loves you is happy you found each other." Was that too mawkish? Naw. This was Mrs. Pinkerton. She and mawkishness went together like bacon and eggs. Or French toast and syrup. Or…Well, you get the idea.

By the time this conversation took place, I was about to fall over from starvation. Not literally, but I'd missed lunch, and I was awfully hungry.

During a surreptitious glance at my wristwatch, which Mrs. P wasn't supposed to see but did, she screeched, "Oh! But I've kept you forever! Oh, Daisy, I'm so sorry! Please, *please* forgive me."

"There's nothing to forgive, Missus Pinkerton. You were having a difficult time, and I'm always available for you when you need me." Sam might eventually have something to say about my general accessibility, but he didn't yet.

"Why don't you go to the kitchen and see if your aunt can fix you a snack or something? Oh, dear, I feel so guilty about keeping you so long!" More tears followed the riverbed pattern her earlier ones had etched in her formerly impeccably made-up face.

"Nonsense. But I will pop in and see Vi if you don't mind. It's about time for her to leave, and I'd be happy to drive her home."

"Wonderful idea! Here, dear. Something extra for *always* being such a special friend to me in my time of need."

And darned if she didn't hand me a hundred bucks. I swear, the woman threw money around as if it were confetti. After I'd almost been murdered on New Year's Day, she'd sent Harold over with not only tons of gifts, but five hundred dollars! For no reason whatsoever, except that she was a big-hearted woman. Which made sense, as the rest of her was also quite portly.

Good Lord! How unkind can one normally pleasant and compassionate spiritualist-medium be, anyway? Awfully unkind, evidently, although I think starvation had something to do with my evil mood that afternoon.

At any rate, after I finally escaped from Mrs. Pinkerton's

drawing room—which, in our family, is a living room; in Mrs. Mainwaring's house, it's the front parlor—I all but staggered down the hall to the kitchen, passing Edie Applewood on the way. Edie and I had been schoolmates once upon a time, and now she worked as Mrs. P's lady's maid. Her husband, Quincy, worked as the caretaker for Mr. Pinkerton's sons' horses.

"Hey, Daisy," said Edie, smiling broadly. "I'll bet you had a heck of a time in there today."

"You'd win your bet," I told her. "How are you and Quincy holding up?"

"Oh, we're fine, thanks. Poor Missus P has been in an awful flap ever since that disgusting daughter of hers got herself locked up." She shook her head. "I know Missus Pinkerton's a nincompoop, but she's a nice lady and really doesn't deserve Stacy."

"Nobody does. I'm sorry the brat's such a sore trial to Missus P."

"Yeah. Me, too. But I'd better get on upstairs. I expect I'll have to re-do milady's makeup before dinner tonight."

"Somebody had better re-do it. Her poor face looks like someone painted riverbeds on it from all the crying she's done today."

With a laugh, Edie tripped up the servants' staircase, and I pushed open the swing door leading to the kitchen. Vi was delighted to see me.

As for me, I was delighted with the supremely delicious aromas emanating from the cardboard box in which Vi had packed the Gumm-Majesty-Rotondo-Prophet dinner. My goodness, but life could be complicated sometimes, couldn't it? We used to be just the Gumms and the Majestys. Then we were the Gumms, Majestys and Rotondo. And now Lou Prophet had more or less joined the family. That was all right by me. I liked Mr. Prophet, even if he was something of an anachronism in staid, peaceful, refined Pasadena.

That evening I stuffed myself at the dinner table, winning odd looks from my family and a gentle reproof from my mother, who said, "Goodness, Daisy, how many people are you eating for?" Then she blushed, because the words she'd spoken might have implied I was "with child," as the picturesque saying has it.

Lou Prophet attempted to smother his chuff of amusement, and Sam gave me a sharp glance.

Fiddlesticks. "I missed lunch today, Ma," I said, whining only slightly. "And I'm starving to death. Well, not *really*." Defiantly, I snatched another biscuit from the bread basket, broke it in half, and slathered butter on it. I did all this whilst displaying excellent manners, too. No slovenly dining for Daisy Gumm Majesty, spiritualist-medium extraordinaire, by golly.

"I like to see a lady with a good appetite," said Mr. Prophet, grinning wickedly.

"Me, too," said Sam, although he didn't sound exactly sure of himself.

"Anyhow, Vi's beef stew is one of the marvels of the modern world, and I should think you'd be glad I appreciate it so much." Turning from my wonderful mother to my wonderful aunt, I said, "Thank you so much, Vi. I don't know what we'd do without you."

"Yes, well, that's the truth," admitted Ma. "I'm just not accustomed to seeing you eat so much at a meal. I didn't realize you missed lunch. How did that happen?"

"Missus Pinkerton."

Solemn nods followed this two-word answer. Everyone understood. Mrs. Pinkerton had been part of our family's history for more than half my life.

"And before Missus P, I spent a good part of the morning with Missus Mainwaring. Her reading turned out to be…well, not great.

According to the tarot cards and Rolly, someone from her past is going to show up and cause trouble for her."

"Her past?" Lou Prophet squinted at me.

"Yes. Her past in Arizona. And, according to Rolly, a couple of other places, too."

"Arizona, eh? What did you say this lady's name was again?" he asked, his brow furrowing, as if he were trying to place her in his memory.

"Mainwaring. Evangeline Mainwaring."

Prophet chewed over the name as he chewed on his biscuit, then swallowed and shook his head. "Never met anyone by that name."

"I guess Arizona is a big place," I said.

"Not that many places fit to live in there, though," Prophet said

"Anyhow, after we finished with the cards and the board, she let me play her grand piano!"

"What fun for you," said Ma.

Almost under his breath, Mr. Prophet said, "A piano-playing lady sounds like someone I might have known way back in my prime, but I still don't recollect that name."

"They sang together, too, and sounded terrific," said Pa.

"How do you know that?" Ma asked my father rather sharply.

"Daisy was gone for so long, and Missus Pinkerton called so often and sounded so desperate, Spike and I went down the street to fetch her home again."

"Oh," said Ma, who had met Mrs. Mainwaring and knew her to be a genuine beauty. I don't think she was jealous, but I wasn't certain. Feeling insecure about one's partner in life was one of the easier traps in which to fall. I knew *that* from bitter experience. Humiliatingly bitter experience, even.

"After you've finished shoveling chow, Daisy, I'd like the whole family—and, of course, Lou—to walk across the street and see the latest thing I've done in the house," said Sam, grinning and trying to sound enigmatic.

"What do you mean, 'done in the house,' Sam?" I asked. *Done in the house?* Hmm. Wasn't sure I liked the sound of his comment. When Spike was a puppy, he had done a few things in the house for which I'd had to scold him.

"You'll see," said Sam, still mysterious.

"You'll like it," said Mr. Prophet, grinning as he buttered yet another biscuit. How come Ma didn't ask *him* why he was eating so darned much?

Never mind.

"That's nice to know," I said uncertainly.

"You'll like it," said Sam, echoing Mr. Prophet. "I can guarantee it."

"Goodness, you two men sound so…What's the word? Mystifying? I guess that's the word I mean," said Vi, working on her own second bowlful of her amazing beef stew.

In other words, it wasn't just I who was making a pig of myself that evening. We all were, and I thought my mother's comment about me stuffing myself and perhaps "eating for more than one" had been unwarranted.

"Mystifying works," I said, my curiosity whizzing out of control.

I needn't have worried. Not that I *had* worried. Exactly. Still…I wasn't altogether certain I approved of Sam's ability to keep secrets from me. I would, after all, sooner or later become his wife and his partner in life. This would make the third or fourth surprise he'd sprung on me since we got engaged. Mind you, all the surprises had been good so far, but… Well, I don't suppose it matters.

Leaving the dishes soaking in the sink, my family and I walked across the street. Lou Prophet opened the gate enclosing the porch, and we trooped inside. Instantly, I saw Sam's surprise.

"Sam! You bought a piano!"

"A baby grand," he said, attempting to sound modest, "because a grown-up grand would, I thought, be too big to look good in this room. But if you want a grand piano, I'll get you one. I figured you'd enjoy having a piano of your own."

"I *love* it!" I all but shrieked with delight. "Oh, Sam, you're *so* good to me!"

I turned and threw my arms around him before he could say, "Damned right," so Lou Prophet said it for him.

Nobody seemed to mind Mr. Prophet's profanity. Truth to tell, we were all pretty much used to his foul mouth by this time. And this, in spite of the fact that he honestly attempted not to swear when in our company. He'd led a wild and woolly, not to mention adventurous, life before he ended up in Pasadena, California. He belonged in Pasadena kind of like a feral hog belonged in a bed of pansies. Not that he was porky. Far from it.

A chorus of delighted thanks issued from my parents and aunt. Sam, trying to detach me and still striving for modesty, told them it was nothing, and that their daughter deserved the very best.

"She does," my father concurred.

"Oh, yes," said Vi.

"Hmmm," said Ma.

But she was pleased, too; I could tell.

"I had a piano-tuner come along with the instrument, so it should be ready to go," said Sam.

"I know we still have to do the dishes and it's getting kind of late, but would anyone mind if I played a tune or two?"

No one minded. At least they didn't say so aloud. Lou Prophet went so far as to say he liked him a good tune every now and then. He'd said that before.

Therefore, after I'd played the scales and a few chords—the piano sounded grand even if it wasn't—I played a hymn I knew by heart, "Amazing Grace." Then, because it was bouncy, I could recall the music, and both Sam and Lou had sung it once when I'd played it on my parents' piano, I struck the opening chords for "Tea for Two." Darned if the two men didn't sing it again!

That turned out to be one of the best evenings of my entire life. The only thing that would have made it better was if I could have remained in Sam's house and not gone across the street to wash the dishes.

Oh, well. One of these days…

SEVEN

The baby grand piano—a *Baldwin*, for goodness' sake—turned out to be the last surprise I received from Sam during the week before our neighborhood party for Angie Mainwaring. Ma and Vi both worked during the day. As Sam also held a day job, even though he didn't need it—I'm honestly not avaricious, but knowing Sam had money gave me such a profound sense of security, it's almost impossible to describe—it was Harold Kincaid and I who took responsibility for arranging the party.

Besides all that, Sam had told me more than once he didn't know beans about party-planning, didn't want to learn, why the heck else would he have suggested the Castleton cater this one, and also why the heck else would he have asked me to call Harold about it? Only he didn't use the word "heck." At any rate, I considered his questions valid. Lou Prophet did a good job of staying out of our way. He appeared a trifle worried, though, as if he feared we might ask him to do something—tell us what our color scheme should be; or, maybe, would he mind donning a waiter's livery and serve guests. Although we hadn't discussed the matter, I figured his party-planning skills and interest in same were about on a par with Sam's.

Wow! I just used a golfing term. And I don't even know anyone who plays golf. I tell you, the reading of novels is educational, and don't let anyone tell you otherwise.

"I'm not much for prettifying places for parties," Mr. Prophet muttered Wednesday morning as he escaped out the back door and fled to his little cottage, carrying a cup of coffee with him.

His absence of prettifying skills was all right by Harold and me. Harold even said, "I think we're better off preparing for this 'do' without him, Daisy. If we left it up to him, he'd probably decorate the walls with his collection of guns, stuffed grizzly bears and mounted moose antlers."

"Harold!" But I laughed. Couldn't help it. "He helped Sam a lot with the floors and the banister and so forth. He sanded and varnished the banister as if he'd been doing such things all his life."

"I thought he used to kill people for a living."

"Not always. I suspect the wanted posters had 'dead or alive' printed on them, although, from what I've managed to gather so far, I believe he preferred the 'dead' option. Dead people probably don't cause too many problems, although they probably stink after a while."

"Daisy!"

"Well, it's true. And if he had to cross a desert to fetch a felon, he'd have to worry about how to feed him and not let him escape. So it would probably be easier to cart a corpse as long as he didn't have to have it slung over his horse for too many days."

Harold's nose wrinkled. "Stop it!"

So I obeyed, only adding, "Anyhow, he must have had some sanding and varnishing experience in his life, because he's really good at it."

"If you say so, my dear." Harold stepped away from a small

grouping of chairs he'd arranged for folks to sit in when they got tired of walking around the house, eating canapés, prying into cupboards, gossiping, etc., studying it critically. "Very nice," said he.

By the way, as the week progressed, I didn't get one tearful telephone call from Harold's mother. When I asked him about this strange forbearance on her part, Harold said slyly, "She doesn't dare. I told her if she wanted to attend the party, she had to leave you alone because the preparations were wearing you down. I also told her you hadn't completely recovered from your run-in with the motorcar and the pepper tree."

"Harold Kincaid! What a monstrous liar you are!"

"One of my many talents," said he, polishing his fingernails on what would have been his lapel had he been wearing a coat.

I agreed with him. Anyhow, I'd also pleaded my left shoulder as an excuse to Mrs. P. It was nice to have a few days free from her moaning and groaning, even if her silence had been produced by a fib. Actually, it was more of a major lie. It worked, though, and that's what mattered.

Although preparing for parties isn't something I do often, Harold planned parties all the time, and he made preparing for this one fun. He and I always had a good time together. The Friday evening before the party, which was set to begin at noon the next day, which was Saturday, the fourth of April, Sam, Harold and I made one last crucial sweep of the house to make sure all was well. It was more than well; it was *gorgeous*.

The Castleton staff aimed to bring tables and more chairs since Sam and I hadn't bought furniture for the place yet—except, of course, the baby grand piano. And if that wasn't the sweetest thing a man has ever done for a woman, I don't know what was.

Oh, and we'd also furnished the master bedroom, but that was our secret. I personally aimed to keep that door locked throughout the party.

However, in light of wanting the house to look good for guests, I'd selected sheer curtains for the living room and dining room windows, and I'd also bought beautiful muted green draperies to pull over the sheers at night.

"Love the draperies," Harold said, observing them with approval.

"Daisy picked them," said Sam, who had been nice to Harold for several weeks by then. I hoped this new appreciation of my best friend would last. With Sam, one never knew.

"Thanks, Harold. I think green and this house naturally go together." I felt like an idiot after I said that.

Fortunately, neither Sam nor Harold considered the statement idiotic. In fact, both men nodded.

"Yes," said Harold. "This house definitely needs green." He turned and touched my arm. "Say, Daisy, you and Sam ought to come with me to that big furniture warehouse in Hollywood. Can't remember the name of the place."

"Fulton's?" asked Sam, surprising me. What in the name of heaven did Sam Rotondo know about where to buy furniture?

Not the least bit shocked, Harold said, "That's the one! Great place, and you can pick up some real bargains there sometimes."

"You and Daisy can shop for furniture," said Sam. "I trust you both to have impeccable taste, and I'd...rather not."

If anyone had told me four years earlier that one day Sam Rotondo would be saying nice things about or to Harold Kincaid —or me, for that matter—I'd have laughed in his or her face after I picked myself up from my faint on the floor. You just never knew what life held in store for you, did you?

"I'd love it," I told my beloved and Harold.

"Whatta you love?" came Lou Prophet's creaky voice from the kitchen. Guess he'd come in while we'd been gazing with admiration at our new draperies. He could be remarkably quiet, considering he had that peg leg to deal with.

"Shopping for furniture with Harold," I said.

"Oh, yeah? Interesting." He spoke in about the least interested voice I'd ever heard issue from a human mouth.

All four of us laughed. Including Mr. Prophet, who then said, "Guess the place does need a chair or a sofa or something. It's pretty bare now."

"We'll have a good time finding chairs, sofas, and lots of other furniture," said Harold. "When Daisy and I get together, there's no stopping us."

"That's for damned sure," mumbled Sam. I gave him a reproving whack on the arm. He then used that arm to pick me up and swing me around. "You can't imagine how afraid I was when I first brought you over here, Daisy. I thought you'd hate the house and me, too. I took a huge chance, you know."

After giving him a whopping smooch, I said, "Oh, you silly man. I love you, and I've loved this house ever since my family bought the bungalow across the street."

"Ain't that sweet?" said Prophet, his voice as dry as the Mojave Desert, which resided a couple hundred miles away from Pasadena.

"Extremely sweet," said Harold, nearly matching Prophet's tone in the dryness department.

"Come along, Sam," I said. "I don't think these two gentlemen approve of us."

"Oh, I approve of *you*, Miss Daisy," said Prophet, all but ogling me. "And Sam and Harold aren't too bad, either. Neither of 'em can hold a candle to you, of course." He winked. By then Sam and I had become accustomed to his teasing ways, so neither of us got our frillies in a twist. That's another one of Mr. Prophet's old-west sayings.

"There's a ringing endorsement if I ever heard one," Sam said, plopping me on my feet again. "Now think hard for a minute, Daisy. Do we need to do anything else in order to prepare for this shindig? I don't want to be rushing around tomorrow picking up things we'll need and don't have."

Digging in the pocket of my once-blue day dress—I'd had it for so long, it was now kind of a grayish color—I withdrew a folded sheet of paper. After reading it and handing it to Harold, who did likewise, we said in unison, "Nope."

Harold went on, "This list covers every little thing we might possibly need. We even over-bought a few items, like napkins and so forth. The Castleton will bring dishes and food, but you never know about napkins."

"Truer words were never spoken," said Prophet, trying to sound serious.

Neither Harold nor I minded. Sam snorted.

"I'm so glad you have lots of money, Sam. It's such fun spending it for you." I smiled sweetly at my fiancé, who grimaced back at me.

"Don't get too used to it," he advised. "I might lose it all one of these days, and then where will you be?"

"With you, my love." I batted my eyelashes at him.

"Good God," Sam said.

"Yeah," said Prophet. "It's gettin' kinda deep in here. I just came in for the latest *National Geographic*. Think I'll go out to the little house before I get sick to my stomach."

"It *was* a little drippy, Daisy," said Harold.

"Yes, it was. I love to tease Sam."

"How well I know it," said Sam. "All right then, I guess we're ready. When will the caterers show up?"

Harold, who knew, answered. "At ten. I think we ought to gather here at around nine-thirty to be on the safe side."

"Sounds good to me," said Sam.

"Me, too," said I.

Lou Prophet, shaking his head in what I assumed to be disgust, had already exited the house.

69

Saturday, April 4, 1925, dawned as clear and bright and beautiful as an April day can get in Pasadena, which is pretty darned clear, bright and beautiful. I loved my city. And I definitely looked forward to the day's amusements. Almost a hundred people had accepted invitations to attend our party. The party Sam was paying for without a single grumble or protest.

It had boggled my mind when Sam had admitted to being a wealthy man, and my mind remained boggled. Until that eventful evening during which he'd revealed all to me, I'd imagined we'd live in a nice little house, probably not in Pasadena, since property in the city had become quite expensive if you're dealing with a police detective's salary.

What had boggled my mind even more than learning about Sam's moneybags, was learning that my father had known Sam's secret (and kept it from me, darn it) for a couple of years by the time Sam revealed it to me. Sam Rotondo, who often reminded me of an irritable granite obelisk or a cold marble statue, had gone to my father and asked for Pa's blessing upon our union! And that was before I'd even learned to like Sam, much less fallen madly in love with him. I think he'd refrained from telling me about his over-flowing coffers because he didn't want me marrying him for his money. As if I'd ever do such a thing.

At least I don't think I'd do such a thing.

Naw. I wouldn't.

Well…

Oh, never mind.

On Saturday morning, as promised, the Castleton catering crew arrived on the dot at ten a.m. They drove to the bungalow in two large covered trucks and began hauling in boxes and boxes of foodstuffs from one truck and a boatload of tables, chairs, dishes, glasses, cups, and saucers, etc., from the other one.

"Wow, these guys are good," I said, in awe of the almost-choreographed precision demonstrated by the Castleton staff.

"You betcha," said Harold. "But I'd better go into the house and tell them where everything goes."

I hadn't even considered doing such a thing. I'm not a party-planner by nature, as mentioned before.

But when I joined Harold and the Castleton folk, Harold was giving orders like a by-golly general, and the Castleton folks were obeying him like privates. Is there a rank lower than private? If there is, that's how they obeyed him.

He directed them to put tables *there*, and to put chairs *there*, and how the lovely white cloths should be placed on the tables, how the napkins should be folded, where the plates and cups and glasses should go, which canapés should be placed where, and how the flatware should be arranged. He had them stick chairs pretty much everywhere including all of the rooms save the master bedroom, which I had already locked. Then there were the vases and vases of flowers Harold had ordered (at Sam's expense) from the most prestigious flower shop in Pasadena, and which Harold directed the staff to place in precise locations in the various rooms.

Harold definitely possessed an artist's eye. The only skill I possessed was chatting with dead people, and I couldn't really even do that.

Well, I was a darned good seamstress, but Harold's organizational prowess impressed me a lot.

As I'd asked her to do, Angie arrived at the house at eleven-thirty.

"This is so wonderful of you, Daisy," Angie said, gazing around with perceptible approval. "Your home is beautiful."

"Harold organized the party," I told her.

Harold, who had just greeted her himself, took a bow. Angie and I laughed. "You're extremely good at this, Mister Kincaid," Angie told him.

"Natural talent," said Harold. Not shy about his assets, Harold. I loved him for it, too.

People began showing up precisely at noon, eager to see the home Sam and I aimed to occupy and to meet the wealthy owner of Orange Acres and the big house down the street. Therefore, Angie and I acted as a two-person reception line at the front door for the first hour or so. After that, we decided to let people fend for themselves and hied ourselves over to the tables laden with food.

Boy, the Castleton did a good job! They'd even prepared trays full of lobster rolls. My father stood stock-still and gazed down upon those particular delicacies in what appeared to me like awe.

"Good Lord, Daisy, this must have cost Sam a blooming fortune! I haven't had a lobster roll since we moved to Pasadena from Auburn." The Auburn Pa meant was in Massachusetts.

"Stuff yourself. You deserve all the lobster you can eat." I caught sight of another delicacy that had been laid out for our party. "And shrimp! Oh, boy, I'm going to have some shrimp with that special sauce the Castleton makes. I love that stuff. And Sam's got lots of bucks, so you don't even have to pay for it."

My mother, standing next to Vi, who stood beside my father, said, "Daisy!" in *that* voice. Ah, well. Sam, who lingered nearby, only laughed, so it was all right.

Besides the lobster rolls and shrimp cocktail, the Castleton staff brought about a million deviled eggs, two huge bowls of mixed fruit, some little sandwiches with their crusts cut off—I hope they at least fed the crusts to the birds and didn't throw them all in the garbage—and some sausage rolls (I'd almost eaten a sausage roll when Harold took me to London on our way to Egypt, but it was difficult for me to eat anything at all in those days, so I'd only nibbled at it). I aimed to actually *eat* one at our party. There were trays of cheeses and cold cuts, stuffed mush-rooms, asparagus spears wrapped in bacon, and tons and tons of other food. I hadn't even known some of those items existed in the world until that day. As many of our guests said, it was quite a spread.

Lots of people from our church came, and I was pleased to see Miss Emmaline Castleton, whose father had built the hospital bearing his name as well as the Hotel Castleton, employees of which business walked quickly here and there, doing things. Emmaline and I had become friends a couple of years back, oddly enough because we'd both loved men who were killed by the war. Emmaline's fiancé died in France, and Billy died in Pasadena, but the war did them both in. In Stephen Allison's case, there; in Billy Majesty's case, here.

Mrs. Bissel brought Mrs. Pinkerton with her, which I considered awfully kind of her. She knew Mrs. Pinkerton as well as I and, while Mrs. Bissel herself had lots of money, she wasn't nearly as addle-pated as Mrs. Pinkerton tended to be. Mrs. Pansy Hanratty, who had taught Spike's obedience class, arrived with her son, Monty Mountjoy, *the* leading Adonis in motion pictures at the moment, causing no end of flutter among the female party attendees. Since I know considerably more about Monty—who was a splendid chap—than anyone else there except Harold, I didn't flutter.

Flossie and Johnny Buckingham brought their little boy, Billy, with them. A darling lad, he'd had a wonderful time with Mr. Prophet some months back. Their appreciation of one another had surprised me, since I hadn't pegged—if you'll pardon the expression—Lou Prophet as a man who enjoyed being around children. Goes to show yet again that nobody knows what goes on the minds (or lives) of others. Even phony spiritualist-mediums. Or should that be media? Good Lord, I didn't even know what to call my own fake profession!

"I'll keep close tabs on him, Daisy," said Flossie, smiling happily. "What a beautiful home you have!"

"Thanks, Flossie," I said, giving her a hug. She was probably the nicest person I'd ever met in my life, barring Johnny, her husband.

"Beautiful," said Johnny, smiling in his own right.

"Is Mistew Pwophet hewe?" Billy asked.

"Soon," I said, thinking he was cute as a bug. Not that bugs are cute, but…Oh, nertz. Don't mind me.

After an hour or two of chatting and nibbling—the shrimp cocktail and those lobster rolls were *very* good—Mr. Floy Hostetter, our choir director, noticed the baby grand in the living room (I presume he hadn't seen it instantly because of the horde of people milling about) and hurried over to me in order to gush about it. Mrs. Fleming, our organist at the church, joined Mr. Hostetter and his wife in singing praises to the piano.

Therefore, because I'm a terrible show-off, I said I'd be happy to play some tunes for our guests. And I did. And everyone applauded. Then I asked Angie if she'd care to sing "The Whiffen-poof Song" with me, and *she* did.

I was having so much fun—and believed everyone else to be likewise employed—when we got to the last chorus of "Whiffen-poof." Then, suddenly, Angie ceased singing, her voice making a funny clicking sound before it stopped altogether. The rest of the room went quiet, too, all at once.

Turning on the piano bench, wondering if a bomb-throwing anarchist had managed to crash the party, I saw Angie, her hand at her throat, staring fixedly at someone or something across the room. So I pivoted a little more and saw Lou Prophet, stock still in the middle of the floor, holding a lobster roll in one of his hands, his mouth agape, staring as if he were Lot's wife after peeking back to see Sodom and Gomorrah flaming away.

Angie said, "Oh, my Lord!"

Lou Prophet said, "God damn sumbitch."

For the record, Mr. Judah Bowman, who had been enjoying himself too up until that moment, looked from Angie to Prophet and back again, puzzlement writ large on his features. I'm sure most of the occupants of the room shared his confusion. I know I sure did.

Then Lou Prophet turned abruptly on his peg leg—he could maneuver with that thing quite gracefully, considering he'd had it for less than a year—and stomped out of the house, carrying his lobster roll with him.

EIGHT

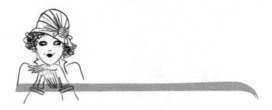

I didn't know what to do. I sat on the piano bench, fingers poised over the keys, and…didn't know what to do.

Finally, Sam came to the fore. "May I help you, Mrs. Mainwaring?" he asked, all but oozing solicitude. "Have you something caught in your throat?"

Since he'd handed her a perfect excuse, Angie ran with it. After coughing a couple of times, she croaked, "Oh, my." Then she forced another couple of coughs and pretended to clear her throat. She glanced at Mr. Bowman and frantically clutched his arm.

"You all right, Angie?" asked Mr. Bowman.

"Perhaps you need a glass of lemonade or something?" I asked, at last having found my speaking voice. I gently withdrew my fingers from above the piano keys and placed them in my lap.

"Yes," said Sam, still oozing. "Lemonade will be just the ticket." He headed to the kitchen.

"Yes," Angie said in a strangled tone. "Oh, Daisy, yes, please. Will you please take me to the kitchen?"

"I think Sam's going to the kitchen. Perhaps we should go out onto the back porch until he brings your lemonade to you."

"Oh. Oh, yes. That will be just what I need. A glass of water. I mean lemonade." She turned to the audience, the members of which were still staring, confused. Smiling sweetly, she said to them, feigning hoarseness, "I beg your pardon. An unexpected frog in my throat. I'll be all right in a minute. Just need a drink of lemonade to soften my vocal cords."

I managed to say, "We'll be back in a jiffy," before Angie grabbed my arm, yanked me off the piano bench and, with Mr. Bowman following, headed to the kitchen. The wait staff from the Castleton crowded the kitchen, running this way and that like frantic rabbits, so I hustled Angie, Mr. Bowman, and Sam onto the back porch. Sam had possessed the presence of mind to bring a glass of lemonade with him, and he handed it to Angie as soon as she'd seated herself on a chair in one of Harold's artistic groupings.

When I glanced around, I was pleased to see no one else on the porch. They were probably still indoors stuffing themselves. Which was precisely what they were supposed to do. I'm not complaining.

After taking a gulp of lemonade and fanning herself with her hand for a second or two, Angie looked at me, almost accusingly. "You didn't tell me you knew *Lou Prophet!*"

"Um…no, I didn't. Why would I?" Because her voice had held an edge of panic, I didn't get angry.

She put her glass down and covered her face with both hands. "No. There was no reason for you to. You're not at fault. I'm sorry, Daisy. But those cards and the Ouija board were absolutely right, although I didn't expect things to happen so quickly. Talk about someone from my *past!* Oh, Lord." I was pleased to note she wasn't a weeper—unlike some of us.

"You know that peg-legged fellow, Angie?" asked Mr. Bowman, a frown creasing his magnificent brow. Well, magnificent in that he was a terribly handsome man. Too old for me, of course.

Smiling at my fiancé, I said, "Thanks for thinking up the lemonade excuse, Sam."

"Sure thing," he said, squinting at me and knowing *precisely* what I'd been thinking. Sometimes I think he knows me too well. But, golly, Sam was a terribly handsome man, too, if not *quite* as decorative as Mr. Bowman. Anyhow, Mr. Bowman looked kind of like what one might call a fancy Dan. Sam was all masculinity.

The four of us straightened in our chairs when we heard the thud-plop-thud-plop of Lou Prophet's leg and peg as he walked past the orange trees lining the gravel pathway leading from his cottage to our back porch. For the record, the trees had blossomed, and the aroma out there was downright heavenly. Mr. Prophet appeared far from heavenly. In fact, he looked mad enough to spit railroad spikes. I don't think that's an old-west saying. I think I got it from my father.

Hoping to avert a duel or something equally catastrophic on the porch, I got up and walked to the porch steps. Standing on the top step, I folded my arms across my chest and barred Mr. Prophet's entry.

"Mister Prophet," I said sweetly. "I get the feeling you and Missus Mainwaring have met before."

"Missus *Who?*" Prophet growled. "That there's no *Missus Mainwaring*. That there's Angela Smith, and she fleeced me of a whole lot of money in Tombstone some years back."

"Now, Lou, don't be like that," said Angie, attempting a sweetness equal to my own and missing by a mile.

"The hell you say!"

"Exactly who *is* this person, Angie?" asked Mr. Bowman, still frowning fiercely. On him fierce looked good.

I probably shouldn't have noticed that, should I? Oh, dear. Sorry.

"For that matter," growled Prophet, looking Mr. Bowman up and down, "who the hell are *you?*"

"All right, let's all settle down," Sam said, rising from his chair, putting on his Italian-Count-Police-Detective mien, and using his I'm-going-to-kill-you-and-dump-you-in-the-ocean-in-cement-over-shoes voice. "Missus Evangeline Mainwaring, this is Mister Lou Prophet. I take it you two have…met before, only perhaps you had a different name then, Missus Mainwaring?"

"Different name, my ass. That's Angela Smith, and she ran the biggest whorehouse in Tombstone! Evangeline Mainwaring, be damned."

Nearly shocked out of my pretty blue pumps, I still managed to say, "Mister Prophet, please!" in an attempt to curtail his profanities, although I already knew the task to be impossible.

"Daisy," said Sam in the same deadly voice. "Shut up."

So I shut up. Didn't dare do anything else. When Sam got into one of *those* moods, it was best to do as he said.

He continued, "Lou, come up here onto the porch and sit down. Let's sort this out. There's no need for violence. Or profanity," he added, shooting me a glance.

"Hellkatoot," said Prophet. But I moved out of his way and he continued up the stairs and sat on a chair as far away from Angie as he could get.

But merciful heavens! Had Lou Prophet spoken the truth? Was Evangeline Mainwaring—or whatever her real name was—*truly* a former scarlet woman?

Oh, boy, I sure hoped so! Evidently Harold had been right about her all along! This was the absolute *berries*!

"Now," said Sam remaining on his feet, probably so he could catch anyone should he or she try to leap up and attempt some variety of brutality on another one of us, "please explain these allegations." He turned to Angie. "Ladies first." He didn't even sound cynical.

"Lady!" spat Prophet. "Hell." He, on the other hand, raised cynicism to a level surpassing any I'd heard before.

"Pipe down, Lou. Ladies first." Sam sounded even deadlier this time, a feat of which I hadn't believed him capable until then.

Grasping Mr. Bowman's hand and squeezing it hard, Angie whispered, "Yes. Yes, he's telling the truth. I ran a parlor house—"

"Parlor house, my ass," Lou interrupted.

Turning his man-mangling gaze upon him, Sam said, "Shut up."

Lou lifted his hands, said, "Shit," and dropped his hands to his lap again. But he shut up. Probably for the best, all things considered.

As if gathering her strength, Angie then spoke more forcefully— although she kept her voice soft enough so as not to be heard inside the house unless someone were eavesdropping, and I hoped like heck nobody was. "Yes. I ran a parlor house in Tombstone. That was at least twenty years ago. Not that it's an excuse, but I was born on the Lower East Side of Manhattan, and...Well, I grew up hard. I scrimped and saved until I managed to leave—at least I had hoped to leave—parlor houses behind me forever. When I moved to Pasadena in 1896, I fully expected to have seen the last of that god-awful life." She licked her lips, picked up her glass in a slightly shaky hand, and took another sip of lemonade. "I...I...Well, I used every trick at my disposal in order to make my escape. I..." Her words trickled off.

When nobody picked up the strands of conversation for her, she went on after what seemed like a year and a half of silence. "If it's true Mister Prophet was injured in some way because of my business tactics...Well, I apologize, but not awfully hard. I wasn't given any chances in this life. I had to make my own. And you," she added, scowling balefully at Mr. Prophet, "chose to make use of the ladies I employed."

"Ladies," said Prophet in a voice brimming with loathing and scorn. "My ass."

"Lou," said Sam.

Prophet said, "Hellkatoot," but shut up after uttering the one word.

"It's true," said Angie. "I ran a parlor house, and *he*"—she shot another glower at Mr. Prophet—"used to come in and purchase time with my girls."

"I see," said Sam, his tone now judicial. He turned to Prophet. "Lou? What do you have to say about this situation?"

"Aw, hell. Yeah, I met that woman"—he pointed at Angie.—"in her *parlor* house. She acted her role like a professional courtesan, by God. And, yeah, I *chose* to *make use* of one or two of her so-called *ladies*. And I sure as hell wasn't the only one she skint."

Skint? I'd ask later.

"I see," said Sam again. "Mister Bowman," he asked, turning to that gent, "did you know about Missus— Well, I guess she's Missus Mainwaring now. Did you know about her past life in Tombstone?"

"Yes, I did," said Mr. Bowman, frowning hideously—only on him nothing looked hideous. "I helped her escape."

"Escape, hell," said Lou Prophet. Then he spat on the porch floor.

"That was *so* rude!" I told him.

Looking at me under thunderous brows, he said, "Sorry, Miss Daisy. Ain't sorry to nobody else." He turned his attention to Angie. "So you managed to escape, did you? How many other men got skint when you did this escaping of yours?"

Angie heaved a gusty sigh. "Many," she confessed. She suddenly turned and looked at me. "Oh, Daisy, you're not going to tell that mob in there about this, are you?" She hooked a thumb at the back door of the house.

"Heavens, no! It's nobody else's business," I said, meaning it sincerely. Heck, I'd kept darker secrets than hers, sometimes to my own personal peril.

"Bless you, child," she whispered, laying her hand on my arm. "Thank you *so* much."

"Although," I said, having thought of something pertinent having to do with someone not entirely unlike Mrs. Mainwaring herself, "you might want to think about talking to Flossie Buckingham. She grew up in circumstances much like your own, and—"

"Daisy," Sam interrupted, his own brow now thunderous. "Before you offer advice, we'd better thrash out this current problem. We've still got a party going on, you know."

"Yes, Sam," I said. I considered batting my eyelashes but thought better of it, thereby proving I can sometimes behave sensibly.

"If you did relieve Mister Prophet of some of his money using sketchy tactics, would you be able to return the money to him?" Sam asked of Angie.

"Of course!" No hesitation at all. "I've made wise investments, and I'll be happy to repay Mister Prophet. With interest, if he'd like."

"Huh," said Prophet, sounding like Sam.

"I mean it, Lou. I mean, Mister Prophet," said Angie. She sounded desperate. "I didn't set out to rob people."

"You had your girls do it for you." The bitterness in Mr. Prophet's voice nearly made my skin itch.

Angie sat straighter in her chair. "Yes, I did. Those poor girls had no more choice in their careers than I did. Even today, I help as many girls as I can to get away from that wretched life."

"You do?" As soon as the words left my lips, I turned to Sam, fearing rebuke.

He didn't seem inclined to scold this time, however. "In what way?" he asked of Angie.

"Yeah. How do you help 'em? You've taught 'em to thieve. What the hell else can you do for them?"

Needless to say, this comment came from Mr. Prophet. Sam

frowned at him. Mr. Prophet rolled his eyes heavenwards. Mr. Bowman sat as if turned to stone. I got the feeling he hankered to shoot Lou Prophet through the heart, but didn't want to cause a fuss. Sensible decision on his part.

"When I can, I bring parlor-house girls who want to escape that awful kind of life here."

"Here?" I asked. "Here, like in Pasadena? In your home? I mean, where do you keep them?"

With a sweet smile for me, Angie said, "No, not in my new home. I generally have three or four girls residing at Orange Acres until they...um...have acquired other skills and are able to secure employment somewhere else. Some of the poor things are...Well, they're..."

"They're addicted to opium or laudanum or chloral hydrate, is what she's tryin' to tell you," said Prophet in a flat voice.

None of us gasped, and Angie seemed surprised by our restraint. I told her, "You have no idea what some of us have seen in the past few years, Angie. You're not alone either, not in your tough life or in your desire to help others."

"Really?" She blinked at me.

"Yeah. She's telling the truth," said Sam, adding a soft, "damn it," under his breath.

"My goodness." Angie appeared very nearly stunned.

"You got any of that left?" asked a snide Lou Prophet. "Good-ness, I mean."

"That's enough of *that*," I told him severely. "We understand you've been wronged by Missus Mainwaring, and she's willing, if not eager, to make amends. However, continuing to berate her will gain none of us anything."

"True enough," said Sam. "Look, Lou, I understand why you're mad, but hold off the whining for a while, will you? We need to get back to the blasted party before people start looking for us."

Good Lord, I'd almost forgotten about the party!

But sure enough, the words had no sooner left Sam's lips than Harold Kincaid stepped out onto the porch. "What's going on out here? You all right, Missus Mainwaring?"

All of us except Lou Prophet, who couldn't, leapt from our chairs and turned to Harold.

"Harold! How nice of you to ask. Angie just got a little choked up. You know. I mean she got a frog in her throat there for a minute," I said, blithering, to judge from the look Harold gave me.

"Need anything?" he asked.

"No, thanks. Sam got some lemonade for Angie. How's the party going?"

"It was going pretty well until all of you left." Dry tones of voice were going around that day.

"Yes, well, we're all coming back now," I told him.

"Good idea," said Mr. Bowman. "Here, Angie, give me your arm."

"Thank you, Judah." She did as he'd suggested and hung on to his arm. I think she tried to pretend she wasn't using it to keep herself upright.

"Yes. We can't let all that good food and lemonade go to waste," said Sam, smiling and trying to look normal.

Harold squinted at him. I whacked him on the arm, and he jumped. "Sorry," said he.

"No matter. Just act normal."

"Oh, good. That gives me plenty of leeway." Grinning like the Cheshire Cat, Harold waltzed back into the house.

"You all go on ahead. Think I'll head to the cottage," Prophet grumbled.

I grabbed his arm so hard, I nearly upended the poor man. I guess he wasn't as steady on his pins as he'd been when he still possessed both legs. "No, you're not. You're coming into the house with us, and you're going to stay there, eating things and pretending to enjoy yourself for...I don't know. Look at the clock in the kitchen, and stay until fifteen minutes have passed. That's an order."

"From a snip of a thing like you?" he asked, gazing down at me. A long way down, as he was at least as tall as Sam, although not nearly as bulky.

"Yes. From a snip of a thing like me, darn you!"

"Oooh, such language." Prophet pursed his lips and tried to look horrified. Didn't work.

"And from me," said Sam, taking Prophet's other arm.

"Aw, hell," said Prophet.

But he walked with us back into the melee.

I mean the party.

NINE

A few people seemed to notice us when we returned to the living room, but thanks to Angie coughing artfully a time or two and clinging to Mr. Bowman's arm, no one asked us what had happened to compel our departure. Angie cleared her throat several times, too, thereby adding to the impression she'd swallowed the wrong way or done something else of a like nature.

"Mistew Pwophet!" shrieked little Billy, who did a better job of diverting the party attendees' attention than any of us who'd left the house and then come back indoors. His chubby two-year-old legs carried him on a wobbly and semi-straight path right to Lou Prophet.

Bless his old and, I'm sure, scarred and at least partially black, heart, Prophet pasted on a smile for the child and said, "How, do, little Billy? Good to see you again." He didn't even sound sarcastic.

"I wuv my wocks," said Billy peering up at the tall man in an almost worshipful manner.

"Glad to hear it," said Prophet. "Let me sit in this here chair, and I'll show you a couple other things you might like."

And darned if he didn't sit on a chair and allow Billy to climb on to his lap. I must have looked as amazed as I was, because I felt a soft touch on my arm, turned, and found Flossie smiling at me.

"Billy hasn't been able to talk about anything besides Mister Prophet ever since we had lunch that day at Mijares."

In case the name doesn't ring a bell—and why should it?—Mijares is a Mexican restaurant in my fair city, and it serves about the best grub I've ever eaten except at our dinner table at home.

"Really? I don't know why I should be so surprised that Mister Prophet gets along well with children, but I am," I told Flossie. I didn't add my suspicion that Mr. Prophet remained a child at heart in spite of his advanced years.

"I know." Flossie wore a sweet smile. "He does seem an unlikely fellow to be such a child-lover, doesn't he? But this just goes to show one can't judge a book by its cover. Look at me, for heaven's sake!" She laughed.

"Oh, Flossie, I'm so happy you're my friend," I said, feeling tears build in my eyes. I blinked them away as fast as I could.

"If it weren't for you, I'd probably be dead now, Daisy. You know that. You and Johnny saved my life."

"Fiddlesticks," I said, my voice somewhat unsteady. "You always possessed a saintly nature. You just needed to get away from…ugly influences."

"So true," she said. Glancing at Angie, she whispered, "I suspect the same might be said of people other than I, as well."

To my credit, I didn't gawp at her, although I did jump a little. Just a little. Really.

"Um…I…"

"Don't tell me," said Flossie, holding her hand up, palm out. "I know from personal experience that you'd never tell another person's story."

I had to gulp twice before I said, "Thanks, Flossie."

With a pat on my shoulder, Flossie walked over to where Mr. Lou Prophet—who, as Harold had so cogently said, used to kill people for a living—was busily entertaining little Billy. I followed her.

"And this here's an arrowhead I got from a Mescalero Injun a few years back."

"What's a Mescawewo?" asked Billy. "What's a Injun?"

"You never saw no Injuns at the flickers, little Billy?" Prophet asked, lifting his eyebrows so high, they darned near climbed into his hairline.

After clearing my throat, I said, "We call them Indians, Billy." I aimed a frown at Mr. Prophet after Billy stopped looking at me. "I believe the Mescaleros are one of the Apache tribes, aren't they, Mister Prophet?"

With a grin that told me he didn't give a good hang—only he wouldn't have used that last word—what I thought about him *or* Indians, Prophet said, "Right you are, Miss Daisy. Apache Injuns fixed these arrowheads to the ends of sticks to hunt for deer and antelopes and—when they were still around—buffalos."

Billy stared hard at Prophet. "Dey hunted?"

"Had to, if they wanted to eat," said Prophet. "They didn't live near any stores or suchlike conveniences."

"Oh," said Billy, his infantile brow furrowing. "No more buffwoes?"

"Not many. Probably folks keep 'em in menageries or zoos these days. But white men killed most of the buffalo. Just shot 'em dead and left their corpses to rot on the ground where they landed. White men killin' all them buffalos made it hard for Injuns to get food."

"White men?" asked a clearly baffled Billy.

"I think he's heard about enough of your history lesson, Mister Prophet," I said, trying to sound firm. Every time I read articles about how we "superior" white folks stole land—not to mention bison and health—from the so-called Indians, I wanted to hit someone. Today I wanted to hit Mr. Prophet, although I kind of, in a way, honored him for at least telling Billy a partial truth. The entire truth would probably make the poor lad sick. It had that effect on me.

"Right you are, Miss Daisy," said Prophet, grinning wickedly. "Lemme see if I have anything else in this here pocket little Billy might like."

When I'd first encountered Mr. Prophet in the side yard of the Methodist-Episcopal Church my family attended, he'd worn a tattered frock coat. After Sam took him to the Salvation Army to meet Flossie and Johnny—without telling me he'd done so, of course—Mr. Prophet had commenced looking darned near respectable. The suit he wore to the party had been obtained at the Salvation Army's thrift shop, so it was used, but it fitted him admirably.

After fumbling in his pocket for a moment or two, Mr. Prophet pulled out a small green object, round and…well, I'm not sure, but it looked as if someone had carved something in the green stone.

"This here's a Chinese dragon, Billy," said Mr. Prophet. "Chinese artists carve this kind of rock—it's called jade—into all sorts of shapes. This here one's a dragon."

"A dwagon?" Billy said, his voice filled with wonder.

"Yep. This is a dragon."

"Oooooooh," said Billy, still awed.

Flossie and I clunked heads as we bent over to better see the object in Mr. Prophet's hand.

"That's gorgeous!" I said, rubbing my head.

"Beautiful!" said Flossie, likewise engaged.

"A pretty Chinese lady give this to me in Tombstone some years back." Prophet winked at us, and I instantly knew the Chinese woman who'd given him the dragon amulet had been no lady.

So did Flossie. She said, "Very pretty, I'm sure, you sly dog."

Prophet threw his head back and barked out an uproarious laugh. Disreputable old man!

But Billy laughed, too, so I guess everything was copacetic. Whatever that means. I'm sure every generation has its own slang, and copacetic was going around not unlike a plague of locusts just then.

I suddenly realized Angie Mainwaring—or whatever her name was—had joined our group. She smiled down upon Lou Prophet, although her smile looked more like a grimace to me.

"Hey, Angie," I said.

"Good day, Daisy. Lovely party, isn't it, Mister Prophet? And where on earth did *you* get a baby? Although I have no doubt you have plenty of them scattered about in various places."

"Keep your voice down. Please," I said frantically scanning the room to see if anyone else was looking at us. To give her credit, Angie's voice, while sounding vicious, had been soft and low.

"Oh, I will," said Angie. "But I think we need to have a little discussion when the party is over." She glanced at Flossie. "Are you Mrs. Buckingham? From the Salvation Army?"

"I am," said Flossie smiling beatifically and holding her hand out for Angie to shake.

Angie shook the hand. Her smile looked slightly less like a grimace than it had when she'd spoken to Mr. Prophet. "It's a pleasure to meet you. Daisy has told me about the good works you and your husband do."

"We try. Daisy's the one who introduced Johnny and me," said Flossie. Then she added, "If she hadn't, I'd probably be dead by now."

Her eyes widening significantly, Angie said, "Really? I'd love to hear your story one day."

"Happy to share," said Flossie.

Because the grownups had disrupted the fun he'd been having with Mr. Prophet, Billy began to fuss. Hardly blamed the kid. Grownups had always got in my way when I was a child, too.

"But I'd best get Billy out of here. You three clearly have some things to chat about."

"Chat," said Mr. Prophet. "Good word." Turning his attention to Billy, he said, "Would you like to keep the arrowhead, Billy? It's made from a stone called flint. Maybe your ma and pa can explain better than me how the Injuns used them things."

Clutching the arrowhead—which was sharp and pointy, darn it —to his childish chest, Bill said in a voice still registering bedazzlement, "Oh, yes. Tank'oo, Mistew Pwophet."

"You're more than welcome, Billy. Any old time."

As Flossie gathered her son in her arms and carted him off, still smiling like the saint she was, we all gazed after her. She was, however, no angel. And that's no disparagement of Flossie Buckingham as a person, a better example of personhood could rarely be found. However, no matter how pure and wonderful a life Flossie had been living since her rescue from that gaggle of vicious gangsters, she'd never be an angel.

I don't know why it peeves me so much, but people keep insisting nice folks who die become angels. No, they don't. There are (or should that be is?) a finite number of angels, they were there from the beginning—according to Christian dogma—and you can't become one. For pity's sake, *Christians* ought to know that, even if nobody else does.

I get upset by the most trivial things, don't I? Well, no matter.

"Listen," said Angie, her voice soft but demanding, "we need to talk. And *you*, Lou Prophet, need to come out to Orange Acres and see for yourself what I'm doing to help the women I used to...I hate the word, but I guess it's true...run." Turning to me, she said, "You, too, Daisy. Please? Honestly, I've changed my life a hundred and fifty percent since my bad old days, and I want to prove it to you in particular." Casting a disdainful glance down at Mr. Prophet —he hadn't risen from his chair—she said, "And I need to pay you back. I hope you've kept good accounting records. *I* certainly have."

In other words, she knew how much she'd skint him for or, perhaps, of—I still had a lot of work to do on my old-west vocabulary—and she didn't aim to be skint in return. She wouldn't pay back more than she needed to if she added interest to the money she or her "girls" had relieved him of. Oh, dear, I just ended a sentence with a whatchamacallit. Can't remember what they are, but you're not supposed to put "of" at the end of a sentence.

Why am I babbling? Don't trouble yourself trying to answer that question, please, because I already know. I'd hoped this party would be trouble-free and a wonderful experience from beginning to end for everyone who attended. Stupid, stupid Daisy.

Yet the party continued in spite of Mr. Prophet, Angie and me. What's more, when I glanced around, I noticed almost everyone smiling, laughing, cramming food into their mouths and drinking lemonade, coffee or tea. By golly, it looked as if the party was truly a success! Thank God!

After letting out a lungful of air, I said, "I'd love to see Orange Acres. And I can bring Mister Prophet in our motorcar." Looking down upon Mr. Prophet, I asked, "Is that all right with you, Mister Prophet?"

Tilting his head slightly and narrowing his eyes, he said, "Yeah. I guess so."

Angie heaved a relieved sigh of her own. "Thank you both. What day would you like to take this little jaunt?"

"Don't make no never mind to me," said Prophet with a grin that should be outlawed. "I'm retired."

Angie said something that sounded like, "Tchah."

"I have to sing in the choir tomorrow morning," I said. "And I don't think my folks or Sam would appreciate me taking off after dinner. Besides, I'll probably be too tired. Maybe Monday or Tuesday?"

"Either day is fine with me," Angie said.

Both of us peered at Mr. Prophet, who'd finally managed to rise from his chair. To be charitable, he probably *did* have more trouble rising from chairs than most of us who have two legs upon which to rely. Then again, I knew him to be a cantankerous old buzzard—he would use a word considerably more vulgar than buzzard—so perhaps he'd remained seated to let Angie and me know he didn't consider us ladies.

I kind of resented that—if my assumption was correct, of course—because *I'd* never been a gangster's moll or the head-mistress of a parlor house. That's supposed to be a witticism. Headmistress?

Never mind.

At that moment, Angie, Mr. Prophet and I were joined by Sam, bringing Mr. Hostetter (choir director) and Mr. Smith (pastor) with him.

"Beautiful home, Missus Majesty. Detective Rotondo has been showing me its various features."

"Thank you, Mister Smith. I love it." I sent Sam a look so sweet, I wouldn't have been surprised if he'd gagged. "Sam is so good to me."

Sam said, "Hmm."

"You *are* good to her, Sam," said Mr. Prophet. "And she's good to you."

"Pastor Smith," I said fairly loudly, "I don't believe you've met Mister Lou Prophet. Mister Prophet has recently resettled in Pasadena."

To my astonishment, Mr. Prophet held out his hand as if someone somewhere, somehow, had actually taught or tried to teach him manners. Mr. Smith took his hand and shook it vigorously. "Happy to meet you, Mister Prophet. Missus Majesty and her family have been loyal members of our congregation for many years, and Detective Rotondo is now one of us, too."

For the record, he stretched the truth a trifle when he included Sam as part of his congregation because Sam hadn't officially joined the church, but so what?

Giving first Sam and then me a sappy smile, he went on, "I hope to perform their nuptials soon. They make a lovely couple. Can we look forward to seeing you in church one of these days?" Mr. Smith's smile lost its sappiness and was now quite charming, considering he was trolling for converts.

To my further astonishment, Mr. Prophet smiled back at Mr. Smith and said, "I'd be happy to join Miss Daisy, her family and Sam at church one of these days. I've been to your church before."

He didn't say when, thank God. Not that it mattered much. Mr. Hostetter had been leading the choir when Sam's nephew had tried to skewer me to a church pew with his stupid knife, and I'm sure Pastor Smith had heard all about it.

Then Lucy and Albert Zollinger strolled up to us, relieving my mind of its fear about either Mr. Prophet or Mr. Hostetter spilling any more beans. I smiled at both of them. Mr. Zollinger was a good deal older than Lucy, but they seemed to dote on each other. After the Great War and the Spanish Influenza pandemic, a girl pretty much had to select from the males available to her. And, since a whole bunch of young men had been killed during the war or shortly after it, most of the then-available males were of the older variety.

Oh, dear. I didn't mean to imply that Lucy had snatched at Mr. Zollinger as a last resort or anything. I swear, some days the world would probably be a better place if I just stayed in bed and didn't dirty it up any more than it was being dirtied already. Lucy loved her Albert. And he loved her. Heck, he'd even given her a coat with a raccoon-fur collar last year. Personally, I'd just as soon no animal sacrifice its life and hide to adorn my person, but I was neither Lucy nor Albert. And I just did it again, didn't I? I swear, you can't take me anywhere!

"Mister Hostetter would like you and Missus Zollinger to sing a couple of duets, Daisy," said Sam. I'd noticed him eyeing our threesome—Prophet, Mainwaring and Majesty—and knew he wanted to know what we'd been discussing. Unlike his bride-to-be, however, Sam could be circumspect when he chose to be.

Lucy and I peered at each other and smiled. "I'd love that!" I said, meaning it sincerely. If I were singing, I couldn't utter any more stupidities.

"So would I," said the equally enthusiastic Lucy.

"I love hearing the two of you sing," said her Albert with a fond glance at his wife.

"Me, too," said Sam, sounding not quite as sincere as Mr. Zollinger.

"Me, too!" said Mr. Prophet. Now *he* sounded sincere as all heck.

Rubbing his hands together, Mr. Hostetter said, "Good, good. Do you have sheet music in the piano bench, Missus Majesty?"

"Um…" I had to think for a second or three. "I'm not sure. Sam? Do we?"

"Why don't I run across the street and get some for you?" said my often-wonderful Sam.

"Great idea," said Mr. Prophet. "I'll join you."

With a profound feeling of liberation, I watched the two men walk out the front door on their way to fetch sheet music. Sam would probably pump Mr. Prophet about what he, Angie and I had been discussing in such soft voices, thus relieving me of that particular onus, although I didn't yet know how Sam would react to our plans. Sam got mad at me for the silliest reasons sometimes. I can't imagine why he'd object to me taking Mr. Prophet to Orange Acres for a visit, especially in light of Angie's declared intention of helping fallen women achieve an upright position in life. Did that sound snide? I didn't mean it to. Sometimes I can't be trusted with the English language.

The two men returned shortly, Sam carrying a stack of sheet music and Mr. Prophet carrying the hymnal I kept at home.

"Here you go," said Mr. Prophet, handing me the hymnal.

"And here's some sheet music," said Sam, giving me the stack of papers. "Didn't know what you wanted, so I just picked up the ones on the piano rack and the top ones inside the bench."

"Thanks, Sam and Mister Prophet. You're both very helpful."

Sam squinted at me. Mr. Prophet gave me one of his devilish grins.

Taking the music and not speaking to either man, I grabbed Lucy by the elbow and led her to the—*my*—baby grand piano.

Darned if we didn't entertain our guests, with both hymns and Broadway musical numbers, for an hour or more. At the end of the day, after the last guest had departed, I was about to fall down dead from exhaustion.

Before collapsing, however, I managed to set up a date to visit Angie's Orange Acres. On Tuesday morning at ten a.m., I aimed to drive Mr. Lou Prophet out to Angie's orange grove. There, I felt sure, we would meet some of the women Angie was attempting to help.

I even dared tell Sam about our planned adventure. He didn't snarl. Guess he was pooped, too.

Oh, and Mrs. Pinkerton had also cornered me and made an appointment for me to see her on Monday morning, bringing with me Rolly, the Ouija board and the tarot cards. I'd expected her attack, so it didn't irritate me. Much.

TEN

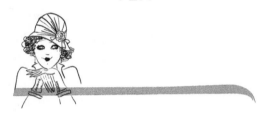

My entire family, including Sam and Mr. Prophet, awoke on Sunday morning still groggy from Saturday's jollifications. Nevertheless, as Vi prepared French toast and sausage patties for our breakfast, I tramped to our back yard and picked some Valencia oranges in case anyone wanted something healthy to eat along with his or her French toast and sausage patties. Thanks to our two orange trees, we had fresh oranges almost all year round. Good thing we all loved oranges.

Spike joined me, not because he likes oranges, but because he adores sniffing around in the back yard. Every now and then he'd find something interesting back there, like a stray opossum, the Wilsons' cat Samson or even, once, a man who'd been shot by Lou Prophet. Fortunately, he found nothing on Sunday morning but a dirty sock that had somehow made its way into our yard. Wind maybe. Or Pudge Wilson.

By the time I got back inside, washed and dried the oranges and began placing them in the decorative bowl we always kept them in on the kitchen table, the entire house smelled heavenly. That's when I noticed Sam and Mr. Prophet's weariness, since they'd entered the house while I'd been out of it. Sam's eyes looked kind of sunken. Since his complexion tended toward an olive hue due to his Italian heritage, the bags under his eyes were a grayish-green; quite unbecoming, actually. Mr. Prophet, being more or less lily-white like my family—that's supposed to be another joke. If Mr. Prophet's skin actually *were* lily-white, it was indubitably the only part of him remaining thus after years and years of rowdy misbehavior—just looked fatigued. Both men stood in the doorway to the kitchen, sniffing the air and reminding me of Spike.

"Oh, my, your party was fun, Daisy, but I'm still exhausted," said Ma, entering the kitchen in her bathrobe and slippers. Nobody minded. By then, both Sam and Mr. Prophet had become honorary members of the family. Prophet would remain honorary. Sam would become a certified member of same. Someday.

"Me, too. If I didn't have to sing a duet with Lucy this morning, I might even skip church."

"You would not!" my mother said with some force. "Just because you hosted a party and it wore you out does *not* mean you may fail in your duties to your family and your church."

"Yeah," said Mr. Prophet.

When I whipped my head to glare at him, he appeared as angelic as an old reprobate like he ever could. Since Sam didn't say it for me, I said, "Huh!"

Sam laughed. So did Pa. For that matter, so did Vi.

So what the heck, I laughed, too. "It's all right, Ma. You know I never miss church unless I'm sick."

After frowning at me for another second or two, Ma shrugged and said, "I do know it, Daisy. I'm sorry. Didn't mean to snap at you. I think I'm touchy because I'm still worn out from yesterday."

"We all are," said Pa. "But that was a darned fun party, and I enjoyed meeting Missus Mainwaring and Mister Bowman. I think I've seen his office there on Colorado but never thought much about it or him."

This time, Sam said, "Huh," so I didn't have to.

"Sam doesn't appreciate private detectives," I told my father.

"Really? Why's that, Sam? They get in the way of the police or something?"

"Sometimes," said Sam. "I don't hate 'em all. Bowman seemed like a nice fellow and, as far as I know, he's never interfered with a police investigation." Giving me a meaningful stare, he added, "Unlike some other people I could mention."

That made everyone laugh again. Except me. I did *not* interfere in his cases, curse it!

"At least, thanks to Harold and Sam, we didn't have to clean up the mess after the party was over," I said, forgiving Sam for his unwarranted slur. In fact, after plopping the last orange in the bowl, I went to him, stood on my tiptoes and gave him a smooch. Right on his lips in the middle of the kitchen doorway in front of my family, Lou Prophet, Spike and God. He kissed me back, and when we finally broke for air, everyone gazed at us adoringly. Except Lou Prophet, who looked as if he might throw up. Nertz to him.

Vi's breakfast was, as ever, delicious. She even heated the maple syrup, our stock of which had been renewed at Christmastime by our relations back in Massachusetts. It was nice of them to send us syrup, because pure maple syrup wasn't easy to find in Pasadena except at Jorgensen's Market, which catered to rich people, and we weren't. Rich, I mean. Vi and the butcher at Jorgensen's, Mr. Larkin, were pretty good pals by this time, and he gave her good deals on lots of stuff, but Vi had told the family the syrup Jorgensen's stocked was far beyond our budget. Or it had been before Sam came into our lives.

Every now and then I still marveled at the thought of my Sam being a rich man. As Harold had said when I'd told him about Sam's shovels-full of dough: "Who'd'a thunk it?"

After we'd finished breakfast, I washed and dried the dishes, and then we all got ready for church. Except for Mr. Prophet, who said he'd commence coming to church in a week or so, but he aimed to rest today. I'd believe it when I saw it. Lou Prophet in church, I mean.

Easter Sunday fell on April twelfth, so we'd already begun singing the dismal hymns appropriate for the Lenten season. I preferred bouncier hymns, but I understood why Lenten hymns weren't jolly. They led up to Good Friday when, according to the Christian Bible, Jesus had been crucified. Things brightened up considerably on Easter Sunday and thereafter.

Anyhow, on that particular Sunday, the fifth of April, Lucy and I were scheduled to sing the anthem, which was, "O Love Divine, What Hast Thou Done," which might not be precisely fun, but it was a heck of a lot more appealing to me than "There is a Fountain Filled with Blood," the first hymn with which Mr. Hostetter had threatened us. I asked him if he would mind picking a less disgusting hymn and, after frowning horribly at me for a couple of seconds, he selected "O Love Divine," whose only redeeming quality in my opinion was that Charles Wesley wrote the words. Somebody else wrote the music. It was still a pretty boring hymn, Charles Wesley notwithstanding.

Probably to get back at me for my teeny-weeny rebellion, Mr. Hostetter made Lucy and me sing all three verses of the hymn. Generally, he only had us sing a duet on one or two verses. That should teach me not to balk at singing hymns I didn't like, but I doubted it would. Anyhow, one of the hymns we aimed to sing that day was "O Sacred Head Now Wounded," which was gloomy enough to suit anyone. The music was also considerably prettier than that for "O Love Divine."

How'd I get on that topic? Ah, yes. I remember. The day was Sunday, by golly!

The moment Sam's Hudson pulled to the curb on the Marengo side of our church—the church itself sat on the corner of Marengo

Avenue and Colorado Street—and I got out to walk to the choir room, people positively *flocked* to greet us. To a person, they thanked us for the wonderful party and told us how much fun they'd had, how delicious the food had been, how lovely our (Sam's and my) house was, and how nice it was to meet the wealthy and refined (if they only knew) Mrs. Mainwaring. Without squashing a single parishioner, Sam managed to park his Hudson and herd the rest of my family inside the church's sanctuary. Good driver, my Sam.

In the choir room, I was likewise besieged. I didn't mind. I took delight in knowing we'd made so many people happy. Everyone raved about the lobster rolls and the shrimp cocktail, by the way. Vi had tucked away a lot of leftovers in the Frigidaire, so her task of feeding us dinner after church and supper that night would be easier than usual. This situation pleased me, too. My aunt had to work too darned hard and, even though she said she loved feeding people, she must get tired of standing on her feet all day, every day, slaving away over a hot stove.

In my opinion, Lucy and I sounded as spectacular as it was possible for us to sound when we sang "O Love Divine." We both smiled and bowed at the end, and went back to our assigned seats. A smattering of applause and a few "Amens" startled both of us, and I whipped my head around to see people clapping. Lucy had more presence of mind and, probably, more poise than I, so she just kept smiling and sat. But really, we Methodists aren't generally so spontaneous and enthusiastic in church. Lucy and I smiled at each other again, however, both of us proud we'd sung our parts well. Mr. Hostetter gave each of us an approving nod, too, so I guess he'd forgiven me for not wanting to sing a hymn featuring a fountain filled with blood.

Due to general fatigue, the family didn't even walk to Fellowship Hall after the church service ended. We just toddled out to Sam's Hudson and piled in.

My mother, the same mother who had berated me for being too tired to go to church, heaved a weary sigh and said, "Glad that's over. I can't remember being this exhausted in a long time."

We all shared her sentiments.

Naturally, Lou Prophet sat on the front steps of our (my parents') bungalow when Sam parked the Hudson in front of the house. Mr. Prophet rose to greet us, and I noticed he had to push himself a little bit in order to get to his foot and peg. I probably shouldn't be so hard on the old geezer, although I sometimes found it difficult not to be. He seemed *such* an odd, uncouth duck in lovely, sophisticated Pasadena. Ah, well. I remained thankful that he'd come into our lives, and not merely because he'd saved my life a couple of times. I also wanted to learn more about his picturesque old-western vernacular.

Also…well, I *liked* the guy. Couldn't seem to help it.

Speaking of which, once we'd unlocked the door and gone inside—we'd never locked our doors until the attacks on my life began on the first day of the year—and after we'd all greeted Spike with love and pats, I asked, "What does 'skint' mean, Mister Prophet?"

"Eh?" he looked at me as if I'd lost what little was left of my mind. "Beg pardon?"

Peeved, probably because of my own state of fatigue, I said perhaps more querulously than was necessary, "Skint! What does 'skint' mean? For pity's sake, you said Angie skint you. I'd never heard that word until yesterday."

"Lower your voice," Sam, who had come up behind me, advised.

Startled into achieving one of my athletic foot-high jumps, I darned near whirled around and slapped my beloved's face. "Darn you, Sam Rotondo! You scared the feathers out of me!"

"Feathers?" Prophet squinted at me as if at a rare and unusual species of bird. Or butterfly. Or maybe rodent.

"Sorry, love," said Sam, not meaning it—I could tell—"but you don't want your whole family to know about our discussion with Missus Mainwaring, Lou, you and me yesterday, do you?"

After my palpitating heart slowed a trifle, I begrudgingly agreed with him. "You're right. I don't." Facing Prophet once more, I whispered, "But, darn it, I *do* want to know what 'skint' means." I dragged him by his coat sleeve to the far south section of our living room where the upright piano sat. He stumbled along behind me and Sam took his other arm, probably so I wouldn't yank him from his perilous upright position. That peg-leg definitely counted as a handicap.

Once we were in the living room and standing before the piano, I plunked myself on the piano bench and said, "So what does 'skint' mean, Mister Lou Prophet?"

He and Sam sat on the sofa facing the piano, while I took the piano bench. Well...I don't mean I took it. I sat on it. English is such an interesting language, isn't it?

"Just means she fleeced me."

"Oh, that helps a whole lot," said I in supremely sarcastic mode. "I remember you saying she fleeced you, too. What does 'fleeced' mean? Does it mean she sheared you like a sheep?" Eyeing him up and down, I said, still sarcastic, "You don't appear particularly woolly to me, Mister Prophet."

"Thanks." He smiled, showing me his stained teeth.

Bending over so as to be closer to the men, I whispered, "I'm going to hit you with my dachshund-headed cane if you don't answer my question." I don't think I meant it, but maybe I did. Exhaustion inevitably plays havoc with people's moods.

By the way, Sam had bought the cunning cane for me when I was recuperating from having been hit by that rotten automobile. He'd even had Arnold's Jewelers fashion the dachshund's head it sported. Sam could be a sweetheart when he wanted to be, which wasn't too often but often enough. Anyhow, who wants a guy who's a pushover? Not I, which was a good thing, since it would take a whole lot more strength than I possessed to topple my Sam.

"I mean," said Prophet slowly and distinctly, "She stole money from me. She skint me. She fleeced me." After pondering his response for a moment, he said, "Guess skint means skinned. Beaver hunters used t'say they skint the beavers, so that's probably where the expression comes from."

Ew. "Why'd they skin beavers?" I asked, feeling sorry for the beaver population of the United States.

With a shrug clearly telling me I knew nothing of the world, Prophet said, "They skint 'em for their pelts, of course. Where'd you think all them beaver hats the toffs used to wear came from? Giraffes?"

"Oh. I guess I forgot men used to wear beaver hats all the time." Because I still felt peevish, I added, "And frock coats. Men used to wear frock coats, too." I didn't stick my tongue out at him, but I wanted to.

"And you're right about 'fleeced,'" he said. It comes from shearing sheep. She fleeced me out of lots of my money."

"How'd she do that?"

"Well, now, I don't know as to how I ought to answer that question. I didn't go to her parlor house for a tea party, if you know what I mean."

"Her parlor house…" I repeated, my memory hazy. Then I remembered. "Oh, yes. She ran a…house of ill repute—"

Prophet snorted, and I smacked his arm. He said, "Hey!"

"Hey yourself," I told him. "She ran a house of ill repute—a house of prostitution, if you want to be persnickety about it—"

"She ran a damned whorehouse," said Lou Prophet.

"Stop swearing in my presence, Mister Lou Prophet!"

"Tut-tut on me," said he.

Scowling ferociously—which either didn't register with him or didn't bother him, confound the man—I said, "So you took advantage of the…the…favors some of the women there offered. Is that correct?"

"They *sold* their *favors* to any feller who paid the price, Miss Daisy."

"Yes, yes. I know. Did they then drug you and take your money? Or did you just get roaring drunk, pass out, and *then* they took your money? If the latter is how it happened, you deserved it." Very well, I'm a prude. I don't want to be. But, as both Angie and Flossie had told me, one's upbringing can't be flung aside at a moment's notice or flicked away like a stray leaf. That goes for good upbringings as well as bad ones.

"Might'a been the one and might'a been t'other," said Lou Prophet, not clarifying things one little bit.

"You're impossible! Did you know that? You're absolutely impossible! How did you get skint? Or fleeced? Or had your money stolen? By means of either of the scenarios I outlined?"

"Probably a little of both. Some good tangleleg with some laudanum mixed in would do the trick."

"And you didn't notice your pockets were lighter when you woke up the next morning?"

"Wasn't feeling too chipper the next morning." Mr. Prophet lifted an eyebrow at me.

"Well, *I* think you deserved to be skint. And fleeced. And stolen from! Taking advantage of women in situations like that!"

"It's how they earned their living," Prophet pointed out.

"That may be so, but I'll bet you anything they didn't *want* to have to earn their livings like that. Who'd want to get so close to a dirty, smelly, drunken man and…Ew. The mere thought makes me sick!"

"Hey, I might'a been a little sloshed, but I wasn't all that dirty and smelly." Mr. Prophet sounded as if I'd hurt his feelings.

"Applesauce! You know exactly what I mean. Bother you and every other man like you!"

"Daisy," said Sam. Guess I'd become a trifle loudish.

Modifying my volume, I said to Prophet. "I despise men who take advantage of women in lowered circumstances, is all I'm saying."

"Didn't know you despised me. I'm sorry 'bout that."

"I didn't mean you in particular, but I *know* you know what I'm talking about."

"Only bought what they was sellin'," said Prophet. "Didn't deserve to be fleeced for it."

"Oh, you're just insufferable! You ought to be stabbed to death in your shriveled, black heart, if there's anything left of it, which I doubt."

"Daisy!" said Sam, in a voice louder than it had been, even though I'd lowered my own voice to a whisper.

Didn't matter. Mr. Prophet only grinned. "It's all right, Sam." To me, he said, "Miss Daisy, you ain't heard nothin' yet. And all's I got in my chest is a scab over my liver, so you can't stab me in my heart. Ain't got one left."

On that note, I rose from the piano bench, turned, stalked through the dining room and kitchen and retired to my bedroom, where I removed my Sunday clothes, hung them neatly in the closet and got into a comfortable house dress. Spike, proving that men stick together and thereby making me mad as a riled sidewinder—I made that one up all by myself, by golly, and didn't even *need* Lou Prophet—remained in the living room with Sam, Lou and my father, who passed by me as I stomped to my bedroom. I think he wanted to ask me what I was angry about, but I didn't give him the chance.

When I'd changed into comfy attire and re-entered the kitchen, Vi stood in before the Frigidaire, gazing at its innards and occasionally picking up something contained therein. The *men* remained in the living room. Guess they thought food appeared by magic, or that Vi never required any assistance when it came to feeding them.

"Need any help, Vi?" I asked sweetly, thinking the men should be asking the same question. Well, except for Spike. He'd probably be happy to help, but he didn't have opposable thumbs and his legs were too short. Also, although I hate to admit this, he'd probably eat everything before it got to the table.

"Just set the table, please," said Vi. She sounded remarkably happy for a woman who had to cook for and wait on people all the time. Perhaps I was a trifle sensitive that day. Well…I know I was. Fatigue has a debilitating effect on my state of mind.

But I set the table, then called everyone in for dinner, which was leftovers from yesterday's party. They were still darned good.

ELEVEN

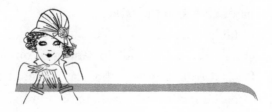

O n Monday morning I awoke about seven-ish, as usual, and
joined my father in the kitchen. Ma and Aunt Vi were in
their respective rooms, dressing to go to work. I had to go to work,
too, but at least I could set my own hours. Spike followed me into
the kitchen, hoping. Full of hope, Spike, and never became grumpy
because he was tired or worn out. I admired that in a fellow.

Looking up from the newspaper he'd been reading, Pa said,
"Vi's having us finish up those deviled eggs and stuffed mushrooms
from the party, and there's some bread there to toast. There's also a
lot of fruit salad, if you want some."

"Oh, boy, that party just never ends, does it?"

"Looks like it," said Pa, laughing.

"I'm glad of it. The Castleton fixed some mighty tasty grub."

"It did indeed."

I decided to heck with toast, got a plate and filled it with
deviled eggs and stuffed mushrooms and some little crackers with
squiggly things on them. I presume someone with a pastry bag or
something akin to it had created the squiggles, which were made of
soft stuff that tasted good. Cheese perhaps? Liver sausage? Both?

Sounded like a lot of work for a cracker that would end up in someone's tummy, but it made me happy to know there were people who liked doing such things, since people like me appreciated them so much. After I'd set my plate on the kitchen table, I got a little bowl and filled it with fruit salad.

By the way, the only reason I know what pastry bags are is because Vi told me what one was as she used one of them to fill chocolate éclairs for our dessert once.

Boy, that was a good breakfast! Mind you, when Vi fixes us breakfast, it's always good, too, but she hadn't had to prepare any of this stuff, which gave it an added appeal. If that makes any sense. Spike enjoyed bits of it, too, because I managed to "drop" a few pieces of egg for him.

Ma and Vi walked into the kitchen as I was stuffing my face with a deviled egg. I'd picked it up, what's more, and hadn't bothered cutting it with a fork. Ma gazed upon me with disapproval because I was using bad manners. But golly, nobody else was in the house, and I figured I could relax the proper etiquette she'd taught me for one single morning.

Rather than scold me, Ma said, "Where's Mister Prophet?"

After goggling at her for about the second and a half it took me to swallow my bite of deviled egg, I said, "I guess he's across the street. Why?"

Putting on her hat and securing it with a hat pin, Ma said, "I just worry about him, is all. The poor man needs nourishment and, as much as I admire your Sam, Daisy, I doubt he has a kitchen stocked with food suitable for an elderly man."

"Sam? Lou Prophet? Elderly?" I goggled a trifle more. "Ma, Mister Prophet's been taking care of himself for longer than any of the rest of us has been alive. I doubt he could have reached his elderly state—if that's what you want to call it—if he didn't know how to take care of himself."

"That's not kind, Daisy," said Ma, her frown deepening.

"When people get older, they often lose some of their abilities. For instance, I'm sure it's much more difficult for him to get around these days, what with one of his legs missing."

Before I could think of a suitable response to this statement, which was true, although having a peg leg didn't seem to bother Mr. Prophet a whole lot, Pa rose from the table and gave Ma's shoulder a squeeze. "I'm sure Sam saved some of the party food in his own Frigidaire, Peggy."

Ma tilted her head slightly, and her frown turned to one of troubled concentration. "That may well be so. But don't you think you should go over there and knock, Joe? Just to make sure Mr. Prophet's all right?"

I'd have grimaced in bewilderment if I didn't know such an expression on my face would invite rebuke. But honestly. Did Ma really think Lou Prophet, former bounty hunter, gunslinger, bedder of every loose woman who ever came his way, I'm sure, with a lot of other things I didn't even know existed, would starve to death if we Gumms and this Majesty (and the one Rotondo) didn't look after him? Maybe she did. I suppose stranger things have been thought by stranger people. My mother, who was practical under all circumstances, also possessed a supremely kind heart.

"If it will make you happy, Peggy, I'll go over there right now," said my father, who was also a kind person, and who didn't allow his wife's odd notions to upset him. Great guy, my father.

"Thank you, Joe." Ma kissed Pa on the cheek and looked happier.

I exchanged a speaking glance with Vi. I do believe our glances spoke the same language that morning.

Nevertheless, I could tell Ma was a happy woman when she and Vi left the house to walk up the street toward Colorado. Ma would make a detour at the Hotel Marengo, where she worked as chief bookkeeper. Vi would continue to Colorado Street, where she'd catch a bus to Mrs. Pinkerton's palace.

Speaking of which...

After I'd finished my lovely breakfast of leftover hotel food, I sat for a few minutes at the kitchen table, chin in my cupped hands, and began contemplating what to wear to Mrs. Pinkerton's house that day. The weather remained fine—I'd already checked on it by standing on the back deck for a few seconds—so I could wear something comfortable. As I anticipated the day's session to be emotionally wrenching for both Mrs. P and me, I spared a moment to be grateful I didn't have to wear anything bulky. Nobody wants to hire a bulky spiritualist-medium. And this particular spiritualist-medium didn't like wearing bulky coats and scarves and so forth. Thinking about my overly stuffed closet, I finally rose from the table, gathered dirty dishes and started washing same.

Before I'd finished cleaning up from breakfast, Pa appeared, towing Lou Prophet behind him. Nertz. Did this mean the man hadn't found anything to eat at Sam's place? I didn't believe it. Frowning slightly, I said, "Good morning, Mister Prophet."

"How-do, Miss Daisy. Your pa was nice enough to offer me breakfast at your place."

"Sam didn't tuck any leftovers in his refrigerator for you to dine on this morning?" I know my tone was snide, and I'm sure my face reflected the same snidity (I don't think that's a word) in its expression.

The fellow looked downright respectable this morning, which surprised me. I knew he'd found some used clothing at the Salvation Army thrift store, but I didn't necessarily expect him to look civilized every day. That's probably pure prejudice on my part.

"Oh, sure," he said. "Sam and me, we had a great breakfast. That hotel caters a good party."

"Yes, it does."

Very well, my snideness (I don't think that's a word, either) hadn't gone unnoticed by Mr. Prophet because, with a wry look for me, he said, "I just come over to see if you could drive me to that library of yours one of these days. I'd like to get me a card there, now that I'm pretty much settled in Pasadena." Tipping his head to one side, he gave me a wicked grin. "Sam told me I can stay in the cottage behind your house and be the caretaker."

"How nice of him," I said. Then, deciding I actually wanted him in that cottage, I gave him a genuine smile and added, "I'll be happy to take you to the library, but it'll have to be after I visit Mrs. Pinkerton this morning. Unless you want to sit inside the library and read or something while I deal with Mrs. Pinkerton."

"Your friend, Miss Petrie, going to be there?" asked Prophet.

I squinted at him, wondering if he aimed to try to seduce Regina Petrie.

But no. That was absurd. He was an old man in his seventies (probably), and Regina was young and pretty and engaged to marry Robert Browning! Studying Mr. Prophet's lined face for another second, I decided I'd put nothing past him. Fortunately, all of my female friends were above reproach in the morality depart-ment. The same could not, I knew well, be said of Mr. Prophet.

"I'm not sure," I told him, wiping a glass dry and sticking it in the cupboard where it resided with its fellow glasses. "She might be. I don't know her precise work schedule. But anybody working at the main desk can help you get a library card."

"Swell. Think I'll do that, then. If you don't mind driving this old reprobate to the library, of course."

"I don't mind," I said. I think I meant it. Actually, I knew I meant it. I don't know why I was carping about Lou Prophet that morning. Just moody, I guess. Peering behind Mr. Prophet, I said, "Where's Sam?"

"Had to go to work. Got a call pretty early."

"Oh, dear. I hope this doesn't mean another gruesome murder."

"Don't know," said Prophet. "I thought Pasadena was a law-abiding community."

"It is, for the most part."

"Guess I'll have to look around until I find the other part then."
He winked at me.

The wicked old man! Oh, very well, I liked him. However, I
also rather disapproved of him, if that makes any sense. It probably doesn't.

"Just stay here with Pa while I get dressed," I told him.

"I'll get us each another cup of coffee," said Pa, smiling and
gesturing for Mr. Prophet to take a kitchen chair. Well, not take
one. Sit on one. English language usage confounds me sometimes.
Think I've already mentioned that once or twice.

So Pa and Mr. Prophet sat at the kitchen table, and I retired to
my bedroom. Spike, sensing no more food would be forthcoming
and not caring for coffee, joined me in my room. I picked him up
and deposited him on my beautifully quilted bedspread. An aunt in
Massachusetts had quilted my bedspread; I can't remember which
aunt, but the quilt was lovely. From his position on the quilt, Spike
could peruse my overflowing closet and help me decide what to
wear that day.

After pondering far too many selections—I probably should
donate a lot of my clothes to the Salvation Army because I sure
wasn't going to stop sewing—Spike and I decided on a relatively
new creation. Sewn by me using a Butterick pattern in a blue-
patterned fabric, both of which I'd bought at Maxime's Fabrics on
Colorado, the creation was called a coat-dress. It buttoned in a
sharp angle to the left. It also had a narrow tied belt, and the skirt
flared below the belt into a sort-of folded-up fan.

While I generally selected single-colored garb for my spiritual-
istic outings, I figured this one was sophisticated enough that I
could get away with it having been made using patterned fabric.
Besides, although I'd never admit it to anyone, I could probably
have shown up at Mrs. P's house stark naked, and no one except
Aunt Vi would even have noticed. Featherstone, Mrs. P's butler,

might have noticed, but he'd never have indicated he had by so much as a blink, much less a stare. Mrs. Pinkerton herself never commented on my clothing, not caring about anyone save herself.

That was unkind of me, too, and I don't really mean it. A generous woman, Mrs. Pinkerton might be a wee bit dense, and she might not notice anyone else's attire, but she'd probably not have been my best client for so many years if I'd clad myself like, say, a hobo or your classical Gypsy fortune-teller, or someone along those lines. In other words, my wardrobe fitted my act. I hoped the blue-patterned material of this particular dress wouldn't put her off.

Naw. She wouldn't notice any difference at all in what I wore, patterned fabric or no patterned fabric. After Spike and I had come to this conclusion, I put on my flesh-colored stockings, got my black bag and black pumps from the closet, clapped on a black-felt cloche hat—adorned this day with a ribbon fashioned from the same blue-patterned fabric as the gown—grabbed the beautifully embroidered bag containing my Ouija board and tarot cards, and exited the bedroom alongside Spike, whose tail wagged in supreme appreciation of my attire. I'm sure that's why he wagged. His wag had nothing to do with the plate of deviled eggs sitting on the kitchen table.

"I thought you'd both already eaten breakfast," I said to the seated men, eyeing the platter.

"We did, but these eggs are good," said Pa.

"They are," agreed Prophet.

So, to make it unanimous, I took one also and downed it in two bites. Well, one and a half bites since I gave Spike a half of my half. He appreciated it.

After swallowing, I asked Prophet, "Ready to go?"

"I am," said he, rising and giving me a bow. "You look mighty pretty today, Miss Daisy."

"You do, sweetheart. Is that a new dress?"

I felt my cheeks catch fire and burn with embarrassment. Every time anyone complimented me on my appearance, I felt guilty. And there was no reason for me to feel guilty, confound it! Every single garment I owned had been sewn by my own two hands with fabric purchased at a discount in one of a number of stores during their annual or semi-annual sales. The costume I wore that day had probably cost a whopping dollar to make. Maybe seventy-five cents.

I felt guilty anyway. Lifting my chin slightly, I said, "Yes, it is. I got this material on sale at Maxime's when they had their year-end sale. That's where I got the fabric for that pretty dress I gave Ma for Christmas, too. And the lovely pink bathrobe I gave Vi for Christmas. And the dresses I just mailed to Polly and Peggy to wear at Easter." Polly and Peggy are my sister Daphne's two children in case you wondered. Daphne, her husband Daniel, and the two girls lived in Arcadia, about twelve miles east of Pasadena. They generally came to our house for holidays.

"You're always a wise shopper," said Pa. I could tell he wanted to laugh at how hard I was defending my clothing addiction.

"Dress matches your eyes," said Mr. Prophet, looking me up and down and tilting his head slightly as if he were trying to figure something out. I didn't ask him what, although his scrutiny made me a little nervous. When he'd stopped staring at me, he put the flat of his palm on a stack of books. "Picked these up at the table beside the front door. Joe says they're books you want to return to the library."

"Yes, they are. Thank you."

"Any old time," said he, scooping the books into his arms and rising from the kitchen chair. I noticed he used the hand not holding books to steady himself by grasping the back of the chair. I really shouldn't be so hard on the old guy.

Naw. He deserved it.

Anyhow, we exited the house via the side door, Spike mournful and telling me he didn't understand why dogs weren't allowed in the library. I told him that, while dogs might be allowed in the library, he knew full well he wouldn't want to visit Mrs. Pinkerton's house with me. He agreed wholeheartedly.

And don't tell me dogs can't talk. Spike and I understood each other just fine.

Mr. Prophet set the books on the back seat, maneuvered his leg and his peg into the front passenger's seat, and I backed the Chevrolet out of our driveway. Very carefully, because backing up isn't something I do well.

We'd just turned north on Marengo when Mr. Prophet said, "Say, Miss Daisy, would you mind if I asked you a question?"

Squinting at him for a mere split-second—didn't want to take my attention off the road for longer than that—I answered his question with the truth. "I won't know if I'll mind until after you ask it."

"Huh," he said. I believe he was acquiring the "huh" habit from Sam.

"So go ahead and ask," I said. "Then we'll both know if I'll mind you asking the question or not."

With a shrug, he said, "How come ladies these days want to look like boys? Like they have no…uh…curves?"

"You mean, why do women these days aspire to the straight up-and-down shape? Or lack of shape? Is that what you mean?"

"Well, yeah. I guess so. You don't want men to see your…uh… well, your natural curves?"

The funny—odd-funny, not funny-funny—thing about his question is that I'd asked myself the same one not long back. In reference to this very man! I'd come to the conclusion Mr. Prophet probably preferred the way women looked in the olden days—his day, in fact. He'd probably especially prefer the women if they weren't ladies.

I didn't instantly answer his question because an instant answer didn't occur to me. After pondering it for a moment or two, however, I came up with the truth as I saw it. "Actually, we don't, Mister Prophet. At least I don't. The fashion houses set trends for us, and we're stuck with them. I suppose a woman doesn't necessarily *have* to wear a corset and a bust-flattener, but if she aspires to earn a respectable living, she'd better."

"A what?" he asked, staring at me as if I'd gone 'round the bend. "What did you say ladies wear? I've heard of corsets, but what was that other thing?"

Oh, dear. I'd managed to embarrass myself again. I seemed to do that a lot. Flaming face or no flaming face, however, I answered his question with another bit of honesty. "A bust-flattener. Women today aren't supposed to have…bosoms."

"Oh. That doesn't make any sense to me."

"It doesn't make any sense to me, either, and wearing fashionable clothes can sometimes be downright painful. Especially if a woman is naturally endowed with…curves."

"Yeah. I can imagine. Don't know why anyone would prefer a stick to a curve or two." Shaking his head, he added, "I kind of like ladies' bosoms."

"That doesn't surprise me the least little bit."

He chuckled. "I suspect Sam does, too."

While I knew his suspicion to be true, I'd die before admitting it, especially to this man. Rather, I said, "Have you ever seen a production of *The Pirates of Penzance*?"

"Eh? The pirates of what?"

"*The Pirates of Penzance.* It's one of Gilbert and Sullivan's operettas."

"Oh," said Prophet. I got the feeling he wasn't well acquainted with Gilbert and Sullivan's work.

"Anyhow," I went on, "there's a fellow named Frederic in the operetta who claims he's a slave to duty. We poor women are slaves to fashion, I guess."

"Don't rightly think I'd like to be a slave to anything at all."

"Says the man who fought for the Confederacy during the Civil War."

"The War of North—"

Peeved, I interrupted him. Most impolite, I know. "I don't care what you call it! You fought for the rights of those rich plantation owners to keep slaves."

"Huh."

"Don't 'huh' me. Anyhow, it's men who run the fashion houses, so you ought to complain to them if you complain to anyone. *I* certainly have no sway when it comes to the designs fashion houses decide we women are supposed to wear."

"Well, I don't know as to how I aim to complain to anyone. I just wondered, was all."

"Fair enough. Anyhow, if Miss Petrie is at the library today, would you mind asking her if she could come to our house on Saturday so I can do a final fitting on her wedding gown?"

"You want *me* to ask a lady to come to your house—is that your parents' house or Sam's house, by the way?—on Saturday?"

"Yes. Please ask her if she can come over about eleven. That will give us plenty of time. Oh, and I meant at my parents' house. Then she can take luncheon with us, too, if she wants to." I pulled up to the curb in front of the library steps. Peering at the two short sets of steps he would need to negotiate and then at Mr. Prophet, a smidgen of compunction smote me. "Can you make it up the stairs carrying those books, or would you like me to take the books in for you?"

"Hell, no! I can walk up a few damned steps, for cripe's sake!"

"There's no need to swear," I told him in a voice sounding excruciatingly priggish to my ears. "If you don't need help, all you need do is say so without embellishment."

"Cripes. I don't need help."

"Very well. Thank you."

"Yeah." He struggled from the motorcar, opened the back door of same and hauled out the to-be-returned books.

"And if Miss Petrie has any books saved for me, please check them out!" I called after him.

"Yeah, yeah," he said.

I watched as he began walking up the first short set of stairs and decided he probably wouldn't overbalance himself. After he got up those few steps, he'd have to walk a few paces before tackling the second set of steps, so he'd probably be able to recover from the first set by the time he reached the second one.

Then I worried about the wisdom of allowing Mr. Lou Prophet to enter the Pasadena Public Library at all. By himself, I mean. He was now a known associate of Sam's and mine, after all. If he created a spectacle of himself, the entire city might turn against the both of us. Sam, even though he didn't technically *need* his job, might be annoyed if he were dismissed because of something Mr. Prophet did in the library. And what would people think of *me* if a friend of mine managed to create havoc in the library?

But no. Prophet wouldn't—*couldn't*—do anything of a troublesome nature in a library, of all places. Could he? Oh, dear. I sure hoped he couldn't.

I waited, though, until he'd finished climbing the very last step and hobbled on to the library's front door before I sighed heavily, pulled away from the curb and made my way to Mrs. Pinkerton's house.

As ever, my session with Mrs. Pinkerton left me a wreck and her feeling a whole lot better than when I'd arrived. Maybe I really *should* retire from spiritualist-mediuming after Sam and I married.

But no. Except for mopping, dusting, and sewing, I was a total failure when it came to the domestic arts. If I kept working, I could hire someone to come in and clean for us and do the gardening and, of course, we could always dine on Aunt Vi's cooking. On the other hand, I could probably do those things anyway, because Sam had a lot of money.

But I'd feel like a slothful layabout if he had to pay someone else to come to our home and do housekeeping chores I should be doing.

Bother. Even when things are going well, life can be complicated, can't it?

I hadn't come to any conclusion about the future of my spiritualist business by the time I left Mrs. Pinkerton's mansion and drove back to the Pasadena Public Library. There I found Mr. Lou Prophet sitting on the wall surrounding the library, reading one book and with several more books stacked on the wall beside him.

For the record, if he'd been so inclined, he could have walked across the park-like lawn and taken a seat in the pretty white gazebo beside the library pond. However, perhaps walking on soft grass might be a difficult thing to do for a man with a peg-leg. I decided not to ask, since I didn't want to appear insensitive.

Anyhow, he got up from his seat and didn't speak as he opened the back door to the Chevrolet and deposited the books on the seat. When he climbed into the front seat, he said, "Your friend was there, she gave me lots of books for you, and she said she'd be happy…No. She said she'd be *delighted* to come to your ma and pa's house on Saturday at eleven."

"Thank you very much, Mister Prophet. And what's the title of the book you were so engrossed in you when I pulled up to the curb?"

"This?" He held up a book. "*The Call of the Wild,* by a fella named Jack London. I used to like to travel to far-off places. These days, can't do much except read about 'em. Got this one, too." He reached into the back seat, grabbed a book and held up a copy of *Ben Hur, a Tale of the Christ,* by General Lew Wallace. "Should be a good yarn. I was in the territory when he was governor there."

"He who?"

"General Wallace."

"General Lew Wallace was the governor of a territory?" I asked, faintly incredulous, but also fascinated.

"Yes, he was."

"Which territory?"

"New Mexico. It's a state now, like everything else that used t'be wild." He heaved a big sigh. "Civilization's got a big damned footprint, and it's wipin' out all my old stompin' grounds."

I thought about chastising him for swearing, but decided not to waste my breath. Maybe General Wallace's story, *Ben Hur*, might go some way toward civilizing Mr. Lou Prophet.

And if *that* wasn't a silly, useless notion, I didn't know what was.

TWELVE

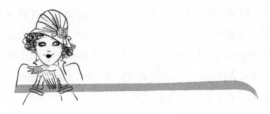

That evening, both Sam and Mr. Prophet came over for dinner. We had a little of the delicious fruit salad still remaining from Saturday's party, but we'd cleaned up most of the rest of the left-over foodstuffs. Therefore, Vi prepared fried chicken and used the last of the deviled eggs in a delicious potato salad. I tell you, the woman was a culinary wonder.

Mind you, I'm a wonder, too, but that's mainly because I wonder how people do the things they do that I *can't* do. Like, for instance, cook. Haven't come up with a satisfactory answer yet.

After we were seated at the table and Pa had said our usual short grace, Sam said, "Tomorrow's the day you two are going to Missus Mainwaring's orange grove, isn't it?"

"Yes, it is," I said as Mr. Prophet chewed on some chicken. "I'll be glad to see it. I understand the orchard is huge, and the home she had built there is another mansion-type place. That's where she houses the women she attempts to reform."

"Women to reform?" asked Ma. Drat. I hadn't told her about Mrs. Mainwaring's good works or former profession. I decided she didn't need to know about the latter.

"She tries to help women who have hit hard times learn... um...legitimate skills, so they'll be able to support themselves."

"Does she know women who don't possess legitimate skills?" Ma again.

Dumb Daisy. "Well, I don't know about that, but she does try to help as many poor women as she can. Not every female in the world comes from a great family like mine."

"I see," said Ma, who clearly didn't.

"From everything I've heard and read, I'm fortunate to have you and Pa and Aunt Vi and all of our kin as...well, kin. If you know what I mean. You know Flossie Buckingham. Remember when she was involved with those horrid gangsters?"

"Ah," said Ma, an expression of comprehension crossing her face. "Yes. Now that you mention it, I do recall her less-than-savory past." She smiled at me. "You did a good service for her, Daisy."

"It was nothing, really," I muttered. A little louder, I added, "Mrs. Mainwaring is trying to help women who are kind of like Flossie."

"That's kind of her," said Ma.

Phew! Got out of that one by the skin of my teeth.

With a squint, Sam said, "You'll have to tell me all about it tomorrow."

"I will."

Mr. Prophet said, "Huh. I'll believe it when I see it."

"Don't be so skeptical. You're judging her before you even know what she does there," I told him.

Naturally this brought a "Daisy" from my mother. Then and there I decided to ask Sam if he wouldn't rather just elope and get our marriage over with so I didn't have to endure my mother's constant censure. He probably wouldn't agree, since he seemed anxious to please my folks. While I was glad about that, I still wouldn't mind being able to speak my mind without my mother's constant, "Daisys," if you know what I mean.

His parents most likely wouldn't care one way or another if we had a grand wedding or got hitched in a judge's office, since they disapproved of me to begin with. It still bothered me that people so close to the man I loved and aimed to marry didn't want me as a daughter-in-law. I'd never been disapproved-of before for no good reason, and I felt sad about it. I mean, Sam's family was important to him, and I was sorry he would be letting them down. Because of *me*, of all innocuous people. Life contains many mysteries, I guess, and this was a whopper for me.

As I washed and put away the dinner dishes, Ma and Aunt Vi picked over the books Mr. Prophet had brought home from the library. Among the haul were *With Lawrence in Arabia*, by Mr. Lowell Thomas (I figured this as being one of Mr. Prophet's picks); *Whose Body*, by Miss Dorothy L. Sayers (from Regina, I was certain); *Dark Frigate*, by Mr. Charles Boardman Hawes (could be from either Regina or Prophet); *Antic Hay*, by Mr. Aldous Huxley (I suspected Regina's selection of this one); *The Rustlers of Pecos County*, by Mr. Zane Grey (I *knew* this to have been suggested by Regina, because I'd heard Mr. Prophet say many unkind words about what he called "so-called westerns"); *Uncanny Stories*, by Mrs. May Sinclair; and *The Rover*, by Mr. Joseph Conrad (again, a toss-up between Regina and Prophet, although I suspected Regina). Anyway, there were quite a number of books to choose from, and I hoped like heck Ma and Vi would leave either *Whose Body* or *Uncanny Stories* for me.

No such luck. However, after I kissed Sam good-night on the lips and pecked Mr. Prophet's cheek, I picked up *Antic Hay*, and took it and Spike to bed with me. I didn't read for long, the day having worn me out some. I think Spike and I were both sawing logs within five minutes of me pulling the quilt up over us.

The next morning, I arose around seven-ish, as it was my usual hour for getting up, and found not merely Pa, but both Sam and Mr. Prophet in the kitchen when Spike and I emerged from my bedroom. I hadn't expected to see the two men, but I'd brushed out my hair and put on a bathrobe and slippers, so I didn't look *too* horrible. Anyhow, the men were so busy greeting the wagging Spike, they didn't pay any attention to me. I used the time they spent on Spike to scurry to the bathroom, wash my face, tidy my hair a little better, and straighten my robe. My robe and night-gown, by the way, had been crafted by me out of a light flannel material that suited the weather. They were also darned pretty, the nightie being a green-patterned number, and the robe a matching solid green. When I walked back to the kitchen, I felt better about confronting all the men in my life. And, of course, my mother and aunt.

"Morning, everyone," said I.

"Good morning, sweetie," said Pa.

"Mornin'," said Prophet.

"Love that green robe, Daisy," said Ma.

"Thanks, Ma. I used the same pattern as the one I made for you."

"Missus Pinkerton said you helped her a good deal yesterday, Daisy," said Vi.

I suppressed an eye-roll.

"You're beautiful, as always," said Sam, rising and coming over to give me a chaste kiss on the cheek.

"Thanks, Sam. You're so good to me."

"I know it," said he, thereby nullifying his earlier comment.

Men.

"What time are we supposed to leave here to see that orange grove?" asked Mr. Prophet. He sounded a trifle tetchy, and I didn't know why, unless he expected Angie to ambush him and shoot him dead when we visited Orange Acres.

Ignoring his mood, I said, "Angie said she'd come up here around ten, and we'll take two automobiles out to Orange Acres."

I noticed everyone was eating or had eaten scrambled eggs, bacon, and toast, so I went to the warming oven and discovered plenty of the same waiting for me. Gee, I didn't think seven o'clock was a frivolous hour, but it seemed as if everyone else preferred rising earlier than I. I tried not to feel guilty, which never works, but I tried anyway.

"Who all is going?" asked Mr. Prophet. This time he sounded suspicious.

"Just Angie, you, Pa and me, I guess."

"Think I'll bow out of this excursion," said Pa. "If you don't mind."

I shot him a quick look and thought he appeared a trifle paler than usual. I decided not to ask him about his health, because he wouldn't appreciate the question in front of so many other people. Therefore, I added, "Not at all. That's okay, Pa. Maybe another time."

"Maybe," he said with a smile.

"Anyway, that makes Angie, Mr. Prophet and me. Maybe Hattie and Mister Bowman."

"Huh," said Sam. "Who's Hattie?"

"Angie's maid, I think. She answers the door and brings trays of food when Angie asks her to."

"Huh," said Sam. "And you don't know if Bowman is going?"

"No."

"Huh."

"Want to come with us?" I asked, trying to sound sweet. Maybe private detectives weren't favorites of policemen, but so far Mr. Bowman had been polite to all of us, including Sam, and I didn't think he deserved any of Sam's huhs.

"No thanks. I have plenty of work to do without deliberately seeking more," said Sam.

I turned from the warming oven and planted my fists on my hips. "And just what does *that* mean, Sam Rotondo? Deliberately seeking more? What do you expect we'll be doing there? Stealing oranges?"

Before she could give me one of her "Daisys," I scowled at my mother. She only shrugged and tied a scarf over her head.

"No. I just have a funny feeling about Missus Mainwaring and her orange grove. And her friends," said Sam. "And then adding you to the mix...I don't know. Sounds more than a little bit toxic to me."

"You're probably afraid Mister Bowman will sweet-talk me," said I, and turned back to fill my breakfast plate with marvelous food.

"No, I'm not," said Sam, surprising me. I thought he'd said what he'd said merely to be annoying. "I don't know why, but I have a strange sense of foreboding this morning."

Evidently I was incorrect about him only wanting to annoy me. "Hmm," I said as I walked with my plate to the table, set it down and sat myself on a kitchen chair. "I don't know why, either, but if Mister Prophet and I see anything fishy going on, we'll tell you about it." I glanced at Mr. Prophet, who was grouchily chewing toast spread with butter and some of Aunt Vi's raspberry preserves. "Won't we, Mister Prophet?"

Looking up from his plate, still chewing, Mr. Prophet said, "Eh?"

"I told Sam we'd report to him if we discovered any fishy goings-on at Missus Mainwaring's Orange Acres."

Returning his attention to his breakfast, Prophet said, "Huh."

"I'm not really worried," said Sam. He got up from his chair, deposited his dirty dishes in the sink, and returned to give me a kiss on the top of my head. "Just stay out of trouble if you can, all right?"

"What do you mean, *if* I can?" I demanded.

"I just know you, is all."

"Sam!" I said. "You sound as though you think I'm *always* getting into trouble!"

"If the shoe fits..." said my beloved as he walked to the front door.

I'd have heaved a shoe at *him*, if I'd had an extra one handy. And if my mother weren't looking. However, all I said was "Phooey," and dug in.

I washed the breakfast dishes, dried them and put them away as my father and Mr. Prophet sat in the living room yakking. Then I went to my bedroom with Spike to decide on the day's wardrobe. According to the *Pasadena Star News*, not always the most reliable weather source on the planet, the April day was destined to be a warm one. That was all right by me, because I had another new frock I wanted to wear.

As I withdrew the rust-colored, flat-silk crepe confection from my closet, I told Spike, "When I get home this afternoon, I'll clean out my closet. Then tomorrow I'll take everything I glean to Flossie at the Salvation Army." I peeked over my shoulder to see if Spike approved of my intentions and discovered him sitting on my bed yawning. Hmm. Guess Spike knew more about the fulfillment of my good intentions in general than I'd hoped he did.

"I will," I insisted.

Spike lifted an eyebrow—and don't tell me dogs don't have eyebrows, either. Those amber dots above Spike's eyes were his version of brows.

"Honest."

Spike curled up into a cinnamon-roll shape and dozed off. Oh, well. At least he hadn't growled. Or laughed. I laid my outfit over the rocker and paid a visit to the bathroom, where I again washed my face, then brushed my teeth, dotted my underarms with lavender water, combed my hair into submission—*much* more easily accomplished now that I'd had the auburn-red mass bobbed—and dabbed on a little bit of pearl powder so my cheeks wouldn't be shiny. I didn't aim to make myself up like a china doll in imitation of the spectacularly gorgeous Angie Mainwaring, but I did want to look good. And there's nothing wrong with that.

Bother. I do believe this lady doth protest too much.

Whatever was going on inside me, I took it all back to the bedroom with me and donned my rust-colored skirt, which was almost the same color as my hair. I tucked a white button-up blouse with a round collar into the skirt, and then shrugged on the light-weight jacket made from the same fabric I'd used for the skirt. The ensemble went smashingly with my hair and the emerald engage-ment ring Sam's father had fashioned for me—against his will, according to Sam, and only done because Sam had given his folks an ultimatum: them or me. I felt bad about that and hoped, if Sam and I ever managed to get married, we'd go back east for our honeymoon and meet his folks. *Surely* they wouldn't hate me if they got to know me. Would they?

I hoped not.

But I decided not to worry about Sam's family for the day. I plopped my straw hat onto my well-groomed head, picked up my tan-colored handbag, slipped my stockinged feet into my tan-colored, low-heeled shoes, and examined myself in the Cheval-glass mirror. What's more, I decided I looked pretty darned good, and the day's plans pleased me.

I was headed to Angie's famous Orange Acres! And, golly, was I looking forward to the trip. If you've never smelled orange trees in bloom, you've missed out on something spectacular. The scent of orange blossoms is probably my favorite in the entire universe. I'd held a bouquet of them when I married Billy. They don't last long, but I still liked to pick some when our orange trees were blooming, bring them into the house and stick them in a vase. I'd have to sweep up the wilted flowers the following morning, but the effort was more than worth it.

Feeling relatively chipper, I woke up Spike, and the two of us joined the gents in the living room. Mr. Prophet glanced at me and winked. "You look mighty pretty today, Miss Daisy." Evidently his mood had improved some.

I curtsied. "Thank you, Mister Prophet. You look pretty spiffy yourself."

"Huh. Don't know what spiffy means, but I doubt I look it. I'm an old man with one leg and a peg, and I can't seem to look like anything else."

"Phooey."

He squinted at me. "Not sure what that means, either."

Pa laughed and rose from where he'd been sitting on the sofa. "Don't worry, Lou. Modern slang is too hard for most of us old folks to understand, I reckon."

"*Modern* slang?" I said. "Heck, I don't know half the words Mister Prophet uses! In fact, I've begun writing them all down. Maybe a publishing house would like to release a dictionary translating old-west sayings into modern English words. I might make a lot of money with book like that."

Another laugh came from Pa, this one even heartier than his first. Prophet merely squinted some more. Guess his good mood had been a temporary thing.

However, the conversation didn't continue because someone scritched our doorbell, and Spike raced to the front door, excited to welcome visitors to the house. Although I'd been frightened to death of people coming to the house mere weeks prior, this time I figured the scritcher was Angie, so I happily trotted after my hound and opened the door. First, of course, I gave Spike the order to sit. He sat. I love my dog.

"Good morning, Angie!" I said with probably more enthusiasm than was absolutely required. Angie seemed startled, at any rate.

"Good morning, Daisy. Ready to pay a visit to my orange grove?"

"You bet I am. So's Mister Prophet."

I waved an arm, ushering her into the house. As ever, Angie looked exquisite. That day she wore a simple, pull-on dress with an embroidered V-neck that appeared as if it were made of pure silk —unlike the fake silk of my own gown. A muted floral print adorned the background color of soft apricot. Angie had pulled her dark hair into a knot held together by what looked like a couple of enameled chopsticks. She seemed to have a passion for Chinese things. That was all right by me. I liked Chinese stuff, too. Especially the food.

"We'll take two automobiles if that's all right with you, Daisy. I'd like to stay at the place for a while and make sure everything's running as it should be. Hattie's going with me."

"I'd already decided we should take two machines, so it sounds like a good idea to me," I told her, securing my straw hat with a hatpin. Wish I had some hatpins with enameled ends, but oh well. I aimed to get Sam to take me to Chinatown in downtown Los Angeles one of these days. Maybe I'd find some pretty hatpins there.

Mr. Prophet and I walked out to Angie's car which, I noticed, was being driven by a colored fellow. Hattie sat in the back seat of the huge cream-colored automobile. I learned later it was a 1924 Haynes Model 60 Sport Touring Car, and Angie used a chauffeur because she didn't know how to drive. What's more, she told me, she'd just as soon not learn.

Her prerogative. I enjoyed the independence given me by being able to drive my own car, but Angie had enough money to be independent even if she didn't know how to drive her own car. I tell you, money is a useful commodity and, if it can't actually buy happiness, it's probably the next best thing.

"We'll just follow you, if that's all right," I said to Angie. The colored fellow had climbed out of her car to open a back door for her. Interesting. Hattie, a black woman, shared the back seat with

131

Angie, a white woman, while a Negro man drove the car. I wondered if he and Hattie were related somehow, although I thought it might be rude to ask. Not sure why.

"Perfectly fine," said Angie. "I'll have Cyrus wait until you back out of your driveway, and then he'll pull ahead and keep you in sight. Orange Acres isn't very far to the east of us here. In fact, it's just off Colorado Boulevard in Lamanda Park, which Pasadena annexed recently."

Pasadena had, indeed, annexed Lamanda Park recently. I'd had a hideous experience in Lamanda Park once, but I didn't like to think about it. It had involved gangsters, Tommy guns and Flossie before she became Mrs. Buckingham. The two of us barely got out of the incident intact, although we'd been coated from head to toe with plaster dust.

"You want to wait here until I back out the Chevrolet?" I asked Mr. Prophet.

Aiming a frown Angie's way, he said, "Naw. I'll just walk there with you. I might only have one leg, but I'm still plenty quick."

"That's fine." He was also plenty touchy.

He opened the driver's side door for me, which surprised me. Mr. Prophet demonstrated so few characteristics one might call gentlemanly that when he displayed one, the action took me aback. Nevertheless, trying not to look astonished, I said, "Thank you."

He said, "Yeah."

Guess gentlemanliness only went so far where Mr. Lou Prophet was concerned.

After he got himself stuffed into the front passenger side of the Chevrolet, I backed it down the driveway, into the street, and pulled over to the curb. Pa stood on the porch, waving, so I waved back. Mr. Prophet clutched his seat as if he didn't trust me not to crash the car into one of Marengo's pepper trees. Huh. And here I'd driven him all over Pasadena only the day before this expedition.

"Your faith in my driving expertise is touching, Mister Prophet," I told him.

"Hellkatoot," said he. "I don't like ridin' around in these things, no matter who's drivin'. Give me a horse any old day. I was in one of these things when that sister of the sheets drove me over a cliff and I lost my leg." He tapped on his peg.

Sister of the sheets? I had a pretty good idea what the expression meant, but I might ask him later in order to be sure. Another day, when he was in a better mood. "I fear the day of the horse is fading fast."

"Huh. Horses are a hell of a lot easier to take care of than these damned machines."

"I *wish* you'd stop cursing with every other word you say. Do you really have to swear all the time?" My mind chanted, *prig, prig, prig*. But honestly, did the man *have* to curse so often?

"Yeah. I think I do."

I sighed and decided to save this conversation and an explanation of the expression he'd used for another day when he wasn't feeling so tetchy. Anyway, I had enough to do, keeping up with Angie's gorgeous automobile. I wondered if her chauffeur—Cyrus? I think she'd said his name was Cyrus—washed and polished it every day. It was sure bright and shiny.

Angie was right in that it didn't take us long to get to Orange Acres. We were there in twenty-five minutes at the most. I could tell when we were approaching the place, because all the trees were blooming like mad, and the heady, toe-curling, heart-thumping scent of orange blossoms filled the air.

Even though I knew I was taking a chance, what with his iffy mood and all, I couldn't help but ask Mr. Prophet, "Isn't that aroma glorious?"

He turned his head and squinted at me.

Irked, I said, "Well? It *is* glorious! Even if you don't like Angie, you must at least appreciate the sweet scent of orange blossoms."

He said, "Huh."

Very well then. I shut up and followed Cyrus, Angie and Hattie through a huge open gate and up a long and winding road. I swear, the scent of those blossoms was about as close to heaven as even our kitchen got when Aunt Vi was in holiday-cookie-baking mode.

When Cyrus pulled the big car to a stop at the bottom of a beautiful porch with steps leading up to it, I parked my car behind Angie's. She got out and walked over to me.

"Do you want to leave your automobile here, or would you rather park it in the shade?"

The weather being as fine as the orange-blossom aroma surrounding us, I said, "I'll just leave it here. But first I'm going to open the windows. The fragrance in the air here is absolutely wonderful!"

Smiling with what looked like approval, Angie said, "I love the scent, too. Orange blossoms are my particular favorites."

"Mine, too," I told her. T'was the truth, by gosh.

Lou Prophet said, "Huh," opened his door, got out of the Chevrolet, and stared around with what looked to me like glumness, perhaps enhanced by a pinch of disgust. Guess he didn't want to give up a good grudge without a struggle.

So be it.

THIRTEEN

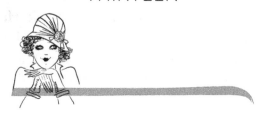

First of all, Angie led us into the house, which was a perfection of a place. I guess you'd call the style in which it was built Victorian. It had several peaked gables, a turret and casement windows. Painted light blue with white gingerbread trim, the place would have looked right at home in a book of fairy tales. Nice fairy tales like those of Mother Goose; not those of the Grimm brothers. The massive front door bore a window with stained-glass image of a peacock in full-tail mode. Lovely.

The door opened to reveal a small entryway where an umbrella stand and a hat rack sat. Although it didn't look to me as if he wanted to do it, Mr. Prophet hung his perky brown fedora on a peg. For the record, he wore a nice-looking brown tweed suit that day. Don't know if he'd picked it up at the Salvation Army or if he'd bought it new, using some of the money he'd earned when he'd captured Sam's nephew, Frank Pagano, after Frank heaved his knife at me. That was the night both Sam and I met Mr. Prophet, who kept a "wanted" poster tucked in his back pocket. The poster bore a photograph of Frank, who was an embarrassing relative to have if you were a policeman.

Anyway, I think Mr. Prophet collected the $500 offered by the law for Frank's capture, even though Frank hadn't been brought to trial yet. Probably Sam had something to do with him getting the money early, if that's what happened.

"Would you like to sit in the front parlor for a moment or two, or would you prefer a tour of the house and grounds first?"

"I'll go on upstairs and see to the ladies," said Hattie, walking toward a stairway ornamented with a rose-patterned runner.

I heard a grunt from Prophet, but pretended I didn't.

"Thank you, Hattie," said Angie. "We'll be on the sun porch in a little while."

"Yes, ma'am," said Hattie.

Angie smiled at both Mr. Prophet and me, but I was the only one who smiled back. I felt kind of like thumping Mr. Prophet on the head. However, even though my mother wasn't there to "Daisy" me, I didn't do it.

"I'd love to see the house," I told Angie, my enthusiasm clear to hear in my tone. "It's just beautiful."

"Thank you. It has an irregular floor plan. The bedrooms are upstairs, and each one has a little balcony off a window. But that's where the ladies reside, so we'll confine ourselves to the lower floor today."

"Ladies," grumbled Mr. Prophet under his breath.

I actually *did* thump him that time, only on the shoulder, not the head. I received a magnificent sneer for my effort, too. Huh, as Mr. Prophet himself might say. Still, he was a guest, and I didn't think it was polite of him to act like a curmudgeon.

On the other hand, maybe he was thinking of the money Angie had skint him of. Or fleeced from him. Or whatever old-fashioned slang expression referred to stealing money from someone. I guess he had a right to be grumpy. Sort of. But he didn't have to carry it to extremes, darn it, especially since Angie had told him she'd pay him back. With interest.

As Angie led us from room to room, I saw what she meant about an irregular floor plan. I don't think any two rooms were the same size or shape. They were all beautifully furnished, however, and I got to thinking I might just take Angie with Harold and me when we went to that furniture warehouse about which Sam and Harold had talked when we'd planned our party.

"And here's my favorite room in the whole house," Angie said as she led us down a hallway ending in a screened-in, tile-floored sun porch. "I like to sit here of an evening and read or just smell those orange blossoms."

"I don't blame you. This is… Well, it's about as perfect as a room can be." In fact, I wanted it. Not that I didn't adore the house Sam had bought for us, but it would be nice to have a sun porch like this in which to sit on a pleasant evening and read a book. Or just look at the sunset. Not that we got great sunsets in Pasadena, but the mountains to the north are always pretty.

"Thank you," said Angie. I could tell she was pleased by my endorsement of her creation. "Let me take you into the orchard now. The gardener here at the Acres is the younger Mr. Wu, my other gardener's son, and he has a little shed back there in an open spot."

Two Wus, by gad. Because I doubted Angie would be as amused as I, I didn't say the two words aloud.

She, Mr. Prophet and I exited the sun porch and found ourselves on a paved walkway wending its way across a small lawn with a white picket fence surrounding it. Roses, entwined with honeysuckle, climbed the fence. The combined scents of honeysuckle, roses and orange blossoms in the yard was enough to make a person swoon.

Noticing one climbing rose in particular because it was absolutely adorable, I touched one of its tiny blossoms. "This is a spectacular rose, Angie. And it smells divine."

"That's my Cecile Brunner rose. It's my favorite."

"I've never seen a rose with little flowers like this one has."

"I planted it in particular because I think it's charming." Angie gazed with adoration at her favorite rose. Boy, I guess she'd really meant it when she'd told me she'd built her present life from nothing.

All in all, I don't think I've ever seen a lovelier back yard. On the spot, I decided to ask Sam to build us something like an arched trellis so I could plant a Cecile Brunner rosebush to climb all over it. Maybe I'd plant the rosebush on one side of the arch and some honeysuckle on the other, and they could mingle in our back yard the way they did in Angie's. We might have a by-gosh rose arbor in our back yard!

I reminded myself Sam and I weren't married yet, and he might want a say in how he wanted the back yard planted. Fiddlesticks.

Anyhow, Angie went to the gate in the little white picket fence, opened it, and gestured the two of us to follow her through it and on into the orange grove.

"Oh, my, Angie," I said, my voice proclaiming my awe at her handiwork, "this is… Well, it's just perfect. Stunning."

She took my arm and spoke confidentially. "I tried my best to make my home as nice as I could. I even wanted the orchard to be pretty. That's probably because there was no prettiness at all in my life during most of it."

I think I heard another "Huh" from Mr. Prophet but wasn't sure.

"And you did this all by yourself? I mean, the planning and hiring of architects and carpenters and so forth?"

"I did."

"What an ambitious project. You've done really well for yourself."

This time I *know* I heard a grumpy "Huh" from Mr. Prophet.

By this time, we'd reached the open space where the gardener's shed stood. Both Angie and I turned around to face Mr. Prophet, I with as hideous a scowl as I could produce on my face. Since I was occupied in glaring at the Prophet of Gloom (sorry about that one), I didn't see the expression on Angie's face, but I heard her peevishness when next she spoke.

"I should have returned your money before we came out to the orchard, I suppose. I apologize, but if you'll contain your carping for another few minutes, I'll give you back all of your money. *With* interest."

"Good."

In this case "good" was no better than "huh," but I didn't thump him again. Even if I'd been so inclined, I couldn't have done it, because at that precise moment Lou Prophet swept out an arm, felling both Angie and me.

I landed hard and opened my mouth to bellow something on the order of "*Hey!*" I didn't get the chance because a gunshot rang out the second we hit the dirt. Therefore, I cowered and covered my head with my arms instead. A split-second later, Mr. Prophet had whipped out his own gun—I have no idea what kind it was or where he'd been keeping it—and pulled its trigger, aiming at what looked to me like a tree branch.

But he hadn't aimed at a branch. Rather, he'd aimed at the man hiding on the branch and who tumbled from the tree a mere heartbeat later. He brought with him a cascade of waxy, sweet-smelling orange blossoms.

"Stay down," Prophet ordered Angie and me as we huddled together on the ground. All right by me. Under the circumstances, I didn't even object to being bossed around or shoved off my feet.

Daring to lift my head a trifle and squinting, I saw Mr. Prophet duck behind an orange tree and gaze sharply around. Looking for more gunmen or other miscreants? I didn't know, but I recommenced cowering and let him do it.

Slowly he emerged from behind the tree, still alert and peering this way and that. I didn't do likewise until he'd inspected every corner of that little open space in the middle of the orchard and said, "I think it's all right for you two to get up now." He didn't offer to help us, but I didn't mind. Under the circumstances, I was kind of glad he was on the alert for other possible gunmen. He could be gentlemanly later. Mind you, he probably *wouldn't* be, but he could be if he wanted.

Oh, Lord, I'm babbling again. Terror does that to me.

Once on my feet, I offered Angie a shaky hand, which she took, and she, too, arose. We both used our hands to clap dust and dried orange blossoms from our clothing. I heard Angie take a huge gulp of air. She said in a quavering voice, "Who in the world is that?" She pointed at the blossom-covered corpse with a finger that quavered as much as her voice.

"Dunno," said Prophet. He walked over to the body and toed it over onto its back. Actually, he pegged it over, but I don't think "to peg" is a legitimate verb; at least not in this context. After gazing at the face thus revealed, he said, "Huh."

"Wh—" Angie's voice croaked to a stop and she cleared her throat. "Who is it? Do you recognize him?"

Prophet turned and gave Angie a bland stare. "Yeah. You do, too."

"I do?"

Still a bit trembly, and sucking in a gallon or two of orange-blossom-scented air, Angie took a couple of small, tentative steps toward the body, Mr. Prophet staring at her the while. As soon as she glanced down, she clapped both hands over her mouth and said, "Oh, my God!"

"Yeah," said Mr. Prophet.

"Who is it?" I asked, finally gathering enough courage to walk over and gaze down at the corpse for myself. "I've never seen him before."

Not that I routinely recognized gunmen, but several members

of the rotten Petrie family had caused Sam and me a whole lot of grief in the recent past. I'd thought they were all either deceased or locked up, but it wouldn't have surprised me a whole lot to see a Petrie lying there, dead, in Angie's orange grove. Speaking of which…

"Is he dead?" I asked in a small voice.

"As a doornail," said Mr. Prophet, pegging at the body again.

When he did it, the body jiggled some before it settled back down. I felt a trifle queasy. "Who is it? I mean he?"

"It's as good as he in this case," said Prophet, sticking his gun—I don't think it was the one he'd called his gut-shredder, but it sure wasn't his long Winchester '73 rifle, either—back into the waistband of his trousers.

No wonder I hadn't known he was carrying a gun. He'd kept it out of sight. On the other hand, I ought to have expected him to come to this get-together armed. After all, I knew he didn't like or trust Angie and used to make his living killing people. That sounds awful and, even though Harold and I had joked about Mr. Prophet's prior line of work, I don't precisely mean it. However, he *had* been a bounty-hunter in his younger years, and he still kept a lot of guns in his arsenal. I know this for a fact because Sam had told me so. I wasn't sure if I approved of him owning all those guns, but my approval or lack thereof wouldn't make any difference to Lou Prophet, even if he knew about it.

"Who is he then?" I asked again.

"This here Jasper is Frank Tucker," said Prophet. "Got a dodger on him at home. One thousand big ones, dead or alive."

Very well, I understood "Jasper" to mean a man and a "dodger" to be a "wanted" poster. I hadn't learned a new language since I'd taken Spanish in high school, but Mr. Prophet was teaching his to me really fast.

"I'll take the money." Prophet gave Angie a penetrating

seconds-long stare, as if he expected her to demand the bounty on Mr. Tucker.

But Angie only shuddered slightly and said, "Fine with me." Then, as if just remembering something, she gasped and said, "Oh, Lord. He probably came for Sally. I'd better check on her. I hope the girls didn't hear the shots."

"Who's Sally and how'd he find her?" I asked.

Nobody answered.

"I hope Sally and Li are in the house," said Angie nervously.

"You'd better call the police, too," I said, my own voice still small, since I wasn't sure precisely what Frank Tucker, Angie Mainwaring, Lou Prophet and Angie's "girls" had to do with each other. But surely if the man was bad enough to be featured on a wanted poster offering a thousand dollars for his capture (or death), this killing was legitimate. Wasn't it?

Lord, I hoped so.

It must be. After all, Mr. Tucker had shot at…Angie? Oh, boy, I didn't know for whom he'd intended his bullet, but he'd fired the first shot.

"I'll call the police as soon as I check on Sally," said Angie, plainly worried.

At that moment, two women appeared on the pathway leading to the place where Angie, Mr. Prophet and I stood around the dead man. Acting quickly, Mr. Prophet shook the orange tree towering over the body and caused another avalanche of orange blossoms to drop onto it. The flowers did a good deal to hide the man on the ground. They also rendered him possibly the sweetest-smelling cadaver in the history of the world. Instinctively, I scuttled over and stood beside Mr. Prophet in an attempt to hide the body from the newcomers.

Giving Mr. Prophet and me a grateful glance, Angie hurried up to the two women.

"What happened? What was that awful noise?"

The speaker, female, appeared to be another person of Chinese extraction. She seemed older than the pale and trembly blonde whose arm she held, but she was lovely all the same. They were both lovely, for that matter. I wondered if they were two of the "fallen" women whom Angie was helping to regain an upright stature in life.

"Li and Sally," said Angie. "Mister Prophet and I were just doing a bit of target practice."

She turned a pleading glance at me, so I smiled idiotically at the women and gave them a little finger wave.

"You remember Mister Prophet, don't you, Li?" said Angie, trying for all she was worth to sound normal. "From Tombstone?"

With a start, the Chinese woman—Li, I presumed—glanced at Mr. Prophet and said, "Oh, my Lord."

"You might say that," grumbled a sour-voiced Lou Prophet.

The Chinese woman seemed relatively calm when she gave Mr. Prophet a curt nod. The other woman was as pallid and shaky as a linen sheet in a high wind. I took her to be Sally. She appeared kind of sickly to me, and I wondered what was wrong with her. All at once, as she peered at Mr. Prophet and me and caught sight of the body, her knees gave out. Before she could sink to the ground, Li grabbed her and propped her up with an arm around her waist.

"Who is that?" Sally's asked in a voice as thin and pale as she was.

"It's just a dummy, Sally," said Angie. "You know, like in the department stores? A mannequin? For target practice."

If Sally bought that one, she was sicker than she looked. Both Li and Sally were exceptionally beautiful women. I felt kind of like a podgy English bulldog in a room full of graceful Afghan hounds. Suddenly I wished I'd brought Spike with me.

Turning to the Chinese woman, Angie sounded like a general giving orders to a raw recruit when she said, "Li? Will you please take Sally to her room? Then come down to the sun porch, if you will."

"Yes. I'll settle Sally and then join you there." Li shot Mr. Prophet a glance I couldn't interpret, although the image of a carved jade dragon flitted into my head. Hmm. Was Li the lady who'd...

How the heck was I going to learn the answer to *that* question? Well, I'd figure something out.

"Thank you," said Angie. Her thanks sounded heartfelt.

As soon as Li and Sally were out of sight, Angie said in her general's voice, "Let's get back to the house. I'll call the police." Turning to me, she said with a note of pleading in her tone, "Do you think you can get Detective Rotondo to handle this? It might be easier on all of us if he did."

Obviously, Angie didn't know Sam very well. Nevertheless, I said, "I'll try."

FOURTEEN

"I have two telephones in the house," Angie said as the three of us hurried to her gorgeous home. "One of them is on the sun porch. I'll call from there. Um…Daisy, you'd better stay with me." She glanced at Mr. Prophet, who stood like a statue of grim death at the door to the sun porch. "Mister Prophet, if you don't mind, would you wait at the door leading onto the corridor. Don't let anyone into the room except Hattie or Li. If you don't mind," she repeated, sounding a trace panicky.

"And If I do mind?"

"Stop being such a pill, Mister Lou Prophet!" I told him, exasperation finally overtaking fear. "Just stand guard at the door so Angie and I can call the coppers."

With a disgusted eye-roll, Mr. Prophet limped over to the door now standing open to reveal the hallway. He shut the door and stood in front of it, thereby blocking anyone's entry, should it be necessary to do so.

"Thank you," I snapped.

"Yeah."

I noticed the crank on Angie's telephone, and realized she probably had to go through an operator in order to be connected to the police department. Therefore, I made a sacrifice of myself.

"Want me to call, Angie? I probably know the girl at the telephone exchange."

"Oh, would you? *Thank* you, Daisy!"

"Sure. I don't mind." I did mind, but I didn't want Angie or Mr. Prophet to know it.

"Um, do you have a party line, or a single line?"

"A single line," said Angie. No surprise there. If she had other people out in the big wide world who wanted to shoot her, she probably didn't want to let her party-line neighbors know about it. And she definitely wouldn't want the would-be shooters to know where she lived, although it looked as if that boat had sailed. Golly, I don't know where I got that expression. It definitely wasn't one of Lou Prophet's.

Anyway, glad for small favors—like not having to shoo party-line sharers off the wire—I asked the telephone exchange to connect me to the Pasadena Police Department. For once, I was glad the operator at the exchange wasn't Medora Cox or any of my other friends. After my request had been fulfilled, I asked the officer who answered the telephone at the police station to connect me with Detective Sam Rotondo.

"Who's this?" the officer had the effrontery to ask.

"My name is Missus William Majesty. Daisy Gumm Majesty, and I am Detective Rotondo's fiancée. This call, however, is not personal. It's important, it's related to an untimely death, and I need to speak to Detective Rotondo. Instantly."

"All right, all right" said the officer, peeved.

I didn't really blame him for his annoyance. I had a pretty good idea Sam was going to pitch a fit when he found out what had happened in Angie's orange grove.

I was right.

"Damnation, Daisy! Why do these things always happen around *you*?"

"I don't know!" I screeched back at him. From the tail of my eye, I saw Angie give a start of surprise, and I lowered my voice. "A fellow was hiding in an orange tree, and he shot at us when we got to the gardener's shed."

"I have *no* idea what you're talking about," grumbled Sam ominously. "A fellow hid in a *tree*? And *shot* at you? Cripes, are there more Petries out there?"

"I don't know!" I caught hold of my alarm and lowered my voice again. "This isn't—wasn't, I mean—a Petrie. He was a…" Stumped, I glanced from Angie to Mr. Prophet.

They chorused, "Frank Tucker."

Mr. Prophet added, "He's got a wanted dodger out on him."

"Angie and Mister Prophet say his name was Frank Tucker and that he is—or was—wanted by the law. I don't know what law where."

"Arizona," said Prophet.

"He was wanted by the law in Arizona. I don't know for what."

"Bank robbery and murder," said Mr. Prophet.

I whimpered. What a big sissy, huh? "Um…He was wanted for bank robbery and murder," I told Sam.

"Good God. Well, stay there. I'll look in our files to see if I can find his information. We probably have a wanted sheet on him filed somewhere."

"Look under the Ts," I whispered, trying to be helpful.

Sam wasn't impressed. "Huh. We'll be there as soon as we can get there. Don't anybody move anything."

"We won't," I promised.

The receiver on Sam's end of the wire slammed into its cradle, making me jump. But honestly. I was *so* tired of people shooting at

147

me and throwing knives at me and running me down with cars. It makes a girl nervous, and I don't think I should be faulted for my reaction. *You* see how calm *you* are after weeks of knowing several people want you dead.

Angie and I sat on a small sofa on her sun porch while Mr. Prophet continued to stand sentry at the door to the hallway. After about twenty minutes, a knock came at the door Mr. Prophet guarded. He opened same, stepped aside and Li joined us. She glanced up at Mr. Prophet when she walked past him and gave him a curt nod. He didn't nod back, but he offered her a magnificent sneer.

Evidently impervious to sneering ex-bounty hunters, Li walked over to Angie and me, hooked the back of a chair and pulled it closer to the sofa upon which we sat.

"Is Sally all right?" Angie asked instantly.

"I think so." Li shook her head. "Her condition is fragile, though. She nearly jumped out of her shoes when she heard those gunshots. I expect she was recalling her time in Tombstone."

"I expect so, too," said Angie. Then she recalled Li and I hadn't yet been officially introduced, so she introduced us.

Sticking out my hand for Li to shake, I said, "How do you do, Miss…um…Li?"

"Li's my last name," she said with a grin, "but don't worry about it. I'm fine, all things considered. And you, Missus Majesty?"

"Oh, please just call me Daisy. Everyone does."

"Thank you, Daisy. Everyone calls me Li."

"Even though it's your last name?" Don't ask me why I asked such a stupid question. Guess my nerves were still kind of jumpy.

"White people don't understand Chinese names," said Li with a cynical smile.

"Oh, that's right. Your patronymic name always comes first, doesn't it?"

"Yes, it does. Most white people don't know that." Li's expression softened slightly. "What's he doing here?" she asked, nodding at Mr. Prophet, who stood scowling at the three of us. However, he didn't desert his post, which I thought was nice of him. Almost noble, even.

Angie said, "Evidently, Mister Prophet was one of the men from whom we took a little more money than he technically owed when he bought our services."

"Hmph," said Li. "I gave him that jade dragon. It's worth a few cents."

Aha! I was right! Li *was* the one who'd given him the dragon!

"Yes, well, it seems he'd prefer to get his money back."

"Yes, I would," growled Mr. Prophet. "With interest."

Angie sighed. "With interest."

Li said, "Hmph," again.

I thought of something that might (or might not) be pertinent. "Have you ever thought about getting a dog, Angie? A dog would bark and warn you when strangers come around."

After exchanging a glance with Li, Angie said, "Some of the girls are afraid of dogs. Sally is, for one."

"Why would anybody be afraid of a dog?" I asked, honestly curious.

"Not all dogs are as nice—or as small—as your Spike, Daisy. I fear some of the girls I try to help have been disciplined rather harshly from time to time, and the men who...ran, I guess is the appropriate term...the houses in which they worked often used... ghastly tactics.

"You mean they sicced *dogs* on them?" I asked, horrified.

"Yes," said Li. "Mastiffs, to be precise."

"Good Lord." My mind, which was already in a precarious state, reeled.

"The man with the mastiff," said Angie, "was a particularly vicious specimen of the type."

"Sally barely escaped with her life," said Li in a matter-of-fact voice. "I had to sneak her out through a third-story window in the middle of the night."

"Good Lord." My own voice was as feeble as my careening wits. "Is Mister Tucker the man in question?"

"He wasn't the one who used mastiffs," said Li. "That was the delightful Mister Adolph Grant."

"Delightful," muttered Angie.

Being the brilliant woman I was, I deduced both ladies were being sarcastic. Fine by me.

"Coppers are here," said Lou Prophet from the door. "Want me to let 'em in?"

"I'll do it," said Angie, rising from the sofa and marching with firm steps to the door.

Mr. Prophet stepped aside to let her pass, but not without making a comment. "I still want my money back."

"You'll get it," Angie snapped, flashing her glorious dark eyes at him.

He seemed unmoved by her rancor. He did, however, relinquish his post at the door and walk over to sit next to me on the sofa. It hadn't occurred to me before that moment, but it might be painful for him to stand in one place for so long, what with having lost his leg rather recently.

Because I'm a compassionate individual, no matter what other people might think, I said, "Are you all right, Mister Prophet? Does your leg hurt or anything?"

With a truly magnificent frown, he said, "Leg ain't there anymore. Stump hurts."

"I'm sorry," I said. I was sorry I'd asked, at any rate.

"How'd you lose your leg, Lou?" asked Li. Not precisely a shrinking violet, Li. Nor did she sound compassionate; only curious. "You had both of them the last time I saw you."

"Yeah, I did." Prophet looked Li up and down in a manner I

thought particularly disrespectful. Li only sneered at him. Maybe these two deserved each other. "Lost it in a car wreck."

"I didn't think you liked motorcars."

"Don't. A woman was driving the damned thing. Drove us off a cliff in Malibu."

"Ah. Well, you probably deserved it."

"Shit."

Thank the good Lord and Sam Rotondo, the police contingent barged onto the sun porch before fisticuffs could commence.

Taking the lead and glaring at me, Sam said, "All right. Where is this body?" He looked at Mr. Prophet. "Lou, you want to tell me what happened?"

"Why don't Mister Prophet and I both walk you out to where it happened," I suggested.

Still glaring, Sam said, "I don't want you to get—"

"I'm *already* involved, darn it, Sam Rotondo! I was *there*!"

"She's right, Sam," said Mr. Prophet, sounding not the least bit happy about it. "But you don't have to shout about it, Miss Daisy."

"I'm not shouting!" I shouted back at him. Then I clenched my hands together and pressed my fists to my mouth to prevent any more bellows from issuing therefrom.

After a fulminating second or three, Sam gave up. "All right. Daisy, Lou, and Oversloot, come with me. Doan, take statements from Missus Mainwaring and Miss..." His voice petered out since he didn't know Li's name.

"Li Ahn," said Li.

"From Missus Mainwaring and Miss Li. Oversloot, come with us."

The way Li's eyes opened wide made me think she'd been surprised to know that, when it came to Chinese folks, Sam understood their last names came before their first names. Huh, as both Sam and Lou (and occasionally I) might say. My Sam was a smart man. After all, he wanted to marry me, didn't he?

Stop snickering, please.

I led the way out to the back yard, marveling again at how beautiful it was, but not saying so to Sam, who, I sensed wouldn't be receptive to comments about how I wanted our back yard to look just then. "Follow me," I said after I'd opened the gate in the picket fence. Sam, Mr. Prophet, and Doan followed me. Down the gravel path and into the clearing I led them, ending up at the gardener's shed. Sure enough, Mr. Frank Tucker still lay where we'd left him. Still covered in orange blossoms, too, by golly.

"There." I pointed at the sweet-smelling body.

"Cripes," said Sam. "How'd he get plastered with flowers?"

"Mister Prophet shot him out of the orange tree." I pointed at the now-unbecomingly bare branch where Mr. Tucker had lain in wait for…Well, I didn't know for whom he'd lain in wait.

"Why was he up a tree?" asked Doan.

"Ask him," I suggested. "I don't know."

"Can't ask him. He's dead," said Prophet the Practical. "Probably wanted to kill Angie."

"Angie said he might have come for Sally," I said, giving Mr. Prophet a frown, which he ignored with easy aplomb, drat the man.

"Who's Sally?" asked Sam.

"Sally is one of the ladies—"

Mr. Prophet guffawed rudely. After frowning at him, I continued telling Sam who Sally was. "She's one of the *ladies* from Tombstone Angie is attempting to help. Um…" I shot a glance at Mr. Prophet, who merely stared back at me, his head tilted slightly to one side. "Um…I think she used to work in a…in a…"

"She worked in a whorehouse run by Adolph Grant," said Mr. Prophet, not mincing his words.

I frowned at him again, which did as much good as it had the time before. "Anyway, Missus Mainwaring is attempting to help Sally and a few other…women"—I decided not to call them ladies

152

again, since I wanted no more uncouth interruptions from Lou Prophet—"who were desperate to get out of that way of life and into a better one."

"Ah," said Sam. "Do you have any idea how many of them are here at the moment? The former…ladies of the evening, I mean?"

At least he hadn't called them whores. Good for Sam. "No. I've only met Sally and Li. I don't know if there are any other women living at the house right now." I thought for a second and added, "I think Li's one of the people who run the place, though. I don't think she's a former…um…" My voice trailed off.

Before Mr. Prophet could tell me I was wrong about Li, Sam Said, "What about you, Lou? Do you know how many females Missus Mainwaring is trying to set right with the world?"

"Nope."

"All right," said Sam. "Guess I'll have to ask her. Take some pictures of the body, Doan."

"Want me to brush off the flowers first?" asked Doan.

Then it was I noticed Doan carrying one of those new Kodak box cameras, and decided then and there to hire someone to take pictures of our wedding, if Sam and I both lived long enough to have one. At least I didn't think Mr. Frank Tucker had been aiming for me. I hoped not; although if his aim had been off, I might be dead anyway. How discouraging.

"Take some of him like that, then brush away the flowers and take some more." Sam turned to Mr. Prophet. "All right, Lou, tell me what happened. Use as much detail as possible, please. I *really* don't want to have to arrest you for murder if you were merely defending helpless women."

"Never met any women less helpless than them three," said Prophet. "Maybe Miss Daisy's—"

"*I am not helpless!*" I roared at Lou Prophet.

Both Mr. Prophet and Sam flinched. Actually, I think Doan did, too.

"All right, all right. Calm down, Daisy," said Sam. "Nobody said you were helpless."

"He was going to!" I pointed a quivering finger at Mr. Prophet. Don't ask me why this one single comment of his had enraged me, unless all my emotions just managed to come together at that precise moment in time and spill out of my mouth.

Ew. That sounds disgusting.

"No, I wasn't," said Mr. Prophet.

I didn't believe him, but I didn't screech again, not wanting to irk Sam any more than I already had.

"Go ahead, Lou. What happened?"

"Missus Mainwaring was showing Miss Daisy and me around her property and took us out to see her orange grove. When we got to this place"—he made a sweeping gesture with his hand meant to encompass the bare area around the gardener's shed—"I saw the sun glint off'n a gun from a feller in that tree." He pointed to the almost-bare branch of the orange tree that had been used for such a nefarious purpose.

"How was it you saw him?" I asked, forgetting I didn't want to annoy Sam. "I sure didn't."

"Let me do the questioning, please, Daisy," Sam requested through clenched teeth.

"All right." I folded my arms across my chest. I probably should have shoved a fist in my mouth.

"I was lookin'," said Prophet.

"What made you look up into the tree?" asked Sam.

"Years of practice," said Prophet. "If ya'd met as many pecker-woods as I have in my life, you'd'a looked, too. I'm used to lookin' around for folks who ain't supposed to be where they are."

And there was another entry into my old-west dictionary. Peck-erwood; which, I presumed, meant a bad man. I didn't ask Mr. Prophet if my assumption was correct, recalling Sam's precarious mood.

"And he shot first?"

"Yep."

"But he didn't hit anyone?"

"Saw him in the tree and shoved the ladies out of range," said Mr. Prophet.

Sam looked at me for confirmation of this ungentlemanly act, which had probably saved two lives. I nodded and then dared elaborate slightly. "He did. I was offended until I realized why he'd pushed us to the ground."

Sam nodded. "Makes sense."

"I was already drawin' my Peacemaker when he shot, but his target wasn't there any longer," Mr. Prophet said.

"You were drawing your what?" asked Sam. I'm glad he did, because I wanted to know the answer to his question, too.

Mr. Prophet reached under his coat jacket and slowly withdrew a gun. It was a longish gun, although not half as long as his *extremely* long gun, with which he'd shot a man hiding in our hibiscus and rosebushes in hopes of murdering me. I think that firearm had been a Winchester '73, about which my father knew a little bit. Pa had never shot men with his Winchester '73, but only squirrels, ducks, rabbits and so forth.

"Ah, now I see. Is that the genuine article?" asked Sam sounding fascinated.

"It is," said Prophet.

Nodding, Sam smiled. "Now here's an interesting piece of history," he said as Prophet handed him the gun, butt (or whatever you call it) first.

"It's my good ol' .45 caliber, horn-handled, Colt Peacemaker. That there's the gun that tamed the west." His lips curled in something that wasn't even a facsimile of a smile.

"Why do they call it a Peacemaker?" I dared ask. "If it was made to shoot people."

"I think he means people used this make and model firearm to tame those old western towns you're so fond of reading about," Sam said, inspecting the gun and not looking at me. He opened the cylinder and perused its innards. "One shot fired." He looked up at Mr. Prophet. "You're a good shot, Lou."

"Had to be," said Mr. Prophet. "Bein' a good shot kept me alive in the old days."

"I guess so." Sam closed the cylinder, handed the gun back to Mr. Prophet and turned to see how Doan was doing.

Doan had actually stopped taking pictures and had commenced gazing in awe at the revolver Mr. Prophet was tucking back into his waistband. When he saw Sam eyeing him, he busily began taking photographs again.

After he'd taken several photos of the late Mr. Frank Tucker from various angles, I helped him brush orange blossoms off the carcass so he could take more pictures of the same dead man from various other angles.

"That'll do, Doan," said Sam after a while. "We can go in and call the undertaker. I don't think we need to ask any more questions of Mr. Prophet."

"You believe him?" asked Doan, a question I thought quite rude.

"Oh, yes," said Sam upon a sigh. "We'll need to talk to Missus Mainwaring and Miss Li, too, but I'm sure they'll confirm Mister Prophet's version of events."

"And I do, too. I was there. I mean here. Well, you know what I mean. At the time, I mean. When the guy shot at us and Mister Prophet shot him from the tree, is what I mean."

Sam didn't even roll his eyes at me, but took my arm and began guiding me along the path back to the house. Mr. Prophet and Doan walked behind us. I don't think Sam held my arm to prevent me from bolting, either, but because he was sorry I'd endured another unpleasant experience.

Maybe I'm giving him too much credit.

Naw. I loved my Sam, and he loved me.

I could have lived happily forever if he hadn't told me later in the day that when I got involved in dangerous situations, I sometimes made myself difficult to love. I think he was kidding, although I'm not sure.

But this current mess wasn't my fault, confound it!

FIFTEEN

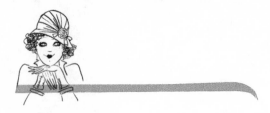

By the time Sam, Mr. Prophet, Doan and I returned to Oversloot and the two ladies in the sunroom, Hattie had joined the gathering. She nodded when told the dead gent in the orange grove was Mr. Frank Tucker, as if she weren't surprised.

"I told you he'd come for Sally," said she.

"Yes, you did. I'm sorry he confirmed your opinion," said Angie. "I don't know how Sally's going to react to this."

"Does she even need to know about it?" asked Hattie.

Chewing on her lower lip, a gesture that surprised me because Angie had always struck me as a woman who knew precisely what to do in any situation, she said, "I...I don't know."

"Might be better to wait and see how she gets along after a day or two," suggested Li, who evidently didn't suffer from Angie's indecisiveness.

I wondered, not for the first time, precisely what Li's role was in Angie's life. She seemed to live here, at the Orange Acres house, but why? What did she do here? Ah, well. Those questions would just have to wait.

"Good idea," said Angie, as if she were glad someone had made up her mind for her.

It was then I noticed Li take Mr. Prophet's arm and lead him to a corner of the room. There she more or less pushed him into a wicker chair, while she sat in another one close to his. He scowled superbly for several minutes until gradually, as Li quietly talked to him, his expression softened. I wondered if he and she had... well...if they'd liked each other in the old days. He'd told me before the love of his life had been a woman named Louisa, who'd had a French last name I can't recall it at the moment, but I also knew he'd been a roué and a cad, so maybe he'd had feelings for Li, too.

Heck, maybe she'd had feelings for him. She'd once upon a time given him a beautifully carved jade dragon, and he'd kept it. Maybe she'd loved him. From a lot of the books I've read over the years, I've concluded women often fall for bounders and womanizers, probably because they could be charming (the bounders and womanizers, I mean; not the women), although I had a difficult time picturing Mr. Lou Prophet ever having been charming. Perhaps the books were talking about men like Mr. Judah Bowman. I can see him charming the socks—and other garments—from susceptible females.

Thank goodness I wasn't one of those women, although I'd produced enough other mistakes to make up for this one oversight on my part. Anyhow, Mr. Bowman seemed firmly affixed to Angie these days. I couldn't imagine her putting up with a man who played around with other women.

Not that it matters, but I'll never understand men for as long as I live. How can a man casually go from woman to woman and not feel anything? Especially if he claims to love a particular woman and then goes out and dallies with another, knowing as he does so he'll break the first woman's heart? Perhaps the men who do those things don't care deeply for the women they're cheating on? Maybe it's because men don't suffer the same consequences as some of the women men casually use and toss aside. Sam has told me more than once he'll never understand women, but I personally think women are *much* easier to understand than men. At least women *talk* about stuff. Men keep everything bottled up inside.

Also, never forget, men can't get pregnant. It's the women who become "with child." Trust me when I tell you if a woman gets pregnant, she knows it, even if the man who got her that way is long gone. There. I said it. Shocking? Perhaps. Chastise me if you will, but it's the truth, and you know it as well as I.

Or maybe I don't know what I'm talking about. Wouldn't be the first time.

As I pondered the differences between men and women—and the list of differences seemed to grow daily—Sam questioned Angie, Li, Hattie and Cyrus about Sally and Frank Tucker.

"Before Li brought her here, Sally was working in a parlor house in Tombstone," said Angie. "Li continues to takes trips to Tombstone periodically, attempting to help women leave the life if they want to. Most of them do."

I heard a grunt from across the room, but when I turned to look at him, Mr. Prophet wore an innocent expression. I frowned at him but didn't say anything.

Sam continued, "So Sally was one of the women you tried to help leave the parlor-house life behind and learn how to…What? Earn a living?"

After a moment's hesitation, Angie said, "Sally has…other problems that need to be addressed before she can be trained for another kind of job. The perfectly *ghastly* man who owned the saloon in which she worked had managed to get her addicted to… well, to drugs."

"Which drugs?" asked Sam.

With a sigh, Angie said, "Mostly laudanum. Chloral hydrate is another one. When Li found her, she'd begun using heroin, which is—"

"Yeah, I know what heroin is. We're seeing more and more of it these days."

This was true. Even I knew what heroin was, although I'd led a sheltered life (as opposed to the lives Angie, Sally, Flossie and many other poor woman had lived) because heroin had been used by a couple of evil men to murder a nice young Pasadena man a year or two earlier.

"I'm sorry to hear it," said Angie with feeling. "At any rate, with Sally, we're trying to deal with the drug issue first. She's not a strong woman, and she'd formed a…I don't know what to call it. She'd formed a relationship, if you can call it that, with Frank Tucker."

"Was he her manager?" asked Sam. Gee, "manager" sounded like such an innocuous word for so pernicious a job.

"No," said Angie. "That honor goes to Mister Adolph Grant, who wants to murder me, too. Tucker was one of his hired guns, and he decided he wanted Sally for his own."

"And Mister Grant didn't object?"

"Of course, he objected, but Tucker was useful to him, so he more or less gave Sally to him."

"But…but that's *slavery*!" I cried. Then I slapped my hand over my mouth, which had gone and done it again. I said, "Sorry, Sam."

Sam, naturally, said, "Huh."

But bless Angie's heart, she said, "Daisy's right. Sally was no better than a slave when Li found her, but she claimed to want out of her way of life."

"You sure she was telling the truth?" Sam asked.

With a nod, Angie said, "She still says she wants to better herself. She understands blind obedience and devotion, and her allegiances shift from day to day. Let's just say I hope we can help her. We'll have to think of some kind of training for her so she'll be able to support herself after we take care of the drug issue. And the reliance-on-a-rat issue."

"Good luck with that," Sam said dryly.

"Thank you." Angie's voice was dry, too. Not unlike the Sahara Desert, in fact.

When he asked to talk to Sally herself, Angie said, "If you don't mind, would you please question her in a day or so? She's extremely fragile, and I worry about her mental state."

"What's the matter with her that makes her fragile? Her addiction?" Sam asked. Blunt and to-the-point, my Sam.

"Yes, and other things, including her so-called love for Frank Tucker. She's been through some truly awful times, Detective Rotondo, and she…" Angie took a deep breath. "Well, we're trying to deal with the drug issue first. Then, with a good deal of love and luck, we may be able to steer her in a new direction. I…I hope you won't make her talk to you today."

"She's telling the truth, Sam," I dared say. "Poor Sally looked as if a gentle breeze would blow her down. In fact, it kind of did, only Li caught her before she hit the dirt."

"That's so," said Li, giving me an approving nod.

"Yeah," said Lou Prophet as if he didn't want to. "She's tellin' the truth."

Li gave him an approving look, too, although he ignored her quite nicely.

Sam nodded as well, not so approvingly. "I'd rather speak to her today, but—"

"She didn't see anything," Li interrupted. "I was with her at the time of the shooting. We were walking in the orchard when we heard the gunfire. Sally nearly fainted. Although I tried to dissuade her, she insisted on seeing what had happened. Fortunately for all of us, Missus Majesty and Mister Prophet tried to hide the body from us, but she managed to catch a glimpse of it. I don't think she knew it was Tucker."

"So this Tucker character was really important to her?" asked Sam.

After giving a ghastly grimace, Li said, "Yes. She thought she loved him."

"Thought?"

"Yes. He's...he was a terrible man. He's the one who began giving her laudanum and chloral."

"Ah," said Sam.

"Anyhow, Sally saw the body. Luckily, she didn't know it was Tucker. There was a whole pile of orange blossoms on Tucker's body. Not sure how they got there, but they disguised his face."

"Mister Prophet shook the tree," I told her. "He didn't want anyone else to see the man lying there dead."

"Did you really, Lou?" Li gazed at Mr. Prophet, plainly pleased with her former whatever-he'd-been-to-her's effort at deception.

"Yeah. Didn't think anybody else needed to know what'd happened."

Li kissed him on the cheek. Mr. Prophet didn't blush, so I did it for him. I know, how silly of me. Sometimes I can't help being a sloppy sentimentalist. Too often, in fact.

Finally Sam agreed to question Sally later, if at all. From the way Angie spoke about both Sally and Mr. Tucker, I doubted Sam would learn much from Sally, whom I had already judged to be a too-tender twig upon which to rely. Unless, of course, I was wrong, and Sally was just a good actress. I didn't think so, though.

"How'd Mr. Tucker know where to find Sally?" I asked somewhere in the midst of these proceedings.

A chorus of "I don't know's" answered my question, which was most unsatisfactory. However, I let the matter slide, knowing Sam would get mad if I butted in any more.

When it was time to leave, Angie said she, Hattie and Cyrus would stay at Orange Acres for a while, if it would be all right with

Sam. By then, Li had a firm grip on Mr. Prophet's arm and didn't look as if she aimed to let it go.

Uncertain what was going on with the two of them or what, if anything, I should do about it, I said, "Um…Mister Prophet, would you like to ride back home with me? In the Chevrolet?"

He glanced down at Li, who glanced up at him, and a slow smile appeared on his face. "I reckon I'll stay here for a bit, Miss Daisy. I'm sure Missus Mainwaring won't mind hauling my sorry butt back to Marengo Avenue later on."

"Not at all, Lou," said Angie, who looked worn out and more than a little tired of the day that had begun so well. "I still have to pay you back. *With* interest." From the way she spoke, it sounded as if she'd rather beat him to a bloody pulp.

"We can negotiate a bit on that," said Prophet. "The interest part, I mean."

All at once I knew precisely how Prophet expected to receive at least partial payment in return for the funds Angie had stolen from him.

I felt my face flame again when Sam walked me out to the Chevrolet. When I glanced up at him, he had a smirk on his face, so I knew he knew, too.

Ah, well, they (whoever "they" are) say prostitution is the world's oldest profession. But I'd thought Angie had left that despicable life behind her. On the other hand, from the way Li hung on to his arm, I doubted she aimed to charge for her services to the old reprobate. Lou Prophet, I mean.

When we got to my motorcar, Sam opened the driver's side door for me. "Would you like Steve Doan to ride with you, Daisy? I have to get back to the department, and I know you've been through a frightening experience."

"Thanks, Sam, but I'm all right." Then I burst out, "But Mister Prophet is *staying* here! Sam, he and Li are—"

With a laugh, he interrupted me. "Yes, they are, aren't they?

Don't worry about Lou. I think he'll be just fine." I'd opened my mouth to ask about Li, when Sam said, "And Miss Li seems to be doing just fine on her own."

"Well…" Since I didn't know what more to say, I remained silent. Doesn't happen often with me, but this was embarrassing ground upon which to tread, if you were me. Heck, Sam and I sometimes did what I expected Mr. Prophet and Li would be doing —and shortly—but Sam and I were going to be *married* as soon as we could be! Mr. Prophet and Li were…

Nertz.

"It's all right, Daisy. Both Lou and Miss Li are grown-ups. Besides, Lou is Lou, and you'll never change him."

"I…I guess you're right, but what about Li?"

"Miss Li doesn't seem to me to be a shy and retiring lady. I have a feeling she won't do anything she doesn't damned well want to do."

I heaved a deep sigh. "You're probably right. But…Well, I…I guess I know from books and stuff that people acted like that, but…well, I'm not used to seeing it in person."

"I'll show you how it's done if you like, although I thought you already—"

"Sam! You know what I meant! It's not the same at all. With us, I mean."

With a wicked grin, Sam said, "Stuff like what's going to go on in Mrs. Mainwaring's house probably happens all the time in Tombstone."

"According to Mister Prophet, even Tombstone is becoming civilized. He doesn't seem to appreciate it, either."

This won a laugh from Sam. "I'm sure he hates civilization. Face it, Daisy, Lou will never become a reformed character. In fact, if you want to know the truth, I don't want him to reform. He's more fun the way he is."

"Fun?" Had Sam just called Lou Prophet *fun*?

By golly, he had. And, also by golly, he was right!

"You're right, Sam. He's a curious character for Pasadena, but I'm glad he ended up here, even if he is kind of a misfit."

"Kind of?"

"Very well. He's a big one."

Mr. Prophet hadn't returned from Mrs. Mainwaring's Orange Acres by the time Vi had dinner ready for us. I'd set the table, and it was just my family (including Sam) who dined on Vi's spectacular chicken and dumplings that evening.

"Where's Mister Prophet?" asked Ma, who seemed determined to take Mr. Lou Prophet, of all unlikely—and probably unde-serving—people, under her wing.

"I'm not sure, Ma," I said, glancing at Sam.

Drat the man, he didn't say a word, so I had to come up with an excuse for the old sinner by myself.

"Um...He met an old friend at Missus Mainwaring's orange orchard. He decided to stay there and...catch up on old times."

There. That was almost the truth. When I again peered at Sam, he had a big grin on his face, the rat.

"Oh, I thought he didn't know Missus Mainwaring," said Ma, who liked things to be clear in her mind.

"It was another...person there whom he knew," I said. Very well, so I stretched the truth a bit on that one.

"My goodness. I had no idea there were people in Pasadena a man like Mister Prophet might know." When she heard what she's said, Ma flushed. "I mean, I didn't think he knew anybody in Pasadena but us."

"He'd met this person before," I told her. "In Tombstone. You remember Missus Mainwaring used to live in Tombstone, too, although she and Mister Prophet didn't know each other there." Leastways, they'd not wanted to admit their acquaintanceship. "The person he wanted to chat with is someone else."

My mother is entirely too smart to allow such enigmatic commentary to pass without remarking on it.

"You keep saying 'this person,' Daisy, and I think you're equivocating unnecessarily. Do you mean she's an old female acquaintance of his? An old flame, perhaps?" Ma smiled and looked demure. She liked a good love story as well as anyone. Even if Lou and Li's wasn't one. A love story, I mean. At least I kind of doubted it was.

"Exactly," I said. "They were happy to re-meet. Or whatever you call it. Get reacquainted, I guess."

I noticed Sam chewing quietly, his shoulders shaking as he tried to suppress his guffaws, and I wished we were already married and in our own home. If we were, I'd throw a dumpling at him. Only I couldn't make a dumpling any more than I could make magic.

Sometimes life is really annoying.

SIXTEEN

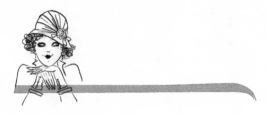

I don't know how long Spike and I had been sleeping the sleep of innocents—or innocence—I'm not sure what the precise term is. Anyway, I probably don't qualify for either one, although Spike sure does.

How'd I get sidetracked already? Don't bother even trying to figure it out.

At any rate, a soft knocking on my bedroom door—the one leading to the deck outside—startled me awake and roused Spike to utter a subdued bark. If he'd been more awake, he'd probably have barked louder, so it's a good thing he wasn't. Half-asleep and groggy, I sort of fell out of the bed and staggered to the door. Spike raced ahead of me, wagging like mad. Wagging on his part generally meant the knocker was a friend; however, because I wasn't completely over my fear that someone might be out there with a gun, ready to shoot me to pieces, I didn't instantly open the door. Rather, I stood close to the crack and whispered, "Who is it?"

"It's me," said Sam. "And Lou. Open up. We need you."

"Wh-what?"

"We *need* you," Sam whispered with some urgency. "Open the door."

"Why?"

"Just open the damned door, will you?" said my charming spouse-to-be.

So, after grabbing my robe from where I'd tossed it on the foot of the bed, I opened the door—very slowly. I wasn't sure what was going on, but I already didn't like it.

Sam and Mr. Prophet shoved me aside and entered the room. Spike started leaping on them, but a sternly whispered, "Spike, sit," from me interrupted his gleeful greeting. He sat. I squinted into the darkness

"What's going on?" I asked in a whisper.

"Is everything all right in there?" came my father's voice from the kitchen. "Are you all right, Daisy? I heard Spike bark."

"Everything's fine, Pa," I said, wondering if I'd just lied. "I rolled over onto poor Spike, and he protested."

My father laughed and said, "All right. Just wondered. Sleep tight."

"You, too. Thanks, Pa."

Then I stared, thinking I must be in the middle of a nightmare when Sam and Mr. Prophet, each carrying a limb of the unconscious Li, walked her to my bed. "What the—?"

"May we lay her on your bed, Daisy? I don't think she's bleeding anymore."

I gaped at my fiancé. "*Bleeding?*"

"She's *not* bleeding," Sam said in a savage whisper. Without waiting for my permission, he told Mr. Prophet, "Put her on the bed, Lou." Turning to me, he said, "Can you boil some water for tea or something?"

"Tea, hell," said Mr. Prophet. "She can sip some of this here good tanglefoot." He took a flask from somewhere on his person, probably a pocket, and uncorked it.

Tanglefoot? I'd heard him call rye whiskey tangleleg. Maybe tanglefoot meant tangleleg, and the two words meant the same thing: whiskey. Three words. However many words there were. I was too groggy to count.

Li had begun to stir. Mr. Prophet went to where her head rested and put one of his big hands over her mouth, I guess so she couldn't cry out or scream or anything. He still held the flask upright and ready. He'd spilled a bottle of what he'd called good rye whiskey on Sam's horrid nephew, Frank Pagano, a month or so earlier, and I guess he was being careful not to spill any of his current stock of the precious stuff on Li.

"What the heck is going on?" I asked again. "What happened to Li?"

"I'll have to tell you later, Daisy," Sam said.

"The heck with later! I want to know, and I want to know now!"

"No sense keepin' it from her, Sam," said Mr. Prophet. Never thought I'd consider him the voice of reason, but in this case I did. "Her brothers come from China to take her back."

"They *what?*" Thinking I wasn't sufficiently conscious yet, I shook my head hard. Didn't help.

"You heard him," said Sam.

"How did they know she was here?" I thought the question pertinent, but neither man answered it.

Sam went on, "When Missus Mainwaring brought Lou and Miss Li back home, three big Chinese fellows were waiting for them, and tried to grab Miss Li. That's the story I got from Lou, anyhow."

"It's the truth, dammit," said Mr. Prophet.

"Oh, stop swearing!" I groused at him. He shook his head and snarled, sounding not unlike Spike when we played a game of tug.

"Leave him be, Daisy. He's worried about Miss Li. According

170

to him and Missus Mainwaring, three men claiming to be Miss Li's brothers were waiting at the gate."

"Yeah," said Prophet. "Good thing Cyrus used to be a championship boxer."

"Cyrus? Missus Mainwaring's chauffeur?"

"Cyrus Potts. Yes. He's Hattie's husband," said Sam. "And he serves as Missus Mainwaring's bodyguard."

"Good Lord. I didn't know she needed one!"

"Ain't you been payin' attention, Miss Daisy?" asked Mr. Prophet, looking at me as if I were one of the duller knives in the drawer of his life. "She used to run a whorehouse in Tombstone, fer cripe's sake, and a man tried to shoot her today. She tries to save whores from their lives of sin and degradation—or so *she* claims. You think the fellers who run them houses are just gonna let her do that without objecting?"

"But...but I thought the man you shot today had come after Sally."

"He probably did, but he aimed to get Angie first," said Mr. Prophet. "Anyhow, there's a lot more where they came from."

"I thought you said this latest batch came from China."

Impatient, Sam said, "Yes. Three of them. They *are* from China, and they damned near carried Li back to China with them. Good thing Lou's got a Bowie knife and knows how to use it. And Cyrus is a fighter. And Missus Mainwaring doesn't mind hitting people over the head with heavy objects."

"Good heavens."

"I doubt good or heaven has anything to do with the current circumstances. Lou tied them all up and came to fetch me. Cyrus is going to see if he can borrow his brother and his brother's truck and drive the three Chinamen to the Port of Los Angeles. There, they'll send them on a steamer back to China. Unfortunately, they managed to hurt Miss Li before Cyrus, Lou and Missus Mainwaring subdued them."

I looked at Mr. Prophet and said, "Did you use your ketch rope?" Don't ask me where that question came from, because I don't know. Lucidity wasn't my best pal after I'd been rudely awakened from my beauty sleep, I guess.

Squinting at me, Prophet said, "My ketch— Who the hell cares?"

I flinched but didn't chide him for his use of bad language this time. Wouldn't have done any good anyway.

He went on, "I tied 'em up, and we're gonna load them into the bed of Cyrus's brother's truck, and they're going to drive them to the ocean and send them back to where they came from."

"You say they came for Li? Why?" If anyone cares, I was still whispering.

"Yes," said Sam, also still whispering. "Missus Mainwaring said they're her brothers, and they wanted to take her back to Canton, because she's worth a lot of money. Evidently, when she left China, she did so because her father aimed to sell her to man she didn't like."

"Her *father* wanted to *sell* her?" Incredulous only partially describes my fuddled thought processes.

"She ran away from home," said Prophet.

"She ran a long way, if she came all the way from China," I muttered.

"Can we talk about this later?" asked Sam. "Missus Mainwaring plans to give the men enough money to make up for Li's father's loss, but we have to get rid of them before morning. We don't want the whole neighborhood to know what's going on."

"Yeah," said Prophet. "Just take care of Li for a few minutes, will you, Miss Daisy? Then we'll come back, and I'll take her to Angie's place."

I looked doubtfully from his face to his peg. He shook his head and said, "Kee-rist! Will you just trust me for a few minutes? Or trust Sam, if you don't trust me."

"Listen, Daisy," said Sam. "I don't like this any better than you do, but if we get the police involved, it's going to get complicated. In fact, it'll probably involve the federal governments in two countries, and I don't want to go through that. Neither do Miss Li, Lou or Missus Mainwaring. And I *really* don't want everyone in the neighborhood to know what's happened tonight."

"I can't believe her father was going to sell her," I said, zeroing in on the main point of Sam's speech and glancing at Li.

Her eyes had opened, and evidently she'd been listening to us chat. If you can call it chatting. "Believe it," she sort of croaked. "Common practice where I come from."

"Oh." Well, all right then, *that* knocked the wind out of my sails.

"Please, Daisy?" Li pleaded. "I'll tell you everything while Lou and your detective get my loathsome brothers out of Pasadena."

"Of course. Of course," I said. "Sure. Happy to help."

What was one more little lie? For the good Lord's sake, I lied for a living. At least I'd be helping Li and Angie with this lie. At any rate, I hoped I would be.

"But you'll have to tell me *everything* when you get back, Sam Rotondo."

With a mock salute at me, Sam said, "Yes, ma'am."

"Shit. Let's get out of here." Mr. Prophet pointed a finger at Li. "And you. Stay here until we get back. Need a shot of this?" He held up his open flask.

After scowling and shaking her head, Li requested Lou do something the words for which I'd never heard issue from a woman's mouth. Or a man's, either, probably because I grew up in refined and respectable Pasadena, California. Anyhow, I don't think it's humanly possible for anyone to do that to himself. Or herself.

I was kind of rattled. Can you tell?

Rattled or not, Li lay on my bed and I didn't. Therefore, after

173

Sam and Mr. Prophet left my room, silently shutting the door behind them, I pulled my rocker nearer the bed, sat on it, and gestured for Spike to join me. He did, then leaned way over and wanted to give Li a little kiss, but I said, "No, Spike. We'd better wait until we know if Li approves of being kissed by dogs."

Li uttered a short laugh, then grabbed her ribs and said, "Ow. Damn, that hurts."

I didn't know very many women who swore, either, but I decided not to be prissy about Li's language. She was injured after all, and she also used to…well, be in a profession most people consider disreputable if not downright sinful.

"Your brothers hurt you?" I asked, thinking my own older brother, George, might like to tease his little sister, but he'd never, ever, hurt me on purpose. In fact, one day when I was on the playground at school, he'd knocked a kid down for bullying me. I love my brother.

"Yes." The way she spoke the word made it sound like a hiss.

"That's…horrible. Why…? I mean, did they *really* mean to take you back to China so your father could sell you?"

"I doubt it," she said. "They were probably just going to throw me into the ocean and redeem the family's honor."

"*Killing* you would redeem the family's *honor*?"

"I ran away and humiliated my family. They lost face."

"Lost face?"

"Honor," said Li with a shrug, which must have hurt, because she then winced. "Respect. It's China. What can you do?"

Since I didn't know, I didn't speak.

"Say, Daisy, do you have a couple of aspirin tablets or something?"

"Oh, my goodness, yes! I'm so sorry, Li."

"No need to be sorry."

"Would you like a cup of tea? I'll be happy to make a pot of tea."

"No. Better not. I don't want to wake up anyone else. I'm sorry Lou and your detective disturbed you. I could have stayed at Angie's, and she'd have taken care of me."

"I don't mind. Probably Angie was busy. Or something. Anyhow, I'll get you a glass of water so you can take your aspirins." I thought of something else. "I also have some morphine syrup left over from—"

"No!" Her whisper was emphatic.

"Well, I don't blame you. The stuff tastes vile."

"It's also caused too many women I know too much trouble."

That was a melancholy thought. Naturally, her words made me think of my late Billy. "I understand completely."

With a wry grin, she said, "I somehow doubt that."

"You shouldn't. My husband was shot and gassed in the war, and he killed himself with morphine syrup." My whisper was perhaps a teensy bit sharp.

"Oh, my goodness. I had no idea. I'm sorry."

"So am I."

"But...I thought you were engaged to the detective."

"I am. Billy killed himself three years ago."

"Oh."

I left Li and Spike, tiptoed to the kitchen and came back with a glass of water. Then I tiptoed to the bathroom, shook three aspirin tablets from the bottle we kept there and brought them back to Li.

"Here you go."

"Thank you." She took the glass in one hand, the aspirins in the other, and swallowed the pills with the water, wincing as she did so. "Ow. I should have thought to take some aspirins at Angie's."

"Things there were probably a bit complicated when Sam and Mister Prophet brought you here."

"Complicated is a good word for it," said Li. "Angie was busy making sure Cyrus didn't kill Fa, Chen and Jian, and I didn't want to interrupt her."

Mercy sakes. The only thing I could think to say was, "Are those your brothers' names? I mean, the ones who aren't Cyrus?"

"Yes. Assholes, every one, so I don't know why I'm glad Angie stopped Cyrus from killing them. Well, I guess Angie and Cyrus would have got into trouble if Cyrus had succeeded, so in that way I'm glad she stopped him. My father is an asshole, too. I ran away thirty years ago. I'm surprised they even remember me."

Deciding to ignore her language, I said, "Thirty years does seem a long time to hold a grudge."

"Grudge, my ass. My father wants the money he'd have made off me. He probably sold his last daughter and decided to send the boys after me."

There was certainly a whole lot I didn't know about Chinese culture. "How did they know where you were living?"

"I have absolutely no idea."

"Wasn't it expensive for him to send his sons here to get you?"

"I doubt it. They probably worked their way over on the ship that brought them."

"Oh." I guess that made sense. "Um...Do Chinese people often sell their children?"

"People the world over sell their children, Daisy. Only folks in some countries are more subtle about it than we Chinese are. Do you think all those young women in England who marry old men *want* to do it?"

"Um...I've never thought about it. *Do* young women in England marry old men? Why do they?"

"Because the old men have already gone through a wife or two and need a young woman to give them an heir. A son. Not a daughter, of course."

"Why not a daughter?"

"Because women can't inherit. Only boys can. So old men who don't have sons will take young wives to give them a son or, preferably, two. I think they call it an heir and a spare."

"But why do the women stand for it? I wouldn't marry an old man just for the sake of giving him male children."

"That's because you were born here, and your parents aren't rich," said Li as if I should have known as much already. "You don't have to secure your family's living."

"I do, too."

Li lifted her head and peered at me. "You do?"

"Well…Yes. I do. My father has a heart condition that prevents him from being a chauffeur to rich people. That's what he used to do, but he can't anymore. We all live in mortal terror that he'll have another heart attack. I don't think I could stand it if my father died. He carries nitroglycerin tablets around with him, but you never know." I shook my head and told myself to stop babbling. "Anyway, both my mother and my aunt also work, but I make more money than either of them."

"As a spiritualist-medium?"

"Yes." A fake one. I didn't speak the last phrase aloud, not knowing precisely how the information would be received.

Musingly, Li said, "Angie said you're a really good spiritualist-medium."

"That was kind of her. Especially since the reading I gave her wasn't…um…rosy, I guess is a good word for it."

Li laughed, cringed, and pressed her arms over her ribcage again. Her hurt ribs worried me.

"Are you sure you don't need a doctor? You keep clutching your ribs. Do you think any of your ribs are broken? Broken ribs can be terribly dangerous. A broken rib might puncture one of your lungs."

"No, none of them are broken. Hattie already checked."

"Is Hattie a physician?" I asked, astonished.

"Not a physician with a degree in medicine, or whatever you call it, but she's the best doctor I've ever known. She gave me a

177

thorough once-over, and she'll keep an eye on me for the next several days."

"So you're going to stay here and not go back to Orange Acres?"

"For a few days, yes."

"Doesn't Angie need you to look after Sally at Orange Acres?"

"There are other people at Orange Acres to look after things when I'm not there. I really didn't want to leave Sally after today's shooting, but…" Her words faded away.

"But you wanted to stay with Mister Prophet a little longer?"

Eying me with an expression I couldn't decipher, Li said after a few seconds, "I suppose I did. I'm *such* a fool about that damned man."

Aha! I'd been right about the two of them.

I'm not sure where Louisa What's Her Name fitted into this picture, but— Wait! I finally remembered Louisa's last name! Bonaventure. Louisa Bonaventure. According to Mr. Prophet, she was probably six feet under by 1925, but he hadn't seemed absolutely sure about the status of her health. Anyway, if she were still alive, she'd probably be in her seventies. As was Mr. Prophet.

Therefore, if one used Li's logic, Louisa Bonaventure, the purported love of Mr. Prophet's life, would be too old for him by this time.

I believe I've mentioned that I'll never understand men for as long as I live.

SEVENTEEN

S am and Mr. Prophet came back to my parents' house about fifteen minutes after they'd left. Spike was ecstatic. Sam appeared slightly disgruntled. Mr. Prophet looked mad as heck.

"There. Dammit, they're on their way to the Port of Los Angeles," said the latter. "Do you need me to carry you back to Angie's place?"

"Daisy gave me some aspirins," said Li. "I think I can walk."

"You probably should bind those ribs first," said Mr. Prophet, eyeing her and frowning hideously.

"Hattie will do it," said Li.

"But you shouldn't walk until you get 'em bound."

"Damnation, will you two stop arguing? *I'll* carry Miss Li back to Missus Mainwaring's house," said Sam in his nobody-had-better-argue-with-me-or-I'll-shoot-you-dead-and-you'll-end-up-being-eaten-by-bears-in-the-foothills voice. Whisper, I mean.

Mr. Prophet, startled, stood up straight.

Li, startled, stared at Sam, her beautiful almond-shaped eyes almost round.

I, on the other hand, smiled at my darling fiancé. "You sure your leg can handle the weight, Sam?"

"Yes." He squinted at me with an expression that quite nicely matched the tone of his voice, which wasn't lover-like.

"Very well," I said meekly. "But you will tell me more about this tomorrow, won't you?"

"You already know everything I know."

"But..."

Glaring at me and shaking his head, Sam said, "All right, confound it. I'll tell you everything." Walking to the head of my bed, he said, "Put your arms around my shoulder, Miss Li. Lou, can you open the door?"

"But—"

In a low, measured tone, Sam told Mr. Prophet, "That wasn't a request. Open the damned door. Now."

So Mr. Prophet opened the (expletive deleted) door, Li lifted her arms, grimacing eloquently, and put them around Sam's neck. Sam carried Li outside, Mr. Prophet following. I followed, too, after I'd given them a big head start and telling my adorable hound to wait for me. I just wanted to see if the excitement at Angie's house had disturbed any of our neighbors.

By golly, not a creature was stirring! And it wasn't even Christmas Eve. That made me happy, because Sam was right about creating a commotion in the neighborhood, not to mention the governments of at least two countries getting involved if anyone else found out what had happened. Since I wore my good old floppy slippers, I didn't even have to tiptoe in order to get to the back of our house, climb the stairs and join my dog in bed after our interrupted night's rest.

Eventually, I got back to sleep, but not until at least an hour had passed. My mind whirled, and I wanted to go down to Angie's right that very minute and find out precisely what had happened at her house, and what was being done about it, other than the little bit Sam and Mr. Prophet and Li had told me. Ah, well, I'd just have wait. I hate waiting. Patience isn't one of my few virtues.

How the *heck* had Li's brothers, not to mention Mr. Tucker, figured out where Angie lived? I'd received the impression she'd tried to hide her early life from everyone and had endeavored mightily to leave no trace of it behind her. Dang. Curiosity is said to have killed the cat, but I doubt it. I think lack of a good and speedy answer had probably done in the feline.

Even though the night hadn't passed particularly peacefully, Spike and I got up at our usual time, which was around seven a.m.

To my surprise, Sam and Mr. Prophet were already seated at the kitchen table, yakking with Pa. Although I hadn't brushed my hair and probably looked like a wicked witch, since I'd already donned my bathrobe and slipped on my slippers—Oh. I think I just realized where the word "slipper" comes from—I joined the three men anyway.

"Morning, all," I said, trying to sound chipper.

"Morning, sweetheart," said Pa, giving me a big smile.

"Mornin'," said Prophet, who gazed gloomily down at a cup full of coffee.

"Morning, Daisy. Did you sleep well?" asked Sam. He didn't sound sarcastic, which surprised me.

I squinted at him for a second before replying, "Yes, thank you."

"Good." His nod was emphatic.

"Oh, wonderful," said Ma, coming into the kitchen dressed for work. "Everyone's already up and about. Let's eat. Vi made us something lovely as usual, I'm sure."

"Go along with you, Peggy," said my wonderful aunt. She used that expression on me a lot, too, and I'm still not sure exactly what it means. "Just eggs and toast this morning."

"Eggs and toast sound lovely to me," I told her. I wished she and Ma and Pa would vanish for a few minutes, which was unkind of me but true.

However, my impatience didn't make anyone eat faster and, in fact, Aunt Vi's omelets deserved to be savored. I almost wrote severed. I think my mind was still jumbled from the preceding night's adventure.

Finally everyone finished eating, and I carried the dirty dishes to the sink, where I aimed to wash them, dry them, and put them away.

Pa said, "Want to go for a walk with Spike and me, Daisy?"

"Sure do, Pa."

Blast. Pa and I always walked Spike in the morning, and I'd managed to forget this salient fact. How in the world was I supposed to get rid of my father? That doesn't sound right, does it? But, darn it, I wanted to find out precisely what had happened last night!

"I have to get going," said Sam. "Supposed to be at work at eight."

Stopping dead-still whilst lifting a plate from the sink of soapy water, I darned near dropped it into the rinse water. I'd be cursed if I'd allow Sam get away from me this easily!

"Hold on a sec, Sam," I said, wiping my drippy hands on my apron. "I need to ask you something before you go."

"Daisy—"

"I'll join you, if that's all right with you, Miss Daisy and Sam," said Lou Prophet.

At least *someone* seemed to be on my side that morning.

"Very well." Sam spoke through clenched teeth; I could hear it in the way he ground out those two little words.

As he, Mr. Prophet and I walked from the kitchen to the dining room and on into the living room, I felt my father's gaze upon us. He knew something was up but, bless the man, he didn't pry.

"So tell me everything," I demanded the instant we were all

three on the front porch. I whispered my demand so as not to alarm any neighbors.

"You already know everything," said Sam, sounding growly. "When Lou and Miss Li came back to Missus Mainwaring's house, three Chinamen were there. They claimed to be Miss Li's brothers, and they said they aimed to take her back to China. They claimed she ran away from China thirty years ago and thereby ruined her family's reputation in the village. Or wherever the hell they lived."

"Yes, Li told me that last night."

"Then what the hell did you want to talk to *me* about?" asked a cranky Sam. "I don't know anything except what you learned last night from Miss Li."

"Them Chinese have peculiar ideas," said Mr. Prophet.

"I guess," said I. "When I asked Li if thirty years wasn't a long time to hold a grudge, she said they probably only wanted to kill her, and that doing so would make her desertion thirty years ago all right again. I still don't understand why."

Squinting down at me, Sam said, "Then why ask me? I'm not Chinese. It's difficult enough being the only Italian in Pasadena, what with all you redheads and blondes running around loose."

"*What?*" I bellowed, forgetting about nosy neighbors in my indignation.

"You heard me," he said. He slapped his brown felt fedora on his head and turned, ready to walk across the street, get into his Hudson and drive himself to work.

I grabbed one of his jacket sleeves, and he turned around with a sigh, frowning down at me.

"What do you *mean*, it's hard being the *only* Italian in Pasadena? Just what precisely do you mean by *that*, Sam Rotondo?"

"Cripes," said my darling, disengaging my hand from his sleeve and rubbing at the wrinkles I'd made. "You tell her, Lou. I've got to get to work."

And off he went. He looked exceptionally fine that morning, if anyone aside from me cares. The warm April air had prompted him to don his light-weight brown-and-tan-plaid three-piece suit. He looked good, but I was mad at him, so I didn't tell him so. Therefore, I turned to Mr. Prophet. "Well? What did he mean by his last crack?"

"Miss Daisy, you're a good woman. Sam's lucky to have found you. But you've gotta admit there ain't a whole lot of Italian folks livin' here in Pasadena. It's got to be tough on Sam, especially since, because of what's going on back east, people think all Italians are gangsters and bootleggers. Hell, that stupid nephew of his *is* a gangster, if a dumb one, poor guy. Sam, not his nephew. I expect folks look at Sam and think, 'Al Capone,' or that other twerp. What's his name? Luciano?"

"But that's silly! Sam's a good man, not a gangster."

"You didn't answer my first question. How many Italian folks you know livin' in this town, Miss Daisy?"

"Um… One."

"Right. The rest of the population, 'ceptin' for some black, brown and yeller folks, look like little white pearls to folks like me, who come from more mixed-up parts of this grand land."

"Little white pearls?" My voice had become faint.

"Yeah. And the black, brown and yeller folks work for you little white pearls. Guess they're the rocks among the pearls or somethin'." And he plopped his own hat, a straw boater that went well with the weather, onto his disreputable head.

"But…but…but that's not true!" I thought about what I'd just said for approximately half a second. "Is it? Really?"

"Yeah, it really is." And he turned and clumped down the porch steps.

When he got to the sidewalk in front of our house, instead of walking across the street as I'd expected him to do, he turned right and headed down Marengo. Aha! I knew what *that* meant!

"Mister Prophet! Just a minute!" I called after him.

I saw his shoulders rise and fall as he sighed and turned around. "Want me to wait for you?" he asked with resignation.

I gave him a huge smile and said, "Yes, please. I won't be but a minute." Remembering I currently wore my bathrobe and slippers and hadn't even brushed my wild mane of russet-red hair (redheads and blondes running around loose, my left hind leg!), I amended my earlier comment. "Maybe two. Come on back inside and talk to Pa while I finish the dishes and get dressed."

"Yes, ma'am."

And he did. I could tell he didn't want to.

When I got back indoors, I discovered my wonderful father had finished washing the breakfast dishes for me. I kissed him on the cheek and thanked him, then hurried to my bedroom, Spike tagging along. It didn't take me long to put on a simple green day dress, brush my bobbed hair, stuff my stockinged feet into my brown walking shoes, plop my own straw hat on my head, and race out to the living room. Spike, needless to say, helped me dress and bounced into the living room with me.

"Ready to go?" I asked Mr. Prophet needlessly. He'd been ready to go five minutes earlier. Honestly, it didn't take me more than that to get ready. Maybe six, but that was it. Really.

"Is Lou joining us on our walk?" asked Pa, sounding pleasantly surprised.

Horsefeathers. I'd forgotten all about Pa and Spike and our daily walk. Well, what the heck. He didn't need to know why Mr. Prophet and I aimed to visit Angie, did he?

Mr. Prophet and I exchanged a speaking glance. His told me I was an idiot. Mine told him I wasn't, either, but I just forget things every now and then. Truth? I think he was right.

"Yes. He's going with us, as far as Angie's house anyway," I told my father, smiling brightly, as if Mr. Prophet visiting the glamorous Angie Mainwaring was an every-day occurrence. Pa was a smart man, and he knew Mr. Prophet and Angie weren't best pals, so this jaunt on Mr. Prophet's part to Angie's place was…odd. Thinking like mad, I added, "She said she'd bring us all some oranges from Orange Acres, and Mr. Prophet is going to pick them up for us." And I'd just have to visit Angie later in the day. Rats.

"Oh?" said Pa, understandably confused, since what I'd said made no sense. Oh, well. I never said thinking madly was a practiced skill of mine, did I? "That's nice. Need help, Lou?" He glanced at Mr. Prophet.

"No, thanks. I can handle a few oranges."

When my father turned his back and went to fetch his own jacket from the hall closet, Mr. Prophet gave me a truly evil-looking scowl. "Oranges?" he said. "Is that the best you could come up with?"

"Yes. Darn it!"

"And you with two orange trees right outside your door. And there are probably six of 'em at Sam's place across the street."

"I couldn't think of anything else on the spur of the moment."

"Kee-rist."

"Stop swearing."

His gaze visited the ceiling, and he shook his head.

Pa joined us. "All right, folks, let's get this walk started!"

Spike leapt with glee as I bent to clip his leash onto his collar. "Want to hold his leash, Pa?"

"Sure."

I could tell my father didn't buy my oranges excuse any more than anyone else with a working brain would have, but it was too late to change the story now. Paltry excuse or not, we started our walk. As we walked up to Angie's mansion, its gate stood open. This seemed strange to me, since something so worrisome had gone on there the night before.

"Why's her gate open?" I asked Mr. Prophet. "It doesn't seem right."

"Why not?" asked Pa reasonably.

"Dunno," said Mr. Prophet. "I'll take a look." And he veered right and on up the long drive.

"Be careful!" I called after him.

He waved, but didn't turn around. He just kept walking.

"What are you worried about, Daisy?" asked Pa, who was a trifle too perceptive for my personal good from time to time.

"Nothing. Not really."

"Come on, Daisy. 'Fess up. Why are you worried about Missus Mainwaring's gate being open?"

"I don't know. I just...am."

"Oh?" He didn't buy my excuse, being the intelligent human being he was.

So I tried again. "Well, I...I mean, why does she have a big fence, a gate that locks and a call box if she's just going to leave her gate hanging open?"

"I have no idea," said Pa, still being reasonable.

We continued our stroll around the neighborhood.

After a few minutes, Pa said, "All right. What's up, Daisy? Is something wrong with Missus Mainwaring? You know as well as I do that we don't need any of her oranges."

Nertz. I figured it wouldn't hurt to tell my father at least a partial truth. After heaving a sigh as big as the entire month of April, I said, "You remember when Spike barked last night?"

"Yes. I wondered if you were entertaining Sam in your bedroom." My father's face was stern.

Mine flamed. I could tell, because it heated up and burned like an oven. "Pa! I would *never* do anything like that! You know it! Don't you?" His doubt of my purity made tears build in my eyes. They didn't fall, which was only appropriate, since my purity at this particular point in my life was a thing of the past.

What a lowering reflection on my morals. But Sam and I *did* aim to marry as soon as we could. Good intentions count for something. Don't they?

"I'm sorry, sweetheart. I do know it."

Naturally, his trust in me made me feel guiltier than sin, if there's anything worse than sin. "But... Well, something disturbing happened at Angie's place last night. Neither Sam nor Mister Prophet wanted to cause a ruckus in the neighborhood, so...um... Well, Miss Li—I don't think you've met her yet. She's a lovely Chinese woman—came over to our place for a few minutes. That's why Spike barked."

"Oh."

When I glanced at my father, I saw him peering at me with a troubled frown on his face. My story needed more added to it, dagnabbit.

"You see, Miss Li, works at Angie's orchard."

"Oh. And?"

"Well, when Angie drove home—actually, she has a chauffeur named Cyrus Potts, who's Hattie Potts's husband. Hattie's Missus Mainwaring's maid, I think, but—" I told myself to stop babbling. "Anyhow, when Angie came home yesterday, she brought Miss Li with her. When they arrived—and I honestly don't know if this is true or not, but I suspect it is—three of Miss Li's brothers had come all the way from China and were waiting for her. They aimed haul her back to China, because she ran away to escape being married to an old man her father wanted her to marry. I guess they kind of pay for brides in China or something like that, and her father was mad because he lost money and... Well, I don't know what you call it, but I guess the family's prestige was damaged by Miss Li's rash act."

"How did Sam and Lou get involved?"

Excellent question. Wasn't sure how to answer it since, as mentioned before, quick thinking wasn't my best friend that day. "Um... I'm not really sure. I think somebody escaped from Angie's house and walked—or probably ran—to Sam's house, and he and

Mister Prophet went down to Angie's house. They brought Miss Li to me because she was slightly injured."

"Injured?"

"Um... Yes."

"By her *brothers*?"

"That's what they said. So I allowed her to rest in my bed while Sam and Mister Prophet went back to Angie's and got Miss Li's brothers packed off to China again. Without Miss Li with them. Sam said he didn't want to get the authorities involved, since those fellows were Chinese, and involving the governments of both the USA and China might make a bigger mess of it than it already was."

"Hmm. Interesting."

"It's the truth, Pa. The truth as I know it, anyway. I guess it's the truth."

"I imagine it is," said my adorable father thoughtfully. "I doubt Sam would enjoy being involved in an international incident. You know, I read an article somewhere—I expect it was in the *National Geographic*—that told of the bride-buying custom still being practiced in China." He shot me a grin. "Aren't you glad we didn't sell you to the highest bidder?"

"Were there any bidders?"

Chuckling, Pa said, "No."

"Didn't think so." I heaved a huge sigh.

I'm sure Pa thought my sigh was one of dejection because no men had pounded on our door, begging my father to allow them to buy me for a small fortune. That was when I was seventeen and married Billy, which seemed like *such* a long time ago. It felt as though those things had happened in someone else's life and not mine.

Out of curiosity, I said, "You allowed me to marry Billy when I was only seventeen. Were you..." I had to stop and think for a minute. "I mean, I was so young. Billy was only two years older than I was. Were you glad we got married? I mean, did you want us to marry? You didn't raise any objections."

After several seconds of silence; seconds that made my nerves jump like water on a hot skillet, my father said, "Your mother and I talked long and hard about the plans you and Billy made. We thought you were far too young to make such a life-changing decision. But we also knew Billy was heading off to fight in a war from which he might not return. We didn't have the heart to object, even though neither of us was happy about it."

Taking a quick swipe at the tears welling in my eyes, I said with the utmost sincerity, "I have the best parents in the world."

"Don't know about that, but we wanted our little girl to be happy."

"That's so sweet. Your little girl was pretty stupid back then, wasn't she?" It hurt to ask the question, although I don't know why. I already knew the answer.

But my father surprised me yet again. "Not stupid. In love and frightened. Nobody knew if Billy would come back from that god-awful conflict or, if he did, how the experience would have affected him."

"In some ways, it might have been better if he'd died over there. I know he often told me he'd rather have died than live the way he had to live when he came home. Maybe he was right."

After another several thoughtful seconds, Pa said, "I don't think so. I know his shell-shock and his ruined body were hard for both of you to deal with, but if he'd been killed in France, I'd bet you'd still be in mourning. The way things happened was rough on you, but at least you didn't have to wonder how—or even *if*—he'd died. Lots of people will never get an answer to that question, but their children or husbands are still missing. It's as if they're living in perpetual limbo."

I mulled over his words for maybe a minute. "You might well be right, Pa. I felt *so* guilty when Billy died."

"I know you did, sweetheart. But you did the best you could, and from the perspective of your parents, you did a swell job."

"Boy, I don't think so. I was so short-tempered with him."

Pa shrugged. "He was an unhappy, crabby, miserable person a lot of the time. But now you're engaged to marry a truly good and honorable fellow, and your mother and I couldn't be happier."

His words made me think of some other words: those both Sam and Mr. Prophet had flung at me earlier in the morning. "Um...does it bother you or Ma that Sam's Italian?"

"Bother us?" Pa sounded surprised. "No, it doesn't bother us. But your mother and I are both from back east. There's more variety back there than there is in Pasadena."

"I guess so. Especially in New York City, where Sam grew up."

"Especially there," said Pa with a grin.

"What would you and Ma have done if I'd decided to marry a..." Oh, Lord, why did I even *begin* to ask this next question?

"Marry a what?" asked Pa.

"Well, if I'd wanted to marry, say, a Chinese fellow. Or one of Mister Jackson's kin?"

"You mean what would we do if you came home with a fiancé of a color different from ours?"

"Yes. I think."

"We wouldn't like it."

"Oh."

"Not for the reason you think."

"Oh?"

"If you decided to marry a man from a different race, your life would be *so* difficult, sweetheart. You know how the KKK went after that poor Jackson fellow a year or so ago. Can you imagine how they'd react if a white woman married a Negro or a Chinese or Japanese man?"

I shuddered. "Yes. I can imagine it. Heck, those horrible Klansmen shot at *me*, and all I did was befriend the Jacksons."

"Exactly." Pa shook his head. "Life is difficult enough without piling unnecessary hardships on it."

"Thanks, Pa. I love you."

With a short laugh, Pa said, "Love you, too, sweetheart."

After deciding God had gifted me with the world's best father and mother, I pondered our conversation. A part of it made me chuckle. "I'm glad my only brother is George. He would never ship me off somewhere because I misbehaved. At least I don't think he would."

With a laugh, Pa said, "I think you're safe with George, sweetie."

Angie's gate still gaped open when Pa, Spike and I walked around the block and looked at it from the other side of the street. The open gate disturbed me a lot, but I didn't say so to Pa. And I wasn't sure why I was so bothered about it.

"I'm going to see how Miss Li is doing, Pa. I'll be home soon."

"Have a good visit," said my marvelous father.

Spike wanted to come with me.

"No, Spike. You go on home with Pa. Be a good boy, and I'll give you a treat!"

The word "treat" always made Spike's tail wag. I loved my dog almost as much as I loved my father.

I walked up to the big porch and climbed the steps. It was then I noticed the coffin door also stood open. This seemed extremely strange to me, but because I'm an idiot—I mean a brave woman—I just went ahead and walked inside.

And *that* proved to be a gigantic whopper of a mistake.

EIGHTEEN

The precise moment I stepped foot onto tiles in the foyer, I felt something poke me, hard, in the back. I jumped a little, and a gruff, New-Yorky voice said, "Hold it right there, sister. Stick 'em up."

Stick 'em up? Did people actually *say* that? Whoever this guy was —did. He also poked me again, so I obeyed his command and held my hands up. "What's going on?"

The man who'd spoken tapped me on the side of the head with something that felt like a bludgeon.

"Ow! *Stop* it!"

He did it again.

"Ow! Cut it out!"

"Daisy!" came Angie's voice from her front parlor. She sounded slightly panicky. "Don't argue! Just do as he tells you to do."

"Smart too late, ain't you, *Angie?*" said the nasty voice. The way he spoke her name made me think she'd meant it when she'd told me she'd made it up. Uh-oh.

"Get in there," said New York Nasty, jamming the hard object into the small of my back and shoving me toward the front parlor.

By that time, I'd figured out the hard object to be the front end of some kind of gun. I'm sure that part of a gun has a name, but I don't know what it is.

Anyhow, I got in there. The scene I walked in on made my mouth fall open. I closed it with a clack of teeth and sought Angie in the tableau. Ah. There she was. Seated on one of her pretty Chinese-patterned chairs, tied hand and foot. Li, looking bruised and much the worse for wear, sat in a chair next to her, likewise bound. I took a breath, intending to speak, saw Angie shake her head furiously, and didn't, even though I wanted to know what the heck was going on. Angie began filling me in.

"Missus Majesty, this is my…" Her voice petered out. Then she said, "He's an old acquaintance of mine."

New York Nasty sneered at her. "You can do better than that, Gingersnap. Tell the lady the truth now."

If looks could kill, New York would be dead as Robert Browning (the poet, not my friend). Unfortunately, they couldn't. Therefore, Angie said, "That *man*"—she put scornful emphasis on the word man—"is my…" her lips pinched together, and she seemed to have to forcefully pry them apart in order to spit out the word, "husband."

Heavens to Betsy!

"Yeah," said New York. "That there's my wife, dammit, and she ain't no fancy-dancy damsel in distress, you can bet on it. She took me for all I was worth and left me back in Brooklyn. But I found you, damn your eyes." He flung the last sentence at Angie, who received it with a flinch as if it hurt. Then New York shoved me at the sofa. I more or less fell on same and peered around.

Mercy sakes. This clearly wasn't a good time to be visiting Angie Mainwaring. It was also clear that neither Rolly nor the tarot cards had been fooling around when they'd told Angie her past would catch up with her. It dawned on me, too, that Angie had made something of a habit of using men for her own purposes. I didn't approve, although men had been doing the same thing to women since the beginning of time. Truthfully, I felt a faint flicker of glee in the understanding that Angie had turned the tables on a few of the men in her life.

This was not the right time for glee, however, so I didn't feel it for long.

"I'll give you money, Raymond!" Angie said. "I already told you I'll give you money."

"I don't want your damned money, you damned whore," said New York. Raymond? Pasadena boasted a Raymond Avenue, but I'm pretty sure Raymond Avenue and this Raymond had nothing to do with each other. "I want you dead."

Mercy sakes again. I glanced at Angie and observed she looked frightened, defiant and absolutely furious. Although I kind of wanted to ask questions, I didn't, thereby reflecting unusually good judgment on my part. I was sure glad neither Pa nor Spike had joined me at Angie's place.

Glancing around the room some more, I saw Hattie standing against the far wall behind the piano. Her hands appeared to be free from constraint, but I suspect she didn't dare move for fear Mr. Raymond would shoot her or someone else. The person I *didn't* see was Mr. Lou Prophet.

Lordy, I hoped Mr. Raymond hadn't killed him. But surely, if this fellow had gunned down Mr. Prophet, Pa and I would have heard the shot. Maybe he hadn't shot him. Maybe Raymond had stabbed Mr. Prophet to death when he first walked into the house, sort of the way he'd ambushed me. Dismal thought. Even though Mr. Prophet swore too much and annoyed me occasionally, I liked him a lot and didn't want him to die.

Anyhow, if Mr. Prophet had been shot or stabbed, a pool of blood would have decorated a floor in the entrance to the house, and I hadn't observed one.

I could see Mr. Raymond's face now. Shoot. What an ugly

customer *he* was. Hair slicked back with some kind of greasy pomade and wearing a loud plaid suit, he looked like a gangster straight out of New York City, which made sense since it sounded as if that's what he was and that was where he'd come from. I remembered Angie telling me she'd had a rough childhood in a bad neighborhood in New York City. Maybe she'd met this fellow when she was young. I'm not good at judging people's ages, but if I had to guess, I'd have pegged him to be about her age. But a whole lot meaner.

"All right," said the Raymond character. "What should I do with all these pals of yours, Ginger? Shoot 'em dead?"

Ginger? Who was Ginger? Yet another question I didn't ask.

"If you want to shoot them *or* me, the entire neighborhood will hear the gunfire, and you'll be arrested, Raymond," said Angie, her tone of voice reasonable. "Why don't you just take a whole lot of money and go away?"

"Because I don't want to *take the money and go away*," said Raymond in a sing-song voice meant to express his disdain. It did a great job. "That's why."

"A detective from the Pasadena Police Department lives right up the street, Raymond," said Angie, still sounding reasonable. "If you shoot any of us, you won't make it as far as the front gate before someone from the police tackles you."

"I don't give a damn, Ginger," said Raymond, sneering magnificently.

Very well then. So much for reason. What now? I soon found out.

Three more men straggled into the front parlor. They were as greasy and gangster-ish as Raymond. Glancing at them, Raymond said, "Find anyone else?"

"No, boss," said a youngish fellow in a flat cap and a loud checked suit. He, too, carried a gun. And he didn't look as if he'd reached his twentieth birthday! I was shocked, which shows yet again how sheltered I'd been while growing up in beautiful, serene, boring old Pasadena.

"Found this broad in the kitchen," said another gangsterish fellow, gun in hand, propelling before him into the parlor a plump, coffee-colored woman. I figured her to be the other Mrs. Jackson. The one who wasn't Joseph Jackson's mother, but the one who worked as Angie's cook.

"Shove her next to that redhead on the couch, Clyde," said Raymond.

So the lout with his gun pointing at Mrs. Jackson's back did as Raymond had bade him, and made Mrs. Jackson sit next to me on the sofa. I nodded at her. She frowned back at me.

"That's it?" asked Raymond. "Where's Gus."

"He's checkin' the attics and the basement," said Mrs. Jackson's shover.

"Aw right. Now, here's what we're gonna do here," said Raymond, sounding smug. "You, Ginger, are gonna come with me. I'm gonna let Clyde and Gus play with your friends here. Don't worry. They won't make any noise."

"Raymond! You can't do that!" Angie cried. "They haven't done anything to you!"

"Maybe not. But you have, and you're going to pay. So are all your friends. Teach you to run out on *me*, damn your eyes."

To this day, I don't know what Mr. Raymond had against Angie's eyes. And where the heck was Lou Prophet? Where the heck was Mr. Bowman? Confound it, where was *Sam*? I wanted Sam!

Too bad, Daisy. Sam wasn't there.

However, something then happened that surprised me more than just about anything else in my life ever had, barring having been dumped into lion's den a few months back. All at once, a white-clad streak burst into the parlor. Before anyone could react— or maybe even notice—the streak hit Raymond, making his gun fly through the air, spinning, looking kind of like a fish leaping from the water. The streak then knocked into Gus, Clyde and the other man, whose name I never did learn. Their guns went flying, too.

As soon as all the bad guys were on the floor, darned if Lou Prophet, Judah Bowman and Sam Rotondo didn't enter the room! Sam and Mr. Bowman held their guns pointed at the fallen villains. Mr. Prophet swung a big rope loop and managed to capture Clyde and Gus in one fell swoop. He then tugged on the rope and jerked the two men off their feet. They both fell with satisfying plops and uttered moans of pain. Made me happy.

"*Sam!*" I shrieked.

"Cripes, keep your voice down," said my beloved. "Nobody move!" He turned to Mr. Bowman and Mr. Prophet. "Check these men for other weapons. Be careful, and be sure to check for boot holsters, scabbards, hide-out guns and so forth."

Boot holsters? Scabbards? Hide-out guns? I didn't even know what those things were.

"Oh, Lou!" cried Li. "You *came!*"

"Yeah. Couple times." Mr. Prophet smirked and added, "Thanks."

I'm not sure why, but Li blushed.

The number of deadly weapons Mr. Bowman and Mr. Prophet gathered from the villains was downright staggering. Not only were several small guns—derringers?—plucked from various places on the vile men's persons, but a vast number of knives was also confiscated, along with brass knuckles (I'd never seen brass knuckles before, although I'd read about them), several small sandbags (Sam said they were also called blackjacks and coshes. Then he had to explain to me what those were) and some metallic handle-like tubes held together with chains. I'd never seen anything like them before, either.

I looked all over the place from my perch on the sofa but didn't see the white-clad person who'd initiated our rescue.

After the villains were certified weapon-free and all bunched together with handcuffs around their wrists and ankles—when one of them griped about the ankle-cuffs, Sam bopped him upside the head with his gun, and he shut up—Sam, Mr. Bowman, and Mr. Prophet came over to free Angie and Li. Hattie instantly ran to Angie, fussing over her. Li reached for Mr. Prophet, and Mr. Bowman made a grab for Angie.

Sam put an end to that. "Stop it! Everybody sit down! Don't anyone move until we get statements from you." He turned his head and hollered over his shoulder, "Doan! Oversloot! Get in here. You, too, Blackman!"

And all of a sudden Officers Doan and Oversloot appeared, notepads and pencils in hand. I'd never heard of an Officer Black-man, but another man entered the front parlor with Doan and Oversloot, armed with a camera. I was impressed by the organizational efforts Sam had expended on this operation. I also wondered how he'd been informed. I suspected Mr. Prophet, but I'd just have to wait to find out, darn it.

"Take as many pictures as you can of everything you see, Blackman. Turn on lights and open the draperies if you need to, but get as many photos as possible without disturbing anything first."

"Yes, sir." And he did.

Nobody spoke for several minutes. I think those of us who'd been in the house when the police arrived were too stunned for conversation. But there was one thing I *really* wanted to know, so I leaned over and whispered a question to Mrs. Jackson, who still sat on the sofa next to me. "Who was that man in white who flung himself around the room and knocked down all those people?"

Turning her head and giving me another pretty good frown, Mrs. Jackson said, "That's Mister Wu. He's Missus Mainwaring's gardener, but he also knows some kind of fighting method he calls... Oh, I can't pronounce it. Gwung fooey, or something like that. Chinese, he says it is. Stupid name, if you ask me, but it seems to work." She stopped speaking and turned away from me to watch the action.

I said, "Oh," and, "thank you." She didn't acknowledge my thanks.

Whatever gwung fooey was, it certainly *did* seem to work. I wondered if all members of Angie's staff were trained in some kind of fighting technique. Mr. Wu was clearly more than a mere gardener. Not that there's anything *mere* about gardening, but... Oh, never mind.

It took quite a while for the police to finish photographing things, and for all the participants in the morning's activities to be questioned—except for Raymond and his cohorts, who would be questioned at the police station. Finally, the police contingent except Sam departed, taking all the villains with them. Sam stayed behind, gun back in its holster, fists on hips, scanning those of us sitting on various pieces of furniture. He shook his head.

I ventured to say, "It wasn't my fault."

His gaze landed on me, and he said, "This time."

"Darn it, Sam Rotondo—"

He held up a hand, and I shut up.

"This mess didn't have anything to do with Daisy," Angie said.

"Yeah," said Sam. "I know it. Lou filled me in on as much as he knew." He walked over to the piano bench gazed upon us one by one.

Li now sat next to Lou Prophet in another, smaller, sofa across the room from where Mrs. Jackson and I had been plopped. Angie had sent Mrs. Jackson off to make tea and bring us some refreshments. She'd had to ask Sam if doing so was permissible first, of course. But Sam, while often grim, wasn't unreasonable, and he'd given his permission for this piece of frivolity. If it can be called that. He hooked the back of a straight chair and sat on it, facing Angie.

"All right, Missus Mainwaring. That fellow, Raymond, said you're his wife. Is that true?"

Mr. Bowman sat on the arm of Angie's chair, and the two held hands. I guess that was kind of sweet. I saw Mr. Bowman give her hand a squeeze, and I *knew* that was sweet.

After exhaling a huge sigh, Angie said, "Yes. I married Raymond Alberts in New York City nearly forty years ago."

"And you're still married? I mean, you never filed for divorce or an annulment in order to put an end your marriage legally?"

"No." Another gigantic sigh from Angie. "But I barely got out of there with my life! He'd have killed me if I'd stayed with him."

"Oh?" Sam lifted one of his dark, bushy eyebrows. The expression made him look rather like a particularly cynical Italian duke. I wished Officer Blackman would come back and take a photograph of him in that pose. A handsome man, my Sam.

But back to the point of this narrative…

Angie continued. "Yes. You're right, though. In order to make certain we were no longer married, I ought to have divorced the man."

"Right," said Sam. "I don't know if what he did today is going to give you any relief, but you might find yourself having to pay that bimbo some of your money."

"I know it. I offered him money to leave me alone."

"Oh? When did you offer him money?"

"Today." Angie glanced around the room. "You all heard me, didn't you?"

Not quite daring to speak yet, I lifted my hand to tell Sam I'd heard her offer Raymond money to go away. Mr. Alberts. Whatever his name was.

"Yes," said Li. "She did. I heard her, too."

"Right. Well, as I said, I don't know if that's going to make a difference. I also don't know if he's wanted for any criminal activity back in New York."

201

"I'm sure he is," muttered Angie. "I know he's a bootlegger."

"Oh? How do you know that?"

"I keep in touch with certain old friends." Angie gave Sam a faint smile.

He didn't return it. Rather, he said, "You know, Missus Mainwaring, your private life is none of my business—until it becomes police business—but from what's happened so far since you moved to this neighborhood, it seems as though you might have a few people who don't wish you well still occupying the world."

"You're right, Detective Rotondo. I...I wish I'd cleaned up better before I moved to Pasadena."

"So do I," said Sam, his tone of voice emphatic. I could tell he meant what he'd said.

"I thought I had," said Angie, her voice small.

"Do you think we can expect much more excitement of this nature? I believe you're attempting to...what would you call it? Fit in? Yes, I suppose that's the right phrase. I believe you want to fit into staid Pasadena society. So far, you're not doing a swell job of it."

I sucked in a breath, wanting to voice a hot defense of my new friend, but a glare from Sam made me blow out the breath accompanied by no words. He was right, darn it.

Shaking her head, Angie said, "I...I don't know. I hope nobody else from my past will find me."

"How *are* all these people finding you, anyhow?" I asked. Nobody answered. I wasn't surprised. Everyone had other things on their minds, I suppose.

"Hope isn't exactly precise, Missus..." Sam shook his head again. "Look, what *is* your name? Are you Missus Alberts or Missus Mainwaring, or something else altogether? It would help if we knew who you were."

"I don't *want* people to know my name!" cried Angie. "Not my birth name. My name is Evangeline Mainwaring. I had it legally changed in Tombstone. I even have a copy of the document. I had to pay Arizona Territory to do it! So I'm Evangeline Mainwaring. Legally."

"I see. Do you suppose anyone else might come looking for you? You under a different name, I mean?"

"I...don't know. If Raymond and Li's brothers could find me, I suppose it's possible other people might be able to do it." She added in a frustrated tone, "But I don't know how they *found* me! I thought I'd covered my tracks so well! Lord, I hope none of the others find me."

"Others? You mean men?" asked Sam drily.

After hesitating a second, Angie nodded. "Men."

"Used a bunch of 'em, did ya?" said Mr. Prophet, giving Angie an ugly look.

"Stay out of this, please, Lou," said Sam. "We don't need recriminations. We need to know the truth and what to expect in the future."

"Huh. The truth ain't in that woman," Lou growled.

Li whapped him, hard, on the arm. He snapped his head around to give her a wounded look.

"Look," said Sam, "I don't know anything about you, but I do know we've experienced three unpleasant incidents in the past two days. If you can think of other people who might hold a grudge against you—and why—please write down their names and their reasons. And their addresses, if you know them."

"But—"

"You can trust me when I tell you I'm not going to tattle, Missus Mainwaring," said Sam in a sarcastic tone and putting slight emphasis on her last name. Her *chosen, legal* last name.

"It's true, Angie. Sam never breaks his word." I smiled at Angie and then at Sam, who evidently didn't appreciate my endorsement of his stellar word-keeping ability.

"Cut it out, Daisy," said he, annoying me. Then he squinted at me. "Maybe you can stay here with Missus Mainwaring and Miss Li for a while and help them compile a list of any other people who might wish Missus Mainwaring harm."

"I'll be happy to!"

"Figured as much," Sam grumbled. He rose from his chair, turned it around again, and glanced at Mr. Prophet. "You staying here, Lou, or would you like a ride home?"

Rising from the sofa he'd been sharing with Li, Mr. Prophet said, "Thanks. Think I'll take you up on the ride. I ain't as young as I once was, and I'm tuckered."

"Won't you stay a little longer, Lou?" asked Li, a note of pleading in her voice.

"I'll be back after I rest up some," he said. He didn't smile at her.

I sensed a quality of lopsidedness to their relationship and wished I could do something to make Mr. Prophet appreciate Li as much as she appreciated him.

Believe it or not, I do possess an inner core of honesty, even though I make my living lying. My inner core jeered at me just then and whispered, *Dream on, Daisy Gumm Majesty*.

Sometimes I hate the truth.

NINETEEN

After Sam and Mr. Prophet had left Angie's house, Mr.
Bowman went outside to lock the gate behind them.

"I'll stay with Wu for a while Angie," he said before he left. "I
want to make sure nobody is lurking in the shrubbery."

"Thank you, Judah." Angie sat slumped in her chair, her head
bowed, elbows on knees, hands covering her face.

"I told you something like this was going to happen," Li
seemed to have recovered from the loss of Mr. Prophet. Resilient
woman, Li.

"I know you did." Angie's voice sounded muffled, which only
made sense as the heels of her hands pressed against her mouth. "I
just hoped you were wrong."

"Huh," said Li, joining Sam, Mr. Prophet and Harold Kincaid
in the growing gallery of huh-ers in my life. "You'd better do what
the detective told you to do, Angie. Try to remember all the men
you bilked."

"That will take forever," mumbled Angie sadly.

"Really?" That word was spoken by me because Angie's statement both intrigued and slightly shocked me, although it shouldn't have. Angie had, I believed, been pretty honest with me about her scarlet past.

With another sigh (there were a whole lot of sighs going around that day), Angie lifted her head from her hands, peered at me and said, "Yes. I'm afraid so."

Because I wanted to be in on all of Angie's dirty secrets, I said in a chipper tone, "How about I take notes? I have—" Nertz. "Um, I don't have my handbag with me. I usually carry a little notebook and a pencil in my bag."

"Angie has paper and pencils," said Li, marching purposefully across the room, perhaps to fetch paper and a pencil.

Looking at me somberly, Angie said, "I don't know, Daisy. Once you know the...well, the particulars of my life, you'll probably hate me."

I shook my head. "Not a whole lot surprises me anymore, Angie. I have friends who...well, who's backgrounds probably wouldn't welcome scrutiny, and a few more who overcame really, really, *really* horrible things." I wasn't going to blab about any of those people to Angie, but I knew them, some quite well. The most important thing my job as a spiritualist-medium had taught me was discretion. I held other people's secrets close to my heart and never told them to anyone. And that, by golly, was pretty amazing, considering the way I blurted out stuff. But at least my blurts weren't about other people's secrets. That sounds odd. Aw, what the heck.

"Are you sure?" She sounded doubtful.

"Oh, yes."

She stared at me for a second or two, then said, "Very well then. Thank you. I appreciate your help."

"You're more than welcome. I don't want anything bad to happen to you or Li. I like you."

"Thank you. I hope you'll still like me when you know more about me."

I only shrugged. Then I remembered something. "Oh! Missus Jackson told me that man who burst in here and made all those awful men drop their guns was your gardener, Mister Wu. Is that so?"

With a nod, Angie said, "Yes, it is. Wu was trained to be a fighter in China. He's kept in practice."

"Missus Jackson said his... What would you call it? His fighting technique? Well, anyway, she said it was called something like gwung fooey."

With a laugh, Angie said, "Yes, it's something like that. I can't pronounce it, either, but Wu practices the skill—or art. I'm not sure what to call it—religiously. And thank God for it. He's come in handy more than once before today."

"Did he come with you from Tombstone?"

"Yes. He, Li, Hattie, and Cyrus Potts and Mr. and Mrs. Wilson —they're caretakers at my house in Orange Acres—all fled Tombstone with me."

"I see." Fled, had they? Interesting word to use in this context.

Li returned with some writing paper and a couple of pencils and said, "Why don't we go to your office, Angie? It'll be easier for Daisy to take notes at the desk than if she has to use her lap."

So go to the office we did. Hattie brought some tea and pound cake—this time it was flavored with oranges and contained, I think, poppy seeds—on a tray and set it down on a table near two chairs. Angie and Li took the chairs. I sat behind Angie's lovely mahogany roll-top desk, pencil poised, several sheets of paper awaiting my script.

Li poured tea for the three of us and handed us each a plate with a piece of orange pound cake and a fork. That pound cake was scrumptious, and I aimed to tell Aunt Vi about it. I took bites in between writing down the names and circumstances related to me by Angie and, sometimes, Li.

After forty-five minutes or so, I'd filled two and a half sheets of paper with handwriting that had begun to deteriorate from overuse, and it didn't look as if the two women were through yet. Good Lord in heaven! I hadn't realized one fairly normal-sized female person could accumulate so many enemies in a single lifetime. Then again, Angie had told me before she'd not been precisely a "good" girl in her former life, so I'd expected to hear about some sordidness. "Some" wasn't a large-enough word for this list. I tried not to let on.

Nevertheless, as Angie and Li compared mental notes and tossed out the occasional name and circumstance that might land the person on my list, I wrote stolidly. Didn't say a single word. And this was only partially because I was stunned. Finally a longer-than-usual spate of silence ensued. I glanced up to see Angie and Li staring at each other, brows furrowed, clearly thinking hard.

Although I didn't want to break whatever spell they seemed to be under, my fingers were beginning to cramp, so I ventured, "Anyone else?"

Lifting a finger to her lips and tapping same, Angie squinted at Li some more. Finally she said, "Li? Can you think of anyone else?"

"No. Adolph Grant would be the most worrisome but, according to Sally when I sneaked her out of Tombstone, he was shot down a year or so ago."

Ew.

"Thank God for small favors," said Angie.

In an attempt to hide my shock at her callous words—or maybe they weren't callous. I didn't know Mr. Grant. Perhaps he deserved them—I peered at the papers upon which I'd been writing, picked them up, and settled them into a tidy stack. "Um, if you can't think of any more names or anything, perhaps I should take these lists home, make a copy for you, and then give this to Sam. Is that all right with you?" I wanted to go home to my father and my loyal dog! I felt guilty for deserting them and staying away so long, not that the staying-away part was entirely my fault.

"Perfectly fine," said Angie. "Thank you so much for your help."

"Happy to be of service," I said. I think I even meant it, in spite of my state of thunder-struckedness. I don't think that's a word.

"And you don't hate me?" Angie's voice was small, and she sounded as if she'd truly miss my friendship if I were to withdraw it.

I laughed. What's more, the laugh was sincere. "No, I don't hate you. I've heard...well, maybe not worse stories than yours..." My voice tapered off as I thought about what I'd just said. By golly, it wasn't true. "Actually, I've heard *much* worse stories than yours. Unfortunately."

"You're exaggerating, aren't you?" said Li, giving me a look of disapproval.

"No, I'm not. I know people who have been sold as slaves to men who wanted to use them for immoral purposes, I've known women who have been almost beaten to death by their lovers or husbands, I've met boys who were kidnapped from their families in far-off places, and I've... Well, I've heard and seen a whole lot. If you don't believe me, you really should talk to Flossie Buckingham. I've mentioned her to you before."

"Yes," said Angie weakly. "Yes, you have. We met at your lovely party."

"And Harold. Harold Kincaid is probably my best friend."

"Good God," said Li. "You know about all that horrible stuff, and you were born and reared *here*? In Pasadena?"

"Oh, yes. And don't forget drug smuggling, incest, abortion, and murder. I've encountered those things a time or two, as well."

"Goodness," said Angie."

"Goodness," I said in a firm voice, "had absolutely *nothing* to do with most of those cases."

"But you won't let on whose stories they were?" asked Li, still appearing skeptical, which irked me at first. Then it didn't. After all, Li hadn't known me for very long.

"Never. I will never tell another person's secret. You can take my word to the bank."

"Thank you, Daisy." Angie had what looked like honest-to-goodness tears in her eyes when she walked to me and took my hand. "Thank you *so* much."

"You're welcome." Then, because I don't quite trust coincidences, even those invented by Mr. Charles Dickens, whose books I loved in spite of the handy twists of fate he came up with, I asked, "You have no idea how all these people managed to find you? All of a sudden, I mean? This is the third of three incidents—frightening incidents—in two days. Three people from your past finding you in two days doesn't seem right to me."

"It doesn't seem right to me, either," said Li in a dry voice.

Angie sat and stared at me thoughtfully. "You're right. All these things seem a little too chancy, don't they? I mean, they're too coincidental to have happened by accident."

Li lifted an eyebrow over one of her beautiful almond-shaped eyes.

"My thought, too. I…" My voice trailed off as I tried to think how to phrase what I wanted to say next. Drat. There was no tactful way to do it, so I just said, "Do you think you might have a traitor in your midst? Could someone you trust be unworthy of your trust? Have you hired anyone new lately? Do you think someone you believe in might have turned on you?"

Angie's eyes opened as wide as pie plates. She and Li exchanged a couple of glances, then she shook her head emphatically. "No. Absolutely not. All the people who work for and with me are loyal to the bone."

"I believe you. That is, I believe you believe what you just said, but I don't know most of the people around you. You might want to take a… I don't know what you'd call it. A surreptitious survey of your staff, just to check and make sure?" My nose wrinkled when I heard my question, although I don't why. I meant it.

"Oh, no. That's not possible!" Angie cried, horrified.

"What about one of the girls you're trying to help? Might any of them betray your trust?"

"Absolutely not!" It looked to me as if the mere thought offended Angie. Whoops.

Then Li said thoughtfully, "I'm not so sure, Angie."

I'd already noticed Li possessed a practical streak. Well, so did Angie. However, I think Angie had planned her life so carefully, fought for it so hard and built it *so much* to her taste and at such a huge cost, she might be prejudiced or, perhaps, unmindful of what might be a cuckoo in her beautiful, impeccably planned and imple-mented nest.

"Li!" said Angie, peering at her in outrage. "It's not possible. You *know* it isn't!"

With a shrug, Li picked up the teacups and saucers and placed them on the tray along with what was left of the pound cake and our dirty dishes. "Wouldn't hurt to look a little closer," she said as she slipped out the door. "I'm not as trusting as you are."

"*Trusting*! I'm not trusting!"

"Yes," said Li. "You are."

"No!"

Li's "huh" floated into the room as she walked back to the kitchen.

Staring at the door Li had just exited, her face a mask of incredulity, Angie said. "No. Such a thing is impossible."

"Well," said I, standing and tucking the papers under my arm, "I know you don't want to believe anyone you know and love might betray your presence to people who want to harm you, but it wouldn't hurt to do as Li suggested."

"No," Angie whispered again.

"I think you should."

"No. I…I can't."

With a shrug, I said, "I hope you're right." I smiled at her and toddled off home. It only then occurred to me to wonder why Pa hadn't come in search of me.

"It's because Sam told me what was going on down there," said Pa when I asked him. "Good gravy, Daisy, you do get yourself into the strangest situations."

I noticed he appeared pale and drawn. He'd had a bad heart attack a few years earlier, and we all worried about his health. I hated to add any stress to his life, although I seemed to do it quite often in spite of my best efforts. "Are you all right, Pa? You look—"

"I know what I look like," he said with resignation. "Sam was so worried after he told me what was going on at Missus Mainwaring's house, he called Doc Benjamin." He patted his shirt pocket. "But I'm a good boy and carry my nitroglycerine tablets with me all the time."

"Good. You took a couple?"

"Yes, I did. And Doc should be here any minute. Sam told him to come, even after he saw me take the tablets."

"Good for Sam. Nothing had better happen to you, Pa. I need you to walk me down the aisle!" I didn't mean to be flippant. In truth, he looked awful, and his appearance frightened me.

However, because Pa hated to be fussed over and I'd made a promise to Angie, I went to my bedroom with Spike, got my notebook and pencil from my handbag, and sat at my dressing table in order to copy the list I'd made at Angie's to give to Sam.

I did take time off from my list-copying to walk Dr. Benjamin out to his automobile.

"Pa looks terrible, Doc. Is he all right?"

Dr. Benjamin looked down at me, his brow furrowed. "Of course, he's not all right, Daisy. He has a touchy heart. He's been good about walking, he tries not to eat too much, and he's stopped smoking those smelly cigars he used to love. All of those things help, but..." His voice petered out.

"But his heart is going to give out one of these days?" I asked, trying not to cry. Blubbering isn't a nice thing to do at your doctor, especially if your doctor is Dr. Benjamin, who is one of the best people on earth.

"I expect so," Doc said after hesitating a few more seconds. "But Daisy, we all have to die of something. Nobody gets out of this alive. Your father isn't getting any younger, and his heart isn't in tip-top shape."

"I don't want my father to die."

"I know you don't." He wrapped an arm around my shoulder and squeezed it. A mere month ago, such a hug would have made me scream in agony. "I don't want him to die, either. Nobody does. And there's no reason to think he'll go any time soon. Keep an eye on him, and make sure he never runs out of those nitroglycerine tablets. I've talked to Peggy about his condition, too, so you can all monitor his health."

"And what does she think about Pa's health."

"About the same as you do," admitted Dr. Benjamin. "But the two of you and Vi can keep an eye on him and make sure he takes care of himself."

"I guess."

"Cheer up, Daisy!" Dr. Benjamin said, a little too heartily in my opinion. "Your father is in great shape."

"For the shape he's in," I muttered.

With a laugh, Doc said, "None of us can ask more than that of life."

"I guess," I said again. Personally, I wanted to grab life around its scrawny neck and shake it until it promised me it would let my father live for another fifty or sixty years.

After I watched his black, doctorly auto make a U-turn on Marengo, probably to head up to his office on Waverly Place in Altadena, I walked back to the house feeling pretty darned lousy.

TWENTY

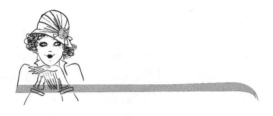

Before I'd finished copying my list, I fielded a call from Mrs. Pinkerton, in a tizzy as usual, and made an appointment to meet with her the next day. I didn't want to meet with her. Ever. But I had to earn a living, so I'd keep the appointment. Therefore, I noted it on my mental calendar and went back to copying the list. My whole hand ached by the time I was through. Don't think I'd ever written so much since I'd done a research paper on sleeping sickness in Africa during my senior year in high school. Having sleeping sickness is probably more awful than having a tricky heart, but acknowledging the truth didn't make my mood any brighter.

In case anyone cares, and I can't imagine why anyone would, my paper—which was well-researched and received a superior grade—was rather slim on details. Something akin to sleeping sickness had been recognized for centuries, but it wasn't until 1917, the year I graduated, that it was isolated and given a name by some Austrian guy. The fact that the man was Austrian didn't bother me when I was in high school. I attended high school before my husband had been murdered by Germans in the war. For many years after Billy came home from that conflict, I lumped Austrians with Germans on my people-to-hate list. It took a long time and some serious blows to my bias before I was forced to admit not all Germanic people were villains.

Harold Kincaid brought Vi home around four o'clock in the afternoon, so at least I got to chat with him for a while. I'd been feeling glum until he showed up, but after we talked for a while, I cheered up a lot.

"That's idiotic, Daisy," Harold said when I told him about my planned visit with his mother on the morrow. "She's already got three appointments scheduled for tomorrow, including lunch with Algie at the Valley Hunt Club, a Shakespeare Club meeting, and a board meeting for the Pasadena Women's Hospital. And Mister Pearlman—you remember him, don't you? One of Stacy's lawyers?"

"I thought he wasn't going to represent Stacy because he doesn't practice criminal law."

"He doesn't, and you're right. However, Mother insists on talking to him about Stacy anyway. Since she's so rich, he obeys her every command."

"Good Lord."

"Something like that. Anyway, he's coming at ten-thirty tomorrow morning to talk to her, and the rest of her day is filled up with other appointments and meetings."

I squinted up at Harold, befuddled. "Really? How come she doesn't seem to know about any of those things?"

"God, *I* don't know! Listen, I'll remind her of tomorrow's social calendar and tell her you'll see her on Thursday. What time's good for you?"

"I guess ten o'clock. Ten was the time we set for tomorrow's meeting."

"Excellent. I'll drive by her place and tell her so. I swear, the woman gets more scatterbrained every damned day."

"Says her dutiful son."

"Hell," Harold growled. "I'm about ready to resign from *that* position. Ever since Stacy got herself locked up, Mother's been more difficult, annoying and blithery than ever. And she was bad enough to begin with."

"Harold!"

"It's true."

"Well, maybe. Maybe you should hire a social secretary for her or something. I've heard of social secretaries."

"She needs a keeper, is what she needs."

"Harold, you're awful!" I laughed, though. Couldn't help it. "Anyhow, you have to admit having a daughter like Stacy would be hard on any woman."

"True enough." Suddenly Harold took both of my shoulders with both of his hands. Gazing down upon me with a ferocious frown, he said, "Daisy, if you and Sam ever have children, promise me you'll drown them if they show any signs of becoming like Stacy."

"Harold!" But I laughed again.

It was a jollier Daisy Gumm Majesty who meandered into the kitchen after Harold left. "Want me to set the table, Vi? Or do anything to help? Help that doesn't require me to cook, I mean."

With a cheerful chuckle, Vi said, "I'd never ask you to do anything requiring you to cook, Daisy. But yes, please set table."

Naturally—this is really stupid, but it's true—her answer swept me right back into the dumps. Which is ridiculous, and I knew it. I knew I was a disaster in the kitchen. Yet when Vi acknowledged my inadequacy, my feelings were hurt. Stupid, stupid, stupid!

"What are we having?" I asked, my voice meek.

Vi turned around and looked at me. "What's wrong, Daisy?"

I shook my head. "Nothing. Nothing, really. I just…I feel bad about not being able to cook. Poor Sam. He doesn't deserve a wife who can't even fry an egg. I can fix toast in our toaster, but when we had to use toasting forks, I *always* burned the toast. To this day

George teases me about the time I tried to fix fried chicken for a picnic. The outside was crunchy, and the inside was raw. Why am I such a bad cook, Vi?" I sounded pathetic. I *felt* pathetic.

"Daisy!" said my aunt, coming over and giving me a quick hug before she went back to the range. "What in the world brought this on? If you paid as much attention to what you're doing in the kitchen as you do when you're at your sewing machine or your Ouija board, you'd be a great cook."

She'd told me the same thing before, and I still didn't believe it. Trying to smile, I said, "You're probably right."

After gazing at me over her shoulder for another couple of seconds, Vi shook her head. "You know, Daisy, not everyone is given the same gifts. You're a whiz at sewing and everything having to do with sewing. When I tried to sew something as easy as a set of table napkins, I nearly killed myself."

This was a revelation. "You did? How?"

"I ran over my thumb with the sewing-machine needle."

"Ow!" I know I made an awful face, because Vi laughed. However, I didn't think running over your thumb with a sewing-machine needle was anything to laugh about.

"It's the truth. And Peggy's no better at cooking than you are. Yet she's a whiz with mathematics, and I'm not."

"I'm not, either. Getting through algebra in high school nearly killed me."

Vi laughed again and continued stirring something in a pot on the stove. "To answer your original question, we're having creamed chicken and noodles. The chicken's all made up and in the warming oven. I added green peas to it, and we'll have cooked carrots on the side. I'm just stirring salt into the water for the noodles now."

"Sounds good. Um…why do you add salt to the noodle water?"

"It's the only way to flavor the noodles. Without salt, they're quite bland."

"Oh." I thought noodles were just naturally bland, and that's why people put stuff on top of them, but I thought it better not to pry further into the mystical art of cookery. Vi's lessons in same had never remained in my brain for any length of time. And honestly, I'd *tried* to concentrate on cooking! I'd even been forced against my will—by, of all people, Stacy Kincaid, which now strikes me as typical of that daughter of Satan—to teach a cooking class at the Salvation Army. The lessons went well only because of Vi's patient, impressive and remarkable tutelage, but her lessons hadn't stuck with me. No matter what Vi told me about various people's various gifts, I knew I was a failure, and that was that.

Needless to say, I'd resumed my state of melancholy by the time Sam and Lou Prophet showed up at the front door. Before they even knocked, Spike had raced, yipping hysterically, to the door. Therefore, I just opened the door when I got to it. Sam had lifted a hand to knock, but he didn't have to.

"Good evening, gentlemen," I said bowing and waving them inside, trying to pretend I felt happy when I didn't.

"It is, is it?" grumbled Sam. But he bent over to pet Spike, so I allowed his grumble to pass unremarked upon. Besides, I was in a lousy mood myself.

"Huh," said Prophet. He, too, bent over and patted Spike. "Like hell it was good."

Very well, then. I decided to stop trying to be cheerful. "Rough day, eh?" I asked.

"You have no idea," said Sam, hanging his hat and coat on the hat rack beside the door.

Mr. Prophet did likewise, only he didn't speak.

Spike had stopped leaping on the two men and now merely stood beside them, wagging his tail and looking happy. One out of four beings at the door was happy. Something seemed out of kilter here.

I asked, "Was your day awful because of what happened at Angie's place this morning?"

"Yes," said Sam. "And what happened yesterday, when Lou shot the man out of the orange tree. Thank God nobody but us knows about the Chinese invasion. But I don't want to talk about any of that stuff. Can anyone think of anything good that's happened today?"

After contemplating his question for a split-second, I said, "Yes. I'd made an appointment to visit Missus Pinkerton tomorrow, but Harold told me she can't make it." I shrugged. "Made me happy."

Sam laughed, hooked an arm around my waist, and drew me to his side. "Good. You can come with me when I go back to that blasted orange grove. I still have to talk to the woman who fainted."

After a mere split-second, I figured out to whom Sam had referred. "Sally?"

"Is Sally her name?" Sam let go of me with a sigh.

"Yes. Sally's the one Li thinks the man Mr. Prophet shot came after." That sentence doesn't look right, but it turned out all right because Sam understood.

"Li's probably right," said Prophet. "That curly wolf was a special friend of Sally's, according to her. Li, I mean."

I already knew what a curly wolf was: a bad man. "Does Sally know he's dead?"

"Dunno. I 'spect either Li or *Angie* might've told her."

Annoyed and feeling challenged by his tone of voice, I said sharply, "I don't like the way you say Angie's name, Mister Prophet. She's changed her ways. She paid you back your precious money, didn't she?"

"Cripes. Yeah, she paid me back."

"Well, then, you can at least speak of her respectfully, can't you?"

Eyeing me with what I could only regard as deep scorn, he said, "Sure. I can do that."

I believed his words about as much as he did. Oh, well. I turned my attention back to Sam. "And you *want* me to come with you? Gee, Sam, usually you try to keep me as far away from your cases as I can get."

"I know. But she might feel more comfortable talking to me if a woman comes with me."

Darned if his words didn't perk me right up again. "Swell! I'll be happy to go with you."

"Figured as much." Sam sounded the least little bit sarcastic. I let it pass.

"I'll go with you, too," said Prophet. "Li asked me to."

When I glanced at him, I do believe he seemed self-conscious. Unless it was my imagination.

It was probably my imagination.

"Let's not talk about work, all right?" said Sam. "I'm sick of the entire city of Tombstone, Arizona, this evening, and I hope nobody from Tombstone ever darkens Pasadena's doors again."

"Amen to that," said Prophet. It was probably the first time he'd uttered anything remotely resembling a prayer in a decade or three.

"Sam and Lou! Good to see you."

This, from Pa, and he'd just come from his and Ma's bedroom. I hoped he'd been resting.

"Evening, Joe," said Sam. "You're looking better than you did earlier in the day."

"Thanks. Feel better, too. Took a little nap. It's heck getting old, Sam."

"You ain't old," said Lou Prophet. "*I'm* old. You're still a pup."

"A pup with a harebrained heart," said Pa.

My own heart squished.

"But Doc Benjamin visited you, didn't he?" Sam sounded anxious.

"Yes, yes. The good doctor visited me. Daisy was here. She can tell you I'm not fibbing."

"He's not fibbing," I said, trying to sound jokey. "I even talked to the doctor myself. He said Pa's doing well, as long as he keeps exercising, doesn't eat too much, and doesn't take up cigar-smoking again."

"You like a good cigar?" asked Mr. Prophet, interested.

"He *used* to smoke cigars," I answered for my father. To Mr. Prophet I said with a meaningful scowl, "They're bad for his heart, so don't you try to get him to start smoking them again."

Mr. Prophet held up his hands in an "I surrender" gesture. "Only just asked, was all. Don't get the fantods and swoon all over the hurdy-gurdy house."

After staring at him for a heartbeat or two, I said, "All right. I won't get the fantods or swoon all over the...what was the kind of house you mentioned?"

"Never mind," said Prophet.

"But—"

With a laugh, Sam said, "Leave him be, Daisy. He's had a rough day, too."

"Oh? Why?"

"You kill a feller who's wanted by the law someday and see if *you* don't have a hard time of it," said Prophet. "Hellkatoot. That bastard was wanted in three states, and the cops *still* treated me like leftover cow shit."

"Do you *have* to use bad language every time you speak?" I asked him, my voice low and fierce.

He scowled at me. "Reckon I can mind my tongue in Joe's house."

In Joe's house. Good enough. "Fine," I said. "Thank you."

"Huh."

I gave up. "But come on in, you two. Dinner's just about ready. You can take your places, and I'll bring out the chow."

Rubbing his hands together, Pa said, "Sounds like a tip-top idea to me. Tip-top."

"Me, too," said Sam.

"Me, three," said Prophet.

I squinted at the latter, but detected no underlying message to his words. Crumb. As if things weren't bad enough, now I seemed to be *looking* for trouble.

However, the men took their places at the table. Ma, who had been chatting with Vi in the kitchen, handed me a big bowl of buttered noodles, which I carried out to the table. I set it at Vi's place, figuring she could dish out the noodles and creamed chicken, and we could pass everything else. Both Vi and Ma seemed to approve of my plan, so I continued, carrying out the bowl of buttered carrots and then a huge tureen of creamed chicken. It smelled delicious. Of course. Everything Vi fixed to eat was delicious. As opposed to... Oh, never mind. I've probably already said too much about my lack of skill in the kitchen. My failure plagued me, though. However, I don't mean to inflict it on anyone else.

Bother.

After we were all seated, Vi at the head of the table, Pa at its foot, Ma and Mr. Prophet seated across the table from Sam and me, Pa said his usual short grace, and Vi started ladling out noodles and creamed chicken. So I passed the plates she loaded and then the bowl of carrots, and we all dug in.

"I'm mighty lucky to have found you folks," Mr. Prophet said at one point. "I never ate so good in my life before this. You're a great cook, Missus Gumm."

"Thank you, Mister Prophet," said Vi, smiling and, I think, blushing a trifle.

Good Lord on high, I hoped to *goodness* Vi wasn't going to fall for the elderly but fascinating Mr. Lou Prophet. What power did the man possess that enslaved women? Perhaps "enslaved" is excessive, but golly. Li Ahn, who had thus far in our acquaintanceship been one of the most sensible, feet-firmly-fixed-on-the-ground women I'd ever met, seemed madly in love with him. Heck, *I* found him attractive, and I didn't even want to.

I guess I'd been staring at the man, because he fidgeted for a second and then lifted his head, frowning and peering at me across the table. "What's the matter, Miss Daisy? Did I use the wrong fork or something?"

"Daisy!" said my mother, aiming one of her looks my way.

I swear to heaven, I couldn't win for losing, as Flossie Buckingham occasionally said. I think it was a saying left over from her stint as a gangster's moll.

"I didn't do anything!" I told Ma, feeling abused and mistreated. "And no, Mister Prophet, you didn't use the wrong fork. I was just thinking about something. I didn't mean to stare at you. In fact, I wasn't staring at you. I was staring past you." One more itsy-bitsy lie couldn't hurt anything, could it?

Prophet looked over his shoulder, then back at me. He said, "Oh."

I didn't say another word all through dinner. Then I gathered up all the plates and serving dishes, flatware and so forth and carried it all into the kitchen. Ma aimed to help me, but I felt an almost punishing need to prove myself good at something, so I told her to go to the living room and chat with Pa and the other men and Vi, although Vi generally retired to her bedroom with a book shortly after we all ate.

The only thing I managed to accomplish that evening was wash, dry and put away all the dishes and pots and pans and give Sam the list I'd made for him. He, Mr. Prophet and I stood on the front porch at the time.

He gazed down upon the several pages, his eyebrows climbing. He had thick, dark eyebrows. He also had long, luxurious eyelashes, which wasn't fair, but what was? "Good Lord. You mean these pages contain lists of people who might have a grudge against Missus Mainwaring?"

"She probably forgot some of 'em," said Prophet, eyeing my notes with disfavor.

"She and Li both gave me the names of everyone they could think of." I frowned at Mr. Prophet. "And they both said they'd tell me if they remembered any others."

"Good God," said Sam in a faintish voice.

"There are quite a few of them," I admitted.

"Yes. There are," said Sam upon a heavy sigh. "Thanks, Daisy. Can you be ready to go about nine tomorrow? I want to talk to that Sally person as soon as I can. I'd like to get to her before Missus Mainwaring and Miss Li can tell her who the dead man was."

"Want me to call and tell Angie so?"

"It's all right, Miss Daisy. I'll take care of it."

Sam and I watched as Mr. Prophet clumped down the front porch steps, walked to the sidewalk, turned right and headed for Angie's house. Oh, well. Li would be pleased. Probably.

"Why do women fall for men like Mr. Prophet?" I asked my fiancé.

"Beats me," said Sam, gazing after Prophet. Then he frowned down at me. "You're a woman. Don't you know?"

"No," I said. "I don't."

Sam shrugged, kissed me and headed across the street to what would be our house one day. Soon, I hoped.

TWENTY-ONE

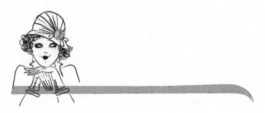

I don't know about anyone else, but I slept like the proverbial log Wednesday night. Having lost a lot of sleep the prior night and having had a frightening and eventful day, I was tuckered. Even though Spike hadn't had as hideous a day as I'd experienced, he slept like a log, too. I think dogs are just like that. They don't fuss and fume and dwell on things and let stuff bother them. Wish I were more like a dog.

On Thursday morning, Sam and Mr. Prophet came over to our house for breakfast. I'd risen at my usual time and had already bathed, brushed my hair, powdered my cheeks (only a little, so they wouldn't shine) and donned a comfortable but pretty, mid-calf length, tan-colored dress with a brown collar and low-waisted belt. I didn't anticipate having to do any running around or fleeing from this or that, but I'd learned long ago one couldn't predict what a day would bring. Days in my life had brought a whole lot of unusual things of late, and I didn't intend to rip anything, get blisters on my feet or trip because of a too-tight skirt if I had to skedaddle in a hurry. Besides, the brown and tan went well with my auburn hair and my beautiful emerald engagement ring. I plopped my brown cloche hat on top of my brown handbag in my bedroom before I joined the men.

"You look lovely, as usual," said my darling father.

"Yes, you do," said my darling fiancé.

"You always look well, Daisy," said Ma. My mother wasn't given to flattery, so her comment surprised me.

"Thank you," I said to everyone in general.

"Vi fried up some ham and cream of wheat for us," said Pa. "It's in the warming oven."

In case anyone doesn't know about fried cream of wheat, it's like fried cornmeal mush, only it's wheat. I mean, you fix cream of wheat as you would if you were going to eat it for breakfast, but instead of eating it instantly when it's soft and hot, you pour it into a loaf pan and put it in the Frigidaire over night. It sets up just like cornmeal mush does, and then you fry it for breakfast. You notice I didn't say *I* fried it for breakfast.

There I go again, bemoaning my lack of cooking skills. I beg your pardon.

"Good. I love fried cream of wheat," I said. "Anybody else want some?"

Everyone except Ma and Vi, who had already eaten their breakfasts, did, so I dished up breakfasts for all the men in my life and me. Even Spike got a little bite of ham. I tried not to feed him too many table scraps, because the long back of a dachshund is difficult enough for a dog to manage. No dachshund needed to haul extra pounds around on those little short legs. It had occurred to me more than once that dachshunds should come equipped with an extra pair of legs in the middle, but then they would look even sillier than dachshunds already looked with only four legs. Their silly-lookingness (I seem to be making up words right and left, don't I?) was one of the reasons I liked them so much.

The men waited for me before digging in, which surprised me. Pa was polite and gentlemanly at all times. Sam had been taught manners and used them every once in a while. I'm not sure what, if anything, Mr. Prophet's mother had attempted to teach him if he'd ever been a child, but I never expected him to behave like a gentleman. On Thursday morning, he did.

After I'd carried my plate to the table, made sure the syrup pitcher was full—Vi had heated the maple syrup, as she always did —and laid out the butter, Pa said a short prayer, and we ate. Yum.

"This is real good," said Mr. Prophet. "Don't think I've ever had this stuff before. What's it called again?"

"Fried cream of wheat," I told him.

"Eh?" His brow furrowed as he looked at me, as if he thought I was making some kind of joke.

"Excuse me." Deciding an explanation would just confuse the fellow, I got up from the table, marched to the cupboard, and got down the box of cream of wheat. Yellow and with a happy-looking Negro fellow on the front, even the box seemed cheerful. "Here. This is a box of cream of wheat."

"Be da-darned," said Prophet.

I didn't laugh as I put back the box and returned to my seat. The man evidently *did* mean to keep his language clean when he was in my father's house. I approved. Mind you, Mr. Lou Prophet wouldn't care one way or another if I approved of him.

"So you're all going out to Missus Mainwaring's orange grove today?" Pa asked as he cut a bite from his slab of cream of wheat.

I answered him. "Yes. Sam needs to interview a woman named Sally. She was too upset the day before yesterday when Mister Prophet killed the man who shot at Mrs. Mainwaring. Then, yesterday, all of that other stuff happened." I shook my head as I tried to figure out what I'd just said.

But my father understood. "I'm sorry these things are happening in our neighborhood," he said with a worried frown on his face.

"With *that* woman in the neighborhood, anything's liable to happen," said Mr. Prophet is a voice leaving his listeners in no doubt as to his opinion of Angie.

I didn't even bother frowning at him, since I knew to do so would be a waste of energy on my part.

"Oh, that's right," said Pa, peering at Mr. Prophet. "You knew her before she moved here, didn't you?"

"Yep."

"But her past doesn't matter at the moment," said Sam in a voice slightly louder than was strictly necessary. "The woman has done nothing in Pasadena to bring any blame upon her. In fact, she's an extremely successful businesswoman. Orange Acres is the biggest and most profitable orange grove still in town. There used to be a lot more orange groves in these parts, or so Daisy tells me." He smiled at me.

I smiled back. "And poppy fields," I said, hoping to get Mr. Prophet off the subject of Angie. "In fact, they're thinking of renaming one of the streets in Altadena Poppyfields, because there used to be so many poppy fields around here. Only they're going to spell it as if poppy and fields are one word. Poppyfields instead of poppy space fields." I ran out of spit and stopped talking.

"Interesting," said Mr. Prophet in a voice that might possibly have sounded more bored, but not without considerable effort on his part.

We didn't talk a lot during the remainder of breakfast. When we were finished dining, Pa said he'd wash the dishes if we needed to get going.

"Thanks, Pa." To Sam, I said, "I'll go brush my teeth and be right with you." I also needed to use the toilet, but the men didn't need to know it.

"Great. Lou and I will get the Hudson and meet you outside."

And they did. After I used the facilities, I detoured to my bedroom to put on my hat and grab my handbag. I spoke comfortingly to my poor pooch, who looked bereft.

"I'm sorry, Spike. I'll take you for a walk when I come home."

Spike wasn't reassured. I could tell. Feeling guilty, I walked into the kitchen to find Pa drying the dishes he'd just washed.

"Don't worry about Spike," said Pa. "I'll take him for a walk."

I got on my tiptoes and kissed my father's cheek. "Thank you, Pa. You're the best." Squatting before my dog, I petted him several times and told him to buck up. "You can go for a walk with Pa this morning, and then I'll take you for another walk this afternoon. Okay?"

Even though he wagged and grinned at me, I don't think Spike quite understood. Ah, well. I've often wished I could speak my dog's language, but I can't. Therefore, I walked outside, making sure the front door was locked behind me, and joined Sam and Mr. Prophet at the Hudson. Mr. Prophet exited the front seat, held the door open for me, and climbed into the back seat as soon as I'd sat in the front seat.

"Thank you," I said politely.

"Yeah," he said.

I gave up.

Sam had just begun to roll his Hudson down Marengo, when he stopped short in front of Mrs. Mainwaring's house. We all stared at a man who stood on the front porch, a pretty bouquet of flowers in his hand, talking excitedly to Hattie.

"Cripes," said Mr. Prophet. "What's going on now?"

"Don't know," said Sam.

"Do you want me to find out?" I asked.

A duet of loud "no's" answered my question. Crumb. You'd think I deliberately set out to get into trouble if you listened those two.

"Let's all go see what's going on." Sam parked his automobile at the curb, and we all exited it. The gate stood open, so we just marched up to the porch where the man still stood, talking heatedly to Hattie Potts.

"But she's my *wife*," the man said.

Sam, Mr. Prophet and I exchanged a trio of speaking glances.

"Not another one," Sam said under his breath.

"Don't surprise me none," said Mr. Prophet in his I-hate-Angie voice. "She's probably got a hundred more tucked away somewhere."

I kept mum, deciding it was probably for the best.

"Mister Godfrey, I don't know what to tell you," said a clearly rattled Hattie. "Missus Mainwaring—"

"Missus *Who?*" the man—Mr. Godfrey, I presumed—said. "She's Missus Godfrey! I'm her *husband*."

We'd reached the porch stairs, and Sam cleared his throat. Mr. Godfrey whirled around, startled. Hattie, standing in the middle of the open coffin door, muttered, "Thank God."

As we climbed the porch steps, Sam said politely, "Is there something we can help you with, Missus Potts?"

"Yes, please," said Hattie.

"Who are you?" the man demanded. "I'm here to see my wife! I just found her after all these years!"

"Perhaps we'd better all go on inside, so we can discuss this matter," said Sam, taking Mr. Godfrey's arm, turning him around and nodding to Hattie.

After her glance paid a visit to the heavens—actually, it was the roof of the covered porch—Hattie stepped aside and said, "Come on in, then. I'll get Miss Angie. She ain't gonna like this one little bit."

"Miss Angie?" Mr. Godfrey sounded confused which, if my surmises were correct, wasn't surprising. "I'm here to see Virginia Godfrey. My wife."

"Come along, Mister Godfrey," said Sam, steering the man toward the front parlor.

He didn't seem to be exerting any particular force, but I knew my Sam. If Mr. Godfrey tried to do anything at all, Sam's strong

hand on his arm would stop him dead. Well, maybe not *dead*, but…
Oh, never mind.

"Why don't you sit right here. Mister Godfrey, is it?" said Sam
in a polite voice, pressing gently on Mr. Godfrey until he plopped
into the chair to which Sam had guided him.

"But—"

"Why don't we wait until the lady of the house joins us." It was
a statement rather than a question, and I thought Sam was pretty
smart not to mention Angie's last name again.

Mind you, Sam didn't know what Angie's last name was any
more than I did. When I'd done my reading for Angie a couple of
weeks ago and Rolly had predicted her past would come back to
haunt her, I'd had *no* idea what her past might contain. At least two
husbands, evidently. Perhaps Lou Prophet was right, and there
were even more of them lurking. Evidently Angie had been a busy
woman before she moved to Pasadena.

"I don't understand any of this," Mr. Godfrey complained.

"Neither do I," said Sam, smiling at the man as he sat in a
chair beside him. Mr. Prophet and I selected seats on the sofa. "So
we'll just wait a few minutes. I'm sure everything will be explained
presently."

Lou Prophet said, "Huh."

We'd been sitting, staring at each other, for a few minutes, when
Hattie appeared. Carrying a tray bearing a silver teapot and
several of Angie's beautiful Coalport cups and saucers, she kept an
eye on Mr. Godfrey as she set the tray on the piecrust table near
the chairs Sam and Mr. Godfrey occupied.

"Miss Angie will be in shortly," she said, and turned and
walked away.

"Who is this 'Miss Angie' that woman keeps talking about?"
asked Godfrey. His voice had taken on a pleading quality.

"Everything will be cleared up soon," Sam promised.

I hoped he was right.

In the meantime, I took a good long gander at Mr. Godfrey. To me he appeared to be maybe Angie's age; perhaps a couple of years older, although not nearly as well-preserved. Maybe in his mid-fifties? I'm not good at judging ages. However old he was, he looked tired, stooped, wrinkled and unhappy. Gray-haired, he also wore a small mustache and sideburns a little longer than was fashionable in 1925. I got the feeling he was still living in the days when he'd been young and bouncy. Any bounce he'd once possessed seemed to have deserted him. Now he only looked old, anxious, worried, and stooped.

Poor guy. I hoped he wasn't really Angie's husband because, upon first glance, he seemed to be a nice fellow. Then again, as with age, I wasn't a good judge or a person's moral fiber. It generally took an act of senseless violence for me to recognize the person committing it as evil.

And I was supposed to be a spiritualist-medium. As Lou Prophet, Li, Sam (or Harold) might have said: "Huh."

"Anybody want tea?" I asked, trying to sound sprightly.

Nobody wanted tea. Very well, then, I poured myself a cup, added just a pinch of sugar, stirred, and sat back on the sofa again. Mr. Prophet frowned at me for some reason.

"What?" I asked, irked.

He only shook his head.

Of course, once I'd poured myself a cup of tea, I didn't know what to do with it. I hadn't really wanted tea; I just thought serving tea might take the edge off the atmosphere. If ever a room was filled with tension, that one was, and tea didn't help one little bit.

After what seemed like a year and a half, Angie appeared in the doorway to the front parlor, clad impeccably as usual and looking beautiful, also as usual. At her age! I don't know how she did it, but if we became better acquainted, maybe she'd teach me. Li, looking equally gorgeous, stood directly behind her. I got the feeling she was acting the role of bodyguard, although I'm still not sure if I was right in my surmise.

"Ginger!" Mr. Godfrey jumped up from his chair, almost strangling the bouquet of flowers in his hands. "It *is* you! Oh, Ginger, I didn't think I'd *ever* find you!"

"Ernest," Angie said, her voice warm, holding out both hands as she walked to Mr. Godfrey.

Li still stood in the doorway, watching the play with what I could only consider cynical detachment. Wished I could do that.

"Ginger. I looked everywhere for you!"

"Oh, Ernest," Angie said mournfully. "I'm so sorry."

"Sorry? About what?" Remembering his flowers, Mr. Godfrey thrust them at Angie, who gave a vigorous start.

Li took one step into the room and stopped. I don't know if Angie signaled her, or if Li was just naturally good at reading people's intentions and had judged Mr. Godfrey's to be benevolent. Wished I could do that, too.

Taking the flowers and gazing down at them as if her heart were breaking, Angie said, "Oh, Ernest, I...I... Well, I have to tell you something. I should have told you years ago, but I was a coward."

"What?" Mr. Godfrey sounded befuddled. "What do you mean? A coward?"

"Come with me, Ernest," said Angie, taking the poor fellow's arm pretty much where Sam's hand had lain not long since.

"Come where? I'll go anywhere with you."

Poor Mr. Godfrey.

Sam said, "I'll join you, if you don't mind."

Both Angie and Mr. Godfrey *did* mind—and so did Li—but Angie knew better than to protest. With a nod, she led Godfrey from the room, Li and Sam following. I wanted to know what was going on, but Sam gave me a glare clearly telling me to stay put. So I did, confound it.

"He'll tell you all about it," said Mr. Prophet.

"He'd better," I said.

"I told you before. The truth ain't in that woman. I'll bet you right now she's telling a story that'll have the poor peckerwood's head spinnin'."

"I wish you didn't dislike Angie so much."

Giving me a look that might have felled a lesser woman, Mr. Prophet said, "I wouldn't piss... Er... I mean, I wouldn't spit in that woman's ear if her brain was on fire."

I blinked twice. Then I said, "Oh."

At least he'd made a stab at not being vulgar.

TWENTY-TWO

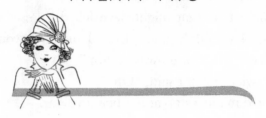

When Mr. Godfrey left Angie's house, the poor fellow was in tears. He appeared bent and defeated and as if he didn't want to live another single second on this earth. I felt genuinely sorry for him.

So, evidently, did Angie. She stood in the front doorway, wringing her hands, her own eyes a bit drippy. Li and Sam stood next to her—that coffin door was wide—and gazed as the beaten man slowly walked down the drive and out into the street. He no longer carried the bouquet he'd brought. I imagine Angie had told Hattie to put the flowers in a vase or something. She wasn't mean enough not to accept them.

Was she?

Holy Moses, I honestly didn't know *what* to think about Angie Mainwaring—or Virginia Godfrey—anymore. Unless or until guided otherwise, I intended to keep liking her. I knew life was hard, especially for woman. Especially for women born into unsavory circumstances.

I wasn't sure I admired Angie's method of using everyone she met to her advantage, but... Well, what did I know about the vicissitudes she'd endured in her life except for what she'd told me? Honestly? I didn't know whether to believe even that much.

Silence prevailed as poor Mr. Godfrey exited through the front gate. I don't know about anyone else, buy my own personal heart ached for him.

Then Angie said, "I'm sorry."

"About what?" asked Sam.

"About bringing my past to Pasadena."

"Yeah," said Sam. "I am, too."

After glancing at Sam, Angie bowed her head and said, "I'm sorry" again.

"All right. Let's get going," said Sam, ignoring Angie's second apology. "Come on, Daisy. Lou."

"Are you going to talk to Sally?" asked Angie. She sounded worried.

"Yes," said Sam. "We didn't get a chance to question her on Tuesday, and then all hell broke loose yesterday."

Mr. Prophet spat on the front porch of Angie's magnificent house and said, "Shit."

I didn't have the heart to scold him.

"Do you want me to come with you?" said Angie. "I really want to make sure she's all right."

"I'll go with them," said Li. "It's my job, after all."

Besides that, she'd get to sit with Lou Prophet all the way from the middle of Pasadena to its eastern edge.

"Thank you, Li." Angie sounded humble.

"See you," I said to Angie, smiling as genuinely as I could.

"Oh, Daisy," she said. "I hope you won't hate me after this."

"I'm sure I won't." My voice was almost intolerably chirpy, probably because I wasn't sure if I'd just lied or not.

At any rate, Li, Sam, Mr. Prophet and I all trooped out to Sam's Hudson. Sam held the front passenger door open for me, and Mr. Prophet held the back passenger door open for Li. We two females—I darned near wrote ladies—slid into the machine, Mr. Prophet joined Li in the back seat, and Sam got behind the wheel once more.

"Cripes," he said as he pulled away from the curb.

Before speaking, I glanced at the back seat, where I saw Mr. Prophet staring out his window and Li staring out of hers. I guess I hadn't expected them to throw themselves into each other's arms; I'd just kind of hoped they would. I think I already mentioned I can be a gooey sentimentalist, didn't I? It isn't a quality I admire in myself.

"Was that fellow really Angie's husband?" I asked Sam.

His lips pinched for a second before he said, "Yes. One of them."

"Oh."

I heard a "huh" from the back seat. I'm pretty sure it had come from Mr. Prophet.

After chugging along in silence for a couple of blocks, I said, "What happened? Did Angie say she aimed to divorce Mister Godfrey or anything? What about the other fellow yesterday? Wasn't she married to him? Or..." I wasn't sure how to say what I wanted to say.

"You mean, did she bother to rid herself of one husband before she married another one?" said Sam.

"I guess so."

"No."

"No? Just no? No what?"

"No, she didn't legally detach herself from either man before she married the other one. I don't know who's legally her husband. She did manage to produce a marriage certificate from New York City to prove to Godfrey she was already married when she married him. She claimed she thought her first husband was dead and when she found out he wasn't, she didn't know how to break the news to him, so she just left Missouri."

"Oh." I didn't know what to say next.

Mr. Prophet didn't suffer from my inability to express myself. "Told you. She's probably got a dozen other husbands littering the world."

When I glanced again at the back seat, I saw he was in the process of fixing himself a quirley. A quirley, in case I haven't yet mentioned it, is a cigarette. Which is also a coffin nail.

Even though I knew myself to be unworthily naïve as I spoke, I said, "Do you really think so?"

Mr. Prophet just looked at me over his cigarette paper and piled-up tobacco.

I said, "Oh," again and turned my head to face forward once more.

"She married him in St. Louis," said Li, surprising me. I'd almost forgotten she was there. "After she got out of New York City. She had to run from New York before Raymond Alberts could kill her."

"She didn't...um, divorce Mister Alberts or anything?"

"No," said Li. "When she got to St. Louis, she met Ernest Godfrey. He was a shoe salesman and a nice man, and he loved her. Angie married him there, in St. Louis. Then Alberts found her, she was scared, and her feet got to itching again. She'd saved up some money, so she pretty much ditched Godfrey."

"He seemed upset when he left her house," I said.

"He was. He loved her." Li shrugged.

"And she didn't love him?"

Stupid question, Daisy Gumm Majesty.

"Angie loves men in her own way," said Li, not clearing up the matter in my mind at all. "But she had goals and she aimed to achieve them. After she left St. Louis and Godfrey, she went to Colorado. Grand Junction, I think she said. She married somebody else there, but I don't remember his name."

"Good Lord," muttered Sam.

"The Lord don't have nothin' to do with that harpy," said Mr. Prophet.

"Maybe not." Li shrugged again. "Angie did what she had to do. She told me she was happy there in Colorado with her Colorado husband, whatever his name was, but he died." Giving Mr. Prophet a hateful glare, she said, "And no, Angie had nothing to do with his death."

After he'd licked his cigarette paper and folded it over the mounded tobacco, Mr. Prophet stuck the cigarette in his mouth and said, "Huh."

Then he scraped the head of a sulfur match against his thumbnail and lit the thing. I do believe I'd heard him call one of those matches a "Lucifer" once. I'd have to ask him to clarify that when he was in a better mood. I swear, my Old West-English dictionary was growing by leaps and bounds!

"Anyhow," Li went on. "The Colorado husband had become wealthy running a silver-mining operation. When he died, he left her with quite a bit of money. So she moved to Tombstone. That's where I met her. It's also where she married Adolph Grant, who's one of the worst men on the face of the earth. Fortunately, Angie got away from him, and she took Hattie and Cyrus and me with her, along with a couple of other people who worked for Grant." Glaring at Mr. Prophet, Li said, "And I don't care what you say, Lou Prophet, Angie Mainwaring is trying to *help* the women she brings to Pasadena. She rescues them. She doesn't want them to have to live the way she did." After a second or two, she added, "Or me."

I didn't correct her grammar. I understood what she meant.

"Yeah, yeah," said Prophet, rolling his window partway down and blowing smoke from same.

I wished he wouldn't smoke in Sam's Hudson because cigarettes were stinky and the smell lingered in the upholstery, but I didn't say anything. More to the point, *Sam* didn't say anything, and it was his car. Things might change when we married, although I wasn't counting on it.

"If Mister Grant was so awful, why did Angie marry him?" I asked, believing the question to be pertinent.

"He's one of those men who don't show their true colors until it's too late," said Li.

Not quite sure how to ask what I wanted to ask next—I didn't want to be vulgar, even if I *was* sitting in an automobile with Lou Prophet and a former... But maybe Li hadn't been a... Bother. "Um...I mean...Um, did he make Angie...um...go with other men?" Nertz.

Fortunately, Li understood my fumbling attempt at asking a question. "No. She was in charge of keeping the girls happy. And that meant...Uh..." Her voice sort of faded to a stop.

"It meant feedin' 'em laudanum, chloral, morphine and liquor to keep 'em from complaining," Mr. Prophet volunteered.

After glowering at him for a heartbeat or two, Li shrugged and said, "Yes. Unfortunately, it did. The girls Angie took in had nowhere else to go. At least Angie gave them a roof over their heads and a safe place to live."

"How did the girls end up in Tombstone? And so...so poor. Or without means. Or...I don't know what I'm trying to say. I mean, did they go there to get a job? Or...I don't know."

"Every girl I ever met in Grant's house was there because she thought she'd have a better life in Tombstone than wherever she came from. I did the same thing. Thought maybe I could open a little restaurant. Ha. Back then, Adolph Grant owned the whole damned town. If he wanted a woman, he'd have her, no matter what she'd come to town for."

"Oh. You like to cook?" I asked, interested.

Both Sam and Mr. Prophet laughed, although I don't know why.

Then Li laughed, too, and I decided I must have said something stupid, although I wasn't sure what it was. People who could actually cook and liked doing it intrigued me.

After she stopped laughing, Li said, "Yes. My husband and I wanted to open a restaurant in Tombstone."

I'm pretty sure my eyes bugged out, at least a little bit. "Your *husband*?"

"Yes, Charles MacDonald. We married in New York City and then moved to Tombstone. Charlie was sure we could make our fortune if we opened a Chinese restaurant there. He said we'd be a novelty." Li shook her head. "We were a novelty, all right." She sounded bitter.

"What happened?" I asked.

"Adolph Grant killed Charlie and snatched me. After that I worked for him. On my back."

Shocked by her plain-speaking—which was really stupid of me under the circumstances—I said, "Oh."

"Angie took care of me. She took care of all of Grant's girls. I was luckier than most of the other girls."

"You mean you were smarter than them," said Mr. Prophet. His words didn't strike me as kindly meant.

Evidently, they struck Li the same way. With a scowl that would have done credit to a gargoyle, she snapped, "You're right. I'm smarter than a lot of people, including you."

Mr. Prophet grunted.

"Anyhow, Angie took care of me, and I took care of her. Grant charmed her. One of his more wicked talents, damn him. He could be charming when he wanted to be, until he had you. Then he showed his true colors. When Angie married him, all of her money became his, of course, because that's the way marriage works."

It did? I didn't ask.

"The laws are changing in some states," said Sam, butting into the conversation so suddenly, I started in surprise. "In fact, more and more of them are becoming community-property states."

"What does 'community property' mean?" I asked.

"It means that when a man and a woman marry, anything either of them produces during the marriage belongs equally to both of them. Sort of a fifty-fifty split."

"And Arizona isn't one of those states?"

"I have no idea," said Sam.

"Is California?"

"Why?" asked Sam shooting a grin at me. "Want all my money? Too bad. I made it before we got engaged."

"I'm not marrying you for your money!"

"Why the hell not?" asked Lou Prophet. I turned my head and glared at him, for all the good it did.

"I know you aren't." Sam reached over and patted my knee.

"Anyhow, Arizona wasn't a whatever you called it. At least it wasn't back then," said Li glumly. "It wasn't even a state. What was Angie's became Grant's, and what was Grant's, he kept, believe me. Including Angie."

"Huh," said Mr. Prophet.

"But Mister Grant is dead now?" I asked.

"Yes. I've been told he was shot to death about a year ago," said Li.

"Do you have any proof? I mean, did you read his obituary or anything?"

"No, but several people, including Sally, told me he was murdered in his parlor house. I know for a fact he was selling illegal liquor there. He probably got in bad with a bootlegging operation, and they killed him for cheating. He cheated everyone he ever did business with."

"Mercy," said I. Silly, I know.

"I don't think mercy and Adolph Grant ever met," said Li in a dry-as-dust voice. "All I know is, he's dead."

"Good." That wasn't nice of me, but Mr. Grant sounded like a truly awful person. I knew from bitter experience slavery existed in the United States, even though people didn't call it that. It always distressed me to learn about another one of slavery's many forms. Sounded to me as if Mr. Adolph Grant had pretty much enslaved Angie and everyone else who'd had the misfortune to become entangled with him and live under his influence. No matter what Mr. Prophet said about her, I thought Angie was a heroine for helping enslaved women achieve their freedom. I suppose it was too bad she'd gone about it in a less-than-honorable manner. But honestly, there are times when honor has to be set aside in order to achieve a loftier goal.

Maybe.

Fiddlesticks. I don't know what I'm babbling on about. All I knew at the moment was Angie Mainwaring, according to Li, helped women in distress. I had no reason to doubt Li's word on the subject and, to my mind, Angie's actions on behalf of other women who were unable to help themselves made her a good person. Kind of like Flossie Buckingham. Only an overall less-good person than Flossie. Maybe I'm wrong. Sorry about blabbing again.

But we'd reached the Lamanda Park section of Pasadena by then, so our conversation and, thank the heavens, my muddled thought processes ceased. Sam slowed down when he got to Orange Acres and turned onto the long drive. The aroma of orange blossoms was as potent that day as it had been on... Good Lord, had we been there only two days ago? By golly, I guess so. So much had happened since then, our first visit seemed as though it had happened in another lifetime.

I smiled as we approached the big old Victorian mansion. It looked like a huge wedding cake, with all its curlicues, gables, turrets, gingerbread trim and so forth. The place was gorgeous, although I don't think I'd like to live in a house so big. Unless one could afford a staff of dozens, it would be impossible to keep the place clean and tidy. Then there were the grounds and the gigantic orange grove. Angie probably *did* employ dozens of people.

And that, I decided on the spot, was one more reason to like her. In order to keep her mansion and orange grove—not to mention the house she'd bought on Marengo Avenue—buzzing along properly, she had to employ a whole lot of people. Although the country had gradually begun climbing out of the economic depression it had fallen into after the war, many people remained unemployed. And if Angie gave jobs to people who used to be all-but-slaves, more power to her!

I didn't voice my opinion aloud, primarily because I didn't want to hear any more snide comments from Mr. Prophet. I don't think Li would have jeered, but I didn't know for sure. In truth, I didn't understand her. She seemed both hard and soft. Ruthless and compassionate. Hateful and loving.

Or maybe I was totally wrong about her, and everyone else found her personality to be as clear and easy to understand as a fresh mountain stream.

Somehow, I doubted it.

When Sam pulled up to the big wrap-around porch, Li got out first. She didn't wait for Mr. Prophet to open her door for her. Mind you, I don't know if he'd have done it if she'd waited, but I guess she wasn't taking any chances.

"Do you know what Sally's last name is?" Sam asked me before the two of us exited the motorcar.

"I don't have any idea. We should have asked Li, I guess."

"We'll learn it," Sam said philosophically. Then he exited the Hudson.

He didn't have a chance to open my door for me like the gentleman he sometimes was, because Mr. Prophet got there first. He'd thrown his quirley away by then, and he wore a sardonic expression on his face when I thanked him for opening my door for me. Drat the man.

TWENTY-THREE

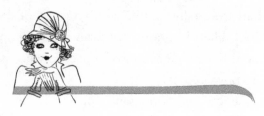

"Miss Li!" Sam called, stopping Li just as she reached out to open the mansion's front door.

She turned and frowned at him.

"Wait there a minute, please."

Li waited, and Sam caught up with her, Mr. Prophet and yours truly right behind him.

"Please don't say anything to Miss Sally except that we want to talk to her," Sam said. "Will you do that? If not, please say so, because I don't want the news about Mister Tucker's demise to come from anyone else before I have the chance to talk to her."

"She might already know," Li said.

"If she does, she does. But I'd like to see her reaction when she receives the news if at all possible."

Hmm. Did Sam think Sally was the cuckoo in the nest? She didn't seem like a viable candidate to me because she'd appeared so darned fragile, both mentally and physically, to think up a dastardly plan to ruin Angie's life all by herself. Maybe she'd had help? From whom? Then again, what did I know? Absolutely nothing, darn it.

"Very well," said Li. She sounded grudging, as if she didn't think a big, burly Italian police detective ought to be delivering sad news to one of Angie's protégées.

Too bad. Sam knew what he was doing.

Did I stick by my man, or did I not?

Li opened the big front door and walked into the entryway ahead of us. She called, "Clara? Clara, I'm back."

A bustling noise came from the staircase, and I looked up to see a woman who might have been Hattie's twin sister coming down the steps. I found out later that she and Hattie were sisters, but not twins.

"Miss Li? Glad you're back."

"How have things been here?" Li asked the woman.

"Calm."

The woman whose name was Clara smiled such a benevolent smile, I instantly felt as if I'd been blessed. Some people are just like that, I reckon.

"Thank God for small mercies," said Li. "Is Sally upstairs?"

"Yes. She's with Nancy and Brenda in the upstairs parlor. They're playing Old Maid."

I don't know why the card game the three women were playing struck me as funny, but I darned near burst out laughing. It's a good thing I didn't because Sam would probably have killed me if I had. I don't mean literally.

"Thanks, Clara." Turning to Sam, Li said, "Do you want me to fetch Sally?"

"In a minute." Sam turned to the woman whom I assumed to be Clara. Holding out his police credentials, he said, "Ma'am, I'm Detective Sam Rotondo, from the Pasadena Police Department. I want to question Miss Sally about the incident that occurred in the orchard on Tuesday."

"Yes, sir. I understand. Miss Angie said you'd be coming

around in a day or so. I'm Clara Wilson." Clara held out her hand for Sam to shake.

"Happy to meet you, Miss Wilson," said Sam, shaking the woman's hand gently.

"It's Missus Wilson, but it's all right," she said, beaming another benevolent smile upon all of us. I swear the woman was a walking benediction.

"Missus Wilson. Thank you. Is there a good place where we can talk in private for a minute or two?"

Private! *Private*? "Sam, you're going to need me with you when you talk to Sally."

Smiling at me, far from benevolently, Sam said, "Oh? Why's that?"

"Well, because…because you need a woman with you, that's why. You said so yourself! Sally's…fragile."

"Miss Li's a woman," Sam pointed out.

"Aw, let her go with you," said Mr. Prophet, surprising me. "She's nicer than Li. Sally'll be likelier to talk to her than to you or Li."

Shocked, I turned upon Mr. Prophet. "That's *so* unkind! How can you say such a thing about Li, Mister Prophet?"

With a shrug, he said, "Because it's the truth?"

"Never mind, Daisy," said Li. "Lou's Lou, and there's nothing anyone can do about him."

"But he's being—"

Sam put a hand on my arm before I could lambaste Mr. Prophet anymore.

"Leave it be, Daisy. Lou wants you there, so I'll allow you to sit in. If you cause any trouble, I'll kick you out."

"*Trouble*! I'd *never*—"

"Shut up, Daisy," Sam advised, interrupting my rant, "or I might change my mind."

Frustrated and angry, I shut up. He was being unkind and unfair—according to me—but I wanted to be in on his interview with Sally. Besides, he'd told me he *wanted* me there! Had he been lying? Darn the man!

"Do you want me to go with you, too?" asked Li.

"Might as well. But let me do the talking, please."

"Happy to," said Li. I got the feeling she meant it.

"Come along with me." Smiling with as much benevolence as she'd earlier displayed, Clara Wilson led us all to a parlor off the entryway.

The room was furnished beautifully. Nothing ostentatious; everything just seemed perfect. I don't know much money Angie had earned—or, perhaps, stolen—over her many marriages and her fifty-some years, but it must have been a bundle. I don't think I'd ever seen such pretty furnishings, including the draperies. The windows were open half-way, and a gentle breeze wafted the scent of orange blossoms into the room as it made the sheer curtains billow softly. The place was about as much like heaven as anywhere on earth could get, if you asked me. Not that you did. Just thought I'd mention it.

"Please take a seat in here," said Clara. "Would you like to ask me any questions before Li goes to fetch Miss Sally?"

"Yes, please," said Sam, holding a round-backed armchair for Clara to sit in. The chair, naturally, was beautiful, a dusky rose color. It was one of a pair.

Sam sat in the chair's mate and gestured for Li, Mr. Prophet and me to take a seat nearby. So we did. I saw a nearby filigreed sofa with a patterned fabric that went well with the chairs and sat on the end closest to Sam and Clara. Li sat next to me and folded her hands in her lap. She looked so demure, you'd never have guessed she'd once been in an unsavory business. Mr. Prophet sneered down at another beautiful chair near our sofa, its cushion patterned like the sofa, before he sat, too. I have *no* idea what he had against pretty furniture.

"Very well, Missus Wilson," Sam began. "How long have you worked for Missus Mainwaring, and what is your position in her employ?"

"I've been working for Miss Angie for pretty much twenty-five years now," Clara answered promptly. "I manage the Orange Acres house. Miss Angie, she brings ladies who need help here from time to time."

"I see. Did you come from Tombstone, too?"

Clara blinked, as if surprised Sam knew about Angie's connection with Tombstone, then said, "Yes, sir. I... Do you know why Angie brings ladies here?"

"According to her, she's attempting to save them from a life of degradation," said Sam. He didn't sound sarcastic, and I was proud of him.

"Yes, sir. That's exactly what she does. She's saved a lot of women, including me and Li and Sally. We have two other ladies with us right now, too. Brenda and Nancy."

"I see. How long has she been performing this rescue service?"

"Oh, my, let me see." Clara shut her eyes for a second or two. "Ten years, at least. Her and us come out here twenty-five years ago, I reckon. For a long time she'd been investing in the Indiana Company. That's an orange company."

"Yes. I've heard of it," said Sam, taking notes as Clara talked.

Gee, I'd never heard of the Indiana Company, and I'd lived in Pasadena my whole life. I'd ask Sam about it later.

"Well," Clara continued, "she'd been savin' money and investin' money, and finally she took Hattie, Cyrus, Li, me and my husband Gabriel and ran. She snuck us out of that house and into a train she ordered special. We was workin' in a...bad house in Tombstone."

"A parlor house?" Sam asked mildly.

After peering at Sam with her eyes kind of squinched up, Clara evidently decided he wasn't being judgmental, but only asking for information. "Yes, sir. That there parlor house was a bad place. Hattie and me, we was cooks there. Hattie's man Cyrus, and my husband Gabriel, they did the hard-labor work."

"I understand from Missus Mainwaring that a fellow named…" Sam flipped a couple of pages in his notebook. "Ah. Here it is. A man named Adolph Grant owned and ran the parlor house. She also said he pretty much used women as his slaves."

"That he did. If anyone tried to escape, Mister Grant, he'd kill her. Or him. Didn't matter. He was a bad, bad man. And he hired more bad men to do his bad work for him."

"But he's dead now?"

"Yes. When Li brought Sally here, Sally said somebody'd gunned him down. Served him right. Didn't happen any too soon, if you ask me. I can't think of another single person who's ruined as many lives as Mister Grant did."

"I see. So you and Mister and Missus Potts, along with Miss Li, came to Pasadena with Missus Mainwaring?"

"Yes. Me and my husband Gabriel. We all lived here in the orange grove for nigh on to twenty years. Then Miss Angie decided to move closer to the middle of town. She wanted to save more lost souls, bless her heart, so she moved out of here and into there, and that made room for another girl or two."

I heard Lou Prophet grunt, but he didn't say anything; therefore, I didn't kick him.

"Did you know the fellow who was shot in the orchard on Tuesday?" Sam asked.

Shaking her head, Clara said, "Not to say I knew him. I knew *of* him from Miss Angie and Li. He was almost as bad as Mister Grant. I heard he used Sally something awful."

"When did the women get here? Miss Sally and the other two?"

"Sally, she come about a month ago. Nancy and Brenda have both been here for about a year. Li, she went and fetched them from Tombstone, too, when Miss Angie heard they wanted her help."

"How did she know they wanted help?"

Clara tilted her head. "Honest? I don't rightly know. Li can tell you." She looked at Li. So did the rest of us.

"Have you ever heard of the Underground Railroad, Detective Rotondo?" Li asked.

"Yes."

"Well, Adolph Grant's parlor house in Tombstone has something akin to the Underground Railroad. Girls take their lives into their hands when they try to send messages, but every now and then a message will get through, and Angie will act on it."

Sam asked Li, "Is that how you knew Sally wanted to leave Tombstone?"

"It's how we found out about all the girls Angie's helped."

"Through messages…what would you call it? Smuggled out of the parlor house?"

"Smuggled is as good a word as any," said Li with a shrug. "If Grant had intercepted one of those messages, whoever wrote it would have met a quick end." With a masterful sneer, she added, "That was the only good thing about Adolph Grant. He didn't torture people when he killed them. He just shot them dead. The torture was *living* when you worked for him."

How horrible. I didn't say so because I didn't want Sam to kick me out of the room.

"I see." His notebook on his knee and his pencil resting on his notebook, Sam looked into Clara's face. "Thank you, Missus Wilson. Several of Missus Mainwaring's enemies have shown up recently and caused trouble in her life. Do you have any idea who might have told those people where she lived? Can you think of anyone who might hold a grudge against her? According to Missus Mainwaring, she cut ties with everything in her past, chose a new name, moved to Pasadena, started over, and believed she'd severed all connections to her past. But her past seems to have found her in spite of her best efforts."

"That's right. She did all of those things. Nobody was supposed to know where she lived or what she called herself."

"And you don't know anyone who could have discovered her whereabouts? Or how and why?"

"Well, I reckon I know the why, but I don't know the who or the how. I 'spect any one of them men who used those poor girls might hate her for takin' them away, but she's doing good by doing that, so I just don't know."

"You've heard about the trouble she's been having in her new home, right?"

"Oh, yes. Li and Miss Angie have both called here to check on the girls. Miss Angie was agitated she didn't get to come out here yesterday, because she's worried about Sally." Clara shook her head again. "And I don't blame her. Sally's kind of a flimsy gal. Don't rightly know how she's going to turn out."

"I see. And no strangers have appeared here recently? You can't think of anyone new? Anyone you don't know who's been hanging around?"

"No, sir. Just us. Mister Wilson—he's my husband—and me. The three girls and Li. And the younger Mister Wu. Mister Gonzales—he manages the orange grove—lives in a little place out near the back of the orchard with his wife and two little boys. Ain't seen nobody else. Didn't see that Tucker fellow, neither, but he snuck in somehow. Miss Angie, she's got guards posted, so I don't know how he got in."

Sam's dark eyebrows soared. "She has guards posted?"

"Mercy sakes, yes! She knows she's made lots of enemies in her life, but nobody'd want those enemies as friends because they're all black-hearted scoundrels. But Miss Angie, she pays her people good, and they stay and are loyal to her."

"You can't think of anyone who might have been bribed to turn against Missus Mainwaring?"

"Pshaw. No. Nobody'd turn against Miss Angie. She's too good and helps too many people."

Another soft grunt issued from Lou Prophet. That time I kicked him, but not hard.

He said softly, "Hey!"

I frowned to let him know he should keep his opinion of Angie to himself. Naturally, he rolled his eyes at me. Don't know why I even bothered with the man.

"Thank you, Missus Wilson. What is Sally's last name?"

"Sally? Peterson, I think, but you never know about them women. They might have a thousand names."

"Oh? How so?"

With a shrug, Clara said, "They call themselves whatever other people call them's, all I know."

Such a thing seemed strange to me. Then again, so many things did.

Sam turned to Li. "Would you please ask Miss Sally Peterson to come here, Miss Li?"

Li rose from her end of the sofa as if she'd been goosed. Guess she was a little nervous or something. "Yes. I'll get her now."

"And please," said Sam, "don't tell her anything I don't want her to know."

Moving so quickly, she'd nearly made it to the door by the time Sam spoke, Li stopped short and whirled around. "What the hell does that mean? What don't you want her to know?"

"Anything. Just tell her I need to talk to her for a few minutes. Don't tell her anything else or mention any names."

With a shrug and a hefty sigh, Li said, "All right. I'll get her." And she left the room.

After sitting there for a few moments in silence, Mr. Prophet said, "How come you don't tell *her* not to swear? You're always bitchin' at me about swearing."

"I'm always *what*?" I knew a bitch to be a female dog. Except for a couple of times when Harold had called his sister a bitch—which I believed to be an insult to all dogs everywhere—I'd never heard the word used in any other context.

"He means you complain to him about his use of bad language," said Sam, thoughtfully translating for me. Grinning, he added, "And he wants to know why you don't carp at Miss Li about *her* use of bad language."

He had a point. After mulling it over for a second or three, I decided I'd never tell him so. "Because Li doesn't come over to our house all the time. Besides, she's a lady."

With a guffaw that made me want to snatch him bald—can't remember where I first heard that quaint saying—Lou Prophet said, "She's about as much of a lady as I am."

"Well, you don't seem to mind spending time with her," I said huffily.

"Don't mind at all." This time Mr. Prophet gave me a smile that made me want to shoot him dead.

"Associating with you is bad for my moral fiber," I told him.

He and Sam both laughed. Clara only gazed at us, puzzled.

She said, "You need me anymore, Detective? I can get more tea and so forth. Might make Sally feel more comfortable if she had a nice cup of tea."

"That would fine. Thank you for thinking of it."

"Chloral'd do a better job of making that harpy comfortable," muttered Prophet.

So I kicked him again.

"Hey!" he cried, pulling his one shin out of kicking range.

"Hey yourself, you awful old man."

"Now that just ain't nice, Miss Daisy."

255

"Neither are you."

Sam said, "Cut it out, you two." He grinned as he said it, which I didn't appreciate.

However, Mr. Prophet and I quit bickering when Li ushered Sally into the room.

TWENTY-FOUR

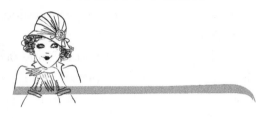

Sally didn't look any better on Thursday than she had on Tuesday. Her wispy blond hair had been cut into a Castle bob, and it didn't suit her. Her face was sort of pretty but far too pale, her torso so skinny you could practically see through her, and she seemed wobbly on her pins. Li had one hand on her arm and another on her shoulder, and I got the feeling she was guiding Sally for fear she might get lost otherwise. Or blow away, maybe. I felt sorry for her. Sally, I mean, not Li.

Sam and Lou rose to greet the newcomers. Sam's gentlemanliness didn't surprise me. Mr. Prophet's did, but that's probably only because he'd recently annoyed me.

Walking to her, Sam held out his hand. Sally looked at it as if she didn't know what to do with it. Or maybe she was practicing good manners. After all, the woman's supposed to initiate the hand-shaking ritual. Giving up on the hand-shake, Sam placed his hand on her arm, his other on her back, and I realized he was taking over guiding duties from Li. Sally glanced in panic at Li, but Li smiled reassuringly at her. I realized suddenly that Li's smile could be darned near as benevolent as Clara Wilson's. The woman (Li, not Clara) continued to baffle me.

"There's no need to worry, Miss…Peterson, is it?" Sam asked gently.

Li answered for Sally. "Peters. Her last name is Peters."

"Thank you." Sam nodded at Li. "There's no need to worry, Miss Peters. I only want to ask you one or two questions."

In a whisper, Sally said, "Very well."

After leading Sally to the chair Li had recently occupied, Sam lightly pressed her shoulder, and she dropped into the chair kind of like an autumn leaf. Not with a solid whump, in other words. She sort of drifted onto the chair. She wore a modern tube-style dress, and I'd wager she didn't need to use a bust-flattener, as some of us did, in order to eradicate any unsightly womanly curves. Sally must have weighed six pounds! Her dark brown eyes seemed huge, although they might have appeared so large because her face was so narrow and pallid.

"Don't worry, Sally," said Li in a sweet voice. "I'll be right here." Glancing at Sam, she said, "It's all right if I stay here, isn't it, Detective Rotondo?"

"Here" in Li's case was right behind Sally's chair, I presume so Li could catch her if she floated away or wilted or did anything of a like nature. I doubted Li would have to catch her if she jumped and ran, because Sally didn't look capable of either of those feats.

"Yes. But let me ask Miss Peters the questions, please."

"Of course," said Li, acquiescing, although I got the feeling she didn't want to.

"Thank you," said Sam. Smiling at Sally, he said, "I understand you've lived at Orange Acres for about a month. Is that correct, Miss Peters?"

A second passed before Sally's almost inaudible "Yes" lifted into the air.

"And you came here from Tombstone, Arizona?"

Sally nodded.

"While you were in Tombstone, I understand you worked for a fellow named Adolph Grant."

Casting a swift look up at Li, Sally didn't answer until the other woman nodded. Then she nodded, too.

"But Mr. Grant is now deceased?"

Sally seemed puzzled by the last word Sam used, so he rephrased the question.

"You told Mrs. Mainwaring and Miss Li that Mr. Grant is now dead. Is that correct?"

After licking her lips, Sally whispered, "Yes."

"He's been dead for about a year?" said Sam.

Sally tilted her head back to look up at Li, who nodded again. So Sally said, "Um... Yes."

"Very good." I'd never before heard Sam Rotondo sound so gentle. I was proud of him. "And you requested Missus Mainwaring's help in getting you away from the life you were forced to lead at the late Mister Grant's establishment?"

"I..." Another glance up at Li produced another nod from Sally.

Probably because he was irked that Sally didn't seem able to produce answers without Li's approval, Sam said, still using a kindly tone of voice, "You needn't be afraid of me, Miss Peters. I'm only here to ask you a few simple questions. I'm not going to hurt you or allow anyone else to hurt you."

"It's all right, Sally," said Li. "Just answer the detective's questions."

With a big gulp of air, Sally nodded. "All right," she said.

Evidently Sam didn't consider Sally's earlier nod any clearer than did I, because he said, "You mean you *did* ask for Missus Mainwaring's help to get you away from Mister Grant's parlor house?"

"Yes," Sally said without waiting for Li's signal.

"I see. And how did you get in touch with Missus Mainwaring? I understand Mister Grant's employees kept a close watch on the women who worked at his parlor house."

"Yes. They did." Sally licked her lips, which were not tainted by lip rouge or natural coloring. The woman was a veritable wisp.

"But you managed to get a message out of his house to a person who could relay it to Missus Mainwaring?"

Another nod from Sally.

"Would you mind explaining to me how the process worked? I'm interested, because it seems some of Mister Grant's employees have come to Pasadena, and they're causing a little trouble and making themselves unwelcome. I'm not, of course, talking about you or the other women in Missus Mainwaring's refuge."

I wondered if Sally knew what a refuge was but didn't ask.

"Um...I...Another girl told me to write a note, and she'd make sure it got to Miss Angie."

"I see. What was this young woman's name?"

"Um...I don't...Frieda, I think."

"But you don't know for sure?"

Sally shook her head.

"Do you recall Frieda's last name?"

"No."

"I see. Were you informed when Missus Mainwaring received your note?"

"No."

"But she did get it, or you wouldn't be here. Right?"

"Yes. Miss Li came to get me. She had to sneak me through my bedroom window."

"Ah. That must have been a frightening experience."

Showing more animation than I'd yet seen from her, Sally shuddered and whispered, "Yes."

"After Miss Li got you away from Mister Grant's parlor house, what happened?"

"She hid me in a wagon."

Lifting his dark eyebrows again, Sam said, "Did you ride all the way from Tombstone, Arizona, to Pasadena, California, hidden in a wagon?"

Sally shook her head.

Li said, "I—"

Sam held up his hand, and Li ceased speaking. Guess she'd aimed to tell Sam how she'd managed to get Sally out of Arizona. I also guess Sam wanted to hear Sally's story from Sally.

"Please let Miss Peters relate her own story, Miss Li."

Told you so.

"Very well." Li's words were sweet. Her expression would have killed Sam if it had been a sharp implement.

"Miss Peters?" Sam prompted.

"Um, what?"

"What happened after Miss Li got you away from the parlor house and into the wagon?" Sam was showing incredible patience. Shoot. Didn't know he had it in him, but the quality boded well for our future life together, mainly because I didn't have any. Patience, I mean.

Licking her lips again, Sally said, "She hid me in a wagon. Then she got me onto the train."

"Do you know if anyone came looking for you? Did you go straight from Mister Grant's establishment to the wagon and then directly to the train?"

"Uh…no. I mean, Li took me to a hotel and made me change clothes. She gave me a dark dress and made me wear a hat with a veil so nobody would recognize me." She paused to think for a heartbeat. "And a big coat."

Wow. Those constituted a whole lot of words from this source. And they were coherent. All at once I wondered if she still took whatever drugs she'd been addicted to at the parlor house. Perhaps Angie and Li were trying to wean her gradually from her bad habit. Because I valued my head and wanted it to stay on my neck, I didn't ask. I did, however, lift a hand to touch my juju. A couple of months prior, it had heated up when I was in the presence of an evil person. I didn't truly suspect Sally of being evil. Exactly. She had begun to annoy me, though. I think that's because my lack of patience was making its presence known.

"I see. So you were made up to look like someone else." Sam nodded. "Makes sense."

"Yes. I guess," said Sally as if she personally wasn't altogether sure if anything made sense.

"So, by the time you got to Pasadena, you had severed all ties with anyone you'd known in Tombstone?"

"Um...Yes. Sure."

After she spoke the words Sally's gaze wandered around the room, and all at once I didn't believe her. And I possess no spiritu-alistic gifts. But I got the distinct impression she'd just told Sam a big, fat lie. Again I felt my juju. Again nothing happened. Stupid juju. If it would work all the time or *not* work all the time, it might actually be useful—or unquestionably un-useful, if you know what I mean.

"Are you certain about that?" Sam asked.

"Yes. Yes. Of course," said Sally.

I didn't believe her again.

"I see."

Sam turned a couple of pages in the notebook he held. I think he only did it to make Sally nervous. If such was his intention, it worked. She squirmed in her chair and clenched her hands together so tightly, they looked as if they were attempting to strangle each other. Li placed a hand tenderly on Sally's shoulder, and the wispy woman stopped fidgeting.

I had *genuinely* begun to take a dislike to Sally, however weak, weedy, willowy and wispy she was. I know. I'm mean. I'm also pretty darned good at alliteration, by golly!

After a few fraught seconds of silence, Sam continued his inter-
rogation, if such it could be called. I thought he was being astound-
ingly gentle to the woman. In fact, I thought he was being too
blasted nice.

"Very well, Miss Peters, do you recall three days ago, on Tuesday, when Mister Prophet, Missus Majesty, Missus Mainwaring and
Mister and Missus Potts visited Orange Acres?"

Sally nodded.

"Good. So you probably remember when you and Miss Li
heard a couple of gunshots. Miss Li said they startled you."

"Yes. I was scared. I thought—" She stopped speaking
abruptly.

"You thought what?" asked Sam, smiling compassionately—I
didn't even know he could do such a thing until then—at Sally.

"Um...I...I guess I thought maybe somebody had come to take
me back."

"Back? You mean back to Tombstone?"

Another nod from Sally.

"Why did you think that?"

After licking her lips again, Sally said, "I...I thought maybe
someone might have come after me."

"Do you know who might do such a thing? Come after you to
Pasadena and then take you back to Tombstone?"

"Um...Well...I...No."

"You don't sound too sure of yourself, Miss Peters. Are you
sure you don't know anyone who might want you to return to
Arizona?"

"Well...I..."

"May I ask a question, Detective Rotondo?" Li didn't sound as
if she aimed to force Sam into acquiescence, but she sure looked
like she wanted to. Small wonder she'd decided to stand behind
Sally so Sally couldn't see her expression, which was...vehement, I
suppose is the correct word.

With a hesitation so small I'm not even sure it occurred, Sam nodded and said, "Yes, if it will help."

"I think it will," Li said to Sam. To Sally she said, "Weren't you close to a fellow named Frank Tucker, Sally? When you lived in Tombstone?"

"F-Frank?"

All at once Sally looked scared. How odd. Or maybe it wasn't. I suppose it depends on how she'd been treated by the dastardly Mr. Tucker. This wasn't an assumption on my part—Mr. Tucker's dastardliness, I mean—because he'd darned near killed Angie and/or me, and the attempt had constituted a dastardly act.

"Yes," said Sam, taking over from Li. "Miss Li and Missus Mainwaring both said you were close to a man named Frank Tucker when you lived in Tombstone."

Sally swallowed and said, "Y-yes. Yes, I was. He..." Her feeble voice trickled out.

"He what?" Sam encouraged. Soothingly.

He was being so gentle with the idiotic woman, I suddenly wondered if he'd be as gentle with a baby. Our baby. Stupid time to get sentimental, but I can't seem to help myself sometimes.

"He...Um...He loved me," whispered Sally.

Li erupted. "He beat the hell out of you! He didn't love you!"

Tears trickled down Sally's ashen cheeks. "He said he did."

"Please, Miss Li," said Sam, any whit of gentleness gone. "If you want to remain in the room while I question Miss Peters, you'll have to refrain from talking."

Li's lips writhed with fury, but she eventually nodded.

Sam resumed. "So, Mister Tucker loved you?"

"Y-yes." Sally sniffled and lifted a hand to wipe tears from her face. Li hauled a clean handkerchief from a pocket and reached over Sally's shoulder to hand it to her. Sam didn't object. Sally dabbed at her tears with Li's hankie.

"Very well. So Mister Tucker loved you. And did you love him?"

Lifting her clenched hands to her nonexistent bosom, Sally said, "Yes," in a voice that might have been the flitting of a bee. Or a butterfly. Bees had stingers. Sally didn't strike me as having much of anything at all.

There I go, being mean again. I'm sorry.

I saw Li swelling up as if she were about to erupt all over Sally again, but Sam stopped any words she'd aimed to spill with a pointed look. It was kind of dagger-like, actually.

After quelling Li, Sam said, "According to Miss Li, Mister Tucker treated you unkindly. Do you remember him hitting you?"

"Well...He didn't...I mean..." Sally sniffled loudly. It was the loudest noise she'd made since entering the room. "He didn't mean to."

"He didn't mean to beat you?" Sam sounded noncommittal, which I considered a sterling achievement under the circumstances. He was a professional, my Sam.

"No. He...I mean...He loved me."

"But he beat you?"

"Well, but he didn't mean to."

Oh, brother.

Sally added, "Afterwards, he always said he was sorry and he loved me."

"I see," said Sam, his attention on his notebook—probably to keep from snorting in disgust, although I might be wrong about that. "When was the last time you saw Mister Tucker, Miss Peters?"

Blinking and looking as if she hadn't understood the question, Sally eventually said, "When?"

"Yes. When was the last time you saw Mister Tucker?"

"Um...I'm...I'm not sure."

"But you haven't seen him since you moved to Pasadena?"

She didn't hesitate, but said, "No," in a voice that, while not firm, wasn't as gelatin-like or feathery as it had been up until then.

"I see."

Silence filled the room. I felt my juju again. Nothing. Nertz.

Sally began to fidget. Except for my hand and Sally's bottom, nothing else moved. Mr. Prophet looked as if he'd been carved from especially old wood. Li looked angry. Sam wore the most unrevealing expression I'd ever seen on a human face.

After long enough to make me want to smack Sally out of her chair—where do I get these violent impulses, anyhow?—Sam said, "So no one had told you it was Mister Frank Tucker who was killed in Missus Mainwaring's orange grove on Tuesday?"

Sally's pale blue eyes widened. "F-Frank? D-*dead?*"

"Yes. He tried to kill Missus Mainwaring, and Mister Prophet shot him."

Sally folded up like a concertina and fell out of her chair.

"Damnation!" Li bellowed. "Now look what you've done!"

"She's the one," I said to Sam.

Glancing at me mildly, Sam said, "The one what?"

"The one who told Tucker where to find Angie."

Kneeling beside Sally and briskly rubbing one of her skinny hands—I don't know what the rubbing of hands is supposed to do to a fainting maiden, but I've read in books about people doing it—Li shot me a glance meant to murder. "Don't be ridiculous! How could Sally tell Tucker anything?"

"I have no idea, but I'll bet you she did."

"Nonsense." Li turned to Mr. Prophet. "Lou, will you come here and help me get Sally upstairs. We'll have to carry her." Facing Sam again, she spat out, "Damn you, Detective Rotondo! Do you see what you've done? We're trying to *help* Sally, not kill her!"

"You think telling her about Frank Tucker's death might kill her?"

"Hell, *I* don't know!" said Li. Irrationally, I thought. "The woman thought she loved him! She's weak! She needs *care*, not verbal abuse!"

Verbal abuse? I was about to say something in Sam's defense, but Mr. Prophet spoke before I could.

"Hellkatoot. If tellin' the stupid woman that curly wolf's dead was gonna kill her, she's probably better off dead." He eyed Sally, who gracefully reclined on the floor. His eyebrows were furrowed and his brow wrinkled. "Don't rightly know as I can help you carry her upstairs. I don't bend so good anymore."

With a sigh, I said, "I'll help carry her, Li." What the heck. I didn't want Mr. Prophet to stumble on a stair with his peg leg, fall down and kill himself. Even though I got mad at him a lot, I didn't want him to die yet. He was quaint.

All at once, a gravelly, growly voice I'd never heard before spoke. It said, "Everybody just stay where you're at. I've got business with that woman." When I looked up, startled, I saw Angie stagger into the room, having been pushed by a tall man wearing what looked like an expensive business suit and holding a gun.

Li cried, "Adolph Grant!" and let go of Sally's shoulders. Sally weighed so little, her body made only a teensy whispering sound as it slipped to the floor again.

And my stupid juju started burning my chest.

TWENTY-FIVE

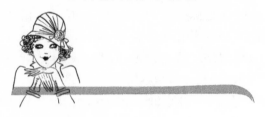

Standing up abruptly, Li said, "Angie! I thought that bastard was dead!"

The man I presumed to be Adolph Grant shoved Angie once more, she staggered farther into the room and fetched up against a wall. I saw she'd sustained a black eye and a bruised cheek, and I wanted to murder Mr. Adolph Grant. And while we were at it, Mr. Frank Tucker could come back to life, and I'd kill *him* again, too. Unfortunately, I possessed no magical powers.

With a leer, Mr. Grant said, "Sorry, Li. I ain't dead."

"Damn," said Li.

Sam slowly rose from the chair he'd occupied. "You're Mister Adolph Grant? From Tombstone?"

"I am," said Grant. "And I'm here to get my damned money back."

Sam tossed Angie a frown. Leaning against the parlor wall, she looked shaky; as if she'd been knocked around vigorously. I noticed blood on her chin and realized it oozed from a split lower lip. What a horrid man!

"I suspect you can get your money back without threatening anyone with a gun," Sam said drily.

"To hell with that. I not only want my money. I want this damned bitch to suffer. She's my *wife*, dammit!"

"Actually," said Sam in a more-than-reasonable voice, considering he was talking to a man holding a deadly weapon, "she probably isn't. She married a few men before she got to you and never legally rid herself of any of them."

Grant stood mute for a second, appearing a trifle stunned. Then he took a giant step toward Angie, yanked on her arm—which elicited a cry of pain from her—and slapped her head with the butt of his gun. Another pained wail issued from Angie's mouth, and she started sliding down the wall. "I-I'll pay you whatever you want, Adolph." Her words sounded mushy.

"Did you beat Angie?" I demanded of Grant. "A big man like you beat up a *woman*? You don't deserve to be called a man!"

Lou Prophet had softly clumped up behind me, and he poked me in the back. "Shut up," he rasped in my ear. "Ain't you got no sense at all?"

Clearly, I did. Have no sense at all, I mean, since two negatives make a positive and they were what Mr. Prophet had uttered in his sentence. Oh, dear. Babbling again. Sorry.

"Well, aren't *you* a feisty little thing," said Grant, giving me a truly superlative sneer. "And you're smart, too. I heard this feller talking to Sally there for some time, and you're the only one who got it."

"Got what? That Sally was the weak link? Anyone with half a brain could figure *that* out!" I cast a scornful glare at Sally, who was unconscious and couldn't appreciate it.

"Shut up, Daisy," Sam ground out between his teeth.

"Don't aggravate the man, fer cripe's sakes," Mr. Prophet growled at me.

"He's already aggravated," I told him. I just hate bullies, and

Mr. Grant was clearly a big one. "Any man who would beat up a woman doesn't deserve to be called a man!"

Grant lifted his gun and aimed it at me. I decided not to speak anymore. It was then I discovered I'd been wise too late—I think one of Angie's many husbands had said the same thing of her, but I can't remember which one—because suddenly Lou Prophet shoved me out of the way. A shot rang out, and Mr. Prophet said, "God *damn!*"

I guess this was too much for Sam to bear with affability—not that he'd been affable to begin with—because the instant Mr. Grant turned his attention to me, Sam bent over at the waist and charged straight at Grant's stomach. Bless his heart, he hit the man with all of his considerable weight, and Grant went down with a thud, hitting his head on a table before he landed on the floor.

"*Adolph!*" screamed Sally.

Still on the floor and wondering how many bruises I'd have after this latest episode, I turned to see Sally struggle to her feet—she had to balance herself on the chair she'd sat on, I presume because she was such a puling weakling—and, after picking up a lamp, reeled an erratic path toward Sam and the fallen Adolph Grant.

"Grab her!" I shouted at anyone who might be standing and mobile. "She's got a lamp, and she's going to brain—" I winced as Sally whacked Sam—who had begun ridding Mr. Grant of weapons—over the head. "—Sam with it," I finished too late.

"Stop it!" hollered Sam.

"No! No! No! *No!*" The lamp was evidently too heavy for the fragile Sally to handle, because she dropped it, thereby breaking it. It had been a darned pretty lamp, too. Then she took off stumbling toward to the staircase. Sam made a grab for her, but just missed grabbing one of her legs.

"Daisy!" Sam glanced at me and jerked his head in Sally's direction, so I got up from the floor, aiming to dash after Sally.

Only then did I realize I had blood on my sleeve. I looked up to see Mr. Prophet holding his left arm with his right hand. Blood seeped from between his fingers. "Oh, my heavens, did that man *shoot* you?"

"No," Prophet said with heavy sarcasm, "I pushed you out of the way of a wasp."

"There's no need to be mean about it. Do you need me to get you a…I don't know. A bandage or something?"

"*Daisy!*" Sam hollered again. "Get that damned woman!"

"I'll get her!" Li rushed across room and headed after Sally.

"*No!*" bellowed Sam. "*Daisy!* Lou's all right. Stop Li, and get Sally."

Thus directed, although I'm not sure precisely why Sam wanted me to get Sally rather than have Li get her, I raced after Li. Li raced after Sally. By that time, Sally had made it to the staircase and had begun climbing, holding on to the banister rail as if to keep herself upright. I had *no* idea what she wanted to do upstairs, but I trusted Sam to have had a good reason when he'd told me to fetch her.

"Li!" I hollered, grabbing Li's arm as it reached for the newel post. "Go take care of Mister Prophet. He's been shot. Sam wants me to fetch Sally."

"But—"

"*Go*" I shrieked, thereby both alarming and delighting myself. Didn't know I could sound so fierce until then.

After jumping as if she'd been jolted by an electrical current, Li stopped and stared at me.

I hollered, "*Go!*" once more, and she went.

Even though my right thigh and hip hurt from having connected so hard with the floor in Angie's parlor, I galloped up those stairs as if I were running from a demon out of hell. Or a graceful antelope prancing across a prairie.

Turned out, what I was running was a race. I reached the top of the staircase just as Sally grabbed a door jamb and hauled herself into a room. I thundered after her. Quicker and stronger than she, I managed to get into the same room just as Sally lifted a bottle to her lips. I whacked the bottle out of her hand and shoved her onto a nearby bed.

"No!" she whimpered. "No. No. No."

"Yes," I said firmly. "What's in the bottle?"

Sally folded up on the bed, hugging her middle, crying and saying, "No, no, no." I wanted to smack her mouth shut.

"Never mind," I said and bent to reach the bottle myself. I looked at the label as I picked it up. Chloral hydrate. A fairly large bottle of the stuff. Probably enough to make all the citizens in the city of Pasadena sleep for at least a week or two. Turning to Sally, still shivering on the bed, I said, "Were you going to drink this whole bottle?" From the looks of the rug next to the bed, the bottle had been either full or almost full.

Still shaking and moaning, Sally didn't respond to my question. I guess it didn't matter, since she couldn't get the bottle or its contents now.

Li entered the room, looking madder than a wet hen—my father comes out with this little gem from time to time. "Is Sally all right?" she asked, clearly concerned about Sally's wellbeing, which is a lot more than was Sally. Or me, for that matter. I guess I should have written I and not me, but it sounds funny that way.

"I neither know nor care," I told Li honestly. "She's the rat, and she was going to drink this."

Li took a glance at the bottle I held, turned again to Sally, then whirled around to face me again. "Where'd she get *that*?"

"How the devil should *I* know?" Really cranky by this time, I didn't feel like being grilled by Li or anyone else. "Did you take care of Mister Prophet? That ghastly man shot him after Mister Prophet shoved me out of the way." Which made the second time the rascally old scoundrel had saved my hide in three days. Very well. I decided to be nice to Mr. Lou Prophet from then on, no matter how much he provoked me.

"What? Lou?" Li stared at Sally, and I think she was beginning to arrange the same pieces I'd fitted together several minutes prior. Distractedly, she said, "Lou's all right. The bullet merely grazed his left arm."

"Huh."

Good Lord, now *I* was doing it!

Turning again to me, Li said, "You think Sally was in touch with Frank Tucker all the time, don't you? And through him, Adolph Grant. She lied to us, didn't she?"

"Ask her," I said peevishly. "I'm going to... No. I'd better not leave the two of you alone in the room together. Sam would kill me."

Outraged, Li said, "Do you think *I*—?"

"I have no idea," I said, interrupting her grouchily. I know, how rude, huh? However, by then, I didn't care. "Can you get that asinine woman to shut up and go downstairs again? I'll follow you."

For a second or two, Li looked as if she aimed to rebel. I guess she sensed I was ready for her, because finally she let out a breath, slumped, and said, "All right. Come on, Sally. Come with me." She reached down for Sally, who cringed away from her as if Li carried bubonic plague or some other dread malady.

"Just grab her," I suggested. "She's no use to anyone, and I doubt she'll obey you or Angie. I have a feeling she's served her purpose, and not even Adolph Grant will want her anymore."

Oh, my goodness, I don't think I'd ever sounded so hateful in my life. Worse, I was kind of proud of myself for it.

It took a long time to sort everything out, but eventually it transpired Sally *had* been the cuckoo in the nest, although she'd been coached by Frank Tucker, who had been paid by Adolph Grant. When she'd made her so-called escape from Mr. Grant's saloon—which he'd turned into an ice-cream parlor after Prohibition was made the law of the land—Frank Tucker had followed her. She'd also lied about Mr. Grant being dead, although it still puzzles me why neither Li nor Angie had discovered the truth. They were pretty good at finding out things. Oh, well...

The ice-cream parlor had sold ice cream. It also sold illegal liquor and women. Which meant it was a real, live parlor house! In the sense that a parlor house is a house of ill repute, I mean.

Aw, fuzz. Forget I said that.

Anyhow, it was Tucker who'd found all the other men in Angie's life and sent them to her in Pasadena. He'd even managed to find Li's brothers in China, for heaven's sake. At, of course, Adolph Grant's instruction. Evidently, Mr. Grant never let go of a good grudge unless forced to do so, and he was mightily irked with Angie for leaving him. Sally, the weakest link in pretty much everybody's life, had told the man she loved (Frank Tucker) how other girls had been smuggled from Adolph Grant's pseudo-ice-cream parlor. Tucker had told Grant, and the evil chain reaction had begun, Sally remaining its weakest link. In the chain. Get it?

Forget I said that, too, please.

When all had been revealed at last, it turned out Mr. Grant had spent a fortune or two just to get back at Angie. I personally think people with a whole lot of money and time on their hands would be better served by doing good deeds with their assets. For example, feeding children starving to death in Russia. Bringing medical services and doctors to the Appalachians. Finding cures for various diseases like, for instance, sleeping sickness. You know, stuff like that. As ever, no one asked for my opinion about what to do with his or her excess funds, a situation that happens all the time, and one I still consider downright annoying.

Sam, Lou Prophet and I were all about to drop dead by the time everything had been explained and Angie and Lou had visited Doc Benjamin's office to get their wounds attended to. Prophet didn't like being in the same doctor's office with Angie, but Sam told him—quite gruffly, too—to get over his distaste and allow the doctor to bandage him. I was there the entire time, and I could tell Mr. Prophet never did get over it. Too bad for him.

Angie said she felt terrible about having brought all of her Tombstone (and New York and St. Louis and Grand Junction and the Chinese Province of Canton) problems to Pasadena. Sam said he did, too. He couldn't very well charge her with anything, however, since none of her husbands had brought charges against her. Technically, her marriage to Adolph Grant was illegal, because she'd still been married to... Lord, I can't even remember the name of the first man who'd showed up in her house. Raymond? Alberts? Raymond Alberts? I think that was it. Or maybe she'd been married to Mr. Godfrey. But no, her marriage to him had been illegal, too.

Good Lord. I'd only been married once so far, and that one time had practically done me in.

After Dr. Benjamin doctored Angie's wounds, given her an eye patch he told her to wear for a week, and ordered her to stay in bed for at least two days, Angie seemed subdued when Sam pulled up to her front porch. Li helped Angie get out of the car.

"Thank you," Angie said in a tired voice. "And I'm sorry again."

"It's all right, Angie," said Li. "None of this was your fault."

By then, I expect three out of the three people remaining in Sam's Hudson (Sam, Mr. Prophet and I) disagreed with Li on the point, but none of us said so. Sam growled a little. I didn't blame him.

At any rate, Sam, Mr. Prophet and I straggled into my parents' bungalow at around dinner time Thursday evening. I'd called Pa from the police station to give him an abbreviated version of what had happened at Orange Acres, so Ma had already set the table for dinner by the time we arrived. I felt guilty for making her perform this service, since she worked hard at her job every day and didn't need my chores piled on top of her own.

"Don't be silly, Daisy," Ma, a gracious and loving soul, said when I confessed to my feeling of guilt. "It wasn't your fault you were late." She shook her head. "I don't understand how these things always happen around you, though."

If I hadn't been so darned tired, I'd have asked her what she meant by her remark. Or maybe I wouldn't have. I already knew what she meant.

Anyway, we all sat at our places at the table, Pa said grace, and we dug in. I was awfully hungry by that time.

"Delicious dinner, Vi," said Sam.

"Thank you, Sam," said Vi.

"It's great," said Mr. Prophet.

"Thank you, Mister Prophet. I enjoy cooking for my loved ones."

Her loved ones? Did she include Mr. Prophet in the group? I didn't ask.

Dinner Thursday night was Swiss steak with fried onions and tomatoes. Vi had thoughtfully cut up Mr. Prophet's steak for him before she'd handed him his plate. She did so because Dr. Benjamin had put his left arm in a sling and told him to keep it there for a week. He'd also told him not to use the arm for a few weeks, even after he no longer needed the sling. Mr. Prophet had grumbled under his breath a few times in the doctor's office, but when he glanced over to see Sam and me smiling unkind smiles at him, he'd acquiesced with an "Aw, hell."

"Are you too exhausted to attend choir practice, Daisy?" Ma asked. She sounded solicitous, but I think she'd have been annoyed if I'd bowed out of my duty just because someone had attempted to kill me a few hours earlier. My mother expected her children to fulfill their obligations unless they were bedridden or dying.

Therefore, although I *really* didn't want to, I said, "Oh, no. I'll go. I always enjoy choir practice." To prove it, I smiled at everyone. When my gaze hit Sam, he crossed his eyes at me. He'd probably have stuck out his tongue, too, if my parents weren't present.

"That's my girl," said Pa, with an approving grin of his own.

Sam said he'd drive me to choir practice, bless his heart. He had to have been at least as worn out as I was, but when I told him he didn't need to drive me, he said, "Don't be crazy. I want to make sure you don't get into any more trouble."

I wanted to kick him under the table but, as mentioned above, my parents were present.

Mr. Prophet didn't join us when we went to the church for choir practice. He wanted to get into his cozy little cottage, he told us, and read for a while. I had a sneaking suspicion he might want to visit a bottle of tangleleg he'd stuffed away somewhere in the cottage, too, but I didn't let on. What the heck.

While I'd been all for Prohibition when it was first propounded as a law of the land, mainly because I didn't want my war-wounded and shell-shocked husband to fall into a bottle, I'd begun to doubt the good of prohibiting anyone from doing anything—barring murder, slavery, and a few other choice sins. It seemed to me Prohibition only promoted crime. Look at all the bootleggers running around in those days if you don't believe me! Well, you can't, but I'm sure you understand what I mean.

"It'll be all right," said Sam as he parked his Hudson near the Marengo entrance of the First Methodist-Episcopal church on the corner of Marengo and Colorado. "I'll drive you right home, and then you and Spike can sleep in tomorrow morning."

"Can't sleep too late," I said morosely. "I have an appointment with Missus Pinkerton at ten."

"Well, sleep until eight then." He laughed and exited the car.

Because I felt so drained, I let him walk around to my side of the Hudson and open my door. He helped me out, since my right leg and hip hurt a lot, too. I'd peeked at my nether limbs in my bedroom mirror and so far, the right one had taken on a sort of dark pink color. I suspected that by the following morning, I'd be black and blue from my waist to my right knee. Phooey.

Anyway, Sam walked me to the choir room, then detoured to the sanctuary where he took a pew next to Lucy Zollinger's husband, Albert. The two men greeted each other with smiles, shook hands warmly, and suddenly I absolutely *loved* Sam Rotondo! I don't know why, but just seeing him there, blending in with my own personal community—in spite of his being an Italian from New York City—gave me a mushy feeling in my heart. In fact, I darned near burst into tears.

Clearly, I was *extremely* exhausted.

I didn't have time to think about it, because as soon as she saw me, Lucy Zollinger rushed over to me, clutching a book in her hands.

"Look at this, Daisy!" cried she, thrusting the book at me.

I looked. My nose wrinkled. The book's title was *Eating Your Way to Health*. I gazed at it for a moment, then glanced up at Lucy again. "Ah." I didn't know what else to say.

"Oh, Daisy, I read about this book in one of Albert's periodicals! It's just been published, and Albert went to Grenville's books and bought it for me when I asked him to. He's so good to me." Lucy paused to sigh happily about her Albert before continuing, "It's got a *lot* of tips about how to get and stay healthy. It even offers exercises!"

I said "Ah" again.

Peering at me in astonishment, Lucy demanded, "Daisy, don't you *see*?"

"See what?"

"This will be a wonderful opportunity for us."

"It will?" I'd begun to wish I'd stayed home that night, Ma's approval or no Ma's approval.

"Yes! At fellowship last Sunday, Missus Dermott and Missus Benjamin and I were talking about how nice it would be to estab-lish a ladies' exercise class. We could hold it here at the church, either in the parlor or in Fellowship Hall. Most of us need more exercise than we get, and this book can tell us *exactly* how to go about it. And if we do it as a group, it will be fun! It even suggests exercising to music on a Victrola!"

"Exercises?" I asked feebly. "You want to start an exercise class? Here? At church? With a Victrola?"

"Yes!" Lucy sounded excited.

I think I said, "Ah" one more time, but I'm honestly not sure. Thank the good Lord, Mr. Hostetter called the choir to attention then. I was so glad of it, I nearly burst into tears again.

However, one of my more fervent wishes had come to pass during the week—a week that wasn't even over yet. I'd met a real, honest-to-God scarlet woman. Doing so had proved strenuous and painful, and I wasn't sure if I was glad if it or not, but at least I now knew scarlet women looked pretty much like all the other women in the world.

How disappointing.

EXERCISED SPIRITS

A DAISY GUMM MAJESTY MYSTERY, BOOK 16

The second time I drove through the big, wrought-iron gate at the Pinkerton mansion that day, I stopped to chat with Jackson, the Pinkertons' gatekeeper.

"Good to see you, Miss Daisy," said Jackson, his big pearly-white smile gleaming in his dark face.

"You, too, Mr. Jackson. How's your mother doing?"

"She's just fine, thank you, Miss Daisy. She's been saying special prayers for you and your auntie, too."

I felt my eyes widen. "Has she? Why's that?"

Laws, I don't know, Miss Daisy. She gets these notions in her head, and there's no telling why. But she told me to tell you to keep your juju close by."

I lifted the chain upon which my Mrs. Jackson-made juju hung and showed the juju to Jackson. "I wear it all day, every day. Please tell her so. And if she ever lets on why she thinks Aunt Vi and I need special prayers, please let me know, okay?"

With another laugh, Jackson said, "Sure will, Miss Daisy. I sure will."

"Thank you!" said I, and drove up the long drive to the front of the Pinkerton palace. The bright yellow sports car I'd noticed when I'd dropped Vi off earlier in the day still sat in the circular drive. This fact seemed odd to me. And, because it seemed odd to me, I wondered if it had anything to do with why Mrs. Jackson's deemed it necessary to say special prayers for Aunt Vi and me. Then I told myself not to be an idiot, parked the Chevrolet, grabbed my bag of tricks, which contained my Ouija board and tarot cards, and walked up the stairs to the massive porch's massive door. I patted one of the massive marble lions on my way to the door then rang the chimes. Sometimes, because it was there, I'd use the brass lion's brass knocker on its brass knocking plate, but that morning I felt like chimes.

Lo and behold, Harold Kincaid opened the door!

"Good Lord!" I cried. "Where's Featherstone!"

"And a bright and cheery good morning to you, too," said Harold with something of a snarl.

"I'm sorry, Harold. I'm just so accustomed to Featherstone opening the door, you surprised me. Besides, I didn't see your car."

"Yes you did, unless you're blind as a mole," Harold told me.

"Are moles blind?" I asked, honestly curious.

"How the devil should *I* know. You're blind as a bat then. Is that better?"

"I don't understand," I told him, confused.

"You saw my car, dammit!"

"What?" I turned around and scanned the circular drive and surrounding grounds. They were beautiful, but I saw no bright red Stutz Bearcat lurking anywhere. Turning back to Harold, I said, "Where?"

"Right in front of your eyes, Daisy."

I whirled around again and stared at the circular drive. "That yellow thing?" I asked, astonished.

"That *yellow thing*, as you so inelegantly call it, is my brand new Kissell Six Forty-five Gold Bug Speedster. For your information."

"Wow! I didn't know you'd bought a new car, Harold!"

"I told you I was going to."

"Well, yes, I know you did, but I didn't think you'd buy a new car and not tell me about it." I felt a trifle hurt, actually, although I'd never let on to Harold. We were great friends and all, but I guess he didn't *have* to tell me everything he did every time he did it.

"I had planned on popping by this afternoon to give you a ride in it, actually."

These words made me feel better. "Thanks, Harold. What does Dell think about it being bright yellow?"

"He hates it, but I already told him I wouldn't buy a Ford just because it's black. I like a machine that reflects my personality."

"Interesting. So you used to have a bright red personality, and now you have a bright yellow personality?"

Harold rolled his eyes. Sam does the same thing a lot. "Something like that."

"But what are you doing opening the door? Where in the world is Featherstone?"

"For the love of God, don't just stand there interrogating me!" Harold snapped. "I opened the damned door so you could come inside." And darned if he didn't take me by the arm and yank me indoors.

"Goodness sakes! You're a bit miffy today, aren't you?"

"I'm a *lot* miffy today, and goodness has nothing to do with it," he chuffed, shutting the door behind me. It closed with a sound that will always and forever remind me of money: solidly. No slamming, no crashing, no squeaking, no clinking; just a good, solid, quiet clunk. The sound of money.

"What's wrong, Harold? You're not mad at me for some reason, are you?"

"Good God, no!"

"Well, I'm glad, but what the heck's the matter?" Harold had shoved my sleeve out of whack when he'd pulled me inside, so I smoothed it down again. It wasn't like Harold to be irrational and irritable, or to manhandle people. He had a temper, as do we all, but I'd never known him to get into a tizzy. Tizziness was his mother's specialty, not his.

"There was an incident here today," he said, not clearing up the matter one little bit.

"An incident? What kind of incident? Calm down, Harold, and just tell me about it."

Wiping his brow with a hastily-grabbed-from-a-pocket handkerchief, Harold sucked in a huge breath. "I'm sorry, Daisy. But Featherstone and the new chauffeur were injured, and your poor aunt's been busy all morning making tisanes for my idiot mother and cold compresses for poor Featherstone's bruised knee and O'Hara's head. Doctor Benjamin just left. He said the knee's not broken, but it's definitely strained, and poor Featherstone will have to take it easy for a few days. No butlering for him for a while. At least O'Hara doesn't have a concussion, according to the doctor."

"Good Lord!"

"The good Lord has nothing to do with it, either, if there is one, which I doubt, but don't tell Del I said so."

"Del already knows," I told him. It was true. Del Farrington, Harold's life partner (sort of like Ma and Pa are life partners, if you know what I mean) was a strict Roman Catholic and attended Saint Andrews Catholic Church every Sunday. I'm not sure what the Roman Catholic Church might have to say about Del and Harold being life partners, but I also don't care. I've held a grudge against the Catholic Church ever since Sam told me his parents disapproved of me because I'm not a Catholic. "Now tell me what the heck is going on, Harold Kincaid!"

"Sit here," Harold said, shoving me onto a magnificent hall bench, the seat of which had been upholstered in a beautiful brocade fabric. I felt almost as if I were desecrating it by putting my hoi-polloi-ish bottom on it. But my bottom was clothed gorgeously—because I'm a crackerjack seamstress—so I don't suppose I should have even entertained the thought. Besides, the bench wouldn't care anyway.

Harold sat next to me, sprawling, his legs stretched out, his head tilted back, and his arms dangling. This posture was most unlike him.

Available in Paperback and eBook from Your Favorite Bookstore or Online Retailer

AUNT VI'S BEEF STEW WITH DUMPLINGS

Stew Ingredients:

- 5-pound aitchbone (cheap piece of beef for stewing or braising)
- 4 cups potatoes chopped into one-inch cubes
- 1 cup turnips chopped into one-inch cubes
- 1 cup carrots chopped into one-inch pieces
- 1 small onion, chopped
- ½ cup flour
- Salt
- Pepper

Preparation for Stew:

1. Remove beef from bone and cut into one and one-half-inch cubes. Wipe beef, sprinkle with salt and pepper and dredge with flour.

2. Cut some of the fat in small pieces and try out (fry) in iron frying pan. Add meat and stir constantly so that the surface is quickly seared. When well browned, put in kettle.
3. Rinse frying pan with boiling water, making sure to save all the flavorful bits and pieces.
4. Add remaining fat to meat along with bones sawed in pieces; cover with boiling water and boil five minutes. Then cook at a lower temperature until beef is tender (approximately 3 hours).
5. Add carrots, turnips and onion along with salt and pepper during the last hour of cooking.
6. Parboil potatoes for 5 minutes and add to stew 15 minutes before removing kettle from fire.
7. Remove bones, large pieces of fat, and then skim.
8. Thicken with 1/4 cup flour, diluted with enough cold water to pour easily.
9. Pour into deep hot platter and surround with dumplings.

Dumpling Ingredients:

- 2 cups flour
- ½ tsp. salt.
- 4 Tbsps. baking powder
- 2 tsps. Butter
- ½ cup milk

Preparation For Dumplings:

Mix and sift dry ingredients. Work in butter with tips of

fingers and add milk gradually, using a knife for mixing. Toss on a floured board, pat and roll out to one-half inch thickness. Shape with biscuit cutter first dipped in flour. Place closely together in a buttered steamer, put over kettle of boiling water, cover closely and steam twelve minutes. A perforated tin pie-plate may be used in place of steamer. OR you can put the dumplings on the stew pot, cover for twelve minutes, and then uncover and cook another ten minutes.

Send a photo of Aunt Vi's Stew to alice@aliceduncan.net and Aunt Vi just might share her recipe for Scotch Shortbread cookies in return.

ALSO BY ALICE DUNCAN

The Daisy Gumm Majesty Mystery Series

Strong Spirits

Fine Spirits

High Spirits

Hungry Spirits

Genteel Spirits

Ancient Spirits

Dark Spirits

Spirits Onstage

Unsettled Spirits

Bruised Spirits

Spirits United

Spirits Unearthed

Shaken Spirits

Scarlet Spirits

Exercised Spirits

The Mercy Allcutt Mystery Series

Lost Among the Angels

Angels Flight

Fallen Angels

Angels of Mercy

Thanksgiving Angels

ABOUT THE AUTHOR

Award-winning author Alice Duncan lives with a herd of wild dachshunds (enriched from time to time with fosterees from New Mexico Dachshund Rescue) in Roswell, New Mexico. She's not a UFO enthusiast; she's in Roswell because her mother's family settled there fifty years before the aliens crashed (and living in Roswell, NM, is cheaper than living in Pasadena, CA, unfortunately). Alice would love to hear from you at alice@aliceduncan.net

www.aliceduncan.net

 facebook.com/alice.duncan.925

CPSIA information can be obtained
at www.ICGtesting.com
Printed in the USA
LVHW032153200120
644239LV00001B/178